JUN   2004

LT M HESS
Hess, Joan.
Muletrain to Maggody :
an Arly Hanks mystery

WITHDRAWN

Muletrain
to
Maggody

Also by Joan Hess
in Large Print:

Martians in Maggody
Malice in Maggody
Out on a Limb

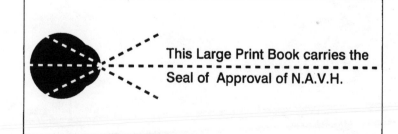

This Large Print Book carries the
Seal of Approval of N.A.V.H.

Muletrain
to
Maggody

An Arly Hanks Mystery

Joan Hess

Thorndike Press • Waterville, Maine

ALAMEDA FREE LIBRARY
2200-A CENTRAL AVENUE
ALAMEDA, CA 94501

Copyright © 2004 by Joan Hess

All rights reserved.

This book is a work of fiction. Names, characters, places, and incidents either are products of the author's imagination or are used fictitiously. Any resemblance to actual events or locales or persons, living or dead, is entirely coincidental.

Published in 2004 by arrangement with Simon & Schuster, Inc.

Thorndike Press® Large Print Mystery.

The tree indicium is a trademark of Thorndike Press.

The text of this Large Print edition is unabridged.
Other aspects of the book may vary from the original edition.

Set in 16 pt. Plantin by Al Chase.

Printed in the United States on permanent paper.

Library of Congress Cataloging-in-Publication Data

Hess, Joan.
    Muletrain to Maggody : an Arly Hanks mystery / Joan Hess.
        p. cm.
    ISBN 0-7862-6402-0 (lg. print : hc : alk. paper)
    1. Hanks, Arly (Fictitious character) — Fiction.
2. Maggody (Ark. : Imaginary place) — Fiction.   3. Police —
Arkansas — Fiction.   4. Police chiefs — Fiction.
5. Policewomen — Fiction.   6. Arkansas — Fiction.   7. Large
type books.   I. Title.
PS3558.E79785M79 2004b
    813′.54—dc22   2004043964

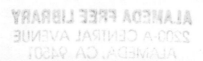
ALAMEDA FREE LIBRARY
2200-A CENTRAL AVENUE
ALAMEDA, CA 94501

For Ken Smith
with fondness and respect

National Association for Visually Handicapped
------------------------ *serving the partially seeing*

As the Founder/CEO of NAVH, the only national health agency solely devoted to those who, although not totally blind, have an eye disease which could lead to serious visual impairment, I am pleased to recognize Thorndike Press* as one of the leading publishers in the large print field.

Founded in 1954 in San Francisco to prepare large print textbooks for partially seeing children, NAVH became the pioneer and standard setting agency in the preparation of large type.

Today, those publishers who meet our standards carry the prestigious "Seal of Approval" indicating high quality large print. We are delighted that Thorndike Press is one of the publishers whose titles meet these standards. We are also pleased to recognize the significant contribution Thorndike Press is making in this important and growing field.

Lorraine H. Marchi, L.H.D.
Founder/CEO
NAVH

* Thorndike Press encompasses the following imprints: Thorndike, Wheeler, Walker and Large Print Press.

Acknowledgments

Okay, listen up: This is not a book about the Civil War. If you want a book about the Civil War, mosey over to the nonfiction section and find something written by a historian and published by a very earnest university press. This is a book about Civil War reenactors. It contains references to the War, but the more scholarly of you will no doubt swoop down on numerous errors and inaccuracies. Please do not feel any obligation to share them with me.

W. C. Jameson's *Buried Treasures of the Ozarks and the Appalachians* (Promontory, 1993) planted the seed in the nether reaches of my mind some years ago. Although lacking documentation, romantic legends of lost Confederate gold have always abounded. One significant battle took place in my area of Arkansas, which meant my premise, although improbable, wasn't totally implausible.

Confederates in the Attice: Dispatches from

the Unfinished Civil War (Pantheon, 1998) by Tony Horowitz, provided me with wonderful insights into the attitudes of those who, in one way or another, have never recovered from the War of Northern Aggression (as it's still known in some pockets south of the Mason-Dixon Line). Mr. Horowitz's encounters and experiences with reenactors, good ol' boys, and genteel ladies with vintage pedigrees were enormously useful. It's also a highly entertaining read.

Amy Alessio, a reenactor from Illinois, patiently fielded my questions and did her best to guide me through the wacky battlefield of muskets by day and cell phones by night. We even discussed how reenactors capture that authentic patina on their brass buttons.

Dewey Lambdin, an author and historian from Memphis, did his best to educate me in matters of caissons and cannons. All the inaccuracies in the book are of my own doing, not his. Sorry, Dewey. I still wouldn't know a caisson if it bit me on the ankle.

Tim Whitbred of Maryland offered invaluable advice, particularly in matters of Confederate gold coins and the logistics of transporting them.

Linda Nickle, a local friend, loaned me her collection of Civil War material so that I could do my best not to make a total idiot of myself. If I did, it was not her fault.

In my unschooled opinion, the Civil War was the worst tragedy the United States has ever suffered. In this work of comedic fiction, I had to downplay the realities of what happened and focus on those who continue to put on stifling wool costumes and relive those horrible times. Their motives are mixed. Some participate to preserve history and educate those who have only a vague sense of the history of the period. Others participate as a hobby, an opportunity to live for a few days in a simpler environment and visit with old friends. And others, dear readers, are crazier than loons.

1

Once again I found myself trudging toward the high school cafeteria for a meeting. The last one had been courtesy of the school board, and mayhem and murder had followed within a matter of weeks. That, I believe, is a pretty damn good reason to ban all meetings, especially in Maggody, Arkansas (population 755 or so, depending on what you count). I don't object to the Missionary Society getting together at the Voice of the Almighty Lord Assembly Hall to grumble about the heathens over coffee and cinnamon rolls, or the Wednesday night potluck suppers where paper plates runneth over with ham, green bean casseroles, and lemon squares. The ladies of the County Extension chapter are welcome to their weekly discussions of the blatantly biased judging of pickled okra at the fair every fall. For that matter, what business is it of mine if Mayor Jim Bob Buchanon huddles with his cronies to play poker in the back room of

Roy Stiver's Antiques Shop?

But this was an official town meeting, and my appearance as chief of police was mandatory — or so I'd been told by Mrs. Jim Bob only that morning. She'd refused to say what the meeting was about or why I had to be there, but I had a feeling I was neither going to be fired (who else would have my miserable job?) nor presented with a raise (miserable and miserly have a certain similarity). When I'd slunk back to Maggody after a nasty divorce from a Manhattan advertising hotshot who appreciated the finer things in life — as long as they were blond and mindless — I hadn't expected much more than a semblance of sympathy and a whole lot of home cookin' from my mother, Ruby Bee, proprietor of a bar & grill of the same name. I'd declined her offer to let me live in one of the units in the Flamingo Motel out back and had instead rented what was supposedly an efficiency apartment above the antiques shop. It was cold and clammy in the winter, and steamy in the summer. The cockroaches thrived in both climates, and I doubted global warming (or an ice age) would deplete their numbers.

Ruby Bee didn't have a clue about the reason for the meeting, and she knows darn close to every last thing that happens within the city limits, including sneezes, wheezes, and sexual trysts outside the confines of holy matrimony. Her best friend Estelle Oppers owns Estelle's Hair Fantasies out on County 101. What Ruby Bee doesn't hear about in the bar is gleaned there during perms and manicures, when a mere hangnail can lead to sobbing admissions of unrequited love or shoplifting at the supermarket. Growing up in Maggody was always a challenge for someone of a teenaged persuasion who liked to drink a little beer on the banks of Boone Creek and count the lightnin' bugs.

If you don't know what that means, settle for a literal interpretation.

I caught up with Ruby Bee and Estelle at the front door of the high school, and we walked down the corridor together.

"You still don't know what this is about?" I asked them.

Ruby Bee growled. "No, I don't reckon anyone in town except Mrs. Jim Bob knows. Lottie Estes said all the teachers were ordered to attend. None of them's happy about it."

"But this ain't a school board meeting," Estelle pointed out, waggling her red beehive of hair for emphasis. She and Ruby Bee make a very odd couple, since one resembles a fire hydrant atop a fencepost and the other a short stack of unbaked biscuits.

We continued into the cafeteria and sat down at a lunch table in the back of the room. Quite a few folks were already wiggling uncomfortably on the plastic benches, muttering among themselves about how some damn fool meeting was interfering with their constitutional right to vegetate in front of the television. Earl and Eileen Buchanon nodded at us, as did Elsie McMay and a visibly disgruntled Lottie Estes. Darla Jean McIlhaney sat with her parents, Millicent and Jeremiah. Larry Joe Lambertino, who's the shop teacher, and his wife, Joyce, were hissing at each other, which they did a lot.

At a table in the front of the room sat Hizzoner the Moron (aka Jim Bob Buchanon), his wife Mrs. Jim Bob (aka Barbara Ann Buchanon Buchanon), Roy Stiver, and a stout woman with steely gray hair and the expressiveness of a bass beached on a gravel bar in the midday sun.

Ruby Bee nudged me. "Who in tarnation do you think that is?"

"How would I know?" I said, still scanning the room to see who all had been bullied into attending the meeting. A fair percentage of them were Buchanons, but

14

that was not remarkable, since there are more Buchanons in Stump County than flies on a dead possum. Most of them have protuberant foreheads, thick lips, and yellowish eyes, and there's nary a college grad among them, mostly due to the dropout rate long about eighth grade. Nevertheless, a few of them are as wily as pole cats. Raz Buchanon's been running his still up on Cotter's Ridge since the dawn of time. When I'm truly bored, I pack a picnic lunch and go looking for it, but the sumbitch stays a step ahead of me. The Arkansas two-step, I suppose.

Jim Bob banged his fist on the tabletop. "Okay, I'm calling this meeting to order. We're gonna skip the minutes from the last meeting and the treasurer's report and all that crap. Mrs. Jim Bob has the floor, so y'all listen up."

Even though Mrs. Jim Bob has plenty of Buchanon blood, her lips are thinner than paper matches and her eyes are dark and beady. She has never risked eternal damnation by painting her face like a common floozy, and her hair was reminiscent of a style predominant in 1960s high school yearbooks. As usual, she was wearing a starchy white blouse buttoned to the top despite the lack of air-conditioning.

15

She stood up and waited as her audience settled down for what well might be an interminable session. "Thank you for coming," she said with a brief smile. "A most exciting thing is about to happen right here in Maggody, and it's going to require full cooperation from all our Christian, law-abiding citizens. I am pleased that so many of you put aside your self-indulgent and slothful ways to attend this evening."

"Good thing Raz ain't here," whispered Ruby Bee.

Mrs. Jim Bob frowned at her, then continued. "Now I'd like to introduce Miss Harriet Hathaway, who lives over in Farberville and is the president of the Stump County Historical Society. Let's give her our full attention."

She began to clap, so the rest of us dutifully followed suit. Once the pitter-patter faded, the woman stood up and said, "As you were told, I am Harriet Hathaway, and I've been the president of the Stump County Historical Society for fifteen years. The society manages the Headquarters House, which was controlled by both Confederate and Union forces during the Civil War. We also publish a quarterly digest called *Remembrances of Stump County's Past*, provide programs for schoolchildren, and sponsor an ice cream social in the summer. I'd planned to bring slides, but I was informed that a projector and screen could not be made available."

"Hallelujah," mumbled someone off to the side of the room.

"Excuse me?" said Mrs. Jim Bob, rising to her feet. "Do you wish to contribute to the discussion, Earl Buchanon?"

"No, ma'am, it's just that there's a baseball game what's already started, and I was hopin' we'd be done right soon so I can —"

"Then you'd best stop interrupting. Now, Miss Hathaway, if you'll tell us your exciting news . . ."

Miss Hathaway appeared a little flustered, probably because the historical society meetings were exercises in tea and cookies. In Maggody, we're more into RC Colas and Moon Pies.

"Well, then," she said, "as I'm sure many of you know, this year will be the one hundred and fortieth anniversary of the Battle of Farberville, fought primarily on the hillside above the Headquarters House. Over three hundred Confederate troops died or were wounded before the Union forces prevailed."

"Damn Yankees," said Jim Bob, then ducked his head as his wife stared at him.

"So what's this got to do with Maggody?" asked Estelle.

"Three days before the battle, a small unit from the Arkansas Fifth, garrisoned in Little Rock at that time, arrived at the edge of Stump County after an arduous six-day trek. They were bringing two saddlebags of gold to pay the soldiers of General Lambdin's brigade, which was coming from the west to halt a Union attempt to secure the Arkansas-Missouri border. They rode mules because they were pulling a cannon on a caisson and a wagon filled with munitions. Their numbers had been depleted due to swollen creeks and the muddy conditions of the road. Also, according to a journal entry made by a young private named Henry Largesse, they'd gorged themselves on green persimmons and many of them had to remain behind as the rest moved north." She paused for effect, but no one seemed overwhelmingly entranced by the narrative. "When they arrived not too far from here, the lieutenant decided to camp near what is now called Boone Creek and allow the men a full day and night of rest before what would surely be a bloody battle."

Ruby Bee flapped her hand. "So this is what we're all supposed to be so excited

18

about? They came, they camped, and then went and got theirselves shot?"

"If you will please allow me to continue," said Miss Hathaway, her voice as steely as her hair, "I'll be succinct. It seems the soldiers found a small, squalid farm and took a pig back to camp to be roasted. Despite the fact this was an unfortunately common practice on both sides, the rightful owner was so incensed that he threatened them with a shotgun and was severely thrashed for his lack of patriotism. He was quite lucky not to have been hanged. In retaliation, he rode to the Missouri border and informed a Union general named Alessio of the proximity of the Confederate unit, although most likely not in those exact terms. General Alessio immediately dispatched a cavalry troop to ambush the unit from Little Rock and take possession of the cannon, wagon, and mules. It is unlikely that he was aware of the gold in the saddlebags."

Estelle elbowed me and whispered, "This is gettin' kind of interesting, ain't it? One side's got gold and a cannon, and the other side is aiming to bushwhack 'em. I wonder why we never heard any of this before."

"Could be because no one's written a comprehensive history of this meadow muffin of a town," I whispered back. "Re-

19

member when that genealogist tried to chart the Buchanon family tree? Supposedly she had an accident after driving away, but I've always suspected suicide."

"Chief of Police Hanks," chirped Mrs. Jim Bob, "please save your discourteous behavior for a more appropriate moment. My apologies, Miss Hathaway."

Miss Hathaway nodded at her. "Yes, of course. During the night, while the Confederates were sleeping off their fine feast, the Union soldiers took a position in a field near the road and waited for sunrise." She picked up a notebook and flipped it open. "I will now read the pertinent entry from the private's journal, written several weeks after the incident. The journal itself only came to light a few weeks ago, when a family member found it in a trunk and donated it to the historical society. Here is an excerpt: 'Come dawn we got the gear stowed and the mules saddled, then headed out. The lieutenant, scared as the rest of us, said we'd most likely meet up with General Lambdin's troops by nightfall. My second cousin from down by Booneville was one of their gunners, so I was looking forward to seeing him and swapping family news. I found out later he'd died of dysentery only a month earlier, likely without never hearing about his sister's baby.' " Miss Hathaway looked up. "He now digresses about family affairs, and then continues. 'We'd gone mebbe not a quarter of a mile when out of nowhere comes musket fire from a field off to the east. We hunkered behind a low stone wall and tried to figure out where the Yanks was. Custiss volunteered to scout 'em out, but was shot square in the back afore he could take three steps. Some of the boys was shaking so hard I thought they'd pass out, but somehow we all grabbed our muskets and returned fire. This goes on for most of the morning. We could see the bastards, but we was already outnumbered and couldn't seem to force them back. By noon, we were down to six boys and the lieutenant, who was getting mighty grim. He ordered Emil Jenks to take the gold up on the ridge behind us and hide it in a cave so it wouldn't fall into Yankee hands if we dint make it. Soon as Emil got back, all covered with mud and panting like a coon dog, the lieutenant took a hit to the side of his head and took to bleeding like a stuck pig. He ordered us to git ourselves on the mules and get the hell out afore we was all slaughtered, saying we should come back for the gold later. Emil was trying to tell us where he'd hid the saddlebags when a minié ball took him in the throat. I don't reckon I can ever forget the look on his face when he fell. The rest of us lit out like Satan was snapping at our heels and didn't ease up till we was a good mile away.' "

Miss Hathaway stopped reading and said, "The entry goes on to describe how the young private was shot in the thigh during the Battle of Farberville and had his leg amputated by a field surgeon. He managed to survive long enough to make it to his home, where he eventually died of complications from the surgery."

"So what about the gold?" asked Earl Buchanon, who'd clearly forgotten all about home runs and double plays. "Is it still up there?"

Miss Hathaway shrugged. "According to the journal, the private was the only one of the Confederates involved in the Skirmish at Cotter's Ridge to survive the Battle of Farberville, and he was in no condition to be sent back to find the precise location. All he could tell General Lambdin was that there were a few dirt-scratch farms, a creek, and a ridge. That description could fit many of the communities in Stump County, even today."

"We got us a stoplight and a fine supermarket," said Jim Bob.

"I'm sure you do," she said, not turning to look at him. "In order to commemorate the Battle of Farberville, the historical society has received a grant for various projects. We can hardly stage a reenactment of the battle itself, since the hill where it took place is now cluttered with homes and power lines. Therefore, we have decided to make a documentary film of what took place here. With meticulous camera angles and editing, we feel as though we can end up with a reasonably accurate depiction. It will be shown at the Headquarters House as an important part of our educational program."

"Remember when those Hollywood folks tried to make a movie here?" whispered Estelle. "Now that was something."

Ruby Bee leaned around me. "These ain't Hollywood folks, Estelle."

"I doubt this documentary will have any sex scenes," I said drily.

Eileen Buchanon stood up. "So what does this mean to us? Are we supposed to get on mules and gallop around till we get shot?"

"Not at all," said Miss Hathaway. "We put out the word for three dozen reenactors and had more volunteers than we can possibly use. A filmmaker from Missouri has offered his services and equipment in exchange for expenses. Two impressionists with national reputations will arrive a few days in advance to speak at the schools about the hardships realized not only by the soldiers, but also by the civilians. One of them portrays a Southern widow, the other a Northern general. It's a wonderful educational opportunity for the students. They both have very busy schedules, so we were quite lucky to engage them."

"So how many folks are you expecting?" asked Ruby Bee. "I own the one motel in town, and it's only got six units."

"The reenactors will set up their camps so that schoolchildren and interested citizens can tour the facilities and learn how the soldiers lived during those infamous years. Mrs. Jim Bob has kindly offered to provide hospitality to myself, Wendell Streek, who is the treasurer of the historical society, and a few other selected parties. We will need to reserve units for the filmmaker and his assistant. He's told me that he will hire a few of your local teenagers to help them."

"Where we're going to make money," inserted Jim Bob, "is from the tourists coming into town to goggle at this play-acting. Some of 'em might pay to camp on various folks' pastures. The SuperSaver is gonna fix up box lunches and sell fancy bottled water. The pool hall's liable to do some lively business after dark on account of the nearest movie theater being twenty miles away. There's been some talk about the high school having a square dance in the gym, with the profits going to buy new uniforms for the football team." He gave me an evil smile. "And the town's revenue is bound to go up with all the tickets our dedicated chief of police writes for speeding, running the stoplight, illegal parking, trespassing, littering, and whatever else goes on. Maybe the town council will pass an ordinance that forbids spitting in public."

"I'll second that," I said. "You can recruit Raz to be your poster boy."

Miss Hathaway cleared her throat. "We have not publicized this because of the potentially volatile nature of the information in the journal. Members of the historical society have been informed, naturally, and might drive out to watch the filming. The reenactors will bring along a few family members, most of whom will stay in area RV parks and campgrounds. Word of the treasure will leak out eventually, but I doubt Maggody will experience an influx of tourists for a few weeks."

"Just who are these reenactors that are

gonna be running all over town?" asked Lottie Estes. "Are they like actors on a movie set? I don't like the idea of a lot of armed strangers that think the Civil War is just an excuse to get drunk and start throwing punches at each other like those rednecks at the pool hall."

"I asked that question myself. Two members of the society were reenactors before their infirmities forced them to retire. For them, and apparently most of the others, it's a hobby, not a religion or an obsession. They told me there are more than forty thousand reenactors in the nation. The reenactment weekends are clean-cut family activities, camping trips, reunions with friends. They're trying to recapture, if just for the few days, an era of simplicity. Women in long skirts, peeling potatoes and swapping recipes. Children playing tag instead of computer games. Lanterns, campfires, and banjos instead of telemarketers and utility bills. They invest money in their hobby, but perhaps less than fishermen with their state-of-the-art sonar equipment and lures. I don't think we'll have to worry about unruly behavior, especially with such a small group."

"You used the word 'most,' " I said pointedly, being the defender of law and order and all that.

Miss Hathaway looked down for a moment, clearly uncomfortable. "According to Mr. Mazurri, sadly confined to his wheelchair because of rheumatoid arthritis, there is a small faction of what are known as 'hard cores.' They take their roles very seriously, and have nothing but contempt for the 'farbs,' as they call them. The term 'farb' supposedly comes from the phrase 'far be it from authentic.' Whether or not this is true, I cannot say. In any case, none of the reenactors will have ammunition in their muskets, or even paper wadding, due to the danger of pasture fires. It will all be" — she smiled — "smoke and mirrors, in a manner of speaking. Rebels from the South, Yankees from the North, mules, a cannon, a caisson, and of course the two saddlebags of gold."

Estelle, no more interested in the reenactors than the majority of those present in the cafeteria, flapped her hand. "So you're saying the gold might still be up on Cotter's Ridge. Just how much is it worth today?"

"That's impossible to say. What records that were not destroyed imply that the saddlebags contained gold Double Eagles, valued at twenty dollars each at the time. Today numismatists value such coins at anywhere from a few hundred dollars to as much as fifty thousand dollars, depending on the year of mintage and condition."

"You're fuckin' kidding!" said Jim Bob, his yellow eyes glinting like doubloons.

His wife swatted him hard enough to leave his head spinning for several days. "Miss Hathaway, please overlook that crass remark. Our citizens will welcome this opportunity to contribute to the preservation of the significant role our community played in the history of Stump County. We'll do everything we can long about the middle of next week to ensure that the documentary is a fine and fitting tribute."

My turn, as I stood up and said with all the grace of a strangled bullfrog, "Next week?"

Miss Hathaway managed a less than convincing smile. "Yes, I'm afraid we weren't able to give you much notice. It's a delicate matter, historically speaking. Once the journal turned up with the reference to the treasure, we decided that it would be in the best interests of preserving the sanctity of the site to minimize publicity. The journal will not be made available for scrutiny by historians until after the reenactment has been filmed. Perhaps the soldier who takes the role of Emil Jenks will actually find the cave and return with the saddlebags of gold. Wouldn't that be thrilling?"

I drove back to the bar with Ruby Bee and Estelle, waited patiently while the former switched on all the neon signs (including that of the molting flamingo out front with a dubious "V can y" promise), unlocked the cash register, and bustled around until she was satisfied.

"Any chance of a grilled cheese sandwich?" I said wistfully.

Estelle, who'd poured herself a glass of sherry and was now perched on her favorite stool at the end of the bar, said, "I swear, Arly, if you keep eatin' this way, you're gonna end up looking like Dahlia. I wonder how many yards of material she has to use to make one of those tent dresses she wears?"

"At least she doesn't have to buy maternity clothes," said Ruby Bee. "Her and Kevin sure couldn't afford that, what with the way the two of them keep making babies. Kevvie Junior and Rose Marie ain't gonna be much more than a year old when they get a baby brother or sister." She gave me a hard look. "I hear Eileen's tickled pink to have another grandbaby. I suppose any of us would be."

"Maybe she'll sell you one of hers." I

turned my attention to the pies under glass domes. "How about a slice of apple pie?"

Ruby Bee stalked into the kitchen. "Get it yourself," she said as the door swung closed.

I did as ordered, then glanced at Estelle, who was sucking on a pretzel. "So what do you think about this Civil War thing?"

"It might prove interesting. Jim Bob's probably right that it'll bring in some tourists, and gawd knows we can all use the business. Not that I'll see any of it, though. Folks don't think about stopping by to get their hair done before settling down on aluminum lawn chairs to watch a battle."

"It will be thrilling," said Mrs. Jim Bob as she and Harriet Hathaway came across the tiny dance floor. "The Civil War was a pageant of courage, sacrifice, romance, and patriotism. Brother against brother, neighbor against neighbor, lovers cruelly torn from each other's arms, young men losing their lives to protect their cherished traditions. I'll never forget when Scarlett O'Hara stood there on the top of the hill and swore she'd never go hungry again."

Miss Hathaway eyed Estelle's glass and sighed. "Do you think I could have a small drop of sherry? It's been a very long day."

Estelle patted the stool next to hers. "You

just climb right up here, honey, and I'll fetch you one. Would you care for a pretzel?"

This left Mrs. Jim Bob in a most awkward position. Sitting on a bar stool in proximity to alcohol might cost her the presidency of the Missionary Society if the information was leaked — and it surely would be. Then again, she was merely a commissioned officer in Miss Hathaway's brigade. She resolved the dilemma by remaining on the dance floor.

"We went by the police department," she said to me. "It was locked."

I shrugged. "I don't keep evening office hours. All criminal activity must take place between the hours of nine and five, excluding my lunch break. Maybe the town council should hire a deputy."

"Or a new chief of police," Mrs. Jim Bob said with a sniff.

"I hear there's an opening for a constable in Bugscuffle. Maybe I ought to apply for it."

Ruby Bee came out of the kitchen and banged down a plate in front of me. "What's all this about?" she demanded. "You aiming to order Jim Bob to fire Arly? You tell him if he does, he ain't never settin' foot in here again! I can get along just fine without him spilling beer all over the place, telling dirty jokes, spitting on the floor, and pinching women's behinds."

Mrs. Jim Bob stiffened. "I said no such thing. Miss Hathaway merely wants to finalize a few details before she returns to Farberville."

Ruby Bee looked down the bar. "I run a reputable establishment, Miss Hathaway, and you are most welcome — unlike some other folks. What can I do for you?"

"Please, call me Harriet. The documentary crew will arrive in five days, and as far as I've been told, will require rooms for three nights. Mr. Wallace will use one, and his assistant the other. May I assume your rates can be accommodated by our limited budget?"

"Just one assistant?" asked Estelle.

"He assured us that he has done this kind of thing before. Will they be able to have their meals here?"

Ruby Bee glared at Mrs. Jim Bob. "Their only other choices are the Dairee Dee-Lishus, which is run by a right surly Mexican fellow, and the deli at the supermarket, which was closed down during the grand opening on account of food poisoning. You recollect that, Arly?"

I put down the grilled cheese sandwich in

32

order to hold up my hands. "Leave me out of this. I'm just going to arrest people for speeding and spitting, or maybe both."

Mrs. Jim Bob, who was in one sense in the limelight but also in a pink one above the dance floor, took a cautious step forward. "That problem was resolved, but thank you so much for mentioning it, Ruby Bee. Arly, you will need to coordinate with the sheriff's department concerning crowd control and parking. When particular scenes are being filmed, the road will have to be closed to traffic. We cannot have chicken trucks and station wagons inching past the muletrain."

"Oh, heavens no," said Miss Hathaway. "In fact, at least half a mile of the road will have to be covered with dirt in order to re-create the conditions of the era. Even tire tracks would be incongruous."

Estelle smirked at me. "I have a pretty good idea who ain't gonna win any popularity contests when the time comes."

"What else is involved?" I asked Miss Hathaway as visions of tar and feathers danced in my head. "Are you going to drape the bar in camouflage and shut down the supermarket?"

"Nothing like that," she said. "Any glimpses of them on film can be edited out. Most of the action will be limited to the armies' campsites, the half-mile stretch of road, and a pasture that I was told belongs to Earl Buchanon." She smiled at Mrs. Jim Bob, who'd been creeping closer to the bar. "A relative of yours?"

Estelle snorted so fiercely that sherry dribbled out of her nose. "I should say so! If all the Buchanons was to have a family reunion, they could spend six weeks trying to sort out stepsisters and half brothers, first cousins, second cousins, cousins once or twice or three times removed that also happen to be aunts and uncles, not to mention certain paternity issues best left undescribed. Ol' Bigger Buchanon that lived up in Badger Holler fathered six girls and fourteen grandbabies, all of 'em with very distinctive dimples in their chins. Once the social workers saw what was going on —"

"Thank you for sharing that," said Mrs. Jim Bob. "Miss Hathaway would no doubt like to be getting home, so why don't we finish our business?"

"Didn't Posthumus Buchanon meet his wife at a family reunion?" said Ruby Bee, always eager to turn a tense situation into something that might require UN peacekeepers.

Mrs. Jim Bob crossed her arms. "As I said, let's finish our business. The reenactors will arrive on Thursday. That evening the Maggody Chamber of Commerce will welcome them with a picnic on the lawn of the Voice of the Almighty Lord Assembly Hall. Their respective camps, one out past the bridge and the other on the hillside below my house, will be open the following day for sightseers and teacher-supervised field trips for schoolchildren. On Friday evening, all the participants and local dignitaries will be invited to a pig roast, and then the next morning the skirmish will be filmed."

"What Chamber of Commerce?" demanded Ruby Bee, who was clearly still pissed at Mrs. Jim Bob. "Maggody doesn't have a fool thing like that."

"I guess you don't hear quite everything that happens here. The board consists of Jim Bob, Roy, and Larry Joe. Brother Verber is the spokesman for the spiritual community. I myself agreed to represent the various civic organizations."

Estelle turned back to look at her. "Next you're gonna say the Kiwanis and the Rotary clubs have been holding secret meetings out by the low-water bridge, unless you're confusing them with the Ku Klux Klan." She patted Miss Hathaway on the shoulder. "Not that we'd tolerate any of them."

I decided to intervene. "Miss Hathaway, if this private didn't know where they were when the Yankees attacked, why are you so certain it was here in Maggody?"

"Good question," said Ruby Bee. "As you yourself said earlier, there are plenty of other towns in Stump County with a creek and a ridge."

"Historians and scholars have generally agreed that the skirmish took place here, but hardly considered it worthy of more than a footnote. General Alessio's cavalry troop had a fairly concise idea how far south they came, and when they returned north during daylight hours, noted a few communities and landmarks. The route assigned to the Confederate unit was chosen to avoid a few strategically placed Union troops known to be in areas adjoining Stump County. There is very little doubt about the location. The young private's journal, however, was the first link with that particular allotment of gold coins."

"But no clues about what happened to the gold over the next hundred and forty years?" I asked. "No one stumbled across it?"

"Or what if," said Estelle, lowering her voice for maximum dramatic impact, "this lieutenant kept the gold and gave that young fellow a saddlebag filled with rocks?"

Miss Hathaway shook her head. "The journal mentions that the five surviving soldiers took off with nothing more than their weapons, abandoning everything, including their haversacks, canteens, and bedrolls. Henry was quite saddened by the fact he'd been obliged to leave behind a scarf knitted for him by his mother."

Ruby Bee sighed. "Such a terrible thing. It don't strike me as a pageant, but just one long tragedy."

"Perhaps you lack imagination," said Mrs. Jim Bob. "Miss Hathaway, I know you must be tuckered out. I'll take you back to my house so you can freshen up before you drive home. As for the rest of you, I will be delivering your committee assignments as soon as I've decided how best to delegate responsibility."

"Just who told her she hung the moon?" sputtered Ruby Bee as Mrs. Jim Bob and Miss Hathaway went out the front door. "She may be able to boss around the likes of Joyce Lambertino and Elsie McMay, but she'd better be real careful before she tries that with me. If we hadn't had company, I would have said it right to her face!"

"Fat lot of good it would have done," said Estelle. "She'd come back in your face with a Bible verse that gives her a divine right to stick her nose in everybody's business. Speaking of divine, I wonder where Brother Verber was tonight. It ain't in his nature not to jump to it when Mrs. Jim Bob snaps her fingers." She looked at me. "You seen him lately?"

I finished the last bite of my sandwich. "Why, just this afternoon, come to think of it. He was headed toward Cotter's Ridge, wearing a miner's hat with a lamp and carrying a metal detector and a gunny sack. I thought it was peculiar, but now I have a pretty good idea what he was up to. Maybe the Assembly Hall will have a new roof by the end of the summer."

On that note, I ambled out of the bar, managing to ignore their spate of questions. I walked down the side of the road to the PD and went inside to grab a couple of the catalogs that had come that day. My social life in Maggody was on the dreary side, since everybody remotely my age had been married for more than fifteen years and had grubby children, leaky washing machines, unpaid bills, and lifetime subscriptions to *TV Guide* and the *National Enquirer*. I got along fairly well with the teenagers, but I wouldn't be welcomed if I dropped by their hangout (the picnic tables in front of the Dairee Dee-Lishus).

The telephone rang, but I ignored it since I was really, most sincerely off-duty. After a few minutes of thought, I left the catalogs on my desk and drove to Farberville to catch a movie. *Gettysburg* and *Glory* were not on my list.

2

"They're gonna make a movie in Maggody?" Dahlia said as she sat at the kitchen table, surreptitiously eyeing what was left of her mother-in-law's double-fudge chocolate cake. "Doesn't anybody remember what happened last time? There I was thinkin' I was gonna be a famous Hollywood actress, and then things got uglier than Veranda Buchanon's front teeth. I liked to died from the embarrassment."

Eileen dried the last plate and put it in a cabinet. "I don't think any of us are destined for stardom, Dahlia. What's more, you're destined for the emergency room if you don't mind your diet. The doctor warned you that you're at risk for gestational diabetes, especially since you had it during your first pregnancy. If you're still hungry, you can have an apple."

"I ain't hungry." Dahlia wheezed sadly as the cake plate was whisked off the table and tucked out of sight on the top of the refrigerator. "So what's this movie s'posed to be about?"

"It's a documentary." Eileen related what she could recall of the story of the Skirmish at Cotter's Ridge, then concluded, "So a bunch of men dressed up like soldiers are going to set up their camps and then after a couple of days, start shooting at each other. In the end, the rebels skedaddle on their mules and the Yankees take everything that's left behind and head back toward the Missouri line."

"That don't seem fair."

"It was wartime, Dahlia, and that's what soldiers did. They'd even go out on the battlefield after the shooting stopped and take shoes, clothes, and weapons from the ones that had been killed. Neither army had enough fancy uniforms to go around. The rebels in particular were a real ragtag bunch, wearing whatever they brought with them when they volunteered."

"They look real fine in the movies."

Eileen considered trying to explain the difference between fact and fiction, but instead hung the dishtowel on a hook and made sure everything had been put away. Of course Earl would finish off the cake before he went to bed, so later she'd find the plate on the counter, surrounded by crumbs and a dedicated army of ants. In the morning, she'd be wiping up dollops of jelly, smears of butter, and splatters of bacon grease. She caught herself wondering what she'd do if she had a musket the next time Earl gulped down supper so he could race back to whatever foolishness was on TV.

Dahlia remained at the table, her hands clasped and her lips puckered with concentration. "You said the rebels left all this gold somewhere up on Cotter's Ridge. Why ain't anybody found it?"

"Who knows?" said Eileen. "Maybe somebody did, but was afraid to say anything because the government might want it back. I don't know what the law is."

"Well, if I was to find it, you can be darn sure I'd keep it."

"And just how do you aim to find it? The caves around here tend to be no more than muddy pits with spiders and snakes, along with bats hanging upside down on the ceilings. Bats and rats are practically kissing cousins, Dahlia, and I recollect how you carried on something awful over a little mouse in your kitchen. Eula Lemoy swore she could hear you all the way over at the Pot O' Gold trailer park — and that's a far piece."

Dahlia's pendulous chins quivered with indignation. "I was jest worried that it might run into Kevvie Junior and Rose Marie's room and start gnawing on 'em. Besides, I ain't gonna crawl inside the cave. Kevvie can do that part. He ain't afraid of anything" — she paused to reconsider — "excepting maybe Jim Bob."

"You don't know where this cave is," Eileen pointed out. "Cotter's Ridge is a big place, and not that easy to get around since the logging trails were abandoned more than fifty years ago. Raz is probably the only person that knows which ones are accessible — and you'd better not go asking him."

"I don't need the likes of Raz Buchanon to find the cave. My granny went up on the ridge ever' summer for more than eighty years to pick berries and collect roots for her homemade medicines. She ought to know where the caves are."

"Wasn't she madder than a nest of hornets when you moved her into the old folks' home after you and Kevin got married? From what you've told me, she won't even look at you when you visit."

Dahlia chewed on this for a minute, then said, "Well, she don't spit at me anymore, but that may be on account of her losing her dentures. I reckon I'll make her a real fine peach pie and pretend I want to listen to her stories so I can tell 'em to her great-grandchildren after she's dead. That might tickle her." She heaved herself to her feet and headed for the living room, where Kevin, his pa, and the twins were watching wrestling. "At least I got a plan."

"What we need is a plan," said Darla Jean McIlhaney as she sucked on a straw. "The gold's likely to be worth millions of dollars, so we could —" She stopped, wondering what it'd be like to have more money than she'd know what to do with. She was pretty sure she'd be transformed into Britney Spears and fly all over the world in a private jet, ordering her staff to make sure there were fresh flowers in her dressing room, letting them pick up her underwear off the bathroom floor, telling them to set out the garbage and feed the damn dog. If she even had a dog, for that matter. If she did, it would be one of those fluffy little things that slept on a satin pillow and never, ever slobbered on her foot.

Heather Riley and Billy Dick McNamara were sitting on the picnic table across from her, sharing an order of nachos slathered with sliced jalapeños. Neither had been dragged to the town meeting, and they'd listened without much interest when Darla Jean told them about the Skirmish at Cotter's Ridge.

"Get real, Darla Jean. Why would the gold still be there after all these years?" said Heather, who would have been a pragmatist if she could spell it, which she most certainly couldn't. "A hundred and forty years? The only thing that old around here is the dill pickles in Zanadew Buchanon's basement."

"Yeah," added Billy Dick, slapping at the bugs swirling around the outdoor lights in front of the Dairee Dee-Lishus. "You'd think somebody would have found it by now."

If Darla Jean hadn't needed their help, she would have flounced back to her car and left them choking on her dust. "This woman said that nobody knew about the gold until her society got the old journal a few weeks ago. Sure, somebody might have crawled way back into some cave and found it, but on the other hand, the caves around here aren't nothing more than holes. What's more, the soldier was looking for one that would be hard for the Yankees to find. The entrance was probably all hidden by brush and briars."

"And probably still is," Heather said as she licked cheese off her fingertips. "Billy

Dick, is that cousin of yours from Rosebud coming again this summer?"

"Depends on his probation officer."

Darla Jean resisted the urge to fling the remains of her cherry limeade at Heather. "Will you stop mooning over that pimply jerk and think about what I just told you? Do you want to get rich this summer — or pregnant?"

She frowned. "All I know for sure is that I don't want to be writing a paper next fall about how I spent my summer vacation wiggling around in filthy caves. There must be at least a hundred of them up on Cotter's Ridge, ferchrissake. What's more, there may not have ever been any gold. Maybe what's in the journal is nothing but bullshit."

"Yeah," said Billy Dick. "The fellow that wrote it just wanted to make hisself sound important."

"Or maybe it's still there," Darla Jean countered. "Are you gonna spend the whole damn summer sitting here, drinking cherry limeades, slapping mosquitoes, and wondering what you're gonna do after you graduate? Going to college ain't cheap, you know. Sure, you can get a minimum-wage job ripping gizzards out of chickens at the poultry plant in Starley City. After a few years, you can make a down payment on a trailer and hang your laundry on a clothesline so everybody can snicker at it." Appalled by her vision, she paused to take a breath. "That ain't gonna be me. I'm out of here."

"You might as well call Peter Pan and ask him to fetch you," said Heather. "Him and Tinkerbell, that is."

Darla Jean did not smile. "Maybe I'll do just that. In the meantime, I'm gonna try to find that gold." She climbed off the picnic table and tossed her cup into the metal trash can. "The next time you see me," she said as she headed for the car, "I'll be driving a silver Viper toward the county line. Maybe I'll wave, and maybe I won't."

Billy Dick, who was less than attractive even at his best, sniggered. "Just how are you gonna buy a fancy car like that?"

"I've got a plan."

By midmorning the following day, Lottie Estes had baked a lovely pound cake and artfully decorated the slices with her homemade plum preserves and tiny sprigs of fresh mint. Elsie McMay and Eula Lemoy expressed their admiration as they accepted second servings and refills of coffee.

Lottie waited until her guests were settled

back, then said, "I think we need to talk about this gold on Cotter's Ridge."

"It's all anybody was talking about at the vegetable stand this morning," Elsie mumbled through a mouthful of cake. "Amazin' to think there might have been a fortune just waiting up there all these years. Why, we could have picked blackberries not ten feet from millions of dollars worth of gold."

"I wish I could have stayed ten feet away from the chiggers," said Eula. "One time I got bit so bad around the ankles that my ma had me to soak my feet in sump water for a week."

Lottie had put down many an attempted diversion in her home ec classes over the last forty years. "Let's stay focused on the gold. Once this documentary is finished and the journal is made public, folks from as far away as California and Maine are going to start swarming over Cotter's Ridge. Professional treasure hunters will have all manner of sophisticated equipment."

"And we most likely don't have a shovel among the three of us," Eula said. "I used to have a trowel, but I left it outside one evening and those nasty little trailer park trash brats stole it. One of these days they'll come too close and I'll tan their behinds till they carry on like screech owls. They should all be sent to reform school, if you ask me."

"Along with their older brothers and sisters," Elsie added vehemently. "They throw trash in my yard every day after school. You'd think they was raised in a barn."

Lottie let them chatter while she took the coffeepot into the kitchen and rinsed it out. "Now then," she began as she came back into the living room, "we need to think about what to do. The gold has been in Maggody for a hundred and forty years, and I see no reason why some outsider ought to steal it from under our noses."

Elsie shrugged. "I agree with you, but I don't see what we can do. We ain't exactly of the age to go crawling into caves."

"And I'm allergic to mold and mildew," said Eula with a sniffle. "My eyes turn itchy and I can barely breathe. My doctor thought it was asthma, but then he did some tests and discovered I was allergic to not only the mold and mildew, but also dust, oak tree pollen, and a goodly number of other things too numerous to mention. Some days I'm afraid to set foot out of my trailer for fear of ending up in the hospital on a respirator."

"My second cousin Florellen is allergic to cat dander." Elsie put down her teacup and leaned forward as if to report some late-

49

breaking and therefore astounding medical news. "She swears that when she goes into somebody's house for the first time, she can tell right away if a cat has ever lived there, no matter how long ago. Even if it was ten years ago, she starts sneezing!"

Lottie wondered if she was fighting a losing cause, just like the Confederates had once done. "It's a shame your cousin isn't allergic to gold as well. We could tie a rope around her waist and drop her into the caves."

"Oh, I don't think Florellen would care for that. She's always been afraid of the dark. Once, when we were children and she was visiting, the electricity went off and she liked to wet her pants before —"

"The gold," Lottie said through clenched teeth. "We need to figure out how to find the gold."

"Before the gold diggers start showing up," said Eula, giggling. "I hope for their sake they don't wander too close to Raz's operation. They'll end up picking buckshot out of their backsides for a month of Sundays."

"I thought about Raz," Lottie admitted, "but I can't see him helping us — or anybody else, for that matter. But we have to come up with a plan." She picked up a notebook and a pencil. "Let's start by listing the different parts of the problem. One would be that we don't have any idea where the cave is." She wrote that down, then licked the tip of the pencil and said, "What else, Eula?"

"Well, even if we did, we don't have any way to go more than a few feet inside it."

"True. Elsie?"

"We don't have any idea how heavy these saddlebags might prove to be, so even if we did manage to find them, we might not be able to get them out of the cave and down the ridge."

At least they were making progress, Lottie told herself. Making a list always helped. Earlier in the year she'd assigned her sophomore girls to make a list of all the appliances in their houses. They'd been downright flabbergasted when they had finished. "These are good points. Now let's think of ways we might be able to locate the cave. We've already ruled out Raz. Diesel might have information, but I for one am not about to go knock on the door of his cave. Anybody that bites the heads off live squirrels and rabbits is not likely to be neighborly. What else?"

"What all did this young private say about the gold?" asked Elsie. "That woman from the historical society only read a few tidbits from the journal. Maybe she skipped over something because everybody was getting restless."

"Or," said Eula, beginning to bounce on the sofa, "maybe the private remembered something later and wrote himself a note in the margin. If he was delirious on account of the gangrene or blood poisoning settin' in, nobody would have paid it much mind. He might have tried to draw a little map that turned out to look like he'd squashed a spider."

"Very good." Lottie made a few notes. "I do believe you're on to something most promising. All we need to do is get hold of the journal and study it for clues. Then once we've pinpointed the cave, we'll have to find someone trustworthy to fetch the saddle-bags."

"Like ol' Whatsit Buchanon," said Elsie. "He's so thick-headed it would never occur to him to claim the gold for himself. We'll have to pay him, though, and make him swear ahead of time not to breathe a word until the gold is safely locked up in a bank vault."

Eula was still a mite bouncy. "Do you think we'll be on the news, or even one of those daytime talk shows like *Oprah*?"

"What I think," Lottie said as she closed the notebook and tucked the pencil behind her ear, "is that we ought to start by getting hold of the journal. Why don't we plan to go to Farberville tomorrow after church and drop by the Headquarters House for a friendly chat with Miss Hathaway?"

The matter having been settled, they moved on to the rumor that Mrs. Jim Bob had been seen staggering out of Ruby Bee's Bar & Grill the previous night.

"Folks sure were acting funny down at the supermarket this morning," Jim Bob said as he cut a thick slab of meatloaf to make a sandwich. "The checkout girls were buzzing like flies every time I came up to the front, and Joyce and Millicent were snickering when I chanced on them in the produce section. Where's the bread?"

Mrs. Jim Bob sat at the dinette table, papers fanned around her like she'd just claimed the pot in a poker game. "The bread is in the breadbox, and before you bother to ask, the mayonnaise is in the refrigerator, the plates are in the cabinet, and the napkins are in the drawer behind you. Do you think I sneak down here at night and move it all around just to befuddle you?"

"I reckon not," he said, still peeved that

she hadn't bothered to fix his lunch. If she kept this up, he thought as he opened the refrigerator and started hunting for the jar of mayonnaise, he'd take to getting a sandwich at the deli and eating lunch in his office, where he could have a beer and gaze at naked women on the Internet. "What's all that mess you're making on the table?"

"I am seeing to the preparations for the arrival of our guests for the documentary. It is a responsibility that I have taken upon myself, despite the headaches and frustration. If it was left up to you, we'd end up looking like a collection of ignorant bumpkins. It's not that I don't have other things to do, but if it's to be done right, I'll have to do it myself." She looked up at him. "Do you believe the mayonnaise is going to put itself back in the refrigerator? Last time I looked, it didn't have wings."

Jim Bob leaned against the edge of the counter and took a bite of his sandwich. "So what's this about people staying here? I don't want a houseful of folks tromping all over the place when I get home from a hard day at the supermarket."

"You may find yourself sleeping there if your attitude doesn't improve. We are having five guests, not a battalion. Miss Hathaway and Wendell Streek, as you heard

last night. We'll also have the impressionists, since they can hardly be expected to
stay at the Flamingo Motel. Kenneth
Grimley is a history professor from some
college in Ohio and plays the role of a
dashing brigadier general. Mrs. Corinne
Dawk of Charleston, South Carolina, who
plays the role of a widow woman left to run a
plantation, writes historical novels set
during the Civil War. Two of them have
been made into miniseries shown on cable
television. She will be accompanied by her
son's fiancée. None of them will be
tromping around the house or leaving
crumbs on the counter like some folks I
won't name."

Jim Bob stuck the mayonnaise jar back in
the refrigerator and brushed the crumbs in
the general direction of the sink. "Where's
that cobbler we had for supper last night?"

"If you're referring to the cobbler we had
for *dinner* last night, you finished it while
you were watching that ridiculous baseball
game." She studied the list of guests. "I suppose I can put Mrs. Dawk and the girl in my
bedroom, and Mr. Grimley and Mr. Streek
in the little bedroom next to the bathroom,
but that still leaves Miss Hathaway. I'll just
have to put her in your bedroom."

"Which puts us where?"

"On the sofa bed in the living room." Mrs. Jim Bob jotted down the sleeping arrangements, then added a reminder to buy several sets of towels just in case her guests were the sort who expected fresh ones every morning. The Yankee professor wasn't likely to, but genteel ladies from Charleston would. She could only hope they wouldn't expect a maid to unpack their bags, press their frocks, and strap them into their corsets. Perkin's eldest had her limitations.

Jim Bob gulped. "On the sofa bed?"

"You are more than welcome to sleep on a cot in the utility room if that's what you prefer. Married people have been known to share a bed, you know. The Lord approves of conjugal relationships. Adultery, on the other hand, is one of the stepping-stones to eternal damnation."

"I was just thinking how lumpy it is," he muttered.

"Life is lumpy, Jim Bob. I learned that not long after we said our vows." She picked up another piece of paper. "The Missionary Society will see to the picnic on the first night. I can have Ruby Bee provide vegetables, rolls, and desserts for the pig roast the following evening, presuming the Chamber of Commerce can find a few dollars to cover her expenses."

"Chamber of Commerce?"

"I've already explained that to you, but it seems you weren't listening. Maggody has a Chamber of Commerce, with you as president. Roy's the secretary and Larry Joe's the treasurer."

Jim Bob wished he'd taken a couple of swigs from the pint of bourbon he kept under the seat of his pickup. "We have a treasury? How much money do we have?"

"Not enough for you to take that bleached-blond harlot to Las Vegas," Mrs. Jim Bob said, shuffling through her notes to try to figure out how many folks would attend the pig roast. A corn casserole would be nice, she thought, unless the reenactors wanted to roast ears of corn on the grill in some sort of primitive display of authenticity. Baked apples went nicely with pork, as did marinated green beans. Perhaps brownies or carrot cake.

"There's a treasury somewhere up on Cotter's Ridge," said Jim Bob. "Could be millions of dollars just waiting to be found."

She glanced up at him. "And how do you intend to go about doing that?"

"Hell, I don't know," he said, then winced as she glowered at him. "I mean, somebody's liable to find it."

"If it's there."

"That Miss Hathaway said it might be. Buchanons have lived in these parts since before the Civil War. If two saddlebags of gold had been pulled out of a cave, the family would have known. I think the gold's still there."

"You may think whatever you like, but I have more important things to do what with five house guests. I'll have to provide them with breakfast and lunch every day, as well as tea in the afternoon. Perkin's eldest will hardly have time to do much cooking after making beds, cleaning the bathrooms, mopping the floors, and dusting and vacuuming downstairs as well as upstairs. Some days she reminds me of a box turtle creeping down the hall. It's impossible to find adequate help these days. Although I am appalled by the concept of slavery, I find it hard not to see some advantages."

Jim Bob had been wandering. "You know who probably has a real good idea where the gold is? Diesel, that's who. He's been living up on Cotter's Ridge for a long while, and ought to know every cave by now. If he'd stumbled across the treasure, he most likely dumped out the gold and took the saddlebags to make moccasins. I mean, it ain't like he can buy anything up there, so gold wouldn't be any use to him."

Mrs. Jim Bob looked up. "And you're going to go up to his cave and ask him to kindly show you the gold? He'll use your skin for his moccasins and stew the rest of you for his supper."

"You might be right about that. I'll have to come up with something."

"Go ahead," she said, "but don't expect me to cry and wring my hands when they haul what's left of you off the ridge in a plastic garbage bag. Maybe I'll use you to fertilize the azaleas. They're looking peaked this year."

Jim Bob went out to his truck. Rather than driving away, he found the bottle of bourbon and took a few swallows as he gazed at Cotter's Ridge. Damn that Diesel for being so ornery, he thought. After all, they were kin in some tangled way, and kin were supposed to help each other. Hell, they were *obliged* to help each other. Didn't everybody say that blood was thicker than water? The problem was that his blood was likely to prove it if he cornered Diesel without warning. What he needed was someone to soften up the crazy old coot and remind him of his ties to the Buchanon clan.

By the time he started down the driveway, he had a plan.

★ ★ ★

Ruby Bee put the last of the pies in the
oven, made sure the kitchen was nice and
tidy, and went out into the bar. Unsurpris-
ingly, Estelle was seated at the end of the
bar, with a glass of sherry and a basket of
pretzels within reach.

"Ain't you got any appointments this afternoon?" Ruby Bee asked in a most unfriendly tone.

"Got your knickers in a knot? I was supposed to give Joyce a perm, but she had to
cancel. It seems Larry Joe promised to
babysit, but he found a sudden desire to go
squirrel hunting."

"Squirrel season doesn't start up again for
most of a month."

Estelle gazed at herself in the mirror
alongside the back of the bar to make sure
the spitcurls surrounding her face were
lined up, then said, "Joyce doesn't think the
squirrels are in much danger. All Larry Joe
took with him was a spade and a sack of baloney sandwiches."

"Lookin' for gold, is he?"

"Him and half the town, from what Joyce
said. It seems to me that experienced detectives like us ought to figure out a way to use
our wits to find it first."

Ruby Bee cleared her throat. "We haven't

had a string of successes, Estelle. Arly flat out told me that all we've ever done is make a muddle of things. She has a point."

"Well, Miss Priss will change her mind when we show everybody up. The thing is, we need a plan. I tossed and turned all night long trying to think how we should go about this. Instead of counting sheep, I found myself counting caves up on Cotter's Ridge." She rubbed her eyes so Ruby Bee could appreciate her weakened condition, although she was mindful of her mascara and turquoise eyeshadow. "That's not to say I know where they are. I was never one to poke my head in a hole that might be home to a bad-tempered bobcat."

"Me, neither." Ruby Bee went back into the kitchen to stir the chicken simmering on the stove, then returned. "What's more, there are more caves up there than there are hairs sticking out of Alfresco Buchanon's ears. How in tarnation would we find the right one? I doubt this rebel soldier painted a big ol' X above the entrance to the cave."

"I sure could find a way to use a million dollars," Estelle said.

"I reckon we all could. I've been running this place for a long time, Estelle. The only time I've had a semblance of a vacation is when I was closed down by the health department on account of that grease fire in the kitchen. My knees are starting to bother me something awful when I scrub the floor. Just this morning my back felt so rusty I wasn't sure I could get out of bed. I did, of course, because I had to make biscuits and start a pot roast for lunch."

"Feeling your age, are you?"

"Not as much as you are. I know for a fact you're three years older than me."

Estelle bristled like a prickly pear. "And just how do you know that? Was there a time I'm unaware of when you worked at the county clerk's office filing birth certificates?"

"Never mind," said Ruby Bee. "But like you said, we could use a windfall. I just don't see how we can find this particular cave any more than we could find a talking squirrel and sell it to a carnival."

"And I can't see us asking Raz for advice. I'm not fond of having tobacco juice spat in my face. He ought to be put down like a rabid skunk." She popped a pretzel into her mouth and chewed it thoughtfully. "But I can think of somebody else who knows Cotter's Ridge better than most anybody, somebody who had the run of the ridge all his life, someone on speakin' terms with all the copperheads and lizards . . ."

"You'd better not be thinking what I'm

thinking you're thinking," said Ruby Bee, her tongue getting tangled along the way. "We've got all these fancy folks and make-believe soldiers coming to Maggody. I don't have any idea how many tourists will come to gawk at them, but I reckon more than two or three. Mrs. Jim Bob's liable to march in here any minute and tell me she expects cheese grits and cornbread for a hundred people. This movie fellow and his assistant will be staying out back, and they'll probably expect room service and mints on their pillows at night. There is no way on God's green earth that we're going to bring in a hundred pounds of pure trouble. You just put that right out of your head, Estelle Oppers! I ain't having anything to do with this birdbrained scheme of yours, not even for a share of a million dollars!"

"Suit yourself," said Estelle, lifting her chin so she could look down her nose at Ruby Bee with the condescension of European royalty. "I am perfectly capable of doing this by myself. I just hope you recollect the story of the Little Red Hen. She ended up eating her fine fresh bread all by herself."

"Arly will kill us."

"Well, at least we'll be able to afford marble headstones."

★ ★ ★

Brother Verber was stretched out on his sofa, his head propped on a pillow and a glass of sacramental wine nearby on the coffee table. It being Saturday afternoon, he should have been slaving over his sermon for the following morning, but he was having a problem settling on a theme. Lust, adultery, perversion, fornication. None of them grabbed his fancy as they usually did. Hardly a week had passed in all these years since he'd received his mail-order diploma from the seminary in Las Vegas that he'd failed to berate his congregation for one or more of these, odds being he'd hit home in the second or third pew. Why, just watching beads of sweat popping out on someone's brow justified his calling to the cloth. His flock floundered, but he himself was the shepherd that collected up their souls and led them back into the glorious green pasture of righteousness.

And there was that bothersome story about a fortune up on Cotter's Ridge.

Brother Verber kicked off his slippers and took a drink of wine. All that gold, just waiting to see the light of day. It could be put to use in the Almighty Lord's war against evil, he thought as he wiggled his toes. Sin was out there, behind every door and down every alley. Young women pulling off their lingerie for the sake of a few dollars, lurking in houses of ill repute where gentlemen paid for their services, laughing when they should be down on their knees repenting for their sins. And what they did in the photos of the magazines Brother Verber kept in his closet was enough to keep Satan hisself stoking the furnace.

The fortune had to be put to use to combat this pervasive moral degradation, he decided. He struggled to his feet and went into the kitchen to make a cheese and sweet pickle sandwich. Ever since he'd heard about the gold, he'd felt uneasy, as though some foul odor was beginning to taint Maggody. If the gold was to fall into the wrong hands, why, there'd be no telling what might happen. The Pot O' Gold trailer park might be overrun by brassy sluts. The cheerleaders at the high school might take to wearing outfits that exposed their navels and accentuated their perky breasts. Cable television might be introduced, with all its scurrilous temptations. Before too long, his congregation would dwindle to a few emaciated widows and he'd be reduced to living off their charity and deviled eggs.

Brother Verber took the wine bottle with him as he returned to the sofa. He couldn't allow this wickedness to pervade, he concluded as he chomped down on the sandwich. Any fortune lying about on Cotter's Ridge was going to be dedicated to the Lord's work, be it a hospital in some African country, a new roof on the Assembly Hall, or even a double-wide replacement for the current rectory.

But he knew he needed a plan before the Yankees started descending like fruit flies on a ripe banana. He'd never spent much time on Cotter's Ridge, having an aversion to ticks and chiggers, but he was painfully aware of the countless caves. The gold could be in any one of them. After a brief consideration, he figured the Lord wasn't likely to provide a map. No, it was going to require the help of someone likely to know each and every inch of the ridge — and that was Raz Buchanon.

Which presented a problem, Brother Verber admitted to himself as he refilled his glass and stretched back on the sofa. Raz was ornery, foul-mouthed, and most likely a soldier in Satan's army. Raz had never set foot in the Voice of the Almighty Lord Assembly Hall, which was for the best since he'd be struck dead on the spot.

He'd have to be approached carefully, even artfully. He'd have to be connived into

66

letting down his defenses and being tricked into telling what all he knew about the caves on Cotter's Ridge. An offer of a discount baptism and a choir robe wasn't going to do the trick.

Brother Verber knew he needed a plan.

3

I'd opened all the windows (okay, both of them) in the office to air out the sour odor left by Perkin when he'd dropped by earlier to accuse Raz of some convoluted malfeasance involving dawgs. It's hard to follow Perkin when the spittle is flying. I'd learned long ago to duck my face and pretend to scribble notes — as well as keep a box of tissues in a desk drawer.

Now I was flipping through catalogs as I awaited the opportunity to earn my paycheck by foiling an armed robbery at the post office or negotiating a hostage situation at the Suds of Fun Launderette. In that we don't have a post office and there's nobody in Maggody worth taking hostage, I figured I was in for a peaceful afternoon.

There was some potential peril in hanging out at the PD, however. Stump County Sheriff Harve Dorfer could call at any second and wheedle me into writing up a gory car wreck on some back road or fishing a bloated body out of the reservoir. Harve was likely to be more shorthanded than usual, since the weather was balmy and a goodly number of his deputies were fond of fishing (or at least sitting in john boats, drinking beer, and telling lies). Then again, I was going to need Harve's cooperation toward the end of the week. Not only was I going to have to deal with the reenactors, their mules, horses, muskets, wives, children, and whatever they'd stuffed in their haversacks, but also slack-jawed tourists, half a mile of barricaded road, and the good ol' boys at the pool hall whose pickups sported Confederate flag decals. Most of them would be hard-pressed to name the century in which the Civil War took place, but their resentment simmered despite their ignorance.

I wondered how long it would be before I'd have to start hauling people out of caves on Cotter's Ridge. I took my flashlight out of a drawer and determined that the batteries were dead. The only rope at the PD was a piece of frayed clothesline I'd found in the weeds out back. I could tie a square knot and a noose, but neither would be adequate if Dahlia got herself wedged in a rabbit hole. The police academy had offered no courses in rescuing overly enthusiastic treasure

69

hunters, should they deserve to be rescued. There were enough caves to accommodate half the town, or perhaps all of them. After a while, Raz and I would be the only ones left to walk the deserted street and compete for cans of corn and peas at Jim Bob's SuperSaver Buy 4 Less. My face would become gray and haggard as I sat alone on a stool at Ruby Bee's, praying the beer distributor would arrive before there was water, water everywhere but not a drop to drink.

I mention Raz because he most likely had the gold buried in his barn. He uses the caves to store his jars of moonshine until he has a chance to take them to consumers across the county. What's more, his stunted branch of the clan had been doing the same since before the Civil War era. Maybe his great-grandpappy had been hunkered behind a tree when the Confederate private hid the gold. Maybe decades ago a Buchanon bushcolt had wiggled down a passageway in hopes of snagging some critter for supper. Braised groundhog innards *à l'orange*, a popular staple of Ozark haute cuisine.

When the telephone rang, I gazed at it without enthusiasm. Early in the day for a wreck, but the denizens of Stump County didn't necessarily observe the traditional cocktail hour. Late in the day for a body to bobble to the surface, since the crack-of-dawn fishermen usually were the first to spot them. That left my mother.

Sighing, I picked up the receiver. "What?"

"You need to get over here right now."

"Why?"

" 'Cause I say so. There's someone here."

"Who?"

"That man who's filming the documentary. He told me who he was, then ordered a cheeseburger and a beer. Now he's sitting in a booth with Hormel Buchanon and Hormel's uncle Fibber."

I leaned back in my chair and propped my feet on a corner of the desk. "Then it sounds as if the situation is under control, unless, of course, you forgot to mention that he's juggling hand grenades and foaming at the mouth. I'm sure Hormel and Fibber can keep him entertained with their most recent Elvis sighting."

"Now you listen up, young lady! I am your mother, and I want you here in the next three minutes. Do you understand me?"

"Okay," I said, aware that it would be a whole helluva lot easier to go over there than argue with a woman who was less co-operative than your standard-issue mule, be it Confederate or Union. "Maybe I'll give him a traffic ticket for driving inside the city limits without a permit. Jim Bob will be impressed with my dedication to duty."

"I don't know what you're talking about," said Ruby Bee, "but I reckon the clock's ticking. I was planning to make cherry cobbler for lunch tomorrow, just because I know you're smitten with it, but there ain't no law that says I have to. What's more, you need to put on some lipstick and make sure your hair's tidy."

Ruby Bee's talent in areas of blackmail and extortion was legendary. I told her I'd be there before too long, and hung up. Putting on lipstick would require me to go across the road to my apartment, which seemed like a lot of effort to impress a documentary filmmaker from — I thought for a moment — Missouri. Missouri was twenty miles away from where I was sitting; Hollywood was more like two thousand.

In a display of petulance, I waited ten minutes before I went outside and walked down the road toward the peculiar pink building known as Ruby Bee's Bar & Grill. Roy Stiver was parked in a rocking chair in front of his antiques shop, snoozing in the sunlight and waiting for the next tourist to marvel over his quaintness and buy a grossly overpriced piece of flea market crap. Joyce Lambertino was wrestling with a gas pump at the self-service while countless children wrestled with each other in the back of her station wagon. Eula Lemoy was wheeling a cart around the supermarket parking lot, probably in search of her car. Mrs. Jim Bob drove by in her pink Cadillac, too preoccupied to acknowledge the likes of me. Raz rattled by in his pickup truck, with his pedigreed sow Marjorie in the passenger's seat, her snout stuck out the window to enjoy the breeze.

All in all, pretty normal for a Saturday afternoon in Maggody.

"It's about time," Ruby Bee said by way of greeting as I sat down on a stool. "Don't look now, but he's over there in the corner. From what I could hear when I took 'em a pitcher, Hormel's telling him about the Japanese kamikaze pilot he found hiding in his root cellar way back in 1949. Hormel's real fond of that story."

I leaned over the bar and whispered, "How am I supposed to arrest this guy or whatever it is you want me to do if I don't look at him?"

"He's familiar, that's why. I thought I

told you to put on some lipstick."

"Familiar?"

"Ain't you ever bumped up against that word before?" She took a mug from the shelf below the bar. "You want a beer?"

"Yes," I said, "and a quarter for the juke box. Any requests?"

She took a quarter from the cash register drawer. "I'd like to think you won't be gaping at him like some moonstruck girl."

I casually sauntered over to the juke box. After making my selections, which didn't take long since the repertoire hadn't changed since the last mastodon died of old age, I glanced at the booth. The man was watching me, and he was indeed familiar. Maybe not as familiar as the nose on my face or the toasty brown swirls of meringue that Ruby Bee uses to top her lemon pies, but familiar.

Oh yes, familiar.

My knees buckled, but I made it back to my stool. I wasn't surprised when he sat down beside me and said, "Thought I'd run into you."

"Maggody's not quite as crowded as Manhattan," I said. "You could go for years in Manhattan without running into anyone you knew. Now running over someone would be a different matter, but of course no one in Manhattan has a car because of the traffic."

You may be thinking that he was my ex-husband, which he most assuredly was not. No, he was the very intriguing man I'd encountered when I'd been bullied into chaperoning the local teenagers at a church camp not so very long ago. You may also be thinking that I was babbling like an idiot. No argument there.

"I tried to call you at the PD," he said.

I met his gaze in the mirror on the backside of the bar. "I don't always answer the telephone."

"My name's Jack Wallace, for the record."

"Is that another alias?"

He ducked his face, which gave me the chance to ascertain that he was still the slightly disheveled, loose-limbed, squared-jawed guy I'd encountered fishing beside a lake — and about whom I immediately found myself entertaining adolescent fantasies of the sort I would never admit. Lawrence of Arabia's blue eyes. The Sundance Kid's tousled blond hair. Indiana Jones's grin.

I watch a lot of movies featuring guys who seldom shave.

"Ruby Bee said you're filming the documentary," I said ever-so-cleverly.

"That's right. An old friend of mine is a reenactor. When he mentioned Maggody, I thought it might be interesting, so I volunteered my services. I work for an advertising agency in Springfield."

"An advertising agency?" said Ruby Bee, swooping in like a turkey vulture. "Ain't that a coincidence, Arly? That ex-husband of yours worked for an advertising agency, too, didn't he? It was a good thing when you upped and divorced him like you did. Nowadays, you're living here in Maggody as a single woman." She smiled at Jack Wallace, who was looking a little pale. "I'm sure you're not an underhanded sumbitch like Arly's ex-husband. I can't think why she married him in the first place."

My look, or perhaps the way my hand tightened around the mug, was enough to send her to the far end of the bar. "So, Jack Wallace," I said, "if that's your real name, how are your children?"

"They're doing well. My sister looks after them when I'm working. Their mother has supervised visitation and is back on medication. They participate in soccer, baseball, music lessons, all that sort of thing."

"No nightmares about the Moonbeams?" I said.

"No, they thought it was creepy, but they were never abused when their mother took them to live with that cult. They're just happy to be back with their dog, their bicycles, their friends in the neighborhood. They adore my sister and their cousins."

"Convenient for you."

"Especially when I'm out at a car dealership filming a commercial. You wouldn't believe how many of these guys insist on wearing toupees no matter how windy it may be. One of the crew described the last one as another 'flying ferret shoot.' "

I smiled, but I was still struggling to keep my cool. I'd hoped that he would call after our last encounter, but I'd chosen to not answer the telephone on the off chance he would. Ruby Bee would not have found my behavior mature. I took a swallow of beer. "So you volunteered your services to the Stump County Historical Society?"

"I suppose I did."

"And . . . ?"

"I came down today to have a look at the locations so I could make sure to have whatever equipment I need. I've done this kind of thing before."

"Really?" I said, wondering what he meant. Done what kind of thing before? Chanced upon an available female with an inadvertent glint in her eye? Okay, the calculating glint of a Westchester matron eyeing the abs of a new pool boy.

"I've filmed several of these events for my friend, Frank Reinor. He fancies himself to be a colonel in a Missouri regiment, but sometimes he has to be a private. Damn well breaks his heart, but he's a devotee of the war when he's not peddling computers at a chain store. He'd like nothing more than to let his teeth rot so he'd be more authentic, but his wife has her limits."

I was going to respond when Ruby Bee came over and clutched my wrist.

"Jim Bob's on the phone," she said, nearly hyperventilating. "He says there's a crisis at the old folks' home and you'd better get over there right this minute!"

"A crisis? Is that all he said?"

"That's all he said, but he was real agitated. Well, he also said he'd fire you if you wasn't there in five minutes, but I told him a thing or two and he backed off. Still, you'd better go look into it."

I looked at Jack, who seemed amused. "Duty beckons," I said, wildly imagining him swooping me into his arms and declaring that nothing short of some cataclysmic event of galactic significance would prevent him from expressing his passion in one of the motel rooms out back.

"I'll be back in a few days to start filming," he said. "Perhaps we can continue our conversation then."

Rhett Butler would have swooped. Jack Wallace seemed content to nod at us and amble out of the bar.

Ruby Bee dumped the contents of my mug into the sink. "Well, that was interesting, I must say. I recognized him right off, but I don't recall it ever being explained what his role in that mess was."

Rather than enlightening her, I said, "I guess I'd better go see what's got Jim Bob in a tizzy."

"Maybe so," murmured Ruby Bee. "Come by later if you're of a mind. I'm making chicken 'n' dumplings."

Jim Bob was pacing across the porch of the old folks' home when I drove up and parked beside his truck.

"About goddamn time you got here," he said as I got out of my car. "You was hired to do a job, Chief Hanks, and one of them is to look after the citizens."

I smiled sweetly. "And here I've been thinking I was hired to do kidney transplants. Just this morning I pulled a donor out of a pond and packed his vital organs in ice. Is the surgical staff prepared? Are you going to scrub in?"

"One of these days I'm gonna fire your ass — and you'd better hope I don't have a twelve-gauge when I do it!" He banged open the screen door. "Now get inside and hear what Miz Pimlico has to say. She's beside herself with worry."

I followed him into the foyer and then into an office, where Miz Pimlico appeared to be restraining herself from an overt display of distress and was, in fact, eating a bowl of red Jell-O and frowning over a crossword puzzle.

"This here's the chief of police," Jim Bob said. "Tell her what happened before she has you locked up for negligence."

Miz Pimlico, a woman of some years with a girth that rivaled Dahlia's, looked up with a confused expression. "Are you still here?" she said to Jim Bob. "I thought we'd already settled this. Petrol does this kind of thing at least once a month."

"Does what?" I asked her.

"Takes off. He'll be back in time for supper. I was a little surprised that he chose this afternoon, since he'd expressed interest in our four o'clock decoupage class. He's created impressive projects in previous sessions. One of his cookie tins showed quite a talent."

Jim Bob shoved me forward. "Just tell Arly here what happened — okay?"

Miz Pimlico reluctantly put down her spoon. "Petrol was present at lunch. He seemed to enjoy his meal, as did all of our residents. Tomato soup, pimento cheese sandwiches, and dill pickle slices are always popular, as well as nutritious, and Jell-O makes them quite giddy. We had a nice rest period afterward so that the poor old things could digest properly. When this person" — she glared at Jim Bob — "came demanding to visit, Vonetta went to Petrol's room and discovered that he wasn't there. This is not a prison or a psychiatric facility. We are required by state law to leave exits unlocked in case of fire."

"And Petrol's taken off before?" I said.

"Yes, indeed. Sometimes he goes back to his old house. He claims he's checking for vandalism, but I suspect he buried jars of moonshine over the years. He stinks to high heaven when he finally staggers back in time for supper."

Jim Bob growled. "What's his roommate got to say?"

"I have no idea." Miz Pimlico moved aside her crossword puzzle and opened a file. "If you'll excuse me, I need to review this week's invoices. I believe in pinching every penny so that our residents can savor their remaining years in a clean, stimulating environment. And that, as we know too well, takes money."

Jim Bob dragged me out to the hallway. "Maybe Petrol said something to this roommate of his. Go find him and ask."

"Just why are you so interested in Petrol?"

"He's kin, that's why. Buchanons have powerful ties. What's more, we can't let doddery old fools like Petrol get snockered and go stumbling around in the woods. He could be lying facedown in Boone Creek right this minute, with the crawdads and minnows nibbling his eyeballs. You're the chief of police, and it's your job to find him and haul him back."

"Okay," I said, "I'll see if I can track him down — but only if you go back to the SuperSaver. As you said, it's *my* job. I'll let you know what I find out."

"You damn well better," he muttered, then slammed out the front door.

I waited until I heard his pickup truck drive away, then poked around until I found an aide in a lilac polyester uniform. She was around my age, but if I'd gone to school with her, I hadn't had any memorable encounters. "Are you Vonetta?" I asked.

82

Her eyes widened. "Why, yes," she whispered. "Are you here to arrest somebody?"

"Nothing like that. I just thought I'd try to find Petrol and get him back in time for the decoupage class."

"It ain't worth your time. He goes off like this ever now and then. Short of tying him down, there's not much we can do. His room's down at the end of the hallway, and he can slip out the exit door faster'n a snake going through a hollow log. Personally, I always hope the crazy old coot won't come back. He pinches my fanny so hard I get bruises. Today at lunch he snatched up Miz Claplander's Jell-O cup, tumping her iced tea in the process. You never heard so much caterwauling in your life."

"Vonetta," Miz Pimlico said from the doorway of her office, "we do not stand around and gossip about our residents. Shouldn't you be getting ready for the decoupage class?"

Vonetta sold me down the river in a Maggody minute. "But Miz Pimlico, she was asking all these questions, and what with her being the chief of police, I didn't reckon I had any choice but to answer them."

I shot her an annoyed look, then said, "As soon as I have a word with Petrol's roommate, I'll be on my way. His room is by an exit?"

Miz Pimlico pointed at a hallway. "Last room on the left. I'd like to think you won't go upsetting Mr. Whitbreedly. His daughter told him about this upcoming Civil War battle, and he's convinced Yankees are hiding at the far edge of the field."

"I'm just going to ask him about Petrol," I said.

"Well, don't be surprised if he assumes you're a Yankee spy and refuses to speak to you. He thinks Vonetta here is one of those camp followers of ill repute. She had her hands full giving him a sponge bath this morning."

Unable to respond, I went down the indicated hallway and eased open the door. "Mr. Whitbreedly?"

"Who're you?" came a muffled voice from under a thin cotton blanket.

"Chief of Police Arly Hanks. I'm looking for Petrol."

"Then use your eyes, gal." He cackled. "Don't see him, do you?"

"Did he say anything before he left?"

The blanket lowered a few inches, giving me a view of tufts of white hair and fierce blue eyes. "I don't recollect he did. Who'd you say you are?"

"Not someone who's planning to pass your invaluable information to the enemy. Go back to sleep, Mr. Whitbreedly."

"Damn Yankees."

I left him swearing under his breath and went out the exit. All looked peaceful along the tree line at the far side of the field, but I supposed it was remotely possible that an errant band of Yankee reenactors were making their way toward Cotter's Ridge to retrieve the Confederate gold their ancestors had overlooked a hundred and forty years ago. What was more important was that I could see no indication that Petrol had forced his way through the weeds in the direction of Boone Creek.

I decided to swing by Petrol's house and make sure he wasn't hiding behind the woodshed with a quart of Raz's vintage 'shine. I was not about to roll up my jeans and wade down Boone Creek from the bridge north of town to the low-water bridge on County 102. I might have to do so if Petrol was still missing in the morning, but I figured I could declare an emergency and persuade Harve to send out a couple of deputies to help. And Hizzoner, of course, since he'd expressed such fervent kinship with Petrol. Which was odd, I admit, but I didn't much care about his ulterior motive

(I never doubted for a second that he had one).

Petrol's place, and then the PD to analyze my reaction to learning that Jack Wallace would be back in town in a matter of days.

Mrs. Jim Bob rapped with the fury of a ravenous woodpecker on the door of the rectory. "Brother Verber? I need to speak to you this very minute! I don't know what you've been up to, but I'd better not find a hussy inside there!"

After he'd stuck the wine bottle and tumbler in a cabinet, crammed a magazine under a cushion, and smoothed back what hair he had, Brother Verber opened the door and gestured for her to come inside. "Sister Barbara, I don't know how you could even entertain such a sinful idea. I was resting on the sofa while making some notes for my sermon tomorrow. I was thinking about a war theme, maybe comparing the Civil War to the eternal battle between good and evil. 'Course therein lies the problem, since —"

"I'm sure we'll all find it very enlightening," she said, perching on one end of the sofa. "You did not come to the meeting last night. I almost felt like I should apologize to all the righteous members of the congregation for your absence. You are the spiritual leader of our little community, Brother Verber, and you have an obligation to set an example."

He was sure that the truth, which involved movies at a back alley theater in Starley City, would not sit well, even though he'd forced himself to sit through all four of them only in order to broaden his awareness of the depths of depravity awaiting his lambs should they stray. Instead, he hung his head. "I should have been at the meeting, Sister Barbara, but the Lord had a mission for me."

"Which was?"

Which was, in fact, a very good question. Brother Verber tugged on his nose while he thought. "Why, a tent revival on the other side of Hasty, sponsored by the Pentecostal church. I don't agree with some of their positions, but I've always thought they had dandy revivals. I was thinking to make some notes in case we ever decided to have one right here in Maggody. I can just hear us shouting 'Hallelujah!' as the stars begin to flicker and the moon rises above Cotter's Ridge. Can't you feel the rapture, Sister Barbara? Can't you feel it?"

Mrs. Jim Bob wasn't sure he was telling the truth, but let the matter drop since his presence at the meeting hadn't been all that important, anyway. "I need you to help me put together the details for next week. We can't have people darting every which way like headless chickens." She pulled a thick sheaf of papers from her handbag. "Now here's what I have in mind for the opening event Thursday evening right here on the lawn of the Assembly Hall. You'll begin with an invocation asking the Lord to watch out for us in case one of the reenactors accidentally shoots someone. Then —"

"I didn't think they was allowed to load their weapons."

"Well, no, they're not, but there have been some incidents. After that —"

"There've been incidents?" he said as he took a handkerchief from his pocket and blotted his forehead. "Folks gettin' shot?"

"Rarely. Let's move on to more practical matters, Brother Verber. After our regular potluck supper on Wednesday evening, have the teenagers fold the tables and prop them against the side of the church so they can set them up the next afternoon. I think it will be easier to use butcher paper rather than tablecloths. Do you agree?"

"Those big ol' musket balls could do some damage to a body's insides."

Mrs. Jim Bob rattled the papers in irritation. "The hundreds of thousands of boys and men killed during the war would agree if they could do so. Did you check the supply of paper plates and plastic forks like I asked you to? From what Miss Hathaway said, we can expect about forty or fifty people."

Brother Verber felt a searing pain. "Rip right through you, they would. Your guts would go spewing like spaghetti in tomato sauce."

"Is there any hope you can stop this blathering and offer me some guidance? I should not have to take this entire burden on my own shoulders. I need you to pay attention while I tell you what I've decided, and then assure me that it's all under control. The meek may inherit the earth one of these days, but in the meantime we need to get organized."

He wished he could slip into the kitchenette for a swallow or two of sacramental wine, but he could see that he'd be pushing his luck right up to the edge. He squeezed Sister Barbara's knee and said in the solemn, rumbly voice he used at funerals, "I already know in my heart that you've done a right fine job. Just looking at all those lists instills me with admiration for your undeniable talent in matters of organization. That rummage sale we had last summer wouldn't have netted us fifty cents without you overseeing every detail. The Voice of the Almighty Lord Assembly Hall would be lost without you, our guiding angel."

"Well, yes," she said, somewhat appeased. "Here's the menu I'm proposing."

He squinted at her spidery notes. "That looks mighty fine, Sister Barbara."

Mrs. Jim Bob removed his hand before she developed circulation problems and ended up in the hospital like Dingaling Buchanon, who'd had an embolism shoot right up to his brain. It'd taken several days before the staff had realized he'd slipped into a coma, and then it was too late. "Of course it's fine," she said. "On Friday afternoon I'll have a luncheon for our special guests. I'm thinking about a garden party, with round tables set up outside the sun porch. Chicken salad with apples and walnuts, asparagus, and Perkin's eldest's fluffy biscuits with my own grape jelly. I can't decide about the dessert. We could have some sort of chocolate cake, but I don't want anything too heavy. What do you think?"

Brother Verber's mind had been straying, as it often did. When he realized she was staring at him, he sidled in and put his hand on her thigh. "Where would we be without your inspiration, Sister Barbara? It's so easy to wander off the path and give way to Satan's temptations, allowing ourselves to succumb to lust and degradation, but you are always leading us, swinging your lantern to guide us back into the ways of eternal bliss."

"I asked you about dessert, Brother Verber. Should I serve something lighter, like angel food cake?"

"I do believe you should," he said. "Shall we fall to our knees right here and now and ask the Good Lord to bless this menu?"

She stood up. "Another time might be better. I need to catch Joyce Lambertino and see if she'll bring potato salad on Thursday."

When Dahlia arrived at the old folks' home, the decoupage class was in full swing. Snippets of paper cluttered the floor, and several of the residents were decorating not only pie plates but also themselves. She stood in the doorway for a long while, then grabbed Vonetta's arm.

"Where's my granny?"

"Under the table," Vonetta said grimly. "I must have told her a dozen times to stop eating the glue, but she kept sucking on the paintbrush until I had no choice but to take it away from her. Now she's sulking."

Dahlia squatted and waved at her granny. "I brought you a treat."

Her granny glowered like a treed coon. "Like'n I care?"

"I come to visit," Dahlia said, trying to sound all soothing. "I got some cookies."

"Don't like cookies."

"I reckon you like lemon snaps."

"Mebbe I do." Dahlia's granny crept between the thicket of bony legs and emerged from under the table. "Give 'em to me and be on your way, you ungrateful girl! Dumped me here like I was nothin' but a mess of turnip greens, you did. What'd you want from me now? I ain't got any organs to donate, not at my age. I slaved away all my life to take care of your mama, and then, when she upped and died, to take care of you. So how'd you repay me? Why didn't you just put me in a gunny sack and toss me in Boone Creek? It might have been a sight more merciful."

"Amen," chimed in Mr. Whitbreedly. "It would have saved us from all her bitching and whining. The chicken's too dry, the meatloaf's too greasy, the collard greens are too tough, the soap operas ain't to her liking. Go get a gunny sack, girl."

Vonetta dearly wished that Miz Pimlico hadn't gone into Farberville to do whatever she did like clockwork every Saturday afternoon, rain or shine. The fact of the matter was that Shirlee was supposed to have shown up at half past three, but gossip had it that she entertained callers in her trailer at the Pot O' Gold. Minimum wage could lead someone to do that, Vonetta supposed, but that wasn't much help what with the riot brewing in the crafts room.

"I can't believe my ears!" sputtered Dahlia. "Here I am with homemade lemon snaps, and you have the nerve to say something like that! I've a good mind to march right out and never set foot in here again!"

"Suits me," said her granny. "You was always scheming to get what you wanted, even back when you had pigtails."

"Oink," Miz Claplander said, not exactly helping things.

Dahlia realized she could wrap her hands around her granny's throat and choke the life right out of her. As satisfying as it might prove to be, it would not give her any clues about the cave where the Confederate private had hidden the gold.

"Just quit your complaining and come sit out on the porch," she said real nicely, like one of those smarmy ladies selling jewelry on TV. "We'll have ourselves some cookies and talk about when you was a girl."

"And I was Batman," said Mr. Whitbreedly. "Me and Robin, we was a team like nobody'd ever seen before."

"Oink," repeated Miz Claplander, this time for no apparent reason, but seeming to enjoy it. "Oink, oink!"

Dahlia's granny stared at her, then nodded at Dahlia. "I reckon we can sit for a spell. Don't go thinkin' I'm gonna tell you about Tishew Buchanon, though. Some memories are best left out in the back pasture." She took a second look at Dahlia's generous contour. "You still breedin' like a rabbit?"

"Kevvie and I are expecting a child," Dahlia said with as much dignity as she could muster, since Miz Claplander was still oinking like a greased pig at the county fair and ol' Mr. Fondro was tweaking every breast, no matter how deflated, that he could reach. Vonetta was in tears, but nobody was paying her any mind. They never did.

4

Mrs. Corinne Valenthorpe Dawk appeared to be a tiny bit perturbed as she studied the bank statement. Perhaps more than a tiny bit, in that her face was flushed and her blood pressure was shooting skyward like a rocket over Charleston Harbor. She forced herself to put down the paper and gaze out the window at the creamy flowers and dark, shiny leaves of the magnolia tree that was by far the tallest in her neighborhood. No one with functional eyesight could dispute that. There was absolutely no reason to pay for the services of a surveyor, as Lucinda Mettier-Longley had suggested. Corinne made a mental note to exclude Lucinda from her next luncheon, presuming she could afford to have one.

The bank statement lay in a stripe of sunshine, looking as innocent as an invitation to a dinner party or a charming letter written by a fan. It was far from either, however. She picked it up and frowned at the expenditures that Simon had made the previous month. Two thousand dollars at an electronics store, more than six hundred dollars at a men's clothing store, and nearly that much at a sports equipment outfitter. How many ties and tennis rackets did a boy need?

What's more, she was certain that the credit card statements would reflect equal, if not greater, damage. Simon seemed to take great pleasure in treating his friends to lavish dinners and chartered cruises. He was going to have to learn self-discipline, she thought. She'd warned him time and again that her resources were not bottomless, and that money did not grow on the magnolia tree or on the massive azaleas in the front yard.

She was still seated at the desk in her office when she heard Simon and Sweetpea come into the house, laughing as they always did. Such an attractive couple, the envy of so many at the country club, Corinne thought, forgetting her financial woes for the moment. Simon was six feet tall, with curly hair and an adorable smile rivaled only by the marble cherubim in the cemetery. Sweetpea was several inches shorter, so she fit nicely when he draped his arm over her shoulder. She had the

Yarborough family coloring: auburn hair, freckles, and clear green eyes. Both were tanned and healthy, as if they'd stepped off the cover of one of the nicer magazines.

"Hey, Mother," called Simon, "you want to join us for a gin and tonic on the porch?"

Sweetpea, known in formal situations as Frances Butler Yarborough, came to the doorway of Corinne's office. "That mean ol' Simon beat me three straight sets without even working up a sweat. I s'pose I'm going to have to take some more lessons this summer."

Simon appeared behind her. "It won't help. What you need are some sessions with a shrink to get over your irrational fear of fuzzy balls." He raised his eyebrows at Corinne. "Shall I make you a drink?"

"Thank you, dear," she said. "There are fresh limes in the refrigerator. Come along, Sweetpea. I have a few suggestions for the flower arrangements at the reception."

Once they were on the porch, Sweetpea sank into a wicker chair. "My mama's been driving me crazy as a loon. I'm even thinking Simon and I ought to skip out on the wedding and head straight for Aruba. Surely we can find somebody there who can marry us without any folderol. People did used to get married in the parlor, you know, and then serve tea and cucumber sand-wiches. 'Course Daddy'd have a stroke if I canceled the wedding after all the money he's shelled out for deposits. Most every day Mama makes me sit down at the dining room table so we can make decisions about the silliest little ol' things! Just this morning we had the most awful row about the color of the candles."

Corinne smiled uneasily. "Oh, honey, you're just getting jittery like every other bride throughout the ages. Your mother's been gracious enough to keep me informed, and I'm quite sure everything will be per-fect. Let's not have any more talk about eloping."

"Sounds like a fine idea to me," said Simon as he set down a tray on the coffee table. "As long I still get a bachelor party, that is. Parker and Trey are plotting some-thing totally nefarious."

Corinne accepted the proffered drink. "Are the two of you packed for our up-coming adventure? It may be cooler in the mountains than it is here. I'm going to take a sweater and my wool shawl, just in case."

"I still can't believe we're going some-place that's not even on a map," Simon said. "This reenactment business is absurd. When I was on the set of your miniseries and obliged to wait around with these un-shaven, filthy wretches stuffed in stinking uniforms, I was terrified I'd end up with lice. Thank gawd I could go back to a decent hotel every night and take a shower. Most of them insisted on camping out so it would be more authentic. How authentic can it be with cameras, booms, lights, prop girls, makeup trailers, a director and pro-ducer, and even a damn catering trailer serving Dijon chicken and veal scallopini for lunch? Jesus, it was unreal."

"I think it will be interesting," Sweetpea murmured with a sly smile. "When my cousin Yancy Lee over in Mississippi told me about it, I knew right then and there it was something I wanted to see, especially if you had the starring role. Who knows if this documentary might earn some critical at-tention and get shown at film festivals? You could end up being an A-list Hollywood actor. We could end up going to parties with Julia Roberts and Tom Cruise."

"Or not. All I'm going to do is sit around a campfire with a bunch of fat old men who smell worse than the runoff from a hog farm. Their idea of a good time will prob-ably be to see who can rip off the loudest fart."

Corinne clucked her tongue. "It's much

too early in the afternoon for that sort of remark, dear. I thought Sweetpea's idea was very clever. If the documentary is a tasteless disaster, then it will never be mentioned again. If it has any charm whatsoever, we'll have our own little film festival right here, and then I'll see if I still have any connections in Hollywood."

Simon slouched further down. "So everybody in Charleston can watch me make an ass of myself? What could be more entertaining?"

"Now, Simon," Sweetpea said, putting her hand on his knee, "there's no way you're going to make any bigger ass of yourself than you did when you ran my daddy's sailboat into the pier during the regatta last summer. You'll look real dashing in your uniform."

"You haven't seen my uniform. Mother insisted on buying it at an antique clothing store, and wouldn't even allow me to have it dry-cleaned. The coat cuffs are two inches short, and half the buttons are missing. The stains are either blood or shit."

"Simon," his mother said indulgently, "please watch your language. Sweetpea's not used to that sort of vulgarity."

Sweetpea giggled. "It's a good thing you weren't watching our tennis match earlier. I was bitchin' so loud the pro got complaints. I'm afraid I could never be a heroine in one of your books, Corinne. The only time I've ever felt faint was when Daddy gave me a Jaguar on my sixteenth birthday."

"The women in my books do not swoon. They held together the very structure of the Southern way of life even as Yankee soldiers burned their houses, stole their crops, and raped their sisters. My great-great-grandmother took in wounded Confederate soldiers and nursed them until they could continue to their homes. She also insisted that the ladies of Charleston meet weekly for their book club even as Sherman's army advanced."

"My great-great-granduncle freed all his slaves as soon as the war started and told 'em to go North. Only two or three of the house slaves stayed put, and he insisted on them being paid every week. 'Course it was probably twenty-five cents, but it wasn't like they could go to a mall."

Corinne decided to change the subject. "Simon, have you memorized your lines? A sloppy performance on your part will reflect on me. I only agreed to do my presentations if you were given the leading role. This will not be like the mini-series, when you were one out of hundreds of soldiers. This is your only chance to be noticed by important directors and producers."

"Yeah, I know," said Simon. "I don't have a lot of lines on camera. Most of it will be voiceover and I can read from a script in an air-conditioned studio. Too bad the rest of this crappy skirmish can't be staged there, too."

"Mules, dear," Corinne said. "So messy."

Yawning, Sweetpea stood up. "Sorry, but the tennis must have worn me out. Simon, you'd better run me home so I can take a nap before I get ready for the party." She bent over to brush her cheek against Corinne's. "I enjoyed visiting with you. Maybe we can talk about flower arrangements next time. Better yet, after we get back from wherever this town is, we can do lunch and drop by some of the floral design studios. Pamela discovered a divine one run by an Italian who claims to be a count. She said he positively licked her hand."

"Yes, we'll do that. Simon, kindly fetch the copy of the journal before you leave tonight. I barely glanced at it when it arrived the other day. Perhaps I can find a way to incorporate some of it into my presentation. A little local color makes it more interesting for the children."

"As you wish, *ma petite mère*," he said,

proving he had picked up a semblance of culture from the prep schools and colleges that had expelled him over the last six years.

Once they'd left, Corinne took the glasses to the kitchen. She returned to her office and sat down behind the walnut desk. Sunlight now shone on the bookcases lining two walls, bathing the spines of well over a thousand books in a musty glow. Some were collections bound in leather. Others were more mundane but necessary for research purposes. Simon kept badgering her to use the Internet, but it was much more satisfying to pull out the perfect volume and curl up in the overstuffed armchair. Countless of her characters had done so in their libraries, even as war raged in the adjoining county.

Rather than retreat to one of her great-great-grandmother's volumes of poetry, however, Corinne picked up the letter from her agent in New York. She'd read it before, but she forced herself to read it once more before she took it to the barbecue grill in the backyard and sacrificed it to the gods of publishing. Which might be futile, since they were a godless bunch.

Sales down, returns up, interest flagging at her current publishing house, the possibility of a smaller advance for her next book.

She'd received an almost identical letter the previous year. Her sales had shot up after each of the miniseries had aired, but then tapered off. The die-hard historical readers were aging and therefore dwindling; the younger readers preferred contemporary novels with sex rather than romance.

The letter obliquely emphasized the importance of a marriage between Simon and Sweetpea (and her family's money). Ancestry and tradition still dictated Charleston society, but neither paid the bills. Nor would her advances and royalties if Simon was not tightly curbed. Sweetpea had a pretty face, but Corinne suspected she also had an inner layer of icy calculation. She probably knew to the penny what her first pair of white party gloves had cost, as well as the Jaguar her daddy had given her. Not, of course, that she would admit it if she were tied to a stake and knee-deep in kindling. Charleston's finest were oblivious to money, as long as they had it.

Corinne was in the living room, the crumpled letter in her hand, when she saw the police car pull up in front of the house. As she had done several times during the previous few days, she ducked into the kitchen and steeled herself to ignore the peal of the doorbell.

★ ★ ★

At the very same time that Corinne was cringing in her kitchen, Kenneth Grimley was admiring himself in his bathroom mirror. He often dressed in the dark blue uniform, with brass buttons and gold trim, a cape lined with scarlet silk, a broad-brimmed hat with a plume, and always the Colt army revolver and the sword in its engraved silver sheath. Such a dashing figure, he told himself as he squared his shoulders and shot his reflection a bold, if not cocky, grin. General Wallingford Ames, commander of the Illinois Army, leader of the troops that had defended the indivisibility of the nation, grinned back at him.

For the moment, it didn't matter that he was short and chubby, had an unfortunate habit of squinting when he was nervous, and taught nineteenth-century history to students who slept through his lectures and cribbed their term papers from the Internet. That his second wife had moved out and was threatening to get her mercenary little hands on his pension and almost all of his assets. That he'd been turned down as a candidate for the chair in Nineteenth-Century American Studies. That his latest proposal for a book on the impact of the struggle for control of the Mississippi River in 1863 had been rejected by his own university's press. That his cat had run away. That his socks didn't match. That his microwave made a curious humming noise that most likely would lead to an explosion.

General Wallingford Ames was above such concerns.

After half an hour of waving his sword about and posturing, Kenneth put away the uniform and settled for a civilian ensemble of pajamas and a robe. Still a professor at a second-rate school, still wearing one brown and one navy sock, still a loser in all aspects of his life, still worried about the microwave.

He poured himself a glass of wine and sat down at his desk to make sure that his airline tickets were in order. The historical society, wherever it was, had promised to pay expenses as well as an honorarium, which amounted to a nice sum. Speaking to braindead elementary and high school students required minimal energy. The only instances in which he could raise a few eyelids were when he whipped out his sword and slashed about as if a rebel soldier were crouched under a desk. He had yet to discover one.

Kenneth had never given up hope, however. The enemy was lurking. The Confederates had overtly abandoned the Cause, but the South had neither forgotten nor forgiven. Resentment stewed in every cast-iron skillet, in every pool hall, in every meeting hall that hosted weekly gatherings of the Sons of the American Confederacy and provided tables for the Daughters of the American Confederacy to hold their bake sales. Sure, they claimed they were raising money for the upkeep of monuments and cemeteries.

Kenneth knew better. They were slowly and surely arming themselves, weapon by weapon, so that they could wage war against the North and reclaim their pride and independence. They were insidious. They were the maggots that fed off diseased corpses and awaited their time to take wing. He'd met them at reenactments, when they pretended that they were pretending. He knew they were practicing. They'd learned from Bull Run and Gettysburg, and now they were preparing to drive out the lawful government and seize back their plantations, their right to own slaves, their lavish lifestyles of mint juleps and sexual excesses. Even the trailer park scum seemed to feel entitled to some fraction of the decadent past. Kenneth wondered if they had any idea how their venerable ancestors had lived — and died.

He found the photocopy of the journal that he'd been sent. He'd skimmed through it earlier, but it was of minor interest. General Wallingford Ames would not have participated in a minor skirmish, or even noticed it. At best, a lieutenant, a colonel, and a dozen privates had gotten themselves shot over a cannon and a few mules.

The reference to Confederate gold was curious, but unreliable. Kenneth had referred to the records kept by General Alessio's army, but no mention of gold had appeared. What remained of the records from Little Rock was vague. One mostly illiterate private's journal was far from definitive. General Lambdin's army had been coming from the Indian Territories, but there was no evidence they'd been allotted pay.

What was more worrisome was the quiet but nevertheless potentially violent rebellion arising south of the Mason-Dixon Line. No one else suspected, or would admit it, anyway. But if there was a fortune in gold from a federal depository, then it rightfully belonged to the Union. Kenneth Grimley knew he had no choice but to accept the responsibility to recover it before it fell into the hands of the enemy. He owed that much to President Lincoln.

Wendell Streek was as excited as a retired accountant could be, even when confronted with blatant miscalculations in the corporate books. The journal by Henry Largesse was fascinating — no, it was positively thrilling. The names, the dates, and even the family details gave Wendell a heady sense of déjà vu, as if he'd ridden a mule to the very campsite beside Boone Creek and pitched a tent. Fired his musket at unseen Yankee soldiers. Fretted that no one in the unit could use the cannon to return fire. Fled when death was imminent, and sacrificed himself to defend Farberville from General Alessio's army. Felled in the field by a musket ball while charging the artillery line. Left amongst the stubble of corn to curse the Yankees and whisper a final word to the pale-complected girl who prayed nightly for his safe return.

Wendell took out a magnifying glass and made sure that he was accurate in his transcription. The young private had not been impressively skilled in penmanship, and often scratched out words and even sentences. Sloppiness that would not have served him well had he survived and looked for work in a local business. His spelling was at best primitive. The journal, Wendell decided, would hardly merit publication as a document of historical interest. It covered only a few months, from when the private volunteered until he returned home with an amputation wound festering with gangrene. Field surgeons had done what they could without antiseptics or anesthesia. At best, a splash of whiskey had served as both.

What intrigued Wendell were the names sprinkled throughout the fifty pages. Henry Largesse seemed to have convoluted connections with most of the soldiers he encountered. This one was a second cousin, that one was the brother-in-law of a third cousin, the next was the husband of a girl with whom Henry had danced at a fancy party in Little Rock before enlisting. It was as if the South had been an expansive family, in which everyone was related from Richmond to New Orleans. Except, of course, for the slaves and the peckerwoods and the swamp rats who lived in shacks and never came to town.

Wendell was gratified to have traced his ancestors back to sturdy shop owners and blacksmiths loyal to the Cause. It would have been nice had there been a plantation owner among them, or even a banker. Alas, he knew that he was descended from the middle class. But they had been the backbone of the South. For his own entertainment, he'd traced Harriet Hathaway's ancestry all the way back to a colonist who'd arrived in Georgia in the early eighteenth century. Branches of her family had gradually moved westward, farmers for the most part, with an occasional blacksmith, cooper, or schoolteacher. Harriet's paternal great-great-grandfather had owned a newspaper in a small town south of Memphis. In an editorial, he'd condemned the institution of slavery and been horsewhipped in front of the local courthouse.

Wendell's ancestors had been ignored for the most part.

Genealogy could be so very interesting, he mused as he peered at a word that was no more than a squiggle. It was likely to be a name, but almost impossible to decipher. He flagged the page and continued. Henry had conscientiously recorded names whenever he could, presenting Wendell with the delicious specter of months and months of research as he traced each individual as far back as records would permit.

And then, when he'd completed his efforts and could write the definitive work on the Skirmish at Cotter's Ridge, he might find a publisher, if only a small regional press specializing in obscure Civil War history. He might be invited to speak at a conference, or at least at a Stump County Historical Society meeting. He would be the logical candidate to introduce the documentary to groups of schoolchildren touring the Headquarters House.

Wendell blotted his forehead with a tissue, then returned with renewed energy to his task. When his mother warbled his name from the bottom of the staircase, he went down to join her for a cup of tea and a documentary on the History Channel.

Jeb Stewart sat on the front stoop of his trailer, soaking his boots in a bucket of water so they'd be as stiff as beef jerky for the reenactment over in Arkansas. They were a size too small, so he could already rely on them to raise blisters and leave bloody sores, but it never hurt to add a little insurance. The rebs hadn't selected their shoes at a boutique selling sweat socks and wristbands. Once the boots that they'd brought from home fell apart, they'd worn what they could find in the field. A good number of them had gone barefooted, mutilating their soles on prickly weeds and sharp rocks.

He'd already lost fifteen pounds in the last two weeks, eating nothing more than hardtack and a squirrel he'd run down on his drive home from work. Belluccio, his boss, had threatened to fire him for bouts of dizziness, but Jeb didn't give a shit. Crop-dusting didn't demand much more than staying awake for endless passes across a field, sort of like marching in formation for days on end. All those boys had been obliged to do was keep on moving, step by mindless step.

He was rationing himself on water, too. One canteen a day, if that much. He was still drinking tap water, but he was thinking he should be getting his water from the creek behind the trailer park. If it gave him diarrhea, so much the better. He'd had a dandy case at Gettysburg, and been so doubled over with cramps that he could scarcely stumble forward when the order had been given. After he'd been shot, so to speak, he'd lain in the middle of the field for the rest of the afternoon, soiling his pants and ending up with such a bad sunburn that he'd had chills and fever the next few days.

A fine battle, Jeb thought with a smile.

The Skirmish at Cotter's Ridge was going to produce far fewer opportunities for authenticity. According to the information he'd been sent, he and the rest of the unit would stage a scene in which they rode in on mules provided by area farmers. They were to set up camp, and then act out some melodramatic nonsense in which they confiscated a pig to cook for supper. Spend the rest of the day hanging around the camp, cleaning their muskets and splashing in the creek for the benefit of tourists with their camcorders and designer sunglasses. Then, the following morning, they'd draw to determine the order in which they'd get killed and only then get around to some action. Jeb hoped he wouldn't have to go down right at the start. Just lying there, puffing up his belly so he'd look bloated, wishing he could swat the flies off his face but knowing he couldn't — well, it wasn't like crouching behind a wall, shooting at the damn Yankees.

This business about the gold bothered him. He tugged at the tips of his mustache, which straggled well below the corners of his mouth. Confederate gold, rightly belonging to the CSA (or one of its loyal descendants). It sure as hell didn't belong to the federal government, which had swept through the South with its superior weaponry and better-equipped armies. These days, the Yankee soldiers like he'd met at Chancellorsville, had cell phones in their packs and asthma inhalers in their coat pockets. At Pea Ridge, Jeb had overheard one of them who died early in the day talking to his stockbroker. Fuckin' farbs.

The saddlebags of gold were rumored to be hidden in a cave on some nearby ridge. He wasn't real particular to caves, preferring the wild blue yonder above the cotton and okra fields. There might be a chance to slip away and have a look, though. The filmmaker would have to pack up before dark, so they'd be left for the rest of the evening to compare the patina of their buttons and belt buckles, while drinking whiskey out of battered tin flasks. Diarrhea would give him a fine excuse to wander away, presuming there'd be enough moonlight to prevent him from falling off a bluff.

Jeb was more comfortable with the relentless flatness of Mississippi. Still, he figured, if there was gold to be found, he was the one who aimed to do it, before some bastard got lucky, even if it meant quitting his job and heading there a few days early. Then he could sell the contents of the saddlebags to a dealer and finish up his doctoral degree.

Andrew Pulaski's day had been very profitable. His employees had sold three new Cadillacs, and he himself had persuaded a fetching blond divorcée to take a used

Mercedes off his hands at what he'd assured her was an incredible price. Her personal information was written neatly in a notebook he kept at the office. Taking it home would lead to complications if his current wife were to find it. She was a suspicious sort, inclined to leap to conclusions.

But to his delight, she'd left for the evening to attend a benefit for the St. Louis symphony, which meant Andrew could sit on a deck chair on the patio, sip scotch, and smoke a cigar. He finished looking over the information provided by the Stump County Historical Society. Most of it involved inane events he would not attend and discomforts he would not experience. He had contempt (unspoken, of course) for the reenactors who insisted on wearing long johns under bulky wool uniforms, no matter the season. He did not object to a certain display of perspiration, but he had no intention of collapsing from a heat stroke. As the colonel of the cavalry troop, he could remain on his horse, barking orders and cutting a fine figure for the camera. He still received compliments for his demeanor when he'd reported to President Lincoln in *The Blue and the Gray*. It might be time to start a subtle campaign within the unit to be promoted.

It was going to prove interesting to see

who was participating in this minor reenactment. He'd heard that Kenneth Grimley was coming, which was not surprising since Grimley would appear for a garage door opening if he were paid. Frank Reinor, always a bore, a few men from Springfield and Branson, and some unfamiliar ones from Illinois and Tennessee. What Andrew found more intriguing was that Corinne and Simon Dawk were listed as participants. He knew Corinne well, having encountered her at various reenactments and found her chillier than a frozen margarita. Simon was beneath his notice — but his fiancée was not. The lovely Sweetpea, as refreshing as a mint julep, as fetching as a dewy blossom, and as passionate, sweaty, and foul-mouthed as a Tallahassee whore in August, when the nights were so steamy it was hard to catch a breath.

Oh, yes, he thought, puffing on his cigar. Darlin' Sweetpea.

Waylon Pepperstone, an auto parts salesman when not a private first class in a brigade out of Rolla, Missouri, tried again to explain to Gretchen why he was going to be out of town on her birthday.

"They're making a movie," he said, squeezing her hand so hard she winced.

"Well, it's more of a documentary, but there'll be cameras catching every bit of it, and one of these days we can sit right here on the sofa and see it on television. Just imagine seeing me on television. The next thing you know, they'll be asking me to be in some Hollywood extravaganza with Kevin Costner and Bruce Willis."

Gretchen yanked her hand free. "And that's what I'm supposed to tell everybody on Saturday night when they ask where you are? This is my twenty-first birthday, Waylon. My parents bought a case of champagne and ordered a two-layer cake from a bakery. My cousins from Kansas City are coming, and my grandmother all the way from Peoria. But you're going to be playing make-believe soldier in some Arkansas podunk, so you can't bother to be at my party. It's going to be the most humiliating moment of my life!"

"Now, honey," he said, "I've already promised to take you to Sir Sirloin on Sunday night. They have a fine salad bar."

"I don't understand why you do this silly thing, anyway," she said sulkily. "You're a grown man, Waylon. You've got a full-time job and your own apartment. Why do you want to dress up and run around pretending you're shooting people? The Civil War ended a long time ago. Why can't you stop fighting it and let bygones be bygones?"

Waylon sighed. "It's a part of history that we shouldn't forget."

"Why not? Abraham Lincoln freed the slaves and some Confederate general surrendered. Everybody went back home and got on with their lives. I'll bet you ten dollars they didn't all decide to put on their uniforms the next year and go reenact the battles for fun."

"Most likely not," he conceded. "It's just that when I join up with a unit to do a reenactment, I'm not just a salesman in a plaid jacket, offering coffee and doughnuts so I can sell mufflers. It's life and death out there on the battlefield. It's my chance to be a hero, if only for an afternoon. When the order's given, I run forward, yelling like I was hell-bent. Maybe the comrade next to me falls, but I keep on charging the enemy line. All I can hear is cannon fire and screams. The smoke gets thicker, but I don't falter unless I'm supposed to take a hit. When I do, I lie there knowing that I gave my best to defend the Union and everything it stands for."

"Do you want me to go with you so I can sing the national anthem while you writhe on the ground like the snake my father killed with a shovel this morning?"

Waylon most certainly did not want Gretchen to come with him for the reenactment of the Skirmish at Cotter's Ridge. Some of the guys brought their girlfriends along, but he had an agenda. Several years back, when he'd made deliveries for his uncle's appliance business, he'd been in all sorts of little towns in northern Arkansas, including Maggody.

There he'd met a woman that he still dreamed about, especially when the weather turned warm and he could sleep out on the porch and savor the hint of honeysuckle in the breeze. Nothing had happened between them, but he'd seen the gleam in her eyes when she'd tilted her head and smiled at him. Remembering the intensity of the electricity between them still gave him a pleasant tingle.

Had she been dreaming of him, too?

5

The creatures might have been stirring all night on Cotter's Ridge, but I'd nodded off during a particularly silly movie and slept without disturbing dreams. Long about ten o'clock on Sunday morning, I ate a bowl of cereal, crammed my dirty clothes into a couple of pillowcases, and went over to the Suds of Fun Launderette (a misnomer if ever there was one) so that I could kick off the week with clean underwear in case I ended up in the emergency room.

Or the morgue, courtesy of a cannon-ball.

As usual, I lacked an adequate number of quarters and was obliged to argue with Bateyes Buchanon until she gave me change. Once I had several machines chugging along merrily, I used the last quarter to call the old folks' home.

"Is Miss Pimilco there?" I asked.

"She don't come in until noon. This is Shirlee."

I told her who I was, then said, "Has Petrol shown up?"

"Not exactly."

"What does that mean? Did he stop by for a moment to wave from the parking lot, or did you find a few body parts on the porch and now you're waiting for the rest of them to turn up before you patch him back together?"

Shirlee gasped. "Oh, nothing like that, Chief Hanks. His niece called yesterday evening to say she was taking him to stay with her in Drainard for a few days. She was as sweet as could be, and apologized for not telling us the plan. As far as I'm concerned, she can take him to China on one of those real slow boats."

"Did you get her name?" I asked.

"No, I don't recollect that she told me. I got to get back to work now. Miz Pimlico will be back afore too long if you want to talk to her. Have a nice day."

I replaced the receiver, bought a soda and a bag of chips from Bateyes, who reluctantly tore herself away from a tabloid long enough to slap down change, and then settled in to wait. Which is mostly what I did in Maggody, with a few notable exceptions. I gazed at the washing machines, numbly watching the sudsy water swirl like eddies in Boone Creek.

I'd thought long and hard about Jack Wallace, but had arrived at no conclusions. For all I knew, he was engaged, remarried, planning to enter the priesthood, or awaiting sentencing on a felony conviction. Then again, available men were hard to find in Maggody, or even in Stump County. I'd had a few romantic entanglements since I'd come home to brood, but none of them had lasted. Ruby Bee and Estelle were convinced that all I needed was a new hairstyle and a positive attitude. Maybe they were right, God forbid.

I was stuffing sodden jeans into dryers when Joyce Lambertino came into the launderette.

"I got to tell you something," she began, then noticed Bateyes's sharp look and dragged me behind the broken pinball machine. "Larry Joe saw something up on Cotter's Ridge last night."

"Like Raz's still?"

Joyce shook her head so vehemently that her ponytail nearly slapped me in the face. "No, Arly, and you got to listen to me. I told him he ought to track you down and tell you hisself, but he's too embarrassed."

I removed her hands from my shoulders. "How did you know I was here?"

"I called Ruby Bee, looking for you, and she said Eula Lemoy saw you carrying your dirty laundry down the steps from your apartment. We figured out you most likely weren't going to church, what with you being an atheist and all."

"And carrying dirty laundry."

"That, too," Joyce acknowledged with a faint smile. "Don't you want to know what Larry Joe saw last night? I swear, he was shivering like a wet dog when he came stumbling into the house. I couldn't get a word out of him until he'd gulped down a big ol' glass of bourbon."

"What did he see, Joyce?" I asked patiently, prepared to hear about fornicating bears or albino wildcats.

She glanced at Bateyes, who apparently found us more interesting than celebrity exposés and singing cows. "A ghost," she whispered. "He swears he saw a rebel soldier slinking through the trees. He said the figure was all shadowy, but he could make out the gray uniform, gold braid, and squashy hat." She grabbed my shoulders before I could make a prudent retreat. "Do you think maybe all this business about the lost gold has stirred up the private what stashed it there all those years ago? He could have been resting in his grave, all peaceful like, and then realized he had to come back and retrieve it before the Yankees got it."

I pretended to give her theory some consideration as I once again freed myself from her grip. "Let's think this through, okay? Half the town's determined to find the gold, and it's possible that outsiders have heard the legend, too. The ridge could have been a busy place last night, for all we know. Larry Joe might have seen someone in a gray sweatshirt and a gimme cap, or he might have seen a glint of moonlight on a scrub pine and let his imagination go wild. You do remember when he claimed to have seen Bigfoot in your backyard, don't you?"

"That was unfortunate, but you have to keep in mind that all kinds of folks were seeing aliens and flying saucers. Larry Joe wasn't the only one that got all het up. I seem to recall that Ruby Bee saw a shiny silver alien walking on water."

"Look, Joyce, there's not much I can do about whatever Larry Joe thinks he saw last night. If it was indeed a ghost, then it vaporized when the sun came up."

She gave me a disappointed look. "I just thought you'd want to know."

"I'll write up a report," I said, wondering if I had a form for spectral trespassing. "As long as Larry Joe stays off the ridge, he should be safe. I gather he didn't find anything of more substantial value?"

"No, about all he did was twist his ankle and pitch face-first in a patch of poison ivy. He said there's no way on God's green earth that anyone's going find the cave." She looked at her watch. "Gosh, I'd better get going. Larry Joe said he'd get the kids ready for church, but I can't trust him. I've been waiting six weeks for him to do something about the leak under the kitchen sink. There are days, Arly, when I envy you being single and as free as a butterfly. You can just up and leave whenever you want. Myself, I've always wanted to see the Eiffel Tower. The closest thing I've seen is the water tower on the hill next to the airport in Farberville. Not exactly the same."

She left, leaving me to consider how sorry I ought to feel for myself, having seen the Eiffel Tower on several occasions but never the water tower. I returned to the business of transferring my laundry to dryers. Half an hour later I was folding towels when Hizzoner came storming into the launderette.

"I thought I told you to find Petrol," he said.

"I found out where Petrol is," I said

126

evenly. "That should be close enough."

"Well, it ain't. I called out to the old folks' home and they gave me some shit about how he'd gone off with a niece. Petrol may have nieces and nephews from here to Kalamazoo, but not one of them's likely to invite him for a visit. Why would anyone let him into their house, ferchrissake? If he was to set foot in the SuperSaver, I'd throw his ass off the loading dock and make book on how high he bounced off the gravel."

"You'd do that to your beloved kinfolk?"

Jim Bob's eyes narrowed. "I don't need any smartass remarks from you, Chief of Police Hanks. Just find him."

"You planning to put him up in your guest room?"

"No, I ain't planning to put him up in any fuckin' guest room!" Jim Bob noticed the rapt expression on Bateyes's face and lowered his voice to a less-than-endearing snarl. "You get him back to the old folks' home by five o'clock this afternoon or you'll find yourself applying for a job at the poultry plant."

"Probably not that," I said as I resumed folding towels. "I might fill out an application to be a chambermaid at the Flamingo Motel, though. Drop by and I'll tickle your nose with a feather duster."

Jim Bob left. I stacked my laundry, nodded to Bateyes, and went back to my apartment. No Yankees attempted to ambush me as I crossed the road, nor did any grayish hazes await me inside. I would have liked a cappuccino, a croissant, and a copy of the Sunday *New York Times*, but settled for instant coffee and the usual pols and pundits on the morning talk shows.

I was not pleased when the telephone rang, but, as I may have mentioned, I rarely was.

"Yes?" I said into the receiver.

Ruby Bee's sniff was not hard to recognize. "Well, forgive me for being your mother. I just called to say I'm gonna be closed today so Estelle and I can go into Farberville. She wants to look at handbags at Wal-Mart."

I'd been planning to mosey over in an hour or so for meatloaf, mashed potatoes, crowder peas, turnip greens, and biscuits drowned in cream gravy. "Wal-Mart?"

"You got a problem with that? I don't reckon we can go shopping on Fifth Avenue, can we?"

"No, I guess not," I said, "but it's not like you to close the bar and grill to search for the perfect handbag."

"You don't think I deserve a break? You

ain't over at the PD, waiting in case there's an accident or a burglary or something. You don't have any problem lolling around all day watching TV."

"Is something wrong? Is Casper the Friendly Confederate pointing a musket at you and forcing you to make this call?"

"So Joyce tracked you down. It sounds to me like Larry Joe found a stash of Raz's hooch, but I told her she might as well tell you what he said. Maybe you should go up on the ridge this afternoon and have a look for yourself. Now that I think about it, that's a right fine idea."

I did my best not to sound exasperated. "No respectable ghost is going to be wafting in and out of caves at this hour. The ridge may be more crowded than Wal-Mart this afternoon, but I have no intention of greeting treasure hunters as they go by with trowels and shovels. I'm sure Raz will do that in his inimitable way if any of them get too close to his still or start poaching Marjorie's acorns."

"I still say you should go up there," said Ruby Bee. "I'll fix you up with some ham sandwiches, pickles, chips, and a slice of pie. It's a nice, sunny day, and Estelle was saying only yesterday that you looked a little pale. Fresh air would do you a world of good. You don't want to look sickly when that filmmaker shows up again, do you?"

"That's hardly your concern, is it?"

Ruby Bee sniffed again. "So do you want me to fix you a picnic lunch or not, Miss Snippety Britches? You can look like you live in a root cellar if that's what you want."

Since I wasn't going to get a proper meal and had no desire to spend the afternoon in my claustrophobic apartment, I said, "That would be very nice, Ruby Bee. Shall I come over in half an hour or so?"

"Don't bother. I'll fix it right now and leave it on your bottom step as soon as Estelle gets here."

"Are you trying to get rid of me?"

"Now why would I want to do something like that?" she said with just a tad too much indignation to be credible. "I'm worried about you, that's all. A nice afternoon outdoors will put some color in your cheeks. Don't come back till suppertime."

"Okay." After I hung up, I went into the bathroom and peered at myself in the mirror, almost expecting to see a reflection that suggested anemia — or terminal consumption. A little pale, maybe, and with slight discoloration under my eyes. I did not, however, resemble the result of a botched embalming job. I wasn't wearing lipstick, but I never did when washing clothes at the launderette. There had been a period in my life when I'd dressed fashionably and spent an hour on my face and hair before heading downtown to the Museum of Modern Art for lunch in the garden, followed by a leisurely exploration of quaint art and antiques galleries. A gin and tonic in a hotel on Park Avenue South, along with genteel yet fiercely competitive chatter.

I grabbed a couple of magazines and a paperback book that looked intriguing, went downstairs where I found a bulging sack that could sustain me for a week, and drove out to one of my favorite haunts on the banks of Boone Creek. If I was overcome with giddiness, maybe I'd roll up my snippety britches and go wading.

Lottie, Eula, and Elsie stared at the Headquarters House. The sign posted on the door made it clear that it was open only on Saturdays until Memorial Day, unless private tours were arranged in advance.

"Well, I never," Elsie huffed. "This is disgraceful, not admitting folks every day. What if somebody had driven all the way from Des Moines to learn about the Battle of Farberville, and then sees this sign?"

Eula, who was seated in the back, leaned

over Elsie's shoulder. "Didn't Harperlee Buchanon move to Des Moines after her husband was convicted of bigamy the third time?"

Lottie parked in a corner of the small lot and shut off the engine. "I don't think we need to concern ourselves with Harperlee just now, Eula. Our mission is to acquire the journal."

"So we can find the gold," Elsie added cheerfully. "The first thing I'm going to buy is one of those satellite dishes. My second cousin Ramona sez there's all manner of cooking shows twenty-four hours a day. I might just find myself with a wok."

"A what?" said Eula.

"A wok."

"That's what I just said. You have no occasion to be rude, Elsie McMay."

"And you have no business leaving your hearing aid in your bedside table drawer, Eula Lemoy."

"What?"

Lottie was eyeing the house. "I wonder if the doors and windows aren't a little bit flimsy after a hundred and fifty years. We might just be able to slip inside and fetch the journal."

"Slip inside?" echoed Elsie. "Don't you mean *break* inside? That's a crime, and I for one ain't a criminal. I can just hear myself calling my sister from the jail and asking her to bail me out. What's more, there are a lot of unsavory folks in jail, like bikers with tattoos and prostitutes with brassy red hair and skin-tight leather shorts. I have no intention of makin' their acquaintance, thank you very much. I have been teaching Sunday school classes at the Assembly Hall for thirty years. I wouldn't know what to say to 'em."

Lottie continued assessing the window frames. "We're not going to commit some terrible crime, Elsie. All we're going to do is borrow the journal long enough to study it for clues. We'll put it back exactly where we found it, and no one will be the wiser. There's a big difference between stealing and borrowing."

"There's not a big difference between misdemeanors and felonies," muttered Elsie, who watched police dramas, including reruns at all hours of the night. "We could end up doing ten years for breaking and entering."

Eula's lips began to quiver. "I think we ought to leave."

"We're not going to break anything," Lottie said. "I'll bet that window over there will slide right open. We'll have to enter, of course, but we shouldn't be inside for more than a few minutes."

Her reluctant partners in crime followed her to the side yard. The windowsills were high, but someone had left a wheelbarrow near the back porch. Ignoring increasingly agitated whispers from Elsie and Eula, Lottie wheeled it under a promising window, settled it as firmly as she could, then grabbed Elsie's shoulder and hoisted herself up.

"Just as we thought," she said as she rattled the frame. "Once the lock slips, this is going to slide up smooth as silk pie. We'll be in and out in no time." She continued fooling with it, mindful not to crack the panes, until at last it obliged with a creaky grunt. "All right, here I go. As soon as I'm inside, I'll help you all climb in."

She hitched up her skirt and managed to get one leg over the sill. After some floundering and a few heart-stopping moments, she found herself inside what appeared to be a parlor. She put out her head out the window and said, "Let me make sure the coast is clear. Don't either of you dare take so much as one step toward the car."

After pausing to admire a cherry spinet, Lottie started for the doorway into a hall. She'd taken no more than two steps when an alarm began to whoop as if a freight train was bearing down on her. The sound was so loud that she could feel the floor throbbing. A mouse scuttled for safety, coming within an inch of her foot. Luckily, it veered away, since Lottie was incapable of moving, and barely capable of breathing.

"Are you okay?" shrieked Elsie.

Lottie shook her head, since she most certainly was not. Would an armed guard come thundering into the room, his gun pointed at her heart? Would slavering German shepherds appear to rip out her throat?

"Lottie!" Eula howled. "What in tarnation's going on in there?"

As her knees began to fail her, Lottie tried to find a reply to what was possibly the silliest question she'd ever heard in all her born days.

Kevin found Dahlia sitting on the stoop of their back porch, her face all screwed up with misery, her red eyes hardly visible below her swollen eyelids, her nose dribbling steadily. He sat down next to her and took her hand. "What's wrong, my love goddess? Did something happen? Are the babies okay?"

"They're fine. Your mama agreed to look after them so's I could take a nap."

"And did you?" he said, bewildered. "Are you troubled by a bad dream? Should I fetch you a bowl of ice cream?"

"I don't want nuthin'. Just leave me be, Kevvie. I've done something awful, and it bein' Sunday, that makes it double awful. I was greedy, and now I got to suffer for my sins. I just hope this new baby won't be born with Satan's mark on its forehead or cloven hooves and little horns." Tears began to stream down her face, catching on her jowls, and then making a zigzagged path through her numerous chins. "I must have broke two or three commandments today."

Kevin did what he could to blot her tears with his shirt cuff. "What exactly did you do?"

"I lost my granny," she wailed.

"She passed away?" said Kevin, who didn't have a clue why Dahlia might feel responsible, unless she'd gone over to the old folks' home and throttled her, which she'd threatened to do on more than one occasion. "She was real old, sweetums, and it was gonna happen sooner or later. Did someone call? Are we supposed to be making arrangements?"

Dahlia shoved him so hard he nearly toppled off the stoop. "I dint say she was dead! I said I lost her. I swear, Kevin Fitzgerald

Buchanon, if you wasn't the father of our children, I'd move to a city like Farberville and start lookin' for a man smart enough to come in out of the rain! What's more, he'd be real handsome, too, and most likely speak French."

Kevin sat for a moment, racking his brain to figure out what in tarnation she was talkin' about. It wasn't raining, and as far as he knew, she didn't speak French — or German or Mexican or even Canadian. He finally decided her hormones was actin' up. "Why don't we go down to my ma and pa's and visit for a spell afore we pick up Rose Marie and Kevvie Junior?"

"Don't you care about my granny?"

" 'Course I do, but if she ain't dead, well, I don't know what you reckon we ought to do."

"I lost her up on the ridge," Dahlia said grimly. "I sweet-talked her yesterday, and she agreed to show me where the caves are so we could find the gold. I did it for you, Kevvie, so this is all your fault. We can barely afford groceries what with you making minimum wage. Once the baby comes, we're gonna be buying more diapers, more medicine, more booties, more" — she began to hiccup — "more everything! I can clip only so many coupons, you know.

I got blisters on my fingers from using the scissors so we can save five cents here and twenty cents there. If Jim Bob wasn't such an ornery cuss, he'd give us a discount and pay you extra for overtime."

"I still don't understand about your granny," he said, sidestepping a delicate subject. "You took her up on Cotter's Ridge and then lost her? Did she run away?"

"In a manner of speakin'. I promised her that if she was to show me where the gold was, we'd buy her new teeth and a double-wide so she could live in the Pot O' Gold. She seemed real tickled."

"But then something happened?"

She gave him a stony look. "Yes, Kevvie, something happened. When God gave out the brains, were you crouched under the bleachers trying to look up the cheerleaders' skirts? We started here and worked our way up the ridge. She knew of some caves, but they didn't look big enough for a body to squirm inside. Then, about a mile later, she said there was a cave where she used to sit and cool off on hot afternoons. I waited outside on account of my delicate condition while she went inside. Two seconds later she came running out, flapping her arms and squawking like a goose. As best I could tell, she thought she'd seen a ghost in a

Confederate uniform. Afore I could sit her down, she pushed me out of the way and disappeared up the logging trail."

"Did you try to catch her?"

"How was I to catch her? She was movin' faster than a preacher caught with his pants down in a whorehouse."

Kevin gulped. "What about this ghost she sez she saw?"

Dahlia looked away. "Well, I wasn't about to go in the cave, so I came back here. I've been waiting for her ever since. I thought about callin' the old folks' home, but then I figured I'd have to tell them that I'd let her go running off like that and they'd think it was all my fault. She's most likely up there somewhere, bleedin' or already dead, but I don't see how we can find her."

He knew that somehow or other it was all his fault for not finding a job that paid more than minimum wage. "Maybe I should go up to this cave and have a look," he said, popping his knuckles for courage. "This ghost might have been in the act of collecting the gold when your granny saw him."

"And then dropped dead again after a hundred and forty years, leaving the gold just lying there?"

Kevin tried to choose his words carefully.

"It might not have been a real ghost. It could be it was just some feller in a gray shirt. Do you reckon you can show me the cave?"

Dahlia sucked on her lip as she gazed across the field that led to a line of scrub pines. "Maybe, but I ain't sure, since my granny kept darting around picking wildflowers and looking for her old ginseng patches. We must have turned ever' which way for most of an hour, but we was a good ways up the ridge and my legs were aching something terrible when she recognized the ledge over the entrance to the cave."

"Were you anywhere near Robin Buchanon's old shack?"

"I s'pose we could have been."

"All right then," Kevin said, beginning to feel right manly, like a star in one of those movies where soldiers went crawling up walls with grenades between their teeth. "I'll go up there and take a look. Maybe your granny's hiding inside. You go let Ma make you a nice cup of tea and wait for me there."

"What if it was a ghost she saw?"

"Then I'll just rip the gold right out of his hands." He stood up and did as best he could to pull her to her feet. "Now you go on. I'll be there afterwhile with your granny and a million dollars' worth of gold."

All in all, it wasn't much of a plan, but it was the best he could do.

"Arly's gonna be spittin' nails," Ruby Bee said as she pulled up in front of the foster home and parked.

Estelle adjusted the rearview mirror so she could apply a fresh coat of lipstick. "Then we'll buy her an emery board with our million dollars. Do we have every-thing?"

Ruby Bee took the grocery bag from the backseat. "Here's the gray wool shirt with shiny buttons, and that cute little hat we bought at the souvenir store. The drum's in the trunk." She paused, then said, "We don't have to do this, you know. We've got no good reason to think Hammet might have seen these saddlebags filled with gold coins."

"Maybe so, but I called his foster mother and he's ours for the rest of the week. Don't you go pretending you weren't sittin' right there when I called, Rubella Belinda Hanks. I promised Hammet he could be the little drummer boy that led the muletrain into Maggody that fateful morning. We are not gonna break his heart by telling him he won't be in this documentary. He's had a hard life, Ruby Bee, living all those years on Cotter's Ridge with a mama that was nothing but an untamed mountain woman. You remember when Arly had to bring Hammet and his brothers and sisters down to Maggody, doncha? Not one of them had ever seen indoor plumbing, or electric lights, for that matter. I'd seen better-behaved wild dogs than that passel of foul-mouthed bushcolts."

"Yes, but . . ." said Ruby Bee, not sure how to counter this particular argument, since she wasn't sure why borrowing Hammet from his very civilized foster home was compensation for his first ten years with a mama known for moonshinin' and, to put it politely, entertaining gentlemen callers, many of whom had fathered her children. "Well, we don't really have any reason to believe he'll know where the gold is. How long do you think we can keep him hidden until he scampers away to find Arly? He's got this crazy idea that if he keeps pestering her, she'll break down and adopt him, but I don't think that's gonna happen. She got mad when I tried to give her a goldfish, said she'd flush it down the toilet."

"Are you saying Hammet's a goldfish?"

Ruby Bee knew she was losing her grip on the conversation. "I said no such thing,

Estelle. I never said he was a goldfish."

Estelle repositioned a hairpin, then shot a last look in the mirror and opened the car door. "I should hope not. He's not more than eleven or twelve years old these days, but I'm sure he's still real sensitive on account of his upbringing. There's no cause to rub his nose in it."

Before she could take a step, the front door of the house opened and Hammet came bounding down the steps, as bouncy as an oversized puppy. His foster mother followed more sedately, although with ill-concealed enthusiasm.

"Here are his things," she said as Hammet dove into the backseat. "Don't concern yourselves if you need to keep him for a few extra days. There's no school on Monday due to teacher conferences."

"Where's my drum?" demanded Hammet.

"We'll get to that when the time comes," Ruby Bee said. She pulled away from the curb before she lost her resolve — or came to her senses. "You got to get one thing straight, Hammet. Arly doesn't know you're coming. If she catches sight of you, she'll have you right back here before your head stops spinning."

"Her said I was gonna be in a movie," he

said, jabbing at the back of Estelle's head. "Don't Arly know what's happening?"

Estelle turned around to look at him. "She knows about the movie, but that doesn't mean she's expecting you. We thought we'd surprise her long about Thursday evening, when you can have a picnic supper with all the famous actors. I figure we can gussy you up in the uniform and let you come marching down the road, beating on the drum, your face determined but with your little chin aquiver on account of knowing you're in danger of being shot down in the dirt. Arly won't have the heart to send you packing after that."

Hammet slithered halfway over the seat. "Jest what is it I'm s'posed to do until these make-believe Yankees shoot me on Thursday? Whittle drumsticks?"

Ruby Bee took one hand off the steering wheel to catch his ear. "What you're *s'posed* to do is what we tell you. I'm gonna let you have a whole motel room to yourself, with your very own television set to watch whatever you want. I'll bring you nice, hot meals on trays. You just can't go roaming around town or trying to hunt up Arly."

"I ain't sure Jim Bob will be happy to see me, neither," Hammet said as he jerked himself free. "The peckerhead was mightily pissed last time I saw him."

"And when was that?" asked Estelle.

Hammet realized that he might have blurted out something best left unsaid, since Ruby Bee, Estelle, and Arly had been off somewheres when he and Jim Bob came to an agreement that had left one of them so mad he was fartin' out his ears. "Oh, awhiles back. I disremember exactly when." He risked leaning over the seat again. "Why is it I can't see Arly until Thursday?"

Ruby Bee waited for Estelle to come leaping to the rescue with some damnfool lie, but when that didn't happen, said, "Because she doesn't know you're coming to Maggody. She's real testy these days, and we don't want to rile her. You're gonna have to think of yourself as a secret agent right up until we surprise her. Estelle here is gonna entertain you for the next few days. Ain't that right, Estelle? Didn't you say something to me about taking Hammet for a picnic on Cotter's Ridge?"

"First thing in the morning," Estelle said brightly.

Brother Verber had been aching all morning, knowing that those gripped by the deadly sin of avarice were up there on Cotter's Ridge. If any one of them was to stumble across the gold, he wouldn't fall to his knees to give thanks to the Almighty Lord, then go forth to found a mission in Africa, or even send a pittance to the little heathens in need of shoes and eyeglasses. No, the miscreant would most likely slink away and waste the money on gambling, liquor, and pleasures of the supple flesh.

However, he'd been obliged to conduct the morning service, which had been sparsely attended. Sister Barbara had been there, as always, but she'd been scribbling in a notebook the whole time and had hardly glanced up to offer an "Amen" when he'd paused. Joyce Lambertino had brought her unmannersome children and her husband, who looked like he was close to passing out in a hymnal. Lottie, Eula, and Elsie had taken their usual seats in the third pew, but they were squirming like they'd been infested with fleas. Millicent McIlhaney had been in the fifth pew, sitting by herself and looking twitchy. Some other folks had been there, but none of them had looked like they was feeling the glory brought on by the purification of their numerous sins. It had been all he could do not to start scratching his head as he beamed down at them from the pulpit and related in great detail the story of the Good Samaritan.

Brother Verber wondered if he might ought to call an exterminator, since it wasn't far-fetched to think Satan might have enlisted fleas or lice in his battle against righteousness. The mail-order seminary in Las Vegas had never suggested such a possibility, but Satan was wily.

The thing was, Brother Verber thought as he plopped down on the couch, the gold was likelier than not to fall into the hands of the Prince of Darkness if he didn't take steps to rescue it and send at least some of it to the little heathens. After he'd done that, why, he just might take one of those cruises so he could see for hisself all that wickedness and lasciviousness on sultry islands where women bared their breasts and wiggled their bottoms in the moonlight.

He blotted his forehead with his handkerchief, then got up and found the bottle of sacramental wine he kept under the sink. It was gonna take a goodly dose of courage to approach Raz Buchanon and inquire discreetly about this particular cave. He'd gone into Farberville the previous afternoon and bought a few things he hoped might soothe Raz. Moonshine had its place, but a bottle of Kentucky bourbon might be welcome. He figured Raz ate nothing but squirrel and possum, so a nice selection of sausages, crackers, pickled okra, green tomato relish, and mustard might win over his petrified heart. And, of course, the fancy smoked ham.

He could just picture himself sittin' on Raz's front porch, passing the bottle back and forth and eating thick slices of salami. Why, they'd be feeling downright brotherly, and before long, Brother Verber could steer the conversation into matters that might be to his advantage. His and the little heathens', of course. The very first thing he'd do after he got off the phone with a travel agent would be to write a check to some mission or hospital in the middle of darkest Africa, where his generosity would be so deeply appreciated that tears would be streaming down the missionaries' cheeks.

He finished off the last of the wine and got up to open another bottle. It was gonna take him some time to find the courage to approach Raz's cabin, but as a soldier in the Lord Almighty's army, he had no choice.

6

Mrs. Jim Bob was prowling the kitchen when Jim Bob came home for lunch on Monday. Prowling, but not growling, although her jaw was clamped and her forehead was rutted like a forgotten back road.

"It's about time you got here," she said by way of greeting.

Jim Bob stopped in the doorway and listened for the whine of incoming missiles. "It's about noon, same as usual."

"That is not what I meant," she said as she went around the dinette table and into the hallway, then returned with a darker expression. "I am doing my level best to make this reenactment reflect well on our community, but I cannot be responsible when people have the audacity to change their schedules and then expect me to forget all my carefully laid plans and — my lists — my menus — my notes . . ." She reeled around and disappeared into the hallway, but before he could do more than blink several times, she was back, darn close to frothing. "No one else has seen fit to accept this burden, as you for one should know. Perkin's eldest had to leave early today because of her ballet class in Farberville. Am I supposed to change sheets and put out fresh towels? How can I spend the afternoon doing housework when I need to be preparing dinner for these people? Just how am I supposed to do that, I ask you?"

"Dinner for these people?" he echoed, keeping his distance.

Mrs. Jim Bob threw herself into a chair and swept all the pieces of paper onto the floor. "I had this well under control, but now I don't know what to do!"

"About what, exactly?"

She glared at him. "Haven't you heard a word I just said? That woman from Charleston, her son, and his fiancée are arriving in a matter of hours. She called to say that the only decent hotel in Farberville was full because of a conference, and they had no other option but to come to Maggody. Two days early, mind you, but she didn't mention that minor detail. Oh no, she just assumed that it wouldn't inconvenience me the tiniest bit. I was planning to go to Farberville tomorrow to buy new linens and bath soaps. I wanted to be a gracious hostess. I was going to put potpourri in little baskets on the bedside tables so they'd know we aren't barbarians. Who knows what they'll think now?"

Jim Bob gave it his best shot. "It ain't like they don't know they're showing up two days early, so they won't expect much. I'll bring home some food from the deli and we can have a right nice picnic on the patio."

"Are you intending to vacuum the upstairs bedrooms and dust the living room, too?" she said icily. "Does the deli have potpourri?"

"I reckon not," he acknowledged, since he had no idea what damn fool thing she was talking about. It sounded like fancy cat litter, but he wasn't about to say so.

Mrs. Jim Bob cradled her head in her hands. "Will this son and his fiancée expect to share a bedroom? This is a God-fearing house, not some sleazy hotel that caters to sinners bent on depravity under this very roof! I called Brother Verber to ask him, but he couldn't bother to be at the rectory in my hour of need. And you're just standing there, squinting at the refrigerator and thinking of nothing more than last night's pot roast and a slice of chocolate cake. I can see it written all over your face, Jim Bob. All you want to do is fill your belly and get back to your office at the SuperSaver, where you can drink whiskey and flirt with the checkout girls. Don't think for a second that I don't know what you do down there, except when you're off visiting some harlot in a cheap apartment."

Whiskey sounded real good at the moment, but he forced a sympathetic smile and said, "Don't get so all fired up about this. Did she say why they're coming early?"

"Her name happens to be Corinne Dawk, and don't you forget it! All she offered was some lame excuse about how she wanted to spend more time speaking to classes. Why on earth she thinks she can keep their attention for three whole days with her Civil War folderol is beyond me, but I said fine. Then I tried to call Lottie Estes at the high school to let her know, and she wasn't there. The secretary said Lottie hadn't even bothered to call in sick. It seems that Lottie has chosen this day for the first time in who knows how many years to simply not show up. Larry Joe's having to take her home ec classes to the shop to make bird feeders."

"Could be she had a heart attack and died in her bed."

Mrs. Jim Bob stood up so abruptly that the chair toppled over. "That is the last thing I need to hear," she said. "You get on the phone right this minute and call Arly. Tell her to go by and check on Lottie, then call me."

"Mebbe you should be the one to handle this. After all, you're running this dog-and-pony show, not me. I need to eat some lunch and get back to the store to work on the payroll taxes. You don't want the IRS to start sniffing around, do you?"

"At this point, I don't care if the IRS blows up the supermarket and everyone inside it, including you. Now you make this call while I start dusting the living room. All Perkin's eldest does is flip a rag from the doorway. I can probably write your epitaph in the dust on the credenza."

"We have a credenza? What the" — he caught himself — "heck is a credenza? It sounds like a bottle of cheap dago wine."

"You'd better hope I don't find any whiskey bottles under the sofa. What's more, I'd better not find any frilly lace underwear in your bedroom when I empty the dresser drawers. If I do, you'll find yourself wearing it till the cows come home to roost!"

As she snatched up a dustrag and stomped out of the kitchen, Jim Bob tried to think what all she might find in his dresser drawers. Cigars possibly, condoms probably. The pictures of Cherry Lucinda in a red teddy were stashed away in his desk at the supermarket. Realizing his wife would hear him if he tried to creep upstairs, he resigned himself to calling Arly and putting up with her smart-ass remarks. After telling her about Lottie, he could also point out that it was high time she hunted down Petrol and hauled his skinny ass back to town. Hell, Drainard wasn't more than fifty miles away. She could go knockin' door-to-door like a missionary until she found him, then stuff him in the trunk of her car and deliver him to the old folks' home.

He was halfway across the kitchen when the telephone rang. He picked up the receiver and said, "Yeah?"

"Ah, Mayor Buchanon. I didn't expect to catch you. This is Harriet Hathaway from the Stump County Historical Society. We met the other night at the town meeting."

"You backing out of this thing?"

"Don't be silly. I just had a call from the gentleman who volunteered to make the film. He's decided to come a few days early, so I thought I might as well, too. This will give us the opportunity to discuss various sites and camera angles. Wendell Streek is very excited about the opportunity to explore the church cemeteries and family plots for names and dates that may prove relevant to his genealogical research. Please let Mrs. Jim Bob know we'll be there around six o'clock — unless, of course, this might inconvenience her." She paused, then added without enthusiasm, "We could stay at that motel, I suppose. The Flamenco, or something like that."

"What the hell," Jim Bob said, figuring that he was signing his own death certificate. "Y'all might as well come along. The woman from Charleston and her runts are coming today. The more the merrier, long as you don't mind baloney sandwiches and potato salad."

"That will be lovely. We'll see you in a few hours, then. Please let your wife know how much I appreciate her hospitality."

He hung up, then stared at the telephone, waiting for it to ring again in case some platoon of damn Yankees called to say they'd be camping in the backyard and would need a couple of bales of hay for their horses.

Since there'd be hell to pay for years if he didn't tell her, he went to the doorway of the living room. Mrs. Jim Bob was on her hands and knees, wiping the baseboards with a dustrag and muttering under her breath.

"That was Miss Hathaway on the phone," he said. "She and that man from the society will —" He stopped and scratched his head. "What happened to the curtains?"

She glared up at him. "Nothing happened to them. They were looking grimy, so I took them into Farberville to be cleaned. Since when did you start paying attention to the decor? For all you care, I could paint the ceiling black and glue moss on the walls."

"Why would you want to do something like that?"

"Just go on back to the SuperSaver. I'll call Arly, and then Miss Hathaway, who probably wants to tell me she'll be bringing a dozen more members of the society with her, all of them with allergies to dust, dairy products, tomatoes, eggs, and gluten. I don't have time to watch you stand there and gape like Kevin Buchanon swallowing a lemon drop. I'll call you later with a shopping list."

Jim Bob shrugged and went back into the kitchen to make himself a sandwich and return to the SuperSaver. The official Skirmish at Cotter's Ridge wasn't supposed to take place until Saturday morning, but he figured there'd be a few opening rounds exchanged before too long.

"Okay, Harve," I said, wishing I hadn't called him on an empty stomach, "I'll go out to Hazzard and write up the burglary, but you have to help me out this weekend. Do you realize how pissed everyone's going to be when we block the road for half the day? You need to post a deputy at County 102 to divert the tourists on their way to Branson, and another one outside of Starley City to do the same for traffic headed for Farberville. There were no pickups, station wagons, or chicken trucks during the Civil War. Trust me on this."

"I ain't arguing," the illustrious sheriff of Stump County drawled. A match scritched as he lit up a cheap cigar. Smoking may have been outlawed in every municipal and state building in Arkansas, but Harve Dorfer remained as serenely oblivious as a portly Buddha in a rock garden. "How many folks you got coming to this little battle of yours?"

"I won't know about the reenactors until they show up, but perhaps no more than three dozen. There's been no publicity, much to Hizzoner's disgust, so I doubt we'll have much in the way of a square dance at the high school on Saturday night. You and Mrs. Dorfer are more than welcome to attend."

Harve chuckled. "I reckon we got other plans. So if I give you two deputies on Saturday morning, you'll go over to Hazzard today and listen to them moan about their illicitly appropriated begonias?"

"Begonias?"

"Out on the front porch in glazed ceramic pots. A real fine display, or so they claim. They had a yard sale over the weekend, so don't bother with tire prints. What time do you need Les and Willard on Saturday, and how heavily armed do they need to be? Should they be packing muskets?"

"When someone like Navidaddy Buchanon rumbles up in his truck on the way to Starley City to buy layer grit at the co-op like he's done every Saturday morning for thirty years — well, it's hard to say. You have any cannons in the back room?"

"I'll get LaBelle to take a look. Let me warn you about something, Arly. When she heard about this, she figured she could show up and be an extra. She's taken to wearing her hair just like that madam in *Gone With the Wind.*"

I gulped. "LaBelle heard about this?"

Harve was obviously enjoying himself. "She said she heard about it from her brother-in-law, who hangs out at the Dewdrop Inn. The good ol' boys are a mite riled about Yankees showing up again after all these years. Seems the sentiment on their bumpers is "Ferget, Hell!' It also seems to be the only thing anyone's talking about at the bowling alley, the body shops, and the tattoo parlors. You want to reconsider how many deputies you'll need?"

I was about to suggest a cavalry unit when the door opened and in marched an emaciated Confederate soldier in a threadbare, filthy uniform. His greasy hair dangled to his shoulders, and the ends of his mustache hung well below his unshaven chin. Although he was far from puffy, his pallor resembled that of the floaters in the reservoir. "I'll call you back, Harve," I said, then hung up and gave my visitor a wary look. "Can I help you?"

"Private Jeb Stewart," he said with a crisp salute.

"I'm not General Grant."

He saluted again. "I can see that, ma'am."

"At ease, Private Stewart," I said, hoping neither of us was in the midst of a psychotic episode. "Why don't you sit down over there?"

"I'll stand, if you don't mind."

"Well, I do mind, so sit down. Would you like a cup of coffee?"

He pulled off a bulging haversack and dropped it on the floor. His only weapon that I could see was a battered musket that appeared to be of authentic origin (and therefore perhaps not in working order). "I could use coffee. I've been driving since three o'clock this morning."

I went into the back room and poured a mug, then took it back to him. The redolence surrounding him reminded me of Raz Buchanon — a combination of stale urine and swamp gas. He was decades younger than Raz, though, and his dark eyes were disturbingly bright. "I assume soldiers stumbling off the battlefield drink their coffee black," I said. "I'd offer you a bagel, but we're fifteen hundred miles from a really decent New York deli, and besides that, the local supermarket doesn't sell cream cheese."

"This is fine, ma'am. I appreciate it."

"So why are you here, Private Stewart?" I asked as I retreated behind my desk. "Your comrades aren't expected until Thursday."

He slurped the coffee, managing to dunk both ends of his mustache in the process, then looked up at me. "That unit that came up from Little Rock back in '63, they hadn't had a decent meal or a night's sleep for most of a week. Their worst enemies weren't Yanks, but hunger and dysentery. I aim to feel their pain come Saturday morning.

Think how bumfuzzled those farm boys must have been. Here they'd been recruited by a bushy-tailed officer in a crisp gray uniform with polished boots and shiny brass buttons, telling them how they'd save the South and all its traditions. The next thing they knew, they were huddled in leaky tents, gnawing on hardtack, wearing rags, praying the sores on their feet didn't fester." He bent over and yanked off one of his boots. "This is what they ended up with, not medals and parades."

It took a moment for me to regain control of my stomach. "Yes, Private Stewart, I see your point. Would you like to be taken to a doctor in Farberville?"

"Damn field doctors, all they do is amputate. I'm not here to pretend, ma'am. I intend to experience this skirmish just as the original troops did. I stopped by as a courtesy to let you know I'll be camping on the far side of the bridge for a few days. As long as nobody bothers me, we'll get along fine."

"Did you just arrive in town?"

Jeb Stewart, CSA, dropped the boot and stared at me. "Yes, ma'am. Do you have reason to think I didn't?"

I shook my head, although I wasn't sure. "A local claims to have seen a soldier up on Cotter's Ridge on Saturday night."

"Was the report credible? Was the description sufficient to suggest someone dressed as a Confederate? Were there any details?"

"I'm not sure what he saw, Private Stewart. You're welcome to camp in the woods alongside Boone Creek, but I can't promise you'll be left alone. You may have participated in this sort of thing for years. It's a first for Maggody, however, and I won't offer any assurance that you won't find teenagers peeking in your tent tonight. A kind lady from the Missionary Society may bring you fresh cinnamon rolls tomorrow morning and sweetly ask if you happen to know where the gold is hidden."

"Gold?"

"Give me a break." I rocked back so hard that I thumped my head against the wall. "I'm having a tough time believing you came here three days early so you could sit on the bank of the creek and watch your blisters ooze. Despite appearances, we're not all brain-dead in Maggody."

"That remains to be seen. Now, ma'am, with your permission, I'll go set up my campsite. I thank you kindly for the coffee and the warning." He touched the brim of his cap, then scooped up his haversack and boot and limped out of the PD.

I felt a pang of remorse for my failure to pay any attention to Larry Joe's purported sighting of a ghostly Confederate soldier, in that I felt as though I'd just encountered one. I was still considering it all when the telephone rang.

"Stonewall Jackson here," I said cheerfully.

"Don't be ridiculous," said Mrs. Jim Bob. "I want you to go check on Lottie Estes. She didn't show up at the high school today, and I find this worrisome. Lottie is highly responsible, unlike others in the community who fail to abide by their contractual duties to protect the citizenry. Go up to her house, and if she has the flu, see if she needs anything. I don't know how I'm expected to get through the week without a liaison to coordinate with the impressionists."

"I don't make house calls."

"I will expect to hear from you in half an hour," she said, then hung up.

I really hadn't expected the madness to kick in until Thursday or even Friday, but it was obvious I'd been overly optimistic. I decided to stop by Ruby Bee's for lunch, then drive over to Lottie Estes's house and listen to her whimper about her stuffy nose and watery eyes. After that, purloined begonias.

163

Bonnie and Clyde rarely stopped in Stump County.

Ruby Bee was glowering as I came across the dance floor and perched on a stool. "I wasn't expecting you," she said, her nostrils quivering as if I'd brought Jeb Stewart's stench with me. "You want the blue plate special or not? I don't have time to fix something special just because you decide to waltz in like a prom queen and expect me to drop everything and —"

"Whatever's easy," I said.

"Nothing's easy! That man from Springfield called to say he's decided to come this afternoon, which means I'll have to air two units for him and his assistant. What's more, some man from St. Louis called and said he'd be coming today to stay until Thursday, when he's gonna camp out with the Yankees. Here I am, supposed to be cooking and bartending, but —"

"I'll clean a couple of the units."

"You most certainly will not! If you so much as set foot out back, you can count on eating burritos from the Dairee Dee-Lishus for a month of Sundays. The only way you can help is to go on about your business and let me sort it out."

I slid off the stool. "No problem. Will you be needing me later to drive you to a psychiatric facility where you can pound your head against a padded wall?"

Her expression softened for a moment. "I'm just kinda antsy right now. Come by later this afternoon and have a beer with that man of yours."

"He's far from mine," I said drily. "Did he say why he's coming early?"

Ruby Bee shook her head. "He just said that he'd be along around the middle of the afternoon with somebody named Terry. You reckon that's a girl or a boy?"

"All I reckon is that it's none of our business. Have you heard anything about Lottie Estes? She didn't show up at the high school this morning."

"That ain't like her. How'd you hear about it?"

I told her about Mrs. Jim Bob's call, then promised to pass along Lottie's prognosis so that the local version of Meals on Wheels could pound on her door with chicken soup and banana pudding.

Lottie's car was parked in front of her house, but she did not respond to my repeated knocks. I peered in all the windows, but as far as I could tell no one was inside, including her cats. It was curious, I will admit. I wasn't inclined to break into her house, though, since she might have gone off with a niece in the same fashion Petrol Buchanon had done a few days earlier, taking her cats with her.

If I'd had a cell phone, I would have called Mrs. Jim Bob, but the city council had declined to pay for one and I was damned if I would out of my own pocket. As it was, I headed for Hazzard to deal with grand theft botanical.

Waylon Pepperstone froze when he saw the Confederate soldier wrestling with a tent. Wasn't anybody supposed to arrive until Thursday, but here was this guy all dressed up like the reenactment was scheduled to start in twenty minutes. He was thinking what to say when the reb spun around and shouted, "Who the hell are you?"

"Private Pepperstone, Union army. My outfit's out of Missouri. You?"

"Private Stewart, Second Mississippi. Now I know who the hell you are, but I don't know why the hell you're standing there."

"I didn't expect to see you."

"And I didn't expect to see you, either," said Jeb. "Now that we're past the preliminaries, would you care to explain why you came creeping up on me? I've cut some bastard's throat for less."

Waylon tried to swallow, but his mouth

166

was drier than a wad of cotton. "I don't know where you get off saying I crept up on you, Private Stewart. I was looking for a place to camp for a few days, that's all." He reminded himself that he had fought valiantly and to the bitter end most recently at the Battle of Pea Ridge, after which he'd been commended by his superior officer for puking in a most realistic manner. "What you doing here, Johnny Reb?"

"Same as you, obviously." Jeb held up the palms of his hands. "You can camp here if you want, long as you're not some fuckin' farb with a battery-powered DVD player."

"Hell, no," Waylon said, relaxing. "Couldn't afford one if I wanted. You don't mind if I pitch my tent over here? I won't bother you. I was thinking I might try to catch a mess of crappie for supper. I've got some cornmeal in my mess kit."

"And I've got a chunk of lard, though it's probably rancid by now."

Having bonded over the promise of a tasty meal, the two privates from opposing armies pitched their tents, peeled off their homespun, hand-sewn wool jackets (replete with brass buttons with the authentic patina that could only be achieved by a lengthy soak in urine), and found a flat rock alongside Boone Creek in hopes of catching

167

supper.

Kenneth Grimley wasn't at all sure what he was getting into as he came into the bar, which was apparently also a motel and most likely the sort of establishment in which rooms were rented by the hour. Resisting the urge to wipe off the bar stool with his handkerchief, he sat down. The place appeared to be deserted, and for good reason, since the decor was reminiscent of the worst of the fifties. It would not have surprised him if James Dean had swaggered out of the men's room and paused to comb his ducktail before belligerently demanding a burger and a beer.

Therefore, he was surprised when a scrawny boy came out of the kitchen and said, "Who the fuck are you?"

"I might ask you the same question."

"Ain't none of your damn business." The boy went behind the bar and poured himself a glass of soda. "If you're aimin' to have lunch, you're shit out of luck. Ruby Bee's out back, vacuuming on account of folks arriving early for this war thing. She's twittering something awful, like a spider crawled down her back. You want something to drink?"

"Are you old enough to serve beer?"

He lifted his eyebrows. "You old enough to drink it?"

"I believe I am." Kenneth extended his hand. "I'm Kenneth Grimley, here to do presentations at the schools before the reenactment. And you are . . . ?"

"Hammet Buchanon, drummer boy, althoughs they won't give me my drum and keep dragging me up to the ridge like I was on an expedition for" — he stopped and crinkled his forehead — "*National Geographic.* You ever seen them on TV? They're all the time sneaking up on gators or zebras to watch 'em screw. You'd think grown folks would have better things to do."

"No gators or zebras on the ridge, then?"

"I reckon not. You want a beer?"

"That would be fine," said Kenneth, who was, to put it mildly, mystified. "So you've been engaged not only to play a drum, but also to search for wildlife in the midst of procreation? Shouldn't you be in school?"

"I dunno." Hammet filled a mug and set it down in front of his very first customer. "You want some pie, too?"

"Thank you, but no. Can you tell me how to get to the home of Jim Bob Buchanon?"

"What you want with that fuckhead?"

Kenneth recoiled. "Is this your customary

vocabulary?"

Hammet sighed. "I get into all kinds of trouble at school and at the foster home. The social worker keeps saying I'll grow out of it, but I ain't so sure. How 'bout some pretzels?" He scooted down a basket, although this time with less vigor, so that it did not go flying off the end of the bar as it had done the previous night.

"Tell me, Hammet, is there a reason I might not want to locate this . . . Jim Bob Buchanon? Do you have a grievance with him?"

"Might be the other way around. What kind of presentations do you put on? Do you stab damn Yankees?"

"I am a general in the Union army, dear boy. My uniform is blue, and my heart lies with General Ulysses S. Grant and President Abraham Lincoln. This part of Arkansas was evenly divided between the two factions. A good fifty percent —"

"Do you kill anybody," said Hammet, "or do you just bore 'em to death?"

"The latter, most likely." Kenneth took a swallow of beer, although he would have preferred a glass of white wine, even of a recent vintage. "You're a drummer boy, you said. I don't remember such a persona mentioned in the journal."

"It's kinda secret. All I'm s'posed to do until Thursday is go wandering all over Cotter's Ridge with Estelle, huntin' for caves. Just 'cause I growed up there don't mean I know about every hole. I got so damn tired of it that I told Estelle I was gonna take a piss and then snuck back here so's I could watch TV. You wanna come to my room and watch cartoons? We can snitch that apple pie out in the kitchen and take it with us. Iff'n you want, you can take one of these bottles and get snockered."

"You say you grew up on the ridge?"

"Yeah," said Hammet, lifting a glass dome in order to stick his finger into a lemon meringue pie. He sucked on his finger, then smoothed over the meringue and conscientiously replaced the dome so the flies couldn't get to the pie. "I had to grow up somewheres, dint I? I guess your kids grew up in a fancy house and got new bicycles for Christmas every year. The only thing I ever got for Christmas was a smack for talking to the ladies from some dumbshit church. They was always too scared to come up to the cabin, so they'd leave their boxes of old clothes and sacks of canned vegetables at the edge of the yard. Her would have shot 'em if they'd come any closer."

"Goodness," murmured Kenneth, whose

studies in the Civil War era had been confined to battles and back room strategy sessions. The general populace, with the exception of plantation owners and barricade runners, had never interested him. He wasn't sure this feral child did, either, except for the reference to caves on Cotter's Ridge. Federal depositories, one might say. "No, I never had any children, but if I'd had a son, I'd like to think he would have been as clever as you. It must be very difficult to remember all those caves on Cotter's Ridge. Why, I wouldn't be surprised if you're keeping some of them a secret just to trick this woman named Estelle."

Hammet glanced at him. "Why would I want to trick her?"

"Because someone else might make it worth your while."

"How much you talkin' about?"

Kenneth hoped his smirk was not too obvious as he said, "Then you do know about more caves. You are a clever boy, aren't you?"

"Mebbe. How much?"

"That would depend on your degree of success — and your willingness to keep this between the two of us. It would defeat my purpose if word were to get out and we ended up with a dozen people trailing after us."

Hammet figgered it was okay with him if this peckerwood wanted to pay hard cash in order to do something that plenty of other folks was already busy doin', some in uniforms and some, like the old lady he'd seen scampering through the trees, in regular clothes. He was about to name a price when the bar door opened and a tall fellow came ambling across the dance floor.

Kenneth Grimley decided the man looked like the sort who spent months exploring remote jungles and paddling canoes in waters thick with piranhas and poisonous snakes. And going into caves in search of species of blind newts and carnivorous fungi.

"Hey, pal," the man said to Hammet, "you running this establishment these days?"

"Ruby Bee's out back, gettin' rooms ready. You want a beer or somethin'?"

"I'm Jack Wallace," he said as he sat down a few stools away from Kenneth. "I'm filming the documentary for the historical society." He paused to stare at Hammet. "By any chance, are you related to Ruby Bee? Grandson, maybe?"

"I would be iff'n Arly hadn't sent me away," muttered Hammet.

Kenneth felt better now that it had been established that the man was not a professional fortune hunter. He held out his hand and said, "Kenneth Grimley here. I'm one of the two impressionists. Are you planning to film any of my presentations at the local schools?"

"That's up to Miss Hathaway, but I suspect she may be a stickler for authenticity. There were no debonair generals at the skirmish, just weary boys hoping to someday see their mothers and sweethearts."

"And a drummer boy," said Hammet as he disappeared into the kitchen.

Elsie McMay and Eula Lemoy stood in the parking lot outside the county jail. Although they'd discussed possibilities during the drive from Maggody, neither had come up with a remotely credible ploy.

"I think we're sticking our noses in an ant hill," said Eula, who kept trying to edge away. "We're likely to end up sharing a cell with Lottie — if they haven't put her in solitary confinement."

Elsie clung to Eula's wrist. "We don't even know she's in there, and here you are ready to think she's on death row awaiting the electric chair. It hasn't even been twenty-four hours as of yet. It takes years before they can carry out the death penalty. Besides, all she was doin' was trespassing. That's hardly a federal offense."

"There are probably all sorts of valuable antiques in the Headquarters House. They most likely think she was there to case the joint. She didn't exactly buy a ticket and take a guided tour."

"Because it was closed." Elsie took a deep breath, then dragged Eula into the front room of the building. A young deputy looked up from a magazine with a photograph of a deer on the cover.

"Yeah?" he said.

Elsie stepped forward. "We're here to visit somebody."

"Visitation hours are from five to seven weekdays, two to five on weekends." The deputy flipped a page in his magazine. "You better call ahead. Prisoners with too many disciplinary demerits aren't allowed visitors."

Elsie flicked the magazine to get his attention. "Then we need to know if this particular person is here so's we can come back at five o'clock."

The deputy put down the magazine and picked up a clipboard. "Name?"

"I'm Elsie McMay, and this here is Eula Lemoy."

"The prisoner's name."

"We don't know," Eula said bravely, fully expecting to be handcuffed and dragged down a pea green corridor to a cell with an iron cot, a bare lightbulb, and a bucket.

They certainly had the deputy's attention by now. "So you want to visit someone whose name you don't know?" he asked.

Elsie held out her hand. "Why don't you just let me look at the list?"

"So you can pick one? We don't do that. This information is confidential. You have to tell me the name."

"We don't know for sure that this person is here. This person could have escaped out the back door for all we know."

"No one's escaped since before Christmas, and he got out through a window in the rec room. Sheriff Dorfer was fit to be tied." The deputy paused, wondering if he ought to call someone with more experience dealing with senile old ladies. "Now either tell me who you're looking for or stop wasting my time."

"Do the prisoners wear orange jumpsuits?" asked Elsie. "If they do, you got one hunkered down at the edge of the parking lot."

Cursing, the deputy stood up and hurried out the entrance. Elsie snatched up the clipboard, looked down the list, and then hustled Eula outside. "Get in the car," she said as the deputy came panting up to them.

"Where'd you see this guy?" he demanded.

"Why, I must have been mistaken. My eyesight's not as good as it used to be. Back when I was your age, I could read the fine print on an aluminum can in a ditch. These days it's a miracle I can see the ditch at all." With a little laugh, she got into the driver's side and carefully backed up, making sure she didn't run over the deputy's foot. Once they were on the street, she said, "Lottie's name wasn't on the list. I suppose we ought to thank our lucky stars she wasn't arrested after all."

"I suppose so," Eula said doubtfully, "but if she's not in jail, where is she?"

7

When I got back from Hazzard, I stopped at the PD and called Harve to report that the begonias had been recovered behind a church, most likely because the miscreant had been overwhelmed with floral remorse. I was sure the appropriate commandment would be covered in the upcoming Sunday service at said church, with a teary confession ensuing.

Case closed.

"I never much cared for begonias myself," Harve said, "but Mrs. Dorfer's real fond of them. Have you figured out when you'll need Les and Willard? We're always understaffed this time of year, and I can't spare 'em to go sit on their butts and watch make-believe soldiers ride around on mules."

"I'm not sure, but I'm guessing that the arrival of the muletrain will be staged on Friday. There are only about a dozen partic-ipants, so traffic shouldn't have to be delayed too long and I can handle it. Saturday morning is going to be the problem. I'll find out and call you back in a day or two, okay?"

"It may be petunias that she's partial to," Harve said, then ended the conversation with a belch.

I was reluctant to face Jack Wallace just yet, so I called the high school and asked if Lottie had appeared (she hadn't), and then called Elsie and Eula to find out if they'd heard from her (neither was home). If I called Mrs. Jim Bob, I was liable to find myself assigned to hang bunting on the front of the Assembly Hall or to whip up a batch of brownies to welcome the troops when Johnny came marching home, hurrah.

Procrastination being one of my favorite pastimes, I wrote up the begonia-theft report for Harve's office, and was debating whether to stop by my apartment to apply lipstick when the telephone rang.

"Now you listen here, young lady," Mrs. Jim Bob began before I could say anything, "I thought I told you to check on Lottie. Here it is the middle of the afternoon, and all you've done is sit there like a toad under a rock while I've changed sheets, polished furniture, cleaned bathrooms —"

"Lottie's not answering her door and the cats aren't there. If the town council wants to authorize it, I'll break a window to get inside. She may be a bit perturbed when she gets home, though. She's only been missing half a day."

There was a moment of silence. "You're going to have to do something if she's not home by this evening. In the meantime, go over to the rectory and check on Brother Verber. I've been trying to call him since early this morning."

"I am not your social secretary," I said.

"That's well and fine, but you have a responsibility to make sure folks aren't dead in their beds. I'd drive over to the rectory myself, but I simply don't have time."

She hung up before I could respond. I decided to forgo the lipstick and take my chances at Ruby Bee's Bar & Grill. Being the conscientious defender of law and order that I was, however, I walked up the road to the silver trailer next to the Voice of the Almighty Lord Assembly Hall, noted that Brother Verber's car was not parked outside, rapped on the door a few times, and was headed toward the eponymous bar when an unfamiliar car cut me off.

The driver, a woman with ethereal blond ringlets and a magnolia blossom complexion beginning to decline after a few seasons of wear and tear, smiled at me. "Are you a police officer, dear?"

I'd forgotten that I'd changed into my uniform before going to Hazzard. Most days I just pin on my badge, which looks as though it came from a box of Cracker Jacks (and well might have). "I'm Arly Hanks, Chief of Police. Can I help you?"

"I do hope so." She extended a slender hand. "I'm Corinne Dawk. This charming girl beside me is Frances Yarborough, but everybody calls her Sweetpea. The lazy boy in the backseat is my son, Simon. We're here for the reenactment. We've been invited to stay with Mayor and Mrs. Buchanon."

"And . . . ?"

"We don't know how to find their house. I'd be grateful if you could be so kind as to give us directions."

I did so, since giving directions in Maggody rarely involved more than one left or right turn. Then again, to find the crime site in Hazzard, I'd been told to turn left at what had been ol' Madagascar's place before the bank repossessed it, and then turn left again past the pond where the catfish bellied up back in '73.

The young woman cursed with the nickname Sweetpea leaned forward and eyed me as though I were an alien species.

"You're the chief of police? Aren't you sup-posed to have a pot belly and dribbles of drool?"

"You caught me at a bad moment. I do most of my dribbling at night."

Corinne laughed politely. "I'm sure we'll see more of you. We'll be in town until the end of the week. Simon is taking the part of Henry Largesse, the private who left the journal detailing the events at the Skirmish at Cotter's Ridge. You are familiar with it, aren't you?"

"Every word of it," I said, although of course nobody had bothered to pass it along to me. "I didn't expect people to arrive for a few days."

Simon, who'd been sprawled on the backseat, sat up. "Nor did I. Is there any place in this pathetic pothole to get a decent drink?"

"I'm sure Mrs. Jim Bob, as we call her, will be happy to oblige. I've been told she has the best-stocked liquor cabinet in town. She's modest about it, so you may have to twist her arm to get her to admit it."

Corinne nodded at me, then pulled away. Sweetpea waved as if we were parting after a pleasant evening at the symphony. Simon was no longer visible.

He was remarkably handsome, I thought

as I resumed my walk to Ruby Bee's, but entirely too young and obnoxious to be of interest. A man who'd been around, who'd scaled a metaphorical mountain, who'd garnered an emotional scar or two . . . well, he was of interest.

And I knew where to find him.

It would have been only a minor cosmic coincidence had Jack been sitting on a stool at Ruby Bee's, but no one was. I took a perch and glanced at Fibber Buchanon, who was slumped in the corner booth and either dead drunk or just plain dead, then reached for a basket of pretzels. I couldn't ignore the attraction, any more than I could ignore a chicken truck bearing down on me in the middle of the road, but I still had time to throw myself out of harm's way. If that was where I preferred to be.

Ruby Bee came out of the kitchen and put her hands on her hips. "I wasn't expecting to see you."

The last time she'd been so unfriendly involved a kidnapped bureaucrat and all manner of insanity. "Were you expecting to see Scarlett O'Hara?" I asked. "She's at the PD, filing a claim for trespassing and vandalism. It seems these damn Yankees stole her silver tea service and —"

"Maybe I need that padded room." Ruby

Bee filled a mug with beer and set it down in front of me. "I'm so dogged tired I'd just as soon curl up in a corner and let somebody bring me a cup of soup." She sighed just in case I wasn't properly sympathetic. "This man of yours showed up, along with some sickly fellow who looked like he'd been pecked to pieces by a chickadee, and then this fellow from St. Louis who started sputtering on account of the units' not having cable, and then —"

I went around the bar and gave her a hug. "For starters, I can help you clean the rooms in the morning. I can't install cable or provide first aid to the chickadee victim, but we'll get through this. By Saturday afternoon, everyone will be gone and the Skirmish at Cotter's Ridge will once again be a tiny blip of history." I took a napkin and blotted a tear on her cheek. "Why are you taking this so hard? It's not as if you had to move bodies before you aired the motel rooms."

"You don't know the half of it," she said darkly as she moved away. "I don't want you setting foot out back. Estelle can help me, if it comes to that."

I resumed my perch. "Who's the fellow from St. Louis?"

"How should I know? He said he's the

commander of the Union cavalry troop that waylaid the rebels on the morning of the skirmish. I just don't know why he showed up out of the blue today. Ain't none of them needed until the end of the week, but they're all flocking like crows. You'd think there was roadkill from here to Starley City."

"Rumor has it there's gold in them thar hills," I said, "or them thar caves, to be more accurate. You are aware of that, aren't you?"

"I didn't pay all that much attention to what Miss Hathaway said at the town meeting the other night. I've got business to attend to, and that includes putting biscuits in the oven."

And I could crinkle my nose and make Fibber disappear in a wisp of smog.

I was nursing my beer and considering whether I ought to make one more run by Lottie's house — or the rectory, for that matter — when Jack Wallace sat down beside me.

"I was going to offer a quote from *Casablanca*, but I'd bungle it," he said. "That line about all the bars and all the cities."

"We could settle for 'fancy meeting you here,' " I suggested. "I didn't expect to see you again until Wednesday or Thursday."

"Is that a good thing or a bad thing?"

His grin, so wide and wry that I wanted to lick his lips, did little to help me keep my composure. Perhaps I'd felt the same reaction with my ex-husband, but I couldn't recall a moment when I'd resisted an urge to crawl onto his lap and indulge in a public display of indecency. Hell, I'd probably have to arrest myself and drive over to the county jail, where I'd dine on beans and cornbread for forty-eight hours.

"It's a thing," I said. "So why did you show up? Planning to do a bit of spelunking?"

Jack went behind the bar and filled a mug of beer. "No, I'm claustrophobic, and although I find the legend of lost gold entertaining, I doubt there's any validity. Besides that, I'm terrified of bats and crawly creatures."

"Anything else?"

He scratched his chin. "Toyotas, Hondas, telemarketers, Disney World, and monsters in the closet. You?"

"Civil War reenactors, muskets, and mules."

"Sounds as if you might be in for a long week."

"No kidding," I said. "So why did you come early?"

"I rescheduled a few jobs. Are you on duty twenty-four hours a day, or does the badge come off every now and then?"

I tried to convince myself that the flutter in my stomach was due to an infestation of butterflies or, more logically, inadequate nourishment, but even I wasn't buying. "It's been known to find its way into a bedside drawer." Bad choice of words, I thought as I felt my face flush. "I'd give you the grand tour of Maggody, but once I've shown you the remains of the Esso station and the site of Hiram's barn before it burned to the ground and a cheerleader came sprinting out with smoldering panties in her hand, we'll be out of significant landmarks. Well, the low-water bridge can be titillating, but only when the water's not low. A few weeks ago a chicken truck slipped off one side and two hundred chickens did the breast stroke all the way to the Oklahoma border."

"I suppose you're familiar with the decor of the Flamingo Motel rooms."

"Entirely too well. I've got a few things to do, and I'm sure you want to unpack your equipment and all. If you'd like, I can pick you up at six and we can drive around for a while, then grab some bad Mexican food at the Dairee Dee-Lishus and go to my apartment to play Scrabble." I stopped, then added hastily, "Or we can go into Farberville and have dinner. There are a couple of restaurants with a bona fide wine list and linen napkins."

"Are the tamales homemade with hot chili sauce?"

I felt as if hot chili sauce was about to start leaking out of my ears. "Oh, yes," I said as I slid off the stool. "Shall I meet you here at six, then? Do we need to include your assistant?"

Jack shook his head. "Terry started throwing up before we were out of Springfield. All he wants is to be left alone. Six o'clock sounds fine."

Kevin stuck his head into Jim Bob's office. "Kin I talk to you?"

Jim Bob turned off his monitor before looking over his shoulder. "You seem to be doing just that, boy. Whatta you want? You didn't bust another mop, did you? If you did, I'm going to start docking your paycheck."

"No, nothing like that, Jim Bob." Kevin sidled inside and closed the door. "I need to take off the rest of the day. I swear I'll make up the hours later in the week. I put out all the produce and stacked the paper towels like you said. I even oiled that cart that squeals like a pig bein' castrated."

"Can you take off the rest of the day?" Jim Bob said, leaning back and pretending to contemplate the question. "Can you just waltz out of here in the middle of the afternoon, leaving the checkers to deal with busted bottles of vinegar on the floor and cartons of ice cream tucked between boxes of cereal, or carry out Walleye Buchanon's sack of groceries so you can help her find her truck? I ain't sure that's a good idea, Kevin. Jim Bob's SuperSaver Buy 4 Less might not run so smoothly without you to handle emergencies of that nature. Why, we might just have to close down for the day, disappointing all the citizens planning to stop by on their way home to pick up something for supper. Little children might end up going to bed hungry, their bellies rumbling. Husbands and wives might take to snarling at each other. There could be all manner of violence tonight in Maggody if you was to take off the rest of the day."

"I don't think it'd be that bad," Kevin said earnestly.

"You want bloodshed on your hands, boy?"

"I'm gonna have bloodshed on my head if I don't . . . well, find something Dahlia lost yesterday. She ain't smacked me as of yet, but she keeps staring at me like I was a pile of dog crap in the middle of the kitchen floor. I gotta go back to Cotter's Ridge, Jim Bob. Mebbe I could come back later tonight and wax the floors." He hung his head. "I ain't asked for a day off since Dahlia had the babies."

"You get a day off almost every week," said Jim Bob, "along with Christmas and New Year's Day when we're closed. Next you'll be asking for a paid vacation so you can fly off to some island and lie around on the beach. This ain't a charity — it's a business."

"But I got to . . . find something afore . . ."

"Spit it out, you chunk of gristle. Find what? You ain't looking for a couple of saddlebags filled with gold, are you?"

"Not exactly."

Jim Bob swung around in his chair. "You know something about the whereabouts of this cave? You'd better tell me if you do, because otherwise you'll find yourself begging for food stamps at the welfare office. Your mama and papa will be so shamefaced that they'll up and sell their place so they can move to the other side of the county. Buchanons don't take welfare, even if it means they have to live on squirrel and possum. Remember how they found ol' Carismatica Buchanon? She starved to death all alone in her cellar because she wouldn't take any handouts from the government or anyone else. Her body was surrounded by seventeen dried-up cat corpses and what they thought might have been a rabbit. Is that what you want for your family?"

Kevin was having a hard time following how an afternoon off was gonna result in such a scenario. "I don't know anything about a cave. All I was wanting was to leave now."

"I think you do know something." Jim Bob came across the room and grabbed the front of Kevin's shirt. "Tell me what Dahlia lost or I swear I'll hold your head in the toilet until you howl for mercy. Does she have a map or something like that? Spit it out!"

"She lost her granny," croaked Kevin.

Jim Bob's hand dropped. "That crazy ol' bitch? Why the hell would you want to find her?"

"I don't rightly know, but Dahlia sez we have to. Iff'n you're gonna fire me, I reckon you can go ahead and do it." He stepped back and stuck out what little chin he had. "I'm leaving now. The bucket and mop are over in the produce department next to the yams." He didn't wait for an answer, but instead hurried out the back door and down the steps of the loading dock. He was sweating something fierce, though, 'cause he knew he might have just lost his job once and for all. Dahlia'd be mad, but she'd be a sight madder if he didn't find her granny. He'd searched until long past sunset the previous night, when even he had realized it was foolish. He'd tripped over so many logs that one of them could have been her body without him noticin' it.

Things had been mighty chilly when he finally dragged himself home. Supper had consisted of cold collard greens and a slice of bread. He'd been sent to sleep on the couch in the living room, and his whimpers all night had failed to produce a thaw from the bedroom.

So now he had no choice but to suck in his gut and do the right thing.

"So there you are, you little polecat!" Estelle said as she came into the barroom and saw Hammet sitting on a stool just like he thought he was sitting in a pew on Sunday morning. "I have been looking for you up one side of the ridge and down the other for the better of three hours! I was convinced you'd been dragged off by a bear — or worse. Now I find you drinking soda pop and eating a hamburger. I've a mind to turn you over my knee and —"

"Calm yourself," said Ruby Bee as she came down to the end of the bar. "Why don't you visit the ladies' room and do something about your hair, then have a glass of sherry? Hammet told me he got lost, so he came down here."

Estelle was almost sputtering with fury. "Lost? How in tarnation can he say he got lost? You look at me, young man! See these scratches on my face? These bruises on my shins? Here I was worried about you, when all the time you were sitting right here!"

"No, I weren't," Hammet said. "I watched a game show on TV where they tell the folks the answers right up front. I wish my geography teacher'd do that."

Ruby Bee hustled Estelle into the ladies' room. "You got to remember he's still a child. He told me he stumbled across Raz's still and realized he was in danger of a load of buckshot if he lingered. That's what killed his mama, if you recollect. It was real hard on him."

"I'll bet he went so far as to shed a tear, didn't he? I swear, Rubella Belinda Hanks, you'd take in one of those Mafia fellows if he had a convincing story about how his mama couldn't make spicy meatballs so he had no choice but to bury her body in New Jersey."

"Did Hammet show you any caves?"

Estelle dampened a paper towel and dabbed the red welts on her cheeks. "Oh, he showed me more caves than a sow has tits. None of 'em was big enough for a body to squirm into, though. Long about noon, we sat down and had our sandwiches. I did my best to talk about the ridge, but he was turning ornery." She put the towel into the trash can and leaned against the sink. "About then was when we saw somebody."

Ruby Bee gasped. "Who was it?"

"I ain't sure, but he was wearing a Confederate uniform sure as God made little green apples. He was watching us from the bluff above us, and as soon as I looked up, he vanished. I mostly saw his backside."

"And then . . . ?"

Estelle snorted. "Hammet said he was going off to relieve himself, and never came back. I stayed where I was, thinking he knew where to find me, but I started getting worried after half an hour and went to look for him. I can't tell you how many times I ran into brambles or stepped in a hole and turned my ankle. My whole body's black and blue, while he was sitting down here with a soda pop —"

"Don't get all fired up again," said Ruby Bee, more distracted than sympathetic. "What's done is done. The important thing is to figure out who this soldier is and if he knows where the gold is."

"Why don't you march yourself up there and sit on a stump until you see him? I'll wait for you here."

"You have to admit it's curious, what with Earl swearing he saw the same thing on Saturday. Do you suppose it's one of these reenactors?"

Estelle began resetting bobby pins and coaxing curls back into position. "The reenactors ain't arriving until Thursday."

Ruby Bee realized Estelle had been out of pocket most of the day. "It seems plenty of them are already here. Joyce said Mrs. Jim Bob was ripping out her hair on account of the folks from Charleston showing up early, along with Miss Hathaway and that treasurer she mentioned — and the professor from Ohio. The filmmaker and his assistant checked into the motel earlier, as well as a reenactor from St. Louis. Millicent called to say she saw a Confederate soldier going into the PD, and what's more, Joyce saw a Yankee buying tobacco and papers at the supermarket."

"Sounds like we could film this silly thing tomorrow and be done with it."

"It might be for the best," Ruby Bee said, "but there are plenty more soldiers arriving on Thursday. With our drummer boy and this ghost on Cotter's Ridge, it's starting to feel kinda crowded, isn't it?"

Estelle dampened another paper towel to attend to her shins and ankles. "The next thing you know, Bufferin Buchanon will be calling to report Confederates in her attic. She does that every spring."

"This is just charming," Corinne said as she looked out at the garden. "You have so much more room to have a spontaneous effect. In Charleston, I have only my walled backyard and a few azalea beds at the front of the house. It must be exhilarating to be able to plant things without any thought to space or organization."

Mrs. Jim Bob forced a tight smile. "Are you finding your rooms comfortable?"

"Very much so, thank you. I must apologize again for descending on you like this, but we searched all over Farberville for a reasonable hotel. Sweetpea and Simon were quite amused by some of the motels we saw, but I couldn't bring myself to stay in one that offered XXX-rated videos and mirrors on the ceiling. I'm no more fastidious than my great-great-grandmother must have been, but even she made sure bedrooms were free of vermin." Corinne took a sip of tea. "Do you enjoy the peacefulness of a quaint little town? If only I could live in the country, with an office and a view such as this. How many books I could write if I were never interrupted by the commotion of traffic, the streetcars, the gaggles of tourists on my sidewalk, the social demands on my time and energy. The ideas would flow like that charming creek at the bottom of your yard. It's all so rustic."

Mrs. Jim Bob wasn't sure how to take this, and she was trying to come up with a response when Sweetpea came strolling across the yard. "Did you enjoy your walk?" she asked like a proper hostess. "Would you like some lemonade and cookies? I'm afraid they're store-bought."

"I'd love some, thank you," Sweetpea said as she sat down. "It's hard to imagine how terrible it must have been that morning with the confusion, the gunfire, and all those boys dying for the sake of a dozen mules and a cannon. Are any of them buried here? I'd like to lay some wildflowers on their graves."

Corinne sighed. "It was so tragic. More

than six hundred and seventy thousand boys and men died during the war, and less than half of them were identified on the battlefield and taken back home for proper burials. Why, Sweetpea's great-great-granduncle is lying in an unmarked grave somewhere, isn't he?"

Sweetpea nodded as she accepted a glass of lemonade from Mrs. Jim Bob. "From all accounts, he was quite the rake about town before he was pressured to enlist. The story is that he got into all kinds of trouble for havin' dalliances with the general's wife and daughters and was horsewhipped more than once. My great-granddaddy used to roar with laughter when he talked about it, which he did right up until the day he died. My grandmother would sit next to him and try to hush him up, but she might as well have been driving bees with a peach switch."

Corinne was not to be upstaged. "There were two boys on my mother's side, identical twins and rumored to be so handsome they could have any girl in Charleston, who were caught running the blockade and summarily shot. All the girls cried for weeks because they couldn't get bonnets from Paris and Belgian lace for their hankies."

"One of my ancestors back in England

was hanged for poaching on the grounds of a royal estate," Sweetpea countered. "Scotland, I seem to recall."

"Well, one of mine was caught consorting with a lady-in-waiting and locked in the Tower of London."

"One of mine was beheaded there." Having neatly won the game, if not the set and match, Sweetpea took a sip of lemonade. "This is real tasty, Mrs. Jim Bob. My mama insists on making it so tart I just want to pucker up my lips."

"Then go right ahead," Simon said as he came out of the house and leaned over her shoulder.

Corinne pinched him on the backside. "Mind your manners, Simon. Would you care for some lemonade?"

He sat down. "I'd prefer a gin and tonic."

Mrs. Jim Bob stiffened. "I am sorry to disappoint you, Simon, but this is a Christian household. I'll be happy to fetch you some iced tea if you'd prefer that."

Simon glanced at his mother, who was staring sternly at him. "Maybe later. Come on, Sweetpea, let's go for a drive. We can check out the site of the skirmish, or even go climbing up on this ridge to find the buried treasure."

"Oh, what fun!" she said, then smiled at

Mrs. Jim Bob. "If you don't mind, of course. We'll be sure to be back in time to dress for dinner."

"No, don't worry about that," said Mrs. Jim Bob, feeling more and more miserable. "I'm afraid we're just going to have a picnic out here this evening. I wasn't quite prepared for you all, and now it seems Miss Hathaway and Mr. Streek are coming, too. My housekeeper will be here tomorrow, so I'll have time to fix a nice meal."

Corinne patted her hand. "We don't want you to go to any trouble. Perhaps we can all go out to dinner tomorrow."

Mrs. Jim Bob bit back the urge to ask her if she'd prefer country fried steak at Ruby Bee's or corndogs at the Dairee Dee-Lishus. "Oh, I enjoy entertaining. I always look forward to the opportunity to have a dinner party for special guests. Sweetpea, you and Simon need to be back here by six o'clock."

After the two had left, Corinne took off her shoes and massaged her feet. "The young are so energetic, aren't they? Every weekend they play golf and tennis, go horseback riding, sail, and still are ready to spend the evening dancing. I must admit my life is a bit more sedentary. I attend an occasional luncheon or tea, but I spend most of my time at my desk, delving into the societal complexities of the South during the War and Reconstruction. What do you do to amuse yourself, dear?"

Mrs. Jim Bob was about ready to mention scrubbing outhouses and frying chitlins for supper when an unfamiliar man came around the corner of the house. He was carrying a suitcase, which did nothing to elevate her spirits. "Who's that?" she whispered.

"Why, I do believe it's Kenneth Grimley. I didn't expect to see him so soon." Corinne stood up. "Kenneth, darling! What brings you here?"

"The same as you," he said as he kissed her on the cheek. "Shall I assume this is our gracious hostess, Mrs. Buchanon?"

The gracious hostess nodded. "It was my understanding you were coming later in the week. I haven't made up a room for you, so you'll have to take the sofa bed." Which would leave no place for Wendell Streek, unless she put him with Simon. Which meant she might find herself on the cot in the utility room, and Jim Bob free to spend the night with whichever of his floozies was in favor. Unless, of course, she could bully him into staying with Brother Verber, presuming Brother Verber had the decency to

ALAMEDA FREE LIBRARY

appear after being gone all day. "Excuse me," she added, "but I need to go inside for a few minutes. Corinne, would you please offer Mr. Grimley refreshments?"

She stopped in the kitchen to take a handful of aspirins, called the rectory with no success, then tiptoed upstairs to make sure Sweetpea and Simon had not snuck in through the front door and gone to his room to indulge in sinful hanky-panky right under her own roof.

When she returned to the patio, she was appalled to see a bottle of wine on her wrought-iron table. To make matters worse, both this Grimley man and Corinne appeared to be drinking it. She reminded herself that she was aware of Jim Bob's weaknesses of the flesh, whiskey being high on his list, and said nothing as she sat down.

"Could I offer you a glass of passable chardonnay?" Grimley said. "It's not one of the better years, I must admit, but it was not inexpensive and I'm disappointed with it."

"No thank you."

Corinne leaned over to tweak the end of his carefully trimmed beard. "I suppose you're going to try to convince us that General Wallingford Ames never set up his headquarters without a case of wine."

"Cases," Kenneth said with a flourish of

his arm, "as well as cigars, smoked chicken, hams, tins of caviar and salmon, imported cheeses, and pretty wenches to serve him. He weighed well over four hundred pounds when he died of gout in 1889."

Mrs. Jim Bob waggled a finger at him. "I'd like to think that's not what you'll be telling the young folks at the schools. Here in Maggody we don't condone gluttony or dissolute behavior."

"Kenneth always behaves when he's getting paid," said Corinne.

"And so do you, to my regret," he said gallantly, "although I've always wondered if Mrs. Delphinia Tuttle might have cast a longing eye on one of those big black bucks chopping cotton out in the field."

Corinne put down her glass. "That sort of language is offensive, Kenneth."

"As was slavery, which is why President Lincoln saw fit to send in Union troops to put an end to it. You Southerners just can't get over it, can you? You probably dream about sitting on the veranda, being served mint juleps by a servant girl who's been raped by the master since she was twelve years old. Of course, once she got pregnant, you'd have to sell her down the river and buy another one."

"I will not tolerate this!" Corinne wadded

up her napkin and threw it on the table. "If you'll excuse me, I think I'll lie down before dinner."

It was all Mrs. Jim Bob could do to nod as Corinne flounced into the house. For a moment she was tempted to drink the wine remaining in Corinne's glass, but regained her senses and said, "I'd like to think you won't be insulting members of the house party, Mr. Grimley. I must insist on common courtesy at the very least. If you feel unable to abide by that, you can go rent a room at the Flamingo Motel."

"I beg your pardon," Kenneth said, his smirk only vaguely visible beneath his mustache. "I shall treat each and every member of your house party with only the deepest respect. Corinne and I are old friends. We are often invited to appear at the same events, and in the evenings there is little to do at the country inns where we're usually lodged. She's been known to slip out of her petticoats after a few glasses of wine."

"We'll have none of that in this house!" Mrs. Jim Bob hurried into the kitchen to splash water on her face. First the obviously ne'er-do-well son and his fiancée, and now this debauched Yankee "general," most likely with cases of wine and wenches in the trunk of his car. For all she knew, Harriet

Hathaway and Wendell Streek might be overly familiar with the double beds in the Headquarters House, each with a hand-pieced quilt and a feather pillow. Her hand was trembling as she dialed Brother Verber's number, but he still did not answer. Had she not been a God-fearing Christian, she might have cursed him for his lack of consideration in her hour of need.

She snatched up a pen and a notebook, then went into the living room to work on the wording of the blessing she would offer before supper. It might turn out to be lengthy, but she had a long list of rules to be made clear to her guests.

8

"I've got some bad news," Jack said as I sat down on the bar stool next to him.

Ruby Bee stopped drying glasses and stared at him. "Somebody taken poorly back home?"

"Nothing like that. Arly and I have been invited to a picnic. Miss Hathaway seems to think it'll provide an opportunity for all of us to meet each other and discuss the logistics for the week. Both impressionists are already here, along with a smattering of other people."

"And just where is this picnic?" I asked without enthusiasm, since I already knew what the answer would be. Death, taxes — and Mrs. Jim Bob, equally inevitable, but no more palatable. If I were on the path to hell (as she's so fond of telling me I most certainly am), she'd be standing on the shoulder selling asbestos cardigans to raise money for the ignorant heathens in Africa.

"The mayor's house. We can still pick up

some tamales later."

Ruby Bee raised her eyebrows. "And just where are you planning to eat these tamales? Alongside Boone Creek?"

I told myself it would not be seemly to lean over the bar and flick gray dishwater at her. "We'll think of someplace. Come on, Jack; let's get this over with. I do need to know the schedule."

"You better take some bug spray," Ruby Bee said in a smarmy voice meant to annoy me. "The mosquitoes can be mighty fierce this time of year."

"So can I," I muttered as I headed across the dance floor.

While we drove to Jim Bob's house, Jack told me what he knew about the various players, which wasn't much. His friend, who was coming on Thursday, had met most of the players on both sides, since they often attended the same reenactments and put aside their political differences when the flasks came out at the end of the day.

"No swamp water and hardtack?" I asked.

"According to Frank, the camps are closed at five o'clock to sightseers, at which time the steaks are thrown on the grill and the premium booze flows freely. Only among the farbs, of course. The hard-core dudes huddle together in the middle of the pasture and pray for frost."

I could imagine CSA Private Jeb Stewart's reaction if someone asked how he wanted his steak cooked. "Don't you think this is all very creepy?"

"Oh, yeah. If you could hear some of Frank's stories about lying in the weeds all day while his neck turned beet red, because he was unlucky in the draw and had to go down early. Once he forgot what he was doing and fell down on his back. He ended up in the emergency room with a second-degree sunburn on his face and palms. I prefer spending my weekends watching my kids play soccer. And then there's baseball on TV, but I never said I was perfect."

I hadn't assumed as much — at least not yet.

We parked behind several cars and went around to the backyard. Mrs. Jim Bob had assembled quite a crowd. Miss Hathaway pounced on Jack and dragged him away, leaving me at the edge of the patio. I spotted Corinne Dawk and Sweetpea seated at a round table with two unfamiliar men. Simon and Jim Bob were lurking behind a dogwood tree, no doubt passing a bottle back and forth in that timeless tradition of Southern hospitality that supersedes social and economic class distinctions. If Mrs. Jim

Bob saw them, one of them might be sleeping in the garage that night, if he was lucky. I was surprised that Brother Verber wasn't there. Lottie Estes wasn't there, either, but most likely because she was still away visiting a friend or relative and unaware of the premature invasion of both the Blue and the Gray. No one else in town would have been deemed worthy of an invitation.

Corinne beckoned to me, so I joined them. "How lovely to see you again," she said. "You look so much prettier without that drab uniform. With a touch more makeup, you'd be quite the belle at one of our Charleston soirees. Don't you agree, Sweetpea?"

Sweetpea's lips twitched. "I don't make it to too many soirees these days, Corinne. When I'm not with Simon, I'm at the library studying."

My mama had taught me not to judge a book by its cover, even one whose purported autobiographer was named Sweetpea, so I was a bit ashamed of myself. "Where do you go to school?"

"The College of Charleston. I'm doing my undergraduate work in European history, and considering law school."

Corinne managed a halfhearted laugh.

"But only after the wedding, I hope. We wouldn't want to disappoint the flower girl, would we? She's Sweetpea's niece and such a little angel. Her teachers at Ashley Hall say she has the nicest manners of anyone at the school."

Sweetpea's smile was no more sincere than Corinne's attempt at lightheartedness. "No, we wouldn't want to disappoint anyone, including the caterer, the organist at St. Michael's, and the florist. Little Caitland will be absolutely devastated if she doesn't have the chance to sashay down the aisle in her lilac frock and matching shoes. She'll stay cloistered, and presumably a virgin even if she has to be packed away to a relative for nine months, until she comes out at the country club cotillion, dressed in white and clinging to her daddy's arm for dear life. Of course, her daddy's been fucking the maid since Caitland was a daffodil in her first dance recital, and her mother's been crouched in the wine cellar with all manner of dearly departeds. I suppose it's crowded down there. I must be related to most of them."

After a moment of silence of the sort more often associated with eulogies at funerals, Corinne said, "Well, I could certainly use a lawyer in the family, what with all these confusing contracts and now this business about electronic books and POD. I had to hire two lawyers to deal with the entertainment rights when my books were optioned in Hollywood. I thought I'd go crazy as a loon." She turned to the man seated next to Sweetpea. "Are you familiar with the miniseries, Mr. Streek?"

"Please, call me Wendell." He fussed with his wire-rimmed glasses for a moment, then settled them on his nose and nodded at me. "Wendell Streek, as you may have deduced. I'm the treasurer of the Stump County Historical Society, as well as the official genealogist. And yes, Mrs. Dawk, I did watch the miniseries, although I found many of the inaccuracies and distortions depicted on the screen to be downright distressing. At one point I became so agitated that I was compelled to write a letter to the producer, delineating each egregious factual error. After the widespread distribution of the Emancipation Proclamation, for instance —"

"She writes fiction," said the other man. He took my hand and squeezed it until I yanked it free and put it in my lap rather than knock him upside the head, a notion that held some appeal. "I'm Kenneth Grimley, known in classrooms across this

211

indivisible nation as General Wallingford Ames of the Army of Illinois."

"If at first you don't secede . . ." murmured Corinne, then smiled at Wendell. "I do write fiction, but my research is impeccable. I had no control over the production company's decisions to rewrite entire sections of the books to better accommodate the limited attention span of an audience weaned on graphic sex and violence."

Mrs. Jim Bob bustled over to us. "I do think we can begin to partake of our little backyard buffet as soon as I've offered a blessing. Arly, I need you in the kitchen. We have several things to discuss."

"Gee, I'd love to," I said, flashing my teeth at her, "but I'm just dying for a salami on rye and a dill pickle. I've had such a busy day that I haven't had a bite to eat."

"You poor thing," Corinne said. "Let me help you fix a plate. Sweetpea, why don't you fetch some iced tea? Wendell, won't you join us?"

Mrs. Jim Bob was obliged to retreat as we pushed back our chairs and headed toward card tables bearing the brunt of "our little backyard buffet." I refused to allow Corinne to load my plate with potato salad and such, since I was saving myself for tamales in a more congenial setting.

I sat down at a picnic table, and after a minute, Jack joined me. I noted that his plate held only a few spoonfuls of this and that, along with a lone carrot stick.

"Not hungry?" I said innocently.

"Not yet." He stood up as Miss Hathaway joined us. "Have you met Arly?"

"Yes," she said, "when I was here earlier. Have you made arrangements to handle traffic on Saturday?"

"I've been promised deputies, but I'll need the specific times you need to have the road blocked." I glanced at Jack. "Can you edit out the blare of drivers leaning on their horns? I'm afraid it's going to sound like a rainy afternoon in Manhattan."

"If need be, I'll erase the audio and dub in the musket fire in the studio. It's mostly the private's voice, reading from the journal. I've arranged to take Simon Dawk to Springfield tomorrow and cut the tape so he won't have to make a special trip. I don't think he's taken with the bucolic ambience of the Ozarks."

"No," Miss Hathaway said with a pained sigh. "I spoke with him earlier this afternoon, and his attitude is less than enthusiastic. I'm sure we could have found a volunteer who would relish the opportunity to make a contribution to the preservation of the heritage of Stump County, but Simon seems so very uninterested. The only reason he was given this vital role was at Corinne's insistence, as well as her willingness to waive her honorarium. It seems the boy has flunked out of numerous schools and has yet to find a suitable job. I'm not sure this documentary will impress her friends in Charleston, but she believes otherwise."

She, Jack, and I discussed the proposed filming schedule while the others nattered at the wrought-iron table. We agreed that the stretch of road from a quarter mile beyond the bridge to the middle of town would have to be blocked to traffic at six in the morning, when the rebels would break camp and set out toward Farberville. With luck, Jack would have enough footage by noon and the road could be opened.

"What if it rains?" I asked.

Miss Hathaway gave me a withering look. "The Civil War generals did not press the pause button because of inclement weather. The forecast looks good, and we must hope for the best."

"It'll be a problem if it rains, though, since the dirt may wash away," Jack pointed out. "How much dirt did you order?"

"Several tons. It's amazing what you find in the classified ads. I'd never thought someone could sell dirt when there's so much of it lying around. I also noticed that people sell rocks. I found it very peculiar."

I wasn't inclined to explain. "What about the mules?"

"The County Extension office put me in contact with a farmer who has promised to deliver a dozen mules on Thursday afternoon. I'm not sure where we can put them. I doubt Mrs. Jim Bob would take kindly to the idea of having them graze in her backyard for three days."

"No," I said, "I don't think so. You can park them in Earl Buchanon's pasture just across the road from the bottom of the driveway. You'll probably have to pay him a few bucks."

Miss Hathaway took a pad from her purse and wrote a note. "That really covers most of our responsibilities. One of the members of the historical society has agreed to transport the cannon from the lawn of the Headquarters House. It's of historical significance that this cannon is the very one the Confederates brought from Little Rock on their fateful trip. One of the privates intentionally damaged the caisson before they fled. The Union cavalry unit was too eager to rejoin General Alessio's army to be slowed down, so they simply left the cannon behind. Some fifty years later, it was found in a barn and donated to the county chapter of the Sons of Confederate Veterans, who eventually passed it along to us. The reenactors are expected to bring their bedrolls, tents, and whatever else they require. They've had a great deal more experience than I in these matters." She blinked several times, but a tear prevailed and dribbled down her cheek. "It's such a responsibility. The grant was generous, and it's my duty to make sure we are successful in this project. I'd hoped to rely on Wendell, but he seems to be experiencing a midlife crisis, if one could call it that at his age. An 'embarrassment' might be the more appropriate description."

Jack patted her shoulder. "I know exactly what I'm doing, and I can promise you that the Stump County Historical Society will end up with a documentary that does it proud. You'll be listed as producer, and Arly as director. We'll probably win an award at the Cannes Film Festival."

"What?" I yelped. "Do you mistake me for Federico Fellini? The only thing I know how to direct is traffic."

"Then I'll have to examine your credentials at a later time."

Miss Hathaway, who surely had been a

teacher or a librarian before her retirement, eyed us for a moment, then stood up and tapped on her glass with a spoon. "If I may have your attention, please. I assume you've all had a lovely meal and taken time to introduce yourselves. Although some of you have had a long day" — she smiled at Corinne — "I thought it would be nice if Wendell gave us some insights into the personal histories of the participants. One hundred and forty years after this tragic event, we tend to think of it only in terms of quantity — twelve Confederates, twice that many Union soldiers, a dozen mules, one cannon —"

"Don't forget two saddlebags of gold," inserted Jim Bob. He might have been planning to elaborate, but Mrs. Jim Bob yanked his ear.

"Or so the legend goes," Miss Hathaway said, undisturbed. "Wendell?"

Wendell took a spiral notebook from a briefcase on the ground beside his chair and flipped through several pages before clearing his throat. "As most of you know, I'm a genealogist, and I've done extensive research on the family histories of all the Confederate soldiers involved in the Skirmish at Cotter's Ridge." He bowed toward Kenneth Grimley. "My apologies to our friend from above the Mason-Dixon Line, but I have better access to Southern records of births, deaths, deeds, wedding licenses, civil and criminal proceedings, muster rolls, pension applications, and so forth. I thought I'd begin with Henry Largesse, since he is ultimately responsible for our being here tonight."

"Don't anybody look at me," said Simon. "I can assure you I'd much rather be someplace else. Anyplace else, for that matter. The only mules I know about are the ones who transport cocaine from Colombia."

Sweetpea put her hand over his mouth. "I think this will be fascinating, Wendell. Was Henry as much of a rascal as Simon here?"

"Heavens no," Wendell said, turning pink as she fluttered her eyelashes at him. "The Largesse family originally came from France in 1823. After a decade in North Carolina, they moved to Arkansas and were awarded a land grant from President Tyler for eighty acres. Henry's father opened a dry goods store and eventually provided an adequate living for his growing family. Henry, born in 1844, was the youngest of six children, four of them female. His brother and one of his sisters died of typhoid fever before they were five years of age. Another sister, Audrey Louise, married a distant cousin of Judge Isaac Parker, who presided from 1875 to 1896 over the Western District from his courtroom in Fort Smith." He seemed to sense that we were not exactly on the edges of our seats, breathlessly awaiting further details of Henry's siblings. "I have more detailed accounts of the family and of the other Confederates in my files upstairs."

"I'd just love to read all about Henry," Sweetpea said with a wicked smile for Simon, who pretended to be dozing.

"Then I shall be pleased to share the file with you, dear girl. The other privates came from lower-class backgrounds, had little or no education, and most likely had never seen a slave. They were more at home riding mules than they would have been riding horses. The lieutenant, Hadley Parham, on the other hand, was an intriguing character from an upper-class family that can be traced back to England. Due to a poor choice of political alliances, the family lost its fortune after the Restoration, and ultimately emigrated to the colonies in 1770. By the 1820s, they were wealthy and owned a vast plantation that produced an extraordinary income by that period's standards."

"From the blood, sweat, and tears of slaves," said Kenneth, thumping the table with his fist. "Trading in human flesh, treating their animals with better care —

those people make me sick! My ancestors earned every penny through their own toil. My great-great-grandfather worked in a mill from sunrise till sunset, seven days a week, as did his sons when they were old enough to carry lunch pails. That's what the Union was fighting for — the dignity of man! You people just don't understand that, do you? You think this is nothing more than halftime, and that you can continue to attempt to undermine the very structure of the lawful government and resort to —"

"Kenneth," said Corinne, "you're so unattractive when you sputter. Do wipe your chin. Please continue, Wendell."

Mrs. Jim Bob was visibly mortified by his outburst. "Would anyone care for coffee? I don't believe the spice cake's been touched. Joyce Lambertino made it this afternoon and brought it by especially for tonight. I have a pint of vanilla ice cream if anyone would prefer that . . ."

Wendell appeared a little unnerved, but he took a sip of iced tea and said, "Hadley, the family's only child, enlisted in 1862. His record was undistinguished, and he was chosen to lead the Little Rock unit because he was the only officer available — or perhaps expendable — at that critical time in the War. As I'm sure you all know from studying the journal, he was shot late in the morning of the skirmish and his body left behind. This caused Henry much grief, but he had no choice but to retreat with his few remaining comrades."

"Hey, Wendell," Jim Bob said, risking another whack, "doncha think maybe ol' Henry or one of the other survivors went back for the gold once the Yankees cleared out? You can be damn sure they must have mentioned this fortune to somebody. I mean, we ain't talking about a sack of turnips."

"With the exception of Henry, all of the survivors of the skirmish were killed in the Battle of Farberville the following day. There are no records from the field hospital, but Henry's journal has explicit details about his arduous trip home. General Lambdin's troops retreated to Oklahoma. I have pored over the minutiae, and I see no way anyone could have returned to Maggody for several months. Had one of them done so, he would have had no information about the whereabouts of the gold. If you recall, the private who actually went up on Cotter's Ridge was killed before he could describe the location of the cave to the others."

"So you think the gold's still up there?"

asked Kenneth. "The gold that indisputably belongs to the federal government?"

Wendell was clearly more interested in the genealogical mysteries awaiting his scrutiny. "More than likely. I myself plan to spend the next few days wandering in the local churchyards and hunting down family plots. In rural areas such as this one, most families simply buried their dead in a clearing near the household. The wooden crosses are long gone, but I hope to chance upon some stone markers with crudely chiseled inscriptions. From what I've gathered, many of them may bear your family name, Mayor Buchanon. These are the true treasures on Cotter's Ridge."

"If you say so," Jim Bob said, "but you ain't gonna buy yourself so much as a carton of bait with a stone marker. You can spend the next ten years hunting down dead Buchanons from Adolf to Zorastus."

Mrs. Jim Bob twisted his ear until he stopped sniggering. "That was merely a joke, Wendell. All of us in Maggody appreciate the abiding value of history. The Lord tells us to honor our father and mother, and I've always taken that to mean all of our ancestors, may they rest in peace."

"Amen," Simon said with a genteel burp. "I'll bet Jim Bob here wouldn't mind getting a little piece tonight."

Sweetpea grabbed his hand and hauled him to his feet. "Let's go for a drive, darling."

On that note, Corinne announced that she was exhausted and ready for bed. Miss Hathaway and Wendell trooped after her, although I presumed not to the same room. Kenneth seemed content to sit at the table, and Jim Bob to hover in the shadows at the edge of the patio. It seemed likely that the bottle of whiskey would come back into play once Mrs. Jim Bob had taken the potato salad and cole slaw inside to be covered with aluminum foil and tucked away for the night.

Jack and I thanked her for supper, and then left before she could corner me (or tree me like a coon) to demand updates on Maggody's ever-expanding list of MIAs.

"That was interesting," he said as we drove away from the house.

"I won't be surprised if I'm called in the morning to sort through bodies."

"That's your job, isn't it?" he said.

I stared out the window. "I think I'll start faxing my résumé to UN peacekeepers in Bosnia and Afghanistan. At least they can identify the warring factions. These people really don't like each other."

"Not even Sweetpea and her darling Simon?"

"Wake me up when I care," I said.

Shortly thereafter, we arrived at the Dairee Dee-Lishus. While he placed an order, I sat down on a picnic table with Heather and Billy Dick.

"Where's Darla Jean?" I asked.

"At home, I guess," said Heather. "I haven't really talked to her since Friday, when she got all hot and bothered like she had an overdose of PMS or something. She was at school today, but she just walked past me without even noticing I highlighted my hair over the weekend."

"She in trouble at home?"

Heather shook her head. "I dunno, but it's not like she's grounded or anything. I called a couple of times, but her ma said she wasn't home."

Billy Dick made a rude sound with his straw. "I'll betcha she's carrying on with Cooter. He broke up with his cousin over in Emmett. Maybe she's doin' grief counseling on a blanket down by the low-water bridge."

"She wouldn't bother to spit on Cooter," Heather said as she batted at a moth. "I mean, like, who would? He has pustules all over his back, ferchrissake."

I did not allow myself to conjure up a visual image. "Did Miss Estes ever show up today, Heather?"

"No, and it was truly awful. Mr. Lambertino dragged us to the shop so we could watch the boys repair a transmission. I thought I was going to die of boredom. At least Miss Estes lets us make cookies or something. Last week we learned how to use woks. It's not like I ever would, you know, but I sure ain't gonna repair a transmission in this lifetime."

"Wok! Wok!" barked Billy Dick.

Heather and Billy Dick were slapping at each other, albeit in an amiable fashion, as I joined Jack at the window. "I'm afraid my conscience is bothering me," I said. "If you don't mind, I'd like to run by someone's house and make sure she's okay. After that, we can reheat the tamales and play Scrabble until all hours of the night."

He was agreeable, so we swung by Lottie Estes's house. No lights, no cats, no answer to my repeated knocks.

"This is odd," I said as I peered through a window. "She isn't the type to disappear like this. She was a constant in my high school career. The basketball team might lose, the toilets might back up, the cafeteria might be closed down by the health department, the custodian might be arrested for selling drugs, but Miss Estes was always there with a lecture on the importance of owning a complete set of measuring cups."

"Shall we go inside?" asked Jack.

"I'm not authorized to do any damage."

"Oh, I think we can do it without any broken glass." He checked above the doorsill, under the mat, and ultimately found the house key in a flower pot next to the porch swing.

"You sure you're not an operative?" I asked as he unlocked the door.

"For the KGB, the CIA, the FBI, the ATF, or the IRS?"

"I don't know," I said rather peevishly. "You did lie to me, you know."

He gestured for me to precede him inside. "I told you I was a fisherman. If you remember, I was fishing at the time. Rod in hand, flies pinned on my canvas hat, khaki jacket, waders, all that sort of thing. After you left, I did catch a perch, although I had to toss him back so he could finish nursery school."

I realized how ridiculous I sounded, and it wasn't because I was worried we'd discover Lottie Estes decomposing in the bathtub or facedown in a wok, having stir-fried a fatal batch of bok choy. I was worried about the rest of the evening — which might result in the rest of the night. Well, not worried exactly. Something, though.

"Let's just take a quick look," I said.

Jack and I met at the front door less than a minute later, both of us shrugging. Since I could think of no way to take further action in the matter of Lottie's failure to provide instruction in the complexities of home economics, I drove us to my apartment and we settled down to drink beer, eat tamales, and play Scrabble.

Yeah, right.

Andrew Pulaski was sitting in a booth at Ruby Bee's Bar & Grill with a bizarre person who claimed to have been impregnated by alien sex slaves. It was hard for Andrew to imagine anyone (or anything) willing to be intimate with a man of some eighty years who smelled worse than a backed-up sewer and kept digging into his ear with a toothpick. "Did you give birth?" he asked.

"Hell, no! It's still growing in my belly. You recollect that movie when the critter comes ripping out of the woman? It's gonna happen one of these days. You reckon you ought to buy another pitcher of beer? I ain't told you all the details as of yet how they strapped me on this metal table and allowed this scaly green creature to slither all over me. Biggest tits I'd ever seen, all six of 'em. What's more, she —"

"Please stop," said Andrew. Coming a few days early had been a terrible mistake. His wife probably still hadn't noticed his absence (he'd once come back from Baja after a week's deep-sea fishing and she hadn't so much as commented on his tan), but Sweetpea had promised she'd find some time for intimacy. Intimacy with Sweetpea transcended definition. A country inn near the site of the miniseries filming had charged two hundred dollars to repair the damage to the bed and the floral wallpaper.

Oh, Sweetpea, won't you dance with me?

And here he was, with nothing to do for three days but eat fried food, stare at a fuzzy TV, and converse with specimens of what might well prove to be offspring of the missing link, which had no business being discovered.

He was about to retreat to his motel room with its quaintly distressed decor and a shower that did nothing more than spit cold water when Sweetpea and Simon came into the bar.

"Oh, my goodness," she said, "here's Andrew Pulaski. Are you playing a role in this documentary? Simon's the star, you know, the private who wrote that tedious journal with all the whining about gangrene."

Andrew dispatched his boothmate to the floor with a well-executed swipe of his foot. Ignoring muffled curses from underneath the table, he stood up and said, "Sweetpea and Simon, what an unexpected pleasure. Please join me. Yes, I'm to be the officer who led the Union cavalry unit. Sorry, Simon, but we did outnumber you."

"Shit happens," said Simon as he sat down. "Any hope of a gin and tonic?"

Sweetpea sat down next to him, apparently oblivious to the stream of invectives beneath her feet. "Andrew, you're just nothing but a sight for sore eyes. We haven't seen you in a coon's age. How's your wife doing these days? Still spending her time raising money for the symphony?"

"Beer," Andrew said to Simon, trying to sound apologetic. "I've got a bottle of scotch in my room, if you'd rather." He smiled at Sweetpea. "Julia has found a new pet project, something to do with inner-city children and interpretive dance. She tells me it's very worthwhile, so I dutifully write checks."

"You were always such a pushover." Sweetpea giggled with such girlish charm that Andrew would have suggestively rubbed her ankle had it not been for the arms and legs flailing beneath the table.

"Scotch sounds good," said Simon. "I've damn well had my quota of lemonade for the next decade. I'm supposed to go somewhere tomorrow and do the audio tape. I can assure you I'll be back by sunset with a trunk filled with liquor — scotch, gin, tequila, margarita mix, you name it. We can party."

"Oh, yes," Andrew said as he and Sweetpea exchanged looks. "Party, party, party."

"This is all so very exciting," Wendell Streek said as he came into the kitchen the following morning, beaming like a newly elected politician. "I am positively tingling with anticipation."

Mrs. Jim Bob would have made more of an effort to be hospitable had she not spent a very unpleasant night listening for the patter of feet in the hallway. Nevertheless, she'd been up early to start coffee, put biscuits in the oven, scramble eggs, set out jellies and jams, fry bacon, and wonder for a few seconds if Jim Bob had really slept on the couch in his office at the supermarket. It wasn't likely, she told herself as she slammed down some paper napkins and tossed another pound of bacon into the skillet.

"What's so exciting?" Miss Hathaway asked. Simon and Sweetpea failed to feign interest, but Corinne and Kenneth glanced up from the newspaper they were sharing. Corinne found it appallingly conservative, while Kenneth condemned it for failing to quash the blatantly socialist pundits who refused to acknowledge the wisdom of quashing any and all parasitic opposition.

Wendell circumnavigated the dinette before sinking down in a chair. "I was out shortly after dawn, taking a stroll as I am accustomed to doing except when the weather is inclement, and met a woman with a fascinating story about a Confederate officer buried in her family plot. She even drew me a crude map, which I've carefully put in my notebook. I'm absolutely determined to find the final resting place of the lieutenant who supposedly died at the Skirmish at Cotter's Ridge. What a wonderful appendage this will make to my research!"

"Hadley Parham?" asked Corinne, who was wishing she could have hot tea rather than the coffee she'd been presented with. It was, well, generic.

"Oh, most certainly, and there's the possibility he was not mortally wounded, but was nursed back to health by the kindly mountain folk. He may have fathered children. One woman in particular, with the charmingly eccentric name of Hospiss Buchanon, claims that she's a direct descendant of a Confederate officer from somewhere back East, and has a family Bible to prove it. Her great-great-grandmother lived at the far end of a remote hollow, clearly under the most primitive of conditions. According to the version Hospiss was told time and again, after the skirmish her kin and others went to the site to scavenge for clothes and whatever else they could use. The lieutenant was dazed and bloody, but alive. They flung him over a mule and took him with them. He decided to remain at the shack, and eventually agreed for a preacher to legitimize the marriage. The dates are vague, as you can imagine, but it well could have been the young lieutenant. I've found no evidence of any other troops from either side in this particular area."

"Why would the lieutenant have stayed here?" asked Sweetpea. "I mean" — she glanced at Mrs. Jim Bob, who was jabbing at bacon with a vengeance — "why would someone want to stay here? If he'd survived, wouldn't he have gone on and found his unit?"

"Not until after the greedy rebel bastard retrieved the gold," Kenneth said with a sneer. "Then perhaps amnesia kicked in and he spent the remainder of the war in a whorehouse in New Orleans."

Wendell shook his head. "No, I don't believe he could have found the gold without the assistance of Henry Largesse's journal, which remained in the family's possession until it was recently donated to the historical society. I was up most of the night in search of a clue. There's one cryptic reference dated a few weeks after the skirmish that has caused me to believe that Henry may have had an excellent idea where the gold was hidden from the Yankees."

"He did?" Harriet stared at him. "I myself read the journal most carefully and saw nothing to indicate that, Wendell. I realize you've been staying up late for several weeks to study the journal. Your behavior has certainly been erratic these last few days. Perhaps exhaustion is behind it. After all, something must be."

"That's not at all the case," said Wendell, who was enjoying the limelight. The last time he'd received so much attention was when he'd knocked over the coffee urn at a board meeting at the Headquarters House, nearly scalding the resident cat. Later that evening the cat had bitten him so severely on the ankle that he'd gone to the emergency room for stitches and a tetanus shot.

"So where is it?" drawled Jim Bob from the doorway.

"Yeah," Kenneth added, "let's hear it."

Corinne pursed her lips for a moment. "It was some kind of secret code, wasn't it? He must have worried his journal might fall into the hands of heartless Yankee imperialists determined to ravage the South."

"His motive for failing to disclose the location was more likely to be that of personal gain," Wendell said judiciously. "He was a smart lad, and he must have realized that CSA tender would be of no value if the North prevailed, as it appeared to be doing that year." He stood up and took his sweet time ambling to the counter to pour himself a cup of coffee. "Henry and Emil, the private who hid the gold, were very close. They'd been reared in proximity and enlisted the same day. In fact, Emil's older brother was engaged to be married to one of Henry's sisters, a twenty-three-year-old widow whose husband had been killed during a foray into Indian Territory. They married in 1866 and went on to have eleven children, one of whom became a prominent attorney in El Dorado and —"

Jim Bob took the coffeepot from Wendell's hand. "So where is it?" he repeated in the same voice he used to confront grazers in the produce department, most of whom immediately confessed to everything from littering to stealing watermelons while in grade school.

"I must do more research before I'm prepared to say anything further. My hypothesis is tentative, and may not be correct."

"And this is something you found in the journal?" asked Kenneth. "You're not just making this up?"

"Well," cooed Sweetpea, "I know what I'm going to do this morning. Instead of taking my watercolors and a pad down to the creek, I'm going to find a nice sunny spot to read the journal. Would you like to join me, Wendell? We can take some cucumber sandwiches, cookies, and a thermos of iced tea."

Harriet smiled at her. "Wendell wouldn't dare do something like that. He's just recently announced his engagement to Miss Lydia Berle. She's the chairperson of the program committee, isn't she, Wendell? A delightful woman, if you disregard her unfortunate overbite and braying laugh. She's mentioned that she'd like to have the wedding at the Headquarters House, but of course that's impossible. Sites listed on the Historic Register are not for rent. Las Vegas chapels with Elvis impersonators, on the other hand, require no advance notice. All you have to do is drive up to the window. Blue suede shoes are optional, I understand."

"Now, Harriet," said Wendell, "that really is a matter unsuitable for discussion at this moment. These good people are much more interested in Henry's journal and the location of the gold."

"Wendell has many secrets," Harriet said, glancing around the kitchen. "Oh, yes, he's quite an enigma."

Corinne slid a plate of biscuits across the table to Simon. "Aren't you supposed to go to Springfield today to do the audio?"

Simon shrugged. "Yeah, I said I would. Anything more exciting than watercolors on your agenda, Sweetpea? It doesn't sound like ol' Wendell is going to play footsie out in the cow pasture. I'd hate for you to be bored all day." When she ignored him, he added, "I'd better find you here when I get back. Fraternizing with the enemy can be dangerous."

"What the hell are you talking about?" she replied coldly.

Corinne finished her coffee with a delicate shudder. "Well, I do believe I'll drop by the high school and let the coordinator know I'll be available tomorrow. You, Kenneth?"

"Fuck 'em. I'm going to take a walk and familiarize myself with the terrain. Unlike General Ames, I have no spies to report back to me."

"And you, Wendell?" said Harriet. "Hoping to find an underage slut on Cotter's Ridge who can reinvigorate your withered manhood before your honeymoon with Miss Lydia Berle? This woman named Hospiss, or maybe one of her illegitimate daughters? It's too bad the whorehouse Kenneth mentioned last night is so far away. It might do you a world of good."

"I am going to Cotter's Ridge, but only to do further research," he said. "What's more, I don't know what's gotten into you, Harriet. I've never heard you say such things before."

Jim Bob tapped his wife's shoulder, since she hadn't moved in more than a minute and was failing to notice that the bacon in the skillet was beyond crusty. "Guess I'll take a shower and then go to work. If you need anything, call me."

Mrs. Jim Bob turned off the burner with a

click reminiscent of the cocking of a rifle. "I'm going into Farberville to pick up a few things. You all will have to make do with what's in the refrigerator at lunchtime. Perkin's eldest will be here shortly to clean up the breakfast things and vacuum. If you need something, ask her. I should be back by the middle of the afternoon."

She left the room before she was subjected to any more of this bickering and profanity in her own home, where she'd hosted the Missionary Society on numerous occasions. Where Brother Verber had said many a blessing over Sunday dinner, his head bent and his voice quavering with respect for the Almighty Lord. Where she'd always made sure there was a Bible in every bedroom and a fresh roll of toilet paper in every bathroom, along with a booklet of daily meditations. Where this morning she'd found two empty wine bottles in the trash and an unopened one on a shelf in the refrigerator. Let them starve, she thought as she grabbed her handbag and car keys. Let them indulge in their naked depravity for Perkin's eldest's entertainment, presuming Perkin's eldest had a sense of humor.

Mrs. Jim Bob was beyond caring.

9

Jack was sitting on my sofa when I came out of the bathroom, a towel wrapped around my head. My bathrobe was as shabby as an antique teddy bear, but I'd never much cared for silky little wisps that were useless on lonely winter nights in Maggody. This is not to imply I'd been lonely the previous night.

"So what's your schedule today?" I asked.

"I called Simon and suggested that I pick him up, but he wants to meet me at my studio at noon. If he can read in anything but a bored monotone, we should be done by midafternoon and I'll be back here by dinnertime. Would you like to try one of those places with a wine list?"

"That would be very nice," I said, "assuming you won't be too tired."

"Too tired for what?"

I realized my toes were curling. "Dinner, of course, and then, if you're in the mood, a Scrabble rematch. If you hadn't nibbled my neck every time it was my turn, I'm quite

239

sure I would have whomped your ass, as we say in Maggody. What's more, we're going to use a dictionary tonight. None of these esoteric words for Chinese concubines or Moroccan variations of couscous. I'm on to your tricks."

"Then indeed a rematch. Do you have any felonies on your agenda for the day?"

"I suppose I'd better check on some missing persons, none of whom are apt to be in the clutches of foreign agents, then make sure Earl's amenable to having a dozen mules in his pasture. Oh, and I need to run by the bridge and make sure the Confederate private camped there is behaving. If he gets too carried away with role-playing, he's liable to steal a couple of chickens or a pig. That wouldn't sit well with the locals. The guy swears his name is Jeb Stewart, if that gives you a clue."

Jack dislodged my towel as he gave me a kiss that vanquished all thoughts of an agrarian uprising in Stump County. Or couscous.

"Later, then," he said.

"Later," I agreed, as quivery as any preteen who'd caught a glimpse of her idol coming out the stage door.

After half an hour devoted to dressing, drying my hair, and reminding myself that adolescent behavior was not attractive in women over thirty, I walked across the road to Ruby Bee's for bacon, eggs, biscuits, grits, and coffee. A "closed" sign hung on the door. Grumbling under my breath, I went to the supermarket, bought a package of month-old doughnuts, and headed to the PD for the backwoods version of a continental breakfast.

I'd just started making coffee when Millicent McIlhaney came into the PD. She was so pale and wobbly that I hurried over to help her to the chair across from my desk.

"Can I get you a cup of water?" I asked. "The coffee will be ready in a few minutes."

"No, thank you. Just let me sit here and collect myself. The last thing I want to do is take to bawling like a baby." She took a tissue from her pocket and blew her nose. "I'm just so darned worried! Darla Jean's never done anything like this before. She may be mouthy on occasion, and sometimes downright rude, but she's a good girl. I can't believe she'd do something like this! What am I gonna tell Jeremiah?"

"What's she done?"

Millicent began to snivel, but, thankfully, not to bawl. "I wish I knew, Arly. This morning Jeremiah and I had to leave early to go to a co-op prayer breakfast on account of him being on the board of directors. I woke up Darla Jean and told her she'd have to fix her own breakfast and get herself to school. When I got home an hour ago, she was gone. I didn't think a thing about it until the secretary in the office called to verify her absence. I looked all over the house and yard, then searched her room and found her backpack in her closet. She hasn't missed a day of school since she had the chicken pox in second grade."

"It's a pretty day," I said soothingly. "Maybe she and some of the other kids decided to play hooky. They're probably catching crawdads in Boone Creek."

Millicent shook her head. "Not Darla Jean, and besides, I asked the secretary who else was absent. All of her close friends are at school today, including Heather, Billy Dick, Cooter, Ramona, and that slutty Pipkin girl with the purple hair. I can't see Darla playing hooky by her lonesome. I think she must have been kidnapped. What do you aim to do about it, Arly?"

I tried to envision a scenario in which Ruby Bee stopped by the McIlhaney house to invite Darla Jean to skip school in order to go shopping in Farberville. And meet Lottie, Brother Verber, and Petrol for lunch at a quaint café, where they would feast on

242

quiche, arugula, and crème brûlée. I caught myself before I smiled. "I don't think we should jump to the conclusion just yet that she's been kidnapped. I gather she didn't leave a note."

"If she'd left a note explaining her whereabouts," Millicent said darkly, "then I wouldn't be sitting here, would I?"

"I suppose not. Let's be reasonable about this. She was in her bed this morning when you left the house, and sometime thereafter, she decided not to go to school. It's not even ten o'clock, Millicent. It's premature to call in the FBI." I remembered the conversation I'd had with Heather the previous evening. "Has Darla Jean been upset lately?"

She sighed. "Even Jeremiah commented on it, and he's not what you'd describe as sensitive. Last week one of the boys at work shot him in the buttocks with a staple gun, and he didn't even notice till he got home and I saw the bloodstain. But yes, Darla Jean's been acting peculiar. She spent the weekend in her bedroom with the door locked, refusing to answer me or come down for meals, and wouldn't talk to Heather when she called. It was all I could do to convince her to go to school yesterday. I told her that if she didn't snap out of it, I was gonna take her to see the doctor."

I poured a mug of coffee while I thought this over. Darla Jean was far from angelic; I'd caught her and her friends with beer and pot more than once — and I'm talking more than once a month when summer nights are graced with shooting stars, whip-poor-wills, and lightning bugs. Some of the condoms discarded on the banks of Boone Creek undoubtedly bore traces of her DNA. It did not seem wise to share this with Millicent, however.

"Here's what let's do," I said. "You go home and wait by the telephone in case she calls. If you hear from her, leave a message on my machine. I'll drive around town, and if I don't have any luck, go to the high school and pull Heather out of class. She may have some idea what's been bothering Darla Jean."

Millicent wasn't overly impressed with my plan, but allowed herself to be escorted out to her car. "I know I sound as dithery as a grannywoman, but I can't imagine Darla Jean doing something like this. She has eleven gold pins for perfect attendance at Sunday school. She made the honor roll last semester, and has been talking to the counselor about going away to college after she graduates in a year. Jeremiah's not real excited, since he thinks she ought to settle for the secretarial school in Farberville, but he told her that we'd give her something to help with her expenses. Now she has an unexcused absence, which means she can't make up the work. It's just not like her."

"She'll turn up," I said, then waited until Millicent drove away before going back inside the PD to gulp down coffee and gnaw on a desiccated doughnut. Once I'd taken in enough calories to hold me for an hour or two, I called the high school and ascertained that neither Lottie Estes nor Darla Jean had shown up.

I stopped first at Lottie's house, where I had no response. I could have grubbed in the flowerpot for the key and gone inside, but I saw no indication that anyone had been in the house since Jack and I had searched it the previous evening. Folks were beginning to behave oddly, I thought as I made a mental note to ask the health department to make sure a hole in the ozone layer hadn't appeared directly above Maggody. Even Ruby Bee had vanished, as if she'd heard rumors of a Union cavalry unit staking out a position in Earl Buchanon's pasture and fled to Cotter's Ridge to hide the family silver (two souvenir spoons and a misshapen gravy ladle from a flea market).

I sat in the car for a few minutes, then

headed for the bridge. Jeb Stewart had as much physical appeal as a cadaver left to bake in the sun for a week or two, but Darla Jean might have found a way to romanticize him. I hoped not, since I'd have to take her to my apartment and keep her in the shower for an hour. And then come up with an explanation to appease Millicent and Jeremiah. Family counseling was not among my many talents.

A campfire was smoldering at the edge of the woods. There were two pup tents, which surprised me, since I'd assumed Jeb was alone in his melodramatic mission to do himself in before any minié balls found their way to a vital organ. What's more, the soldier who leaped to his feet as I approached was wearing a threadbare blue uniform and was clean-shaven.

"Yes, ma'am?" he said as he snapped to attention.

"Who are you?"

"Private Waylon Pepperstone out of Missouri. I'm not trespassing, am I?"

"No," I said. "I came here to have a word with Jeb Stewart, but I don't see him. Did you shoot him and bury his body in the woods?"

Waylon was gaping at me as if I were Nancy Hanks's great-great-granddaughter. "No, ma'am — I mean, I don't know where he is. He was gone when I got up this morning. His gear's still here, so he'll be coming back. Is there anything I can do for you, ma'am? Would you like some coffee?"

I looked at the rusted coffeepot in the ashes of the campfire. "No thank you. When did you arrive in Maggody?"

"Last night. My truck's parked on the other side of the woods. I had to open a gate, but I was real careful to close it behind me. Has there been a complaint?"

"Lighten up, Private Pepperstone," I said. I brushed past him and looked inside both tents, not at all sure if I wanted to find Darla Jean curled up in a blanket. "So you arrived last night and ended up here. Did anyone from town come out to welcome you?"

He shook his head. "Jeb and me caught some fish for supper, then compared notes about reenactments. We both went to bed pretty early. Last night he said he wanted to do some exploring this morning, so that's where I figure he is."

"Does he have a metal detector?"

"Oh, no, ma'am, he's real hard core. He probably parked his car a couple of miles away so he could hike to town. I gotta tell you, if he doesn't do something about those sores on his feet, he's in for real trouble. My uncle let a blister turn so ugly that he had to go into the hospital for blood poisoning. They amputated his big toe. Afterward, even when he was just standing there, he kinda rocked back and forth."

"Do give him my regards," I said, "and tell Private Stewart that I'd like a word with him as soon as he returns. He knows where to find me."

"And where would that be, ma'am?" said Private Pepperstone.

"He knows." I went back to my car and drove over to the rectory. Brother Verber's car was still absent. I went inside and took a quick look on the off chance I'd find him passed out in a scarlet negligee and high heels, then searched the Assembly Hall more thoroughly in case Darla Jean had decided to hide there for her own inexplicable reasons. She had not.

Ruby Bee's Bar & Grill was still closed, much to the consternation of those parked out front and nurturing visions of fried chicken and scalloped potatoes for lunch. I parked in front of the PD and went inside, hoping I'd find a message on the answering machine that Darla Jean had turned up like either a bad penny or a shiny silver dollar. The evil eye was not flashing. I needed to call Harve about Saturday morning, but I decided it could wait while I reheated the coffee, propped my feet on the corner of the desk, and thought about Jack. The Scrabble had been entertaining, the tamales tasty, and the sex fantastic. At some point I'd have to consider where the relationship, if indeed there was one, might be going. For the moment, I was content to anticipate another night with him, although it might be prudent if he rumpled the sheets on his bed at the Flamingo Motel to lessen the suspicions of the proprietress.

Which reminded me of his sickly assistant, Terry, whose last name had yet to be mentioned. I wrapped up the last doughnut in a napkin and walked down the road to the motel to make sure an ambulance — or a coroner — was not required. The blinds in all the units but one were closed, so I took my chances and tapped on the door.

"Come in," said a weak voice, "but don't get too close. I think I've got dengue fever."

Terry proved to be a boy of twenty-odd years, with watery eyes and a raw, red nose. He looked at me, then slumped back on the pillows and snatched up a handful of tissues. "I want to be buried in Springfield."

"And with luck you will be," I said. "Would you like some hot tea or a soda? A doughnut, maybe?"

"Under a tree."

It took me a second to follow him. "I'm sure there's a nice, shady plot waiting for you. Can I fetch anything for you in the interim? Do you have aspirin and decongestants?"

"All I want is to be left alone to die."

"Very few people die of a head cold. I'll come back later with some soup."

He lifted his head to stare at me. "I can't get ESPN or CNN. Have I already died and gone to hell? Is my punishment for all eternity to be in a motel room with avocado green shag carpeting, prints of kittens taped to the walls, toilet paper made of unprocessed wood pulp, and towels that could double for sandpaper?"

"Chicken noodle soup." I waggled my fingers at him, then left before he could start sneezing and coughing in my direction. The last thing I need was a dose of Yankee germs, especially when the Civil War was heating up in my petty domain.

I'd reached the end of the building when I heard gravel crunch behind me. Fully expecting to find Terry lurching after me like a character in a zombie movie, I turned around in order to strong-arm him. I would have been a couple of feet too high.

"Hammet?" I said, stunned.

"Howdy, Arly. Surprised to see me?"

"That would be an understatement. What on earth are you doing here? Aren't you supposed to be in school?"

"So they keep sayin'." He scuffled his toe in the gravel to avoid my perplexed stare. "I weren't supposed to let you know I was here until tomorrow, but I'm gittin' mighty bored. Any chance the fellow in there's a bank robber what needs to be captured? I've been watching him, and he's acting real funny, like he's afraid the police is closing in on him. If he'd leave his room, I could search it for the stolen loot. Then we could bust in on him, and mebbe shoot him."

"How long have you been here, Hammet?"

"Couple of days, I reckon. Ruby Bee and Estelle collected me at the foster home and promised I could be in a movie. I've got a uniform in my room. Wanna see it? It's real fancy, with shiny buttons and these gold braids. When the rebs come riding down the road, I'm gonna be out in front, beatin' on the drum to lead 'em into battle. I saw this movie where —"

"Where are Ruby Bee and Estelle? I'd like to have a word with them."

"Up on the ridge, along with a passel of

other folks." Hammet eyed me uneasily. "You're slitty-eyed like copperhead. You ain't mad at me, is you?"

"No, Hammet," I said as I clapped his shoulder. "I'm a little bit annoyed with Ruby Bee and Estelle, though. Did they say how long they're planning to be up there?"

"Probably not too long after they figger out I came back here. I was getting hungry, but they kept saying we had to find another cave so's they could poke sticks in it. They're gonna be right sorry if they rile up bats."

I gave him the doughnut. "Eat this, and then we'll go by the Dairee Dee-Lishus and pick up some lunch."

"We ain't gonna shoot that guy?" he asked, pointing at Terry's unit.

"I'm afraid not. I need to save my bullets for worthier targets. How about bean burritos and a chocolate milkshake?"

Brother Verber was not happy with his present situation. In fact, he was miserable, in pain, hog-tied, soiled in his britches, aching from his ankles to his wrists, and not at all sure he was going to get out of his predicament alive. It didn't seem likely. He'd offered up a few rounds of "Yea though I walk through the valley of the shadow of death," but the sentiment wasn't exactly heartening since he figured that's where he was. He'd always imagined a more dignified departure into eternal bliss, maybe in a fancy cathedral or at least in a chapel with a stained-glass window and nuns warbling in Latin.

Except, of course, he had ridiculed the Catholic Church on a weekly basis and therefore had no hope of nuns, stained-glass windows, and a fine requiem mass with brochures listing the details of his accomplishments as a servant of the Almighty Lord. All he could hope for was the mail-order seminary in Las Vegas to mention his untimely departure in one of the annual newsletters, alongside advertisements for holy water and souvenir baptism coasters.

Brother Verber began to nibble despondently. Life was too fleeting to go out on an empty belly.

Hammet was in the back room of the PD, happily looking through gun catalogs, and I was sitting behind my desk, rehearsing my lecture on thoroughly despicable and devious behavior, when Kevin Buchanon stumbled through the door. It was his customary style, so I wasn't alarmed.

"Dead body!" he gurgled.

"Here? I don't think so, but I can check."

"Up on Cotter's Ridge, about a mile past Robin Buchanon's shack. There's a bluff. The body's laying there at the bottom."

"Whose body?"

"I dunno." Kevin sat down across from me and began to wring his hands as if we'd been dropped into an opera (or a soap opera, in his case). "A fellow, I think. Most of what I could see was his arms on account of the brush kinda swallowing him up."

"Did you make sure he was dead?"

"Gosh, Arly, it would have taken me a good whiles to climb down and twice that long to get back up. The drop looked to be twenty or thirty feet smack onto rocks. There ain't no way he's not deader'n a stewed squirrel. Besides, I knew I should tell you right away."

"You did the right thing, Kevin," I said as I sat back and tried to decide what I ought to do. The police car so graciously provided to me by the city council couldn't make it more than halfway to Robin's cabin before fallen trees, stumps, and rocks blocked progress. An hour there and an hour back, even if I didn't attempt to reach the body. "Are you really sure about what you saw?" I asked. "It couldn't have been a piece of discarded clothing or newspaper?"

"I think that mysterious fellow at the Flamingo Motel must have shot him and throwed him off the bluff," Hammet contributed from the doorway. "I saw right away that he was a killer. They was most likely partners."

Kevin nearly fell out of the chair. "What are you doing here?"

"What he is doing," I said icily, "is hauling himself back to his room at the motel to wait until Ruby Bee and Estelle appear. In fact, if he's not out of here in five seconds, I'm going to call the county social services department and have him picked up as a runaway."

"I dint run away!" Hammet protested.

"So I'll cross my fingers when I say you did. I'm counting, Hammet." Once he was gone, I reluctantly returned my attention to Kevin. "All I can see to do is call the sheriff's department, report the body, and request deputies and ATVs. You'll have to go with us to find the site. If this is some sort of joke, you're liable to be doing a lot of time at the county jail. Do you understand?"

Kevin nodded glumly. "I know what I saw."

Harve wasn't any happier than I about the situation, but promised a couple of men and a Jeep as soon as he could round them up.

Once I'd hung up, I quizzed Kevin but he had nothing else to add to his description of bluff and body. He'd neither seen nor heard anyone else. There'd been no indications that anyone had been prowling around Robin Buchanon's derelict shack. Recently, anyway, since the teenagers have been known to buy 'shine from Raz and leave jars scattered in the yard.

"Why were you up there?" I asked. "This buried treasure thing?"

He rubbed his face. "No, nuthin' like that. Do you think I can go over to the Dairee Dee-Lishus and get a burger afore the deputies get here? I ate my last peanut butter sandwich long about midnight, and I'm feeling peckish."

"You were up there all night?"

"It's a long story. I can be back in a few minutes."

"Sure, go ahead," I said. While I waited for the posse to come storming into town in a cloud of carbon monoxide, I went ahead and wrote up the beginning of the report, which would end with either a cursory pronouncement from the coroner regarding cause of death or a great deal of trouble for Kevin Buchanon, who didn't really deserve it — unless he'd concocted his story. If he had, I would cheerfully push him off the roof of the antiques store.

I was admiring my succinct yet colorful prose when Dahlia banged open the door.

"You got to find Kevvie!" she shrieked. She disappeared for a moment, then came backing inside with the stroller and its pudgy occupants. "He's been gone all night! First thing this morning I took the babies down to his ma's so I could go into Farberville for my monthly checkup. The blankets on the couch were folded, so I just thought he'd got up extra early and gone to work. But when I got back to town and stopped by the SuperSaver to pick up some groceries, Idalupino told me that Kevvie dint show up and Jim Bob was nigh onto spittin' nails." She mopped her nose on the back of her hand. "I can't stand thinking of him stuck in a cave or all bloodied on account of falling out of a tree."

"He's at the Dairee Dee-Lishus, Dahlia."

"No, he ain't," she said tearfully. "He's up on Cotter's Ridge, most likely dead. So's my granny, but she was real old and liable to die right soon, anyways."

I stood up. "Sit down and listen to me. Kevin was sitting in that very chair less than ten minutes ago. I saw no evidence of blood. He may have bruises on his butt, but he did not drop his pants to show me. At this

257

moment, he's at the Dairee Dee-Lishus buying a hamburger. He should be back here at any minute. Now what is this about?"

Her eyes kept flitting toward the door as she sputtered out an explanation of how she'd taken her granny up to Cotter's Ridge and subsequently lost her. "It's not like the dead of winter or anything," she added in her defense. "My granny's scrawny but tougher'n a weasel. Ornerier, too."

"And this was forty-eight hours ago? You didn't feel the need to mention it to the staff at the old folks' home — or to me?"

Dahlia gave me a defiant look. "Kevvie swore he'd find her. Me and the babies are going home. You tell him he'd better get his sorry ass there if he knows what's good for him. I've a mind to smack him with a skillet for causing me all this worry. I'm in the family way, so I'm s'posed to stay calm."

I spotted Kevin approaching, a greasy sack in one hand. "Go outside and let him explain why he won't be home for several hours. This is more your fault than his, Dahlia, so I suggest you listen to him, then use the skillet to make cornbread."

"What about my granny?"

"I'll put her on the list," I said with a sigh.

★ ★ ★

It took the rest of the afternoon for the three deputies and me to bring the zippered body bag to the top of the bluff and stretch it out next to the Jeep. Kevin had been sent home on foot hours earlier, when his bleating became intolerable. Now the only sounds were birds, chattering squirrels, and heavy breathing as the four of us sat down on the rocky ground. I was surprised I couldn't hear sweat dripping: The temperature was mild but the exertion had not been.

Corpses can be less than cooperative.

"So what's with this old guy?" asked Les. "What was he doing out here by himself?"

I brushed a spider off my arm. "Wendell Streek is — was — the treasurer of the Stump County Historical Society, which may not have made him a local celebrity. He said last night that he intended to track down private family plots to further his genealogical research. I hate to think how many Buchanons are buried somewhere on Cotter's Ridge. Generations of them, I'd think, all the way back to the early nineteenth century. Buchanons wouldn't have seen any sense in paying for a plot in a proper cemetery. Maybe the ginseng grows so well because the patches are well-fertilized."

"So he was looking for family plots. That

doesn't explain what he was doing down there. I ain't a medical examiner, but I can tell you he hasn't been dead all that long. He didn't get lost in the dark and walk off the bluff."

"I agree," I said as I struggled to my feet. "Let's put him on the backseat and get him to the hospital so McBeen can examine him in the comfort of his air-conditioned morgue. The cause of death is pretty damn obvious, though."

The two younger deputies didn't look pleased to be sharing a seat with the lumpy black bag, but obliged. When we got back to town, Les dropped me off at the PD before heading for Farberville in the makeshift hearse.

The evil eye was flashing. I went into the back room and dampened a paper towel, then sat down at my desk, blotted a few oozing scratches, and punched the button. The first message was from Ruby Bee: It was sputtery and defensive, and in some obscure way, accusatory. I moved on. Darla Jean had come home and gone to her bedroom without so much as a word of apology, if you can imagine. I moved on. Harriet Hathaway was concerned about Wendell. I moved on. Mrs. Jim Bob was concerned about Brother Verber. I moved on. And then, of course, Sheriff Harvey Dorfer, wanting to know what the holy hell had been goin' on for the last four hours and why hadn't he heard from anyone.

That one I couldn't ignore. I wiped my face, tossed the towel into the wastebasket, and called him.

"A guy from Farberville," I told him. "Retired, prissy, a self-proclaimed expert in area genealogy. Not the sort to have a rap sheet for anything more heinous than an overdue library book. His body should be arriving at the morgue shortly."

"So cut to it," Harve said. "I'd like to get home and have supper before the baseball game comes on. Mrs. Dorfer is real adamant that we eat at the table so she can tell me all about the gossip at the quilting club and the neighbor's garbage being scattered all over the damn place."

"Most likely an accident. I met him last night, and he didn't sound suicidal or so addled that he might have been oblivious to the bluff. I'd be hard-pressed to think alcohol or drugs were involved, but I presume McBeen will order a blood test and a tox screen."

"You know how to get in touch with his next of kin? Somebody's gonna have to identify him and sign the paperwork."

I propped my feet on the corner of my desk and tried to ignore the rips in my pants. "Yeah, I'll take care of that, but I don't have time to take this case, Harve. The Civil War is scheduled to break out any day now. General Grant's at the south end of town, and General Lee's moving in from the north. Stonewall Jackson's camping in Estelle's backyard and Sherman just burned Hasty in his march to Boone Creek. I can already hear cannon fire in the distance."

Harve chuckled. "You sound like you're about to swoon, Miss Melanie. Now you just handle informing the next of kin and leave me a message. I got a baseball game to watch."

The sumbitch hung up on me. I was still fuming when Jack came into the PD and stopped.

"Oh dear," he said, eyeing me. "Hard day?"

"I won't be able to go out to dinner tonight," I said. "Wendell Streek's body was discovered up on the ridge. I need to go find Miss Hathaway and ask her how to get in touch with his relatives."

"That pompous little man?"

"That pompous little man, now deceased."

He winced. "Sorry, it just came out. What

happened?"

"I don't know. You'd better go on to dinner by yourself, or settle for something to eat at Ruby Bee's. I promised I'd take Terry some chicken soup, but I didn't get around to it. I'm sure Ruby Bee will fix a tray for him, and probably force-feed him if it comes to that. Why don't you catch up with me tomorrow?"

"Not later tonight?"

My toes curled despite myself. "No. I don't know how long this will take, but once I'm done, all I want to do is take a long shower, check myself for ticks, and fall into bed."

Jack sat down across from me. "Can you tell me what happened to Wendell?"

"His body was found at the bottom of a thirty-foot bluff. He most likely fell this morning, although the coroner will have to determine the time of death. I helped bring up the body, and now I need to inform Miss Hathaway so she can provide information about his family and I can make the necessary calls. I've done this before, but it's nothing I look forward to."

"Was he alone?"

My feet hit the floor as I pushed back my chair. "I'm not in the mood to participate in dialogue from some prime-time cop show.

Call me tomorrow, okay?"

"Maybe I'll go check on Terry. Tomorrow, then."

Wow, now there was a way to nurture a meaningful relationship. I wondered if I ought to take a few lessons from Corinne. Or, heaven forbid, Sweetpea.

10

There were plenty of cars parked in Hizzoner's driveway, including one that was doing irreparable damage to what I thought might have been a tree peony in a very recent past life, and another that had left ruts in the lawn. I hoped the miscreants were long gone by Sunday morning, when Brother Verber thundered about the sanctity of nature from his bloody pulpit. Most of the time his foreshadowings of eternal damnation were centered on whiskey bottles discarded on gravel bars and the debauchery any righteous Christian would infer from such, but if Mrs. Jim Bob harbored an abiding love for her tree peony, it would be the focal point. This is not to imply I attended the Voice of the Almighty Lord Assembly Hall on Sunday mornings to cleanse my soul. I mostly cleansed my clothes at the Suds of Fun, but Ruby Bee and Estelle had heard about the juicier remarks by the time I wandered in for lunch.

The house guests, minus one, were assembled in the backyard. Sweetpea and Simon were standing at the far end, several feet apart and cooing sweet nothings. Miss Hathaway was seated at the picnic table, making notes on a pad. Kenneth Grimley was occupied with a corkscrew and a bottle of wine.

Corinne waved at me. "What a nice surprise to see you, Arly. You look absolutely dreadful. Can we offer you a glass of wine or a tourniquet?"

"I need to have a word with Miss Hathaway." I went to the picnic table and sat down beside her. "I'm afraid I have some bad news."

"Is it about the mules? I don't see how we can —"

"About Wendell Streek," I said softly. "We found his body this afternoon on Cotter's Ridge. It appears that he fell off a bluff."

"Wendell? That's absurd. He wouldn't fall off a bluff. He's deathly afraid of heights. It's all he can do to go up to the attic of the Headquarters House. There must be some mistake."

"I'm sorry. I made the identification myself."

The pen clattered on the concrete. "You must have been confused. I will admit I was concerned when he didn't return this afternoon in time for tea and cookies, but I never once thought . . ."

"What's this?" Corinne said as she stooped over us and put her arm around Miss Hathaway. "Could he have had a seizure? Was he in good health?" She hesitated, then added, "You don't think he could have been depressed, do you? We see this kind of tragedy in Charleston all the time, but it's usually on account of a family history of alcoholism or the uncovering of a scandal. Noah DeVille, just three houses down from me, drank a quart of bourbon and then shot himself in the head because of a drop in the Dow Jones. They found out later that he'd been playing fast and loose with his clients' IRA accounts."

Harriet shook her head. "Wendell was in perfect health, and was hardly likely to do something rash because of a flux in the stock market." She clutched my hand. "Can you tell me what happened?"

I wished I could swat away Corinne, but she was hovering with the tenacity of a gnat. "His body was taken to the Farberville hospital about an hour ago," I said. "I won't know anything until tomorrow or the next day. I need to notify his next of kin. Can you help me?"

Kenneth set down a glass of wine in front of her. "Drink up, woman. It'll settle your nerves."

Harriet's grip on my hand tightened, causing my fingers to begin to resemble albino worms. "His mother, but she isn't well. We had a little party last month for her ninetieth birthday. She fainted while attempting to blow out the candles. This will simply kill her. Wendell has a brother in someplace like Boise or Billings, but I have no idea how to get in touch with him."

Corinne whipped out a lacy handkerchief and thrust it into Harriet's free hand. "We'll do everything we can to help, dear. Might there be an address book in his briefcase?"

"Or we could call his fiancée," suggested Kenneth. "What's her name — Linda or something like that?"

"His fiancée?" I said. "Maybe I should call her."

"Don't be ridiculous!" said Harriet, regaining her color. She picked up the wineglass and drained it without so much as blinking. "They became engaged only three days ago. I have known Wendell for more than twenty years. I darned his socks, stayed with his mother during her bouts of nocturnal incontinence, left casseroles in the freezer, and encouraged him to pursue his interest in genealogy after he retired. I always made him divinity for Christmas. When he lost his resolve, I took his canary to the vet's office to be put out of its misery."

"Perhaps you should have taken his mother as well," said Kenneth.

"That's enough!" I snapped at him. I took Harriet's arm and urged her to her feet. "Let's go inside and find a place where we can talk."

"You're quite sure it was Wendell?" she said as we went through the sun porch. "You couldn't have made a mistake?"

"Quite sure, I'm afraid."

Mrs. Jim Bob was in the kitchen, looking more like a sullen scullery maid than a mayor's wife. "Just what are you doing here, missy? Shouldn't you be out looking for Lottie and Brother Verber? I can only accommodate eight at my dining room table. I used to be able to seat ten until Jim Bob used the extra leaf to make a plaque to mount some fish he caught in a tournament. Why don't you just take yourself down to Ruby Bee's and have some fried grease and gravy for supper? I am preparing a nice dinner for my guests."

"There's been an accident," I told her. "We found Wendell Streek's body on Cotter's Ridge this afternoon."

"That's ridiculous," she began, then looked at Harriet. "Take her to the living room so she can lie down. I'll fix her a cup of tea."

Harriet was staggering as we made it to the sofa, but she sank down before her knees buckled. "I just can't believe this. Not Wendell. He wouldn't so much as climb on a footstool to change a lightbulb. He would never get within yards of the edge of a precipice. He must have had a heart attack."

I propped a pillow behind her head. "That may well be what happened. Had he been diagnosed with heart trouble? Did he take any medication for high blood pressure or allergies?"

"I don't know." Harriet closed her eyes. "If you don't mind, I'd like to have a few minutes to assimilate this. Wendell was so filled with energy and enthusiasm this morning that it was all he could do not to start tap dancing in the kitchen. He did love the Fred Astaire and Ginger Rogers movies."

I was trying to think of something to say when Sweetpea swept past me and knelt by the sofa.

"Oh, Miss Hathaway, this is just the most terrible news," she said. "Is there anything I can do for you? Would you like an aspirin or a cup of tea with a splash of brandy? You're trembling, you poor thing. Can I get you a blanket?"

I took Sweetpea's arm and pulled her aside. "Mrs. Jim Bob is fixing tea, but don't count on the brandy. Please stay here while I find Wendell's room and look for his address book. Someone in the family has to be notified."

She lowered her voice. "He was sharing a bedroom with Simon. Upstairs, second door on the right. You may have to dig through Simon's dirty clothes to find much of anything. Ruthie's been his nursemaid since he was born. He's never dropped a dirty sock in the laundry hamper, made a bed, hung a wet towel on the rack, or even put a dirty dish in the sink. He's in for a shock when we get married, because my name's not Ruthie. I've made it clear to him that we're not going to have full-time help."

"Oh?" I said, not nearly as fascinated as I sounded.

"I've had servants underfoot all my life. Not at boarding school, mind you, but when I'd come home for the holidays, my suitcase would be whisked away, my things unpacked, my nightgown pressed, the covers on my bed turned down. I always felt as though I was staying in a hotel in Paris, if you know what I mean."

"Life's tough," I said, nodding. "If you don't mind waiting here . . ."

"Simon can be such a spoiled brat. He thinks he's entitled to fancy cars, expensive wines, prime tee times, access to the hot clubs in Atlanta. It's like he's never seen pictures of starving children in Africa or those cripples in Vietnam and Cambodia who stepped on land mines. Most likely he just has Ruthie change the channels so he can watch a golf tournament — after she brings him a fresh gin and tonic, of course. I'm always surprised when he manages to slice a lime all by himself. Then again, he's adorable."

"Are my adorable ears burning?" said Simon as he came into the living room. He glanced at Harriet, who'd curled into a fetal position. "She okay?"

Sweetpea glowered at him. "Why do you assume that every conversation I have is about you? Tad is a damn sight more adorable than you, and he was never so much as five minutes late when we were dating. Even Trip, with all his mental problems, always brought me an orchid from his parents' greenhouse. Brad arranged for fireworks over Charleston Harbor on my birthday, but you missed it because you were shacked up with Shelby in Aruba. Sometimes you're barely tolerable, Simon. Now take Arly up to your bedroom and help her find Wendell's address book."

"At your service." He offered me his arm as if we were going into the dining hall. "May I escort you upstairs, Chief of Police? I promise not to be overly adorable."

"And I promise not to be overly impressed," I said. We stepped back as Mrs. Jim Bob came in with a tray, then went upstairs. The bedroom was far from the shambles Sweetpea had led me to anticipate. Both beds were made, due no doubt to Perkin's eldest. One suitcase looked as though it had been rummaged by drunken airport security guards, but the other was tidy. I knew which one merited my attention.

Simon sat down on the nearest bed. "What did Sweetpea have to say about me? That I'm a ne'er-do-well, unscrupulous, after her family's money?"

"She didn't go into detail." I shuffled through starched shirts and neatly folded pairs of boxers. "Are you?"

"That was multiple choice, and the fourth answer is 'none of the above.' I'm a pragmatist, if you understand what that means."

I looked at him. "That's way too many

syllables for a simple gal from the Ozarks. We're more accustomed to descriptions like 'dumb shit' and 'pond scum.' "

"What's your problem? I came all this way to do some pissant documentary, didn't I? I haven't run that pathetic stoplight or crashed into a school and killed squealing toddlers. Would you like me better if I lived in a shack and slept with my sisters?" He lit a cigarette and leaned back. "In this society, Chief Hanks, there are givers, who want to gnaw off their extremities to save the less fortunate, and those of us who are willing to sit back and take whatever comes our way. It's an economic reality. Some of us couldn't be rich if others weren't willing to be poor. Marxism, as amusing as it was, didn't work."

I began to sort through the files on Wendell's bedside table. "I gather you don't work, either."

"Oh, but I do, every day and quite diligently. I handle most of my mother's correspondence and deal with her agents, lawyers, and accountant so that she can devote herself to writing. It may be a minor contribution to the collective opus of literary fiction, but I like to think I do my part. After all, how could the Daughters of the Confederacy continue to thrive without

Corinne Dawk's annual potboiler? If there were no reworked renderings of Scarlett O'Hara, there could be no Rhett Butler waiting to scoop them into his arms and carry them up the staircase. That means they'd have to acknowledge that they're married to good ol' boys with bloated bellies and a fondness for waitresses at the truck stop out by the highway." He stubbed out his cigarette in a crystal bowl of dried leaves. It began to smolder, but the aroma was not unpleasant. "So this guy Wendell fell off a cliff. What's the big deal?"

"Well, he's dead," I said flatly.

"As is Private Henry Largesse."

I resumed flipping through files. Most of them contained only a few pages of names and dates, written in such a cramped style that they were impossible to decipher without a magnifying glass. Not that I cared, mind you. Some day genealogists and historians might hold symposiums to debate the relative merits of Private Custis E. Delaney's ancestry and his contributions to the efforts of the CSA. A weekend might be devoted to Henry Largesse and his fertile sisters.

In the drawer of the table I found an address book. I straightened up the files and looked at Simon, whose eyes were closed.

"I'm going downstairs," I said.

"Don't let me detain you."

We most definitely were not destined to be friends. I slammed the door on my way out of the bedroom, which I admit was petty but all I could do without a musket. In the living room, Corinne and Sweetpea were draped all over Harriet, to Mrs. Jim Bob's visible distress. Jim Bob hovered in a corner.

"What the hell's going on?" he demanded as I tried to flit past the doorway.

I nudged him into the hall, told him about Wendell Streek, and concluded with, "The body's at the morgue, and McBeen's conclusion will be blunt impact trauma. Blood work and tox analysis will have to come from the state lab, and that could take a week, if we're lucky. Until Sheriff Dorfer and I hear otherwise, we're assuming it was an accident."

"This don't look good," Jim Bob said. "I don't want tourists thinking it's dangerous to come to Maggody."

"Tourists don't come to Maggody. Why would they?"

He scratched his chin. "I don't know, ferchrissake. Maybe they want to buy antiques at Roy's shop or pick up sandwiches and chips at the SuperSaver deli and have a picnic."

"Keep telling yourself that, Mr. Mayor. Did Wendell say anything this morning about why he wanted to go to Cotter's Ridge?"

"He was all fired up to hunt for family plots. I dunno why he thought anybody'd give a rat's ass about a bunch of Buchanons that are long dead and buried."

"Or some that are still breathing," I said.

I left him growling and went to the PD to look through the address book. There was no notation of Wendell's mother's telephone number, but there would hardly be since he lived with her. Having heard of her frailty, however, I opted not to track down the number via the ever-friendly employees of directory assistance, and instead called Harve's home number.

"Speak your piece," he said brusquely. "The Cubs are gearin' up to take on the Cardinals."

"You have to send someone to the victim's home to inform his mother. I don't think she's capable of making an official identification, but she should know the name of his fiancée." I took a breath. "We agreed that this isn't my case, Harve. I don't see why I should have to drive to Farberville and do your dirty work."

"But you did say you'd write up a report,

didn't you? Was there anybody else up on Cotter's Ridge who might have been in the vicinity? We're talking potential witnesses."

"Is this a pregame warmup? You give me this, I give you that? One of us takes left field and the other right?"

Harve paused, then said, "Sounds like it, although that's not how the game is usually played. You do the preliminary paperwork and I send a deputy over to break the news to Mother Streek. I also send you two deputies on Saturday to cause much distress to those good citizens of Stump County who don't give a shit about the Civil War. Frankly, it sounds like you got the slicker end of the stick."

"And you're going to sit on your butt and watch baseball."

"I most certainly am, soon as Mrs. Dorfer and I eat meatloaf and butter beans. I'm gonna hold off on the pecan pie until the seventh-inning stretch."

"I'm not going to vote for you next time, Harve."

"As long as you don't think about running against me. You're not near able to fill my britches just yet, little lady."

I banged down the receiver and rocked back. Filling his britches, so to speak, would require thirty years of slapping backs at noontime civic club meetings and riding on the backs of convertibles in local parades. Shaking hands with the prosecutor during press conferences on the steps of the courthouse. Gaining two hundred pounds and developing a fondness for smoky rooms on the third floor of city hall. Winking at indiscretions and sweeping all manner of dirt under the rug.

After a few more minutes dedicated to fuming and sulking, I pulled over a pad of paper and started a list of potential witnesses, or at least those who might have been on Cotter's Ridge that morning. Kevin, who'd already told me what he knew. Private Jeb Stewart. Private Waylon Pepperstone, who could have headed there after I left him. Dahlia's granny. Darla Jean, unless she could explain her whereabouts. Ruby Bee and Estelle. Hammet, for that matter. Raz, most definitely but least appealing.

Take me out of the ball game.

I decided to start with Ruby Bee, since I might have a chance for a decent meal before I put on the thumbscrews and dragged out her confession. In that Jack might be at the bar & grill, I went to my apartment, showered, and changed into jeans and a tee-shirt. I was in a foul mood, but there was no reason to smell like an auction barn on an August afternoon. He was, after all, going to be in town for several more days. And nights.

Ruby Bee glared at me as I sat down on a stool as far away from Estelle as I dared. "I was beginning to wonder when you'd show your face. How hard can it be to return your own mother's calls? You're lucky I ain't on a respirator in the emergency room."

"And she might well have been," said Estelle. "You would have been wracked with the guilt the rest of your born days. If I hadn't been there to pull her out of that cave, why, who's to say what might have happened? She had so many spiderwebs in her hair that she looked like she'd decorated herself for Halloween. I had to hold her head between her knees for a good five minutes."

"And this is my fault?" I said.

"You could have called me back," Ruby Bee grumbled. "I hear you know about Hammet. We only fetched him so he could learn to appreciate his Southern heritage. You should have given a thought to that. These days history books sound like the Civil War was all about slavery. What about courage and sacrifice and —"

"Give me a break, and maybe a grilled

cheese sandwich," I said. "I know exactly why you picked him up at his foster home and brought him here. Where is he?"

"That man of yours took him to Farberville for pizza and a movie."

"As opposed to dragging him all over Cotter's Ridge for the last two days?"

Estelle snorted. "And for all the good it did. I've got chigger bites all the way up to my privates, and I've been obliged to slather myself with ointment until I stink like a locker room. There's no way I can stand long enough to give a perm, or even a shampoo and set. I had to cancel Joyce's appointment on Thursday."

Ruby Bee set down a plate of chicken and dumplings in front of me. "So what's this I heard about someone falling off a bluff on Cotter's Ridge this morning?"

I could have demanded her sources, but it wasn't worth the effort. Once Kevin had told Dahlia, and Dahlia had told Eileen, I could have heard it on NPR, had the radio in my car worked. "Harriet Hathaway's colleague, the treasurer of the historical society. It seems he was hot on the trail of backwoods family cemeteries."

"Buchanons, most likely," Estelle said, then buried her nose in a glass of sherry.

"I heard they showed up early," said

Ruby Bee, "and Mrs. Jim Bob was fit to be tied, since Perkin's eldest always takes off Mondays to go to her dance class. Estelle, do you recollect when we went to her recital at that Unitarian fellowship hall?"

Estelle grimaced. "How could I forget that? Grown women in tutus, pretending they were autumn leaves."

"I thought it was real sweet." Ruby Bee dabbed the corner of her eye with a dishtowel. "At the reception afterward, Perkin's eldest told me that she felt like a sycamore leaf, yellow and mottled, welcoming death and then resurrection as compost."

I finished eating and pushed away my plate. "As much as I would like to explore the topic of the regeneration of the life force, I'm more interested in knowing if either of you saw Wendell Streek or anyone else on the ridge this morning."

"I saw that Confederate soldier," Estelle said, "but he sure wasn't any ghost. That's not to say he wasn't sickly, but he had some flesh on his bones. Once he spotted me, he ducked out of sight quicker than a rooster darting into a henhouse. Ruby Bee didn't believe me, but I know what I saw."

Ruby Bee gave her a cool look. "You also said you saw a bear, a wildcat, and a vampire bat. I kept waiting for you to add

Bigfoot to your list."

"I do not appreciate your attitude, Rubella Belinda Hanks."

I intervened. "Can you give me any idea where you were at the time?"

Estelle took a few seconds to select a pretzel from the basket and examine it for defects before she said, "Maybe a mile or so south of the road that goes past the Pot O' Gold."

"Not near Robin's shack, then?" I said.

"Hard to say, since we were wandering around in circles. It's a miracle Ruby Bee and I found our way back here."

"What about this soldier?" I asked. "Any impression of his height, age, or hair color?"

Ruby Bee set down a piece of apple pie in front of me. "If she saw anything at all. I know I didn't, and I certainly wasn't taking a snooze."

Estelle snorted. "You was taking something, squatted like you were behind some bushes. I hope you didn't grab a handful of poison ivy when you finished."

"The soldier," I said. "Can you tell me anything?"

"No, I just caught a glimpse, like I said. The only reason I even saw him was the sun glinted off the buttons on the front of his uniform."

"You said he was sickly."

Estelle closed her eyes. "Skinny, kinda gangly, sleeves too short to cover his wrists. I didn't see his face."

I decided I'd learned as much as I would, and I wasn't inclined to be there when Ruby Bee stopped huffing and came around the bar to tell Estelle a thing or two about blurting out whatever came to mind, and so forth. Pies and pretzels might be flying before too long.

It was time to allow Darla Jean to explain her recent behavior. I drove to the McIlhaneys' house and rang the doorbell.

Millicent opened the door. "Didn't you get my message, Arly? Darla Jean came home in the middle of the afternoon. She wouldn't say where she'd been or anything else, and locked herself in her room. I couldn't coax her out for supper."

"I can coax her out." I went upstairs and knocked on her door. "Okay, Darla Jean, we can discuss this in the living room with your parents sitting on the sofa, or we can go out to my car and talk."

"I didn't commit a crime," she responded. "You ain't got any call to drag me out of here against my wishes."

"Then you can call the ACLU when we're finished. Now where's it going to be?"

Darla Jean banged open her door. "In your car," she said in a fierce whisper. "Can we please just get this over with?"

I led the way to my car and leaned against the hood. "Okay, what's going on? From what your mother and Heather said, you've been acting really strange for the last few days."

"So you're arresting me for truancy? Didn't you ever skip school?"

"I might have, but that's not the issue. Where were you today?"

She began to snuffle. "I needed to be by myself, so I made a sandwich and took a walk. Is there some crime in that? My ma nags me day and night about chores and homework, and my pa sits in front of the TV in his undershirt and drinks beer till he falls asleep. All they do is criticize me." She gave me a furtive look. "So what did Heather say about me?"

"Only that she was worried. Exactly where did you take this walk? Cotter's Ridge?"

She sank to the ground and leaned her head against the bumper. "Okay, so maybe I thought I might find this gold. All these folks are coming into town this week. I don't see why one of them should snatch the gold from under our noses. I mean, those of us who live here deserve it, don't we? It's been in Maggody for a hundred and forty years. It wouldn't be fair if some Yankee came into town and took it."

"Were you anywhere near Robin's shack?"

"Yeah, I thought Robin or one of her bastards might have found the gold and stuck it under the shack or buried it somewhere. I even thought about searching the outhouse, but there was some critter scratching in there. I wasn't about to open the door and find myself facing a rabid coon or possum. My second cousin in Benish had to have all those rabies shots, and she said it hurt like hell."

"Could someone have been hiding in there?"

She curled her lip at my question. "It's got so many knotholes and rotten boards that it's liable to fall over in the next big wind. I made sure nothing taller than six inches was in there."

"Did you see anyone at all?"

"A guy all dressed up like a rebel soldier came up the logging road, gave me a real dirty look, and kept on going. I was so scared I could hear my teeth chattering. I finally realized he was one of those reenactors, although I couldn't for the life of me imagine what he was doing on the ridge."

"He didn't say anything?" I asked.

"Didn't you hear what I just said? He gave me a dirty look, that's all, like I was the one who didn't have any business being there. I mean, I'm the one who grew up here. You'd think I was trespassing on his private property."

She was beginning to snuffle again, so I gave her a few minutes to get hold of herself before I said, "Did you see anyone else?"

"Some man dressed in a suit and tie, like he got lost on the way to a prayer meeting. He wasn't anywhere near as scary as that soldier. In fact, he sort of reminded me of Mr. Frenchi, who taught math in junior high until he ran off with the vice-principal's wife. He never gave us any homework on Fridays."

"What was this man doing?"

"Sitting on a stump, wiping his neck with a handkerchief and peering at a notebook. I went over and asked him if he was lost. He said he was more like confused by this map he had. It was hard to make any sense of, but then he said he was looking for Hospiss Buchanon's old place. I've never been there, but I told him I thought he was going in the right direction and all he needed to do was keep moving east."

"Did he tell you why he was looking for Hospiss's place?"

"Oh, something about folks buried in her yard. I didn't pay much attention. After he left, I just sat there trying to think what to do, and then I got worried that the soldier was coming back to murder me, so I went back past Robin's shack and came home. Can I go inside now?"

"Not yet," I said, trying to sound sympathetic. "I can understand why you want to find the gold, but it doesn't explain why you locked yourself in your bedroom all weekend and then skipped school today."

"I wasn't in my bedroom. There's a walnut tree outside my window. I spent all weekend looking for . . . well, the gold."

"And that's all you were looking for? Crawling in caves seems haphazard, as well as dangerous."

"I had a plan, but it got all screwed up."

It was beginning to fall into place. "Did it involve Diesel?"

Darla Jean tried to sputter, but her heart just wasn't in it. "Nobody'd be foolish enough to mess with him. He'd be more likely to bite my head off than give me the time of day. There's no way I'd go anywhere near his cave, even if I knew where it is.

Which, in case you're planning to write up some report, I don't!"

"But Petrol might."

"I don't know anything about Petrol. Go ask him if you've a mind to."

"I can't do that, Darla Jean," I said, "since he's gone to stay with his niece over in Hazzard. This niece called the old folks' home on Sunday and apologized for not letting them know he'd be staying with her for a few days. Such a considerate girl she must be."

"So what?" said Darla Jean in a last attempt at bravado, since both of us knew damn well that she had reached the limit of that particular credit card. "You saying I had something to do with this?"

I let her stew for a moment, then said, "Where is he?"

"Like I know. I spent all weekend trying to find him. Most of the time I sat on his porch, hoping he'd turn up. I drove him home on Saturday, but he said he wasn't going anywhere until he had a barbecue sandwich from this place over in Emmet. When I got back, he was gone. It's not like I kidnapped him, Arly. Petrol swore he'd take me to Diesel, and if I'd bring along a sack of food and some CDs, Diesel would tell me where to find the Confederate gold. I should have known better than to trust Petrol. My skin was crawling all the time I was around him. He's like some kind of fungus."

"CDs?" I said despite myself.

"And a blender."

"So you haven't seen him since Saturday, when he slithered away."

Darla Jean grabbed my arm. "It wasn't my fault. He promised to wait until I got back from Emmet, but then he was gone. I kept thinking he'd come back sooner or later."

I detached her hand. "But you called the old folks' home and lied to them."

"I could hardly tell them the truth, could I?" She stood up and brushed off the seat of her jeans. "Maybe I should have told you before now, but it's not like you can do anything about it, either. Petrol's probably hunkered down in Diesel's cave, counting gold coins while Diesel fixes a tasty pot of skunkweed soup. The next time we see Petrol, he'll be driving a silver Viper."

On that rather bizarre note, she went inside and switched off the porch light. I remained where I was, trying to sort through what she'd said. Jeb Stewart had been on Cotter's Ridge at the same time Wendell was searching for Hospiss Buchanon's family plot. Jeb had been less than friendly, but there was no reason to assume he'd been homicidal. Wendell had been on a mission, notebook and map in hand. I'd searched the area around his body and found neither on his person nor on the rocks that had resulted in his untimely demise.

Harriet Hathaway had been adamant that Wendell would never have wandered too near the edge of a bluff.

I was beginning to wonder, myself.

11

I wasn't pleased to find Jim Bob's pickup truck parked in front of the PD. I resisted the urge to turn left at the third star and flap my arms until I arrived in Never-Never Land, where all I'd have to deal with were pesky pirates and crocodiles with ticking bombs in their gullets.

"What?" I said as I went inside.

He was seated behind my desk, entertaining himself by rooting through the drawers. "I was wondering if you'd bothered yourself with this investigation. We don't want Maggody to get a bad reputation, 'cause if it does, pretty soon there won't be any way to pay your salary."

"And I won't be able to keep up my payments on the Jaguar? Gee, Jim Bob, I've been thinking about booking a suite on the *QE 2* next fall."

"That's enough of your smart remarks," he said. "What have you found out about this Streek man's death?"

I sat down across from him and crossed my arms. "Why do you care?"

He leaned back in my chair — my chair, mind you — and regarded me with all the warmth of that tick-tock croc calculating my nutritional potential. "You were there when his body was fetched, weren't you? It seems to me any cop with a lick of sense would have looked around and checked his pockets."

"The deputies and I did so conscientiously. I don't have the list of his personal items, but I seem to recall we found lint, a wallet containing the usual cards and about fifty dollars, a ballpoint pen, fingernail clippers, an asthma inhaler, a packet of tissues, a few coins, and half a roll of breath mints. Peppermint or spearmint — I'm not sure which it was. I can call the sheriff's office and ask if you'd like."

Jim Bob bit back what might have been a most entertaining reply, and after a moment, said, "Did you find a notebook?"

"What notebook?"

"I'm the one asking the questions," he said. "You'd best be the one answering them, unless you want to end up trying to collect unemployment."

"And you'll be the one trying to convince Ruby Bee to serve you a pitcher of beer on

Friday afternoons. I can always find another job." As much as I wanted to drag him out of my chair and stuff him in the wastebasket like a piece of junk mail, I sat where I was. "Why don't you tell me everything Wendell said this morning so that I can figure out whether I'm tidying up an accident or looking into a homicide?"

He managed to repeat the conversation that had taken place in his kitchen that morning, although I doubted the language had been quite that colorful. "He swore he found some clue about the location of the gold," he added in a surly voice, as if I might go dashing out of the PD with a shovel. "He didn't say much, except he wanted to do more research. When I went upstairs to take a shower, I happened across a copy of the journal in one of the bedrooms and took it with me to my office. Far as I can tell, the only thing this private knew about was runny bowels and lice. It didn't sound like he ever killed a single Yankee."

"But Wendell told everyone present that he'd run across a reference that would lead to the gold?"

Jim Bob stood up. "Dumb sumbitch was a helluva lot more excited about family plots. So did you find the goddamn notebook or not?"

"No," I said, "but I have a witness who saw him with it before his death."

"Who?"

I could almost see him pounding on Darla Jean's bedroom door while Millicent shrieked and Jeremiah hunted through the coat closet for his shotgun. "I'm in the middle of an investigation, Mr. Mayor. You'll have to direct your questions to Sheriff Dorfer, but not until after the baseball game is over. The Cubs and the Cardinals, I think he said. I don't think it sounds like a fair match, what with bears going against little red birds, but what do I know? He mentioned that he'd be stretching in the seventh inning. That might be a good time to call him."

After he stomped out, I took possession of my chair and realigned my pens and pads on the desktop, wishing I could realign my thoughts as meticulously. It seemed as though I was going to have to make sure none of Mrs. Jim Bob's house guests — or Jim Bob, himself — had been on Cotter's Ridge, perhaps hoping Wendell would lead him or her to the Confederate gold. It was hard to envision, but then again, their very presence in Maggody was due to a staged production, complete with roles, scripts, costumes, posturing — and violence.

It occurred to me, albeit a bit late in the game, that I hadn't demanded a posse and bloodhounds to search for Dahlia's granny. Which wouldn't help. Cotter's Ridge stretched for ten miles. It had been logged for more than seventy-five years, and was crisscrossed with roads, trails, dried creek beds, ravines, crevices, and, of course, caves. Census takers never even considered it. County social workers knew about a few of the remote homesteads, but rarely could find them.

I decided to focus on Wendell's meanderings that morning. Based on Jim Bob's hazy recounting of the conversation around the dinette, it sounded as though Wendell had encountered Hospiss Buchanon on a stroll before breakfast. It might be interesting to ascertain if he'd actually found her home, or even inadvertently left his notebook beside the family Bible.

Having never encountered Hospiss during my formative years, I called the keeper of the Encyclopedia Maggodica and politely asked for suggestions.

"Why on earth do you want to talk to her?" demanded Ruby Bee. "She's got the brains of a June bug. You don't think she has anything to do with this murder, do you?"

"As of now, there is no murder," I said. "I'm writing up a report about this accidental death. There's some indication that Wendell spoke to her early today."

"He must have run into her at the Methodist cemetery. She steals the plastic flowers from the plots and tries to sell them to tourists driving through town. She usually waits till right after Memorial Day, though."

"And you never mentioned this to me?"

"So you could arrest a senile old woman trying to make enough money to buy groceries?"

"I wouldn't have arrested her, for pity's sake," I said, "although I suppose I might have tried to discourage her."

"Nobody minds, and what's more, I know a few folks who set out canned food along with their sprays of flowers from Wal-Mart. Just last fall Estelle and me took her some sweaters and a few blankets we bought at a flea market. It ain't like any of the high-minded members of the Missionary Society would see fit to help her out. They save their energy to pray for heathens before they sit down to coffee and cinnamon rolls."

I waited until she stopped sputtering, then said, "Do you know how to find Hospiss's house?"

"No, but I know how to find her trailer.

It's at the back of the Pot O' Gold, right by the drainage ditch that runs along the fence. Now if you don't mind, I got to go deal with this smart-mouthed Yankee from St. Louis afore I have a brawl in the middle of the dance floor. Some of the ol' boys that come here for happy hour don't cotton to being ragged about the Confederates gettin' their asses whipped. I ain't so fond of it myself."

I drove over to the Pot O' Gold and parked by one of the more squalid trailers. A few plastic roses were set around the cracked concrete patio. The sole aluminum chair was bent and in need of new webbing. Hospiss did not appear when I tapped politely on the door, or even after I gave it a few thumps with my fist. The windows were too high for me to peer into unless I risked my life by balancing on the chair.

"She's in there," said a thin voice behind me.

I turned around and regarded a scruffy girl perhaps six or seven years old. "Are you sure?"

"No, I ain't sure for sure, but she never hardly goes anywhere. Are you a cop?"

"Maggody's finest," I said as I reassessed my chances of teetering on the chair frame in order to look inside. "Then you know her fairly well?"

"I'm not allowed to on account of she's crazy, but sometimes she lets me come inside and eat crackers with her. She sez I'm her best friend, the only one that believes her. She sez that when she has a big, fancy house, I can come live with her. There's gonna be feather beds and gardens with real flowers and even a swimming pool. We're gonna stay up all night watching TV and eating all the chocolate we want. In the mornings, somebody'll serve us eggs and biscuits on china plates."

"And you believe her," I murmured.

The girl shrugged. "Might as well."

"Will you tell me your name?"

"I'm not supposed to talk to strangers." She gave me a puckish smile, then darted away into the chaos of trailers, bass boats, campers, pickups, sickly trees, dingy laundry flapping in the breeze, and men in undershirts drinking beer and hollering at each other.

I knocked once again on the front door, and then, leery in that I was operating on the utterance of a first-grader, took the tire iron from my trunk and went around to the back door of the trailer.

When I received no response, I pried it open. If the town council wouldn't pay for the damage, I figured Ruby Bee could have a bake sale and Estelle could run a special on pedicures. Ten toes for the price of five.

Hospiss was indeed inside, but she would never again pilfer plastic flowers. Her body was sprawled across the worn carpet, her arms splayed, her thin housecoat tangled around her knees, her bare feet shriveled like dried apples. Blood from the wound on the back of her head had left an irregular brown blotch on her faded gray hair.

The putrid odor and presence of flies suggested as much, but I kneeled down beside her and made sure she was dead. I quickly checked the other rooms in the trailer on the obscure chance someone had lingered, and then drove to the PD to call Harve.

"Did I mention it's the Cubs and the Cardinals?" he said as soon as I identified myself. "Mrs. Dorfer did the dishes and went over to visit her sister, leaving me in the most splendid solitude to sit back in my recliner, pop open a cold beer, and appreciate the poetry of the game. I realize some folks think it's on the slow side —"

I cut him off and told him about the body in the Pot O' Gold Mobile Home Park. I did not spare him the details. "And before you even bother to try to justify sitting there on your butt with all that poetry flickering on the screen, it was not an accident. There's no piece of furniture she could have fallen and hit her head against. I didn't see a weapon, but I was more concerned about making this call than doing a thorough search."

"You want me to come racing out there with flashing lights and sirens, along with half a dozen more official vehicles and an ambulance? How about a helicopter? Maybe I can get some black ones so's to send half the Buchanons in the county scurrying into their bunkers to hunker down and prepare for a UN invasion. Most of 'em wouldn't pop up till Groundhog Day next year."

"You, McBeen, and a couple of deputies to search the pasture for the weapon will do just fine," I said sweetly.

"Score's tied and one of those home run sluggers is coming up in the next inning. How long's she been dead?"

"Some number of hours, but not days. Harve, I'm real sorry about this. I suppose I can sit here in the PD until the end of the baseball game, but I might just pass the time by alerting the media to the crime spree right here in little ol' Maggody. I'll do my best with the reporters, cameras, lights, and microphones. I'll just tell them you're delayed."

He harrumphed. "I'll be on my way soon as I make a couple of calls. Give me directions to the trailer and we'll meet you there."

It was beyond credibility to categorize Hospiss's murder as a coincidence, I thought as I drove back to the Pot O' Gold. Wendell had spoken to her earlier, and both he and she were dead within a matter of hours. Harriet Hathaway had been adamant that Wendell's fear of heights would have kept him at a prudent distance from the edge of the bluff. His notebook, containing not only genealogical notes and a map, but also hints as to the location of the Confederate gold, had disappeared. It did not seem likely that he'd left it at Hospiss's abandoned homestead or failed to notice if it had dropped out of his pocket. And surely he wouldn't have mentioned his encounter with her if he'd followed her back to her trailer and dispatched her. The Methodist cemetery had few visitors at an early hour, or even a much later one. Wendell had seemed harmless, to put it politely. His ancestors would not have ridden with Quantrill's Raiders.

I had a few minutes before Harve and his platoon would arrive, so I stopped at Eula Lemoy's trailer on the off chance she'd noticed anything that morning. I knocked on her door, and was rather surprised when she threw it open, grabbed my arm, and yanked me inside.

"Is this about Lottie?" she demanded. "Is she all right? I haven't been able to eat a thing for two days, not so much as a bowl of soup. I know Elsie and I were cowards to drive off like we did, but we were planning to go back and fetch her if the police didn't show up. There wasn't any reason for all three of us to get ourselves arrested, was there?"

"I don't know," I said, backing away. "Was there a reason why all three of you *should* have gotten yourselves arrested?"

"Of course not. What Lottie did most likely wasn't against the law. Elsie and I was nothing but innocent bystanders, like those folks you see standing behind the yellow tape." Eula sat down and wiped her eyes. "So what have they done with Lottie?"

"Who?"

"Didn't your mother teach you to pay attention when folks are talking to you? Where did the police take Lottie after she was arrested?"

"Arrested for what?"

"Breaking and entering, I suppose, although she didn't break anything. Entering's another matter."

I sat down next to her and waited until she stopped twitching and told me the whole story, from the unauthorized entry into the Headquarters House to the confrontation at the county jail. "It doesn't sound as though she was arrested," I said, frowning. "Could she have ended up at the hospital?"

Eula shook her head. "We thought of that, but we called and they said she wasn't there. Would they tell us if she was locked up on the psychiatric ward, maybe on account of amnesia?"

"The hospital staff would have been happy to share information if they had an elderly patient without a Medicare card." I went over to the window to watch for county vehicles gliding by without the benefit of lights and sirens. It was a little late for melodramatics. "This took place Sunday afternoon? Is there any chance she's still inside the house?"

"Elsie and I went there first thing yesterday morning. This tight-lipped woman came to the door and scolded us for not reading the sign that said the only time to tour was on Saturdays until after Memorial Day. I suppose it's possible that Lottie hid under a bed after the alarm went off, but she wouldn't still be there. I've been sleeping on the couch so's to be by the telephone in case she calls. She might be unhappy with us on account of how we drove off like we did, but she hasn't turned up in more than two days. Elsie's seeing to her cats and I've been stopping by to water her plants."

"Very thoughtful of you," I said. "As soon as I have a chance, I'll call the police department in Farberville and ask them to search the house from attic to cellar, as well as yards in the vicinity in case Lottie took refuge under a bush and lost consciousness."

Eula gasped. "You mean she could be lying in muddy leaves, all wet and cold?"

"Does she have any family or friends in Farberville who might be looking after her?"

"No, her only sister lives over in Blytheville and I seem to think both of her nieces live in Dallas. Do you think she's — no, I can't bring myself to say it. Arly, you got to do something! I won't be able to live with myself, knowing I was responsible. Well, and Elsie, of course. She's the one who dragged me back to the getaway car, and then did the driving."

I went over and squeezed her hand. "I'm sure she's fine, Eula. I'll make some calls, but you and Elsie don't need to worry. Have some tea and keep watering her house plants until she shows up."

"She ain't gonna be happy with us when she does," Eula said glumly.

"Most likely not." I took a breath, then said, "There's been some violence in the mobile home park. Hospiss Buchanon was killed in her trailer this morning. Did you notice anyone unfamiliar walking or driving by?"

Eula blinked at me. "Why would anyone hurt Hospiss? She never bothered anybody. I'm not saying she wasn't above stealing other folks' laundry off the lines, including my favorite brassiere, or going through their trash bags looking for aluminum cans, but mostly she just stayed in her trailer. She wasn't more than a pitiful sparrow. Every now and then I'd have her over for supper, and she was always real grateful. Why would somebody do such a thing? What is the world comin' to?"

"I wish I knew." I gave her hand a final squeeze, then left and drove to Hospiss's trailer. It was past sunset, and the packs of feral children that roamed the Pot O' Gold had been hauled inside, some to be bathed and fed, others to be smacked and sent to bed.

Harve and his posse arrived shortly. McBeen, who was more than chunky, prickly as a pine cone, and lacked the social skills of a troll under a bridge, examined the body. After he'd pronounced her dead at the scene, he stood back while a few photographs were taken and a nervous young deputy collected fingerprints from the doorknob. No one seemed eager to linger, even after a window had been forced open.

"Time of death?" Harve asked him.

"How the hell would I know? I wasn't here, and I presume you weren't, either. Eight to ten hours, give or take. Blunt object to the back of her head. She was so old and frail that her skull just caved in like a ripe melon." He gave me a speculative look. "You're finding all manner of corpses today, aren't you, missy? Are you finished for the day, or should I hang around town and save myself another trip out here?"

"Suit yourself," I said levelly.

Harve took me outside before McBeen and I exchanged more words, some of which were apt to be less than professional. More deputies were poking sticks in the muddy water in the drainage ditch or tromping in the weedy pasture with flashlights. A few gawkers had gathered, but I didn't see the child with whom I'd spoken earlier.

"So what's the connection with her and

that fellow on Cotter's Ridge?" asked Harve.

"He talked to her today, sometime before breakfast. According to what I've been told, she claimed that one of her ancestors had been involved in the skirmish and was buried on her old homestead. She also claimed that she had evidence in the family Bible that she was a direct descendant."

"So what?"

"Wendell was excited about it. He was into that sort of thing." I repeated what Jim Bob had told me, then added, "So he must have gone looking for a stone marker to confirm her story. Someone followed him, or happened to encounter him. Darla Jean said he —"

"Darla Jean?"

"She was up there, looking for Petrol."

"Looking for Petrol?"

"Yeah, Harve, she thought Petrol would lead her to Diesel, who would then take them to the gold. Petrol — or even Diesel — could be this ghost everybody's been spotting. Then again, Dahlia's granny could be wearing a dress with shiny buttons."

"Dahlia's granny is up there?"

I nodded. "As well as Private Jeb Stewart."

"I though he was a general."

I felt as if I were slogging through molasses. "Look, why don't we go to the PD and I'll fill you in. Once the trailer's aired out, have the deputies search for the family Bible. Hospiss wouldn't have left it behind when she moved down here. There's no way we can find her homestead in the dark, but I'll see if Hammet can help me tomorrow."

"Hammet? I thought he was staying with a foster family over in —"

"He is, but at the moment he's here. Now unless you want us to be standing here when McBeen comes out and he and I end up mud wrasslin' in the ditch, you'd better come on to the PD. I'll make coffee, and you can make notes. I'll even loan you my only pencil."

"Am I wrong in thinking I'm the one what's supposed to be giving the orders?"

"No problem," I said. "There's nothing I'd rather do more than go to my apartment, take a long bath, put on my robe, and curl up to watch TV. What channel is this baseball game on? I love poetry in skin-tight pants."

Harve seemed to sense that he, like Wendell Streek, was getting too close to the edge of a particular bluff. "You go on to the PD and start the coffee. I'll tell the deputies to search for the Bible, then knock on some doors and ask if anyone saw something this morning. Give me ten or fifteen minutes."

I figured I'd won the Skirmish at the Pot O' Gold, but not necessarily the Battle of the Stump County Sheriff's Department.

Mrs. Jim Bob eyed her dinner guests, all of whom had seemed to enjoy her chicken casserole with mushrooms, slivered almonds, and imported black olives, as well as her molded cabbage salad and homemade cloverleaf rolls. Under no circumstances could she be blamed for the Yankees' wine bottle in the middle of the table. She'd been putting the empty bottles in a cardboard box in the garage so that they could be left discreetly in a Dumpster in Farberville in the future. "Is anyone ready for pecan pie and ice cream?" she asked, hoping they'd all decline and just go to bed, even though it wasn't yet eight o'clock.

Jim Bob tried to muffle a belch, but with little success. "That was a mighty fine supper, if I do say. Maggody's famous for its warm hospitality and home cookin'."

"Oh, a fine meal indeed," said Kenneth, who was hoping Mrs. Jim Bob had not gone tripping through the woods picking the mushrooms herself. He figured he'd find out within an hour or so. "So, Corinne, are the schools expecting us tomorrow?"

Corinne shook her head. "The teacher in charge of all this has gone missing, and no one else in either the elementary or high school seems to have a clue. I really don't know what we're supposed to do."

"I'll see to it," Mrs. Jim Bob said numbly.

"Maybe I ought to fix a plate for Harriet," said Sweetpea. "The poor thing looked so pale this afternoon that I was worried she might collapse. Maybe soup might be better. What do you think, Corinne?"

"Let's allow her to rest for the time being. Such a terrible shock for her, I should think. I do believe that she was emotionally involved with Wendell, and had expectations of a permanent arrangement. The announcement of his engagement to another woman was as devastating as his demise."

"God, Mother," Simon said as he tossed down his napkin, "this is not one of your novels. Do you suspect this spurned spinster followed him up that mountainside and pushed him off the bluff? Doesn't that seem a bit far-fetched?"

"I said no such thing."

Simon smirked. "Well, it sounds like somebody did, but more likely to get his hands on the notebook and find the treasure. What about you, Jim Bob? Where were you this morning?"

"At Jim Bob's SuperSaver Buy 4 Less, with half a dozen employees to vouch for me. What about you?"

Sweetpea pushed back her chair and stood up. "This is not some silly parlor game! That nice man died this morning. I am not going to sit here and listen to any more of this."

"Sit down," Simon said curtly. "It's a very entertaining little game. What about you, Kenneth? You said you were going to familiarize yourself with the terrain or some such shit. Did you take a little hike?"

"I did. I went out to the area by the bridge, where the Confederates will be camping in two days. Strangely enough, I encountered a Union private who claimed he was sharing the site with a rebel. That would never have happened. I told him as much and ordered him to move his tent elsewhere, but he refused. There was something about him that made me uneasy."

"Did he have a copy of the journal?" asked Corinne.

"He said all of the participants were sent one." Kenneth refilled his glass and leaned back. "I don't seem to recall that Simon explained where he was today."

Simon reached across the table for the

wine bottle. "I was supposed to do the audio in a studio in Springfield, but I couldn't find the place. Eventually I had lunch in some fast food joint and came back here to take a nap. I have to be rested for this reenactment thing, you know."

"You ever ridden a mule?" asked Jim Bob, snickering. "Unlike your fancy thoroughbreds, they're as bony as anything you'd find in a pit behind a slaughterhouse. You're gonna end up with bruises on your butt till the fireworks fade on the Fourth of July — and that's if you're lucky. You might be walking bowlegged till Christmas."

Mrs. Jim Bob was on the brink of losing what little composure she'd clung to for the last twenty-four hours. She'd imagined a dinner party in which music and literature would be the topics, or at least documentaries on PBS. "I do believe it might be nice for us to go out to the patio for dessert and coffee. I'll be out there as soon as I've cleared the table."

"Let me help you," said Sweetpea. "You've been so lovely about our unexpected arrival. Dinner was divine. Is there any chance I can wheedle that recipe out of you? I was thinking it would be perfect for my bridesmaids' luncheon."

Corinne began stacking plates. "You boys

just go on outside and smoke your smelly ol' cigars. We'll join you after a while."

Kenneth picked up the wine bottle and his glass. "Come along, boys."

Harve ended up with several pages of notes, but he was still scratching his head and mumbling to himself. "Lotta crazy folks doing a lotta crazy things, all for the sake of this fairy tale about lost Confederate gold. You don't reckon it's still up there, do you?"

"What skimpy evidence there is suggests that it might be," I said wearily. "It's the least of my problems at the moment. Did you have someone go by Wendell's house and tell his mother what happened?"

"Yeah, I sent LaBelle, thinking she might be more tactful than any of my boys. They'd most likely just spit it out and leave without waiting to see if the old lady collapsed. LaBelle said it was painful, but there was someone else there, a family friend, who started fluttering around like a nurse."

"I've got Wendell's address book. You can send some photos to the brother and let him make the official ID." I looked at the scribbles I'd made on a legal pad. "Next item on the agenda is to locate Lottie Estes. While I was waiting for you, I called the Farberville PD, but I don't think they're impressed with the urgency. Can you send a deputy over to search the Headquarters House tonight?"

"Tonight?"

"And I don't mean after the baseball game. She could have made it to the basement or even crawled into a closet and lost consciousness. It's been more than seventy-two hours. Dehydration could be a factor."

"It's liable to be locked up tighter'n a tick at this hour. You saying I ought to order a deputy to break into the only Civil War site in Farberville? That ain't gonna sit well with the locals who take their heritage seriously."

I raised my eyebrows. "Who might just vent their displeasure at the polls next November?" When he responded with a wheezy nod, I said, "There have to be several keys floating around. I'm sure Harriet has one, but I don't want to disturb her tonight. Wendell surely had one, too. He didn't have a key ring when we found him, and I didn't see one when I searched the bedroom for his address book. He probably left it at home. Have a deputy go by Mrs. Streek's house and ask this family friend to look around."

"I s'pose that might work." Harve made the call while I refilled our mugs, and when I returned, said, "We're on it. She lives just a couple of doors down from the Headquarters House, so we should hear something afore too long. Satisfied?"

"You got my vote."

"And you owe me," he said as he lit a cigar and tossed the match into the wastebasket. "Now from what I can sort out from all these hen scratches I made, Wendell met Hospiss early in the day. She told him about the Confederate officer buried up at her old place and went so far as to draw him a map. As you know darn well from your experiences with Raz, Buchanons can be a tight-lipped lot, not likely to tell secrets to a stranger. So why'd she blab all this?"

I tried not to be distracted by the thin ribbon of smoke rising from the wastebasket. "It may have been nothing more than an impassioned desire on her part to qualify for membership in the Daughters of the American Confederacy, or the chance to be a footnote in Wendell's historical blockbuster. Maybe she believed she'd be given a role in the documentary. Her story is that her great-great-grandmother appeared after the rebels fled, slung the lieutenant's body over a mule, and took him back home with her. But Harriet wouldn't have strayed from the account in that damn journal unless Wendell found proof." I made a square with my thumbs and forefingers and peered through it like a pretentious Hollywood director. "Yes, I can see it. The last echoes of musket fire have faded to an eerie silence. A haze of acrid smoke still lingers from —" I jumped up and poured my coffee into the wastebasket. "Goddamn it, Harve! Feel free to burn down your own office, but not mine. The town council would decide to set up my office in Raz Buchanon's barn."

He grinned. "And then you could hire that pedigreed sow of his to be your second in command."

I made sure the fire was out before I sat down. "Or I could organize a write-in effort to get her on the ballot for county sheriff. Nobody would notice the difference."

His grin disappeared. "What you need to do in the morning is get statements from all those folks staying at Mrs. Jim Bob's house about what all they did after breakfast today. Have a talk with that Stewart fellow, see if he ran into Wendell and heard something of interest. Then find Hospiss's old place and see if you can find anything that hints of Wendell having been there. After that —"

"Wait just a minute. This is your case."

"All I want you to do is talk to them. I can't see any of my boys sweet-talking those ladies from Charleston or getting anything out of Harriet Hathaway without reducing her to hysteria. Tact ain't their strong point. You, on the other hand, are all refined, having lived in New York City. Mrs. Dorfer keeps harping about us taking a trip there for our anniversary, but I'd just as soon spend two weeks at the state prison farm, chopping cotton and picking up litter alongside a state highway."

"You're a weasel," I said.

"But you got to admit I'm a genial weasel."

The telephone rang before I could offer a rebuttal. It proved to be the deputy who'd searched the Headquarters House and adjoining yards, and found no trace of Lottie Estes or anyone else. Harve told him to go back on patrol, then stood up and said, "You just talk to those folks tomorrow and call me if you learn anything of interest. I'll check with the hospital and the homeless shelters in case this fugitive might be hiding there. You might think about changing your coffee filter every few months or so."

After he left, I made sure the coffeepot was turned off and was about to turn off the lights when the phone rang again. As much as I wanted to ignore it and go hide in my bathtub, I answered it.

"What's this about Hospiss?" demanded Ruby Bee.

"Talk to Eula."

"I already did, but she knows next to nothing beyond the pitiful little thing was killed."

"I'll see you in the morning," I said, then hung up and left before she could call me back.

Enough, already.

12

The next morning I inspected my many bruises in the bathroom mirror, then gingerly dressed and went over to the PD to find out if Robert E. or Ulysses S. had left any messages of significance. Neither had bothered, but the day was in its infancy (or infantry, perhaps). Mrs. Jim Bob had left a hysterical message demanding to know the whereabouts of Lottie and Brother Verber. All I knew about Lottie was where she'd last been seen, and to some extent, where she wasn't. As for Brother Verber, I'd noticed while crossing the road that his car had not reappeared. As far as I knew, he could be anywhere in the tri-state area, indulging in things I didn't even want to imagine.

I went to Ruby Bee's and sat down in a booth with Jack. "Enjoy the movie?"

"Was the child raised by wolves?" he said.

"Pretty much." I told him about Hammet's upbringing on the ridge, then paused as a sleek, silvery man came to the table. He looked as though he could afford the high-maintenance costs of disguising his age.

"Andrew Pulaski," he said to me. "I'm one of the reenactors. Do you mind if I join you for breakfast?"

I told him who I was as he pulled up a chair. "Are you the Yankee who was stirring up trouble here last night?" I asked. "You're lucky you didn't find a bunch of rednecks with baseball bats waiting outside for you."

"Just having a bit of fun with them." He picked up a menu. "I suppose I'd better have oatmeal and dry toast. My cholesterol level has been climbing steadily since I arrived. How do you keep yourself so trim, my dear? Diet pills, aerobics, bulemia?"

"Mostly hiking on Cotter's Ridge. You been up there in the last day or so?"

Ruby Bee came over to the table with three coffee mugs and a full pot. "You might think twice before you come to happy hour again," she said to Andrew in an icy voice. "You pull that kind of crap again, I'll just duck behind the bar and let them beat you until you're seeping like a rotten tomato. Why don't you go to Mrs. Jim Bob's house and spend the evening with your friends?"

I glanced at Jack, who was observing the

scene with muted amusement, then looked at Andrew. "You're acquainted with some of Mrs. Jim Bob's houseguests?"

"The trio from Charleston. I met them when I was on the set of the miniseries. Corinne dashed about, trying to get the director's attention, while Simon complained about the heat, the mosquitoes, and his uniform, which he felt failed to accentuate his abs and pecs. Sweetpea, in contrast, spent her time sitting on a quilt in the shade, sketching the action. She's really quite talented."

Ruby Bee rumbled. "Are y'all gonna order? I got other customers, you know."

"Oatmeal, with skim milk," said Andrew.

Jack grinned at me. "I'll have whatever you're having."

I could feel Ruby Bee's stare as my face turned warm. "We'll have the works."

"Is that what you call it these days?" she said, then stomped away.

"So," I said to Andrew, "did you decide to do this reenactment so you could see your dear friends Corinne, Simon, and Sweetpea?" I gave the third name a nuance of emphasis, just to see if he squirmed.

He did not oblige. "In fact, I did. Sweetpea was kind enough to drop me a note about this particular reenactment. I'm hoping to take the three of them to lunch today or tomorrow in a somewhat more upscale dining environment. Can you recommend a place?"

"You came all the way from St. Louis for an upscale dining environment?"

"Oh, I do several of these reenactments a year, as long as I'm not expected to run around a pasture in blistering heat. In the upcoming skirmish, I shall stay on a horse and ride up and down the lines, shouting encouragement. Because of my unflagging leadership, my men will prevail."

"I didn't notice a horse trailer out back," Jack said.

Andrew took a sip of coffee. "A comrade from the Missouri unit provides one for me. Not a thoroughbred, but a good, sturdy animal. I own a highly successful car agency, which is both physically and emotionally draining. Sometimes I like to escape and indulge in childish fantasies. Even though I'm obliged to camp out, I do not deprive myself of basic comforts."

"A farb, huh?" I said drily.

"Of the worst kind."

Ruby Bee returned with our food. While we ate, Andrew tried to sell Jack a Mercedes and me a 1992 pickup with low mileage and new shocks. As soon as I'd had enough food to sustain me, I told Jack I'd see him later and left before Ruby Bee could haul me into the kitchen to demand details about Hospiss.

Although I knew I was going to have to question the houseguests, I decided to cover a few other bases first. I did a posthaste tour of Lottie's house and determined she had not come home. I then tossed a mental coin and drove out to the bridge to talk to Private Jeb Stewart.

He and Private Waylon Pepperstone were sitting by the campfire, drinking coffee out of battered tin cups. I hoped they'd enjoyed their hardtack as much as I had my heady dose of cholesterol. Both leaped to their feet as I approached.

"Sit down," I said. "There were two deaths yesterday, one in town and the other on Cotter's Ridge. I want to know exactly where each of you were in the morning."

"I was right here," Waylon said, gulping. "Well, after you left, I went into the woods, thinking I might be able to catch a rabbit for supper."

Jeb hooted derisively. "With your bare hands? Or were you planning to set a snare with a piece of fishing line? God, boy, you wouldn't last three weeks in a real war unless your mama sent you packages with granola bars and clean pajamas."

"Tell me more precisely where you went," I said to Waylon, ignoring the rude noises from the far side of the campfire. "Up on the ridge?"

He shook his head. "No, I mostly stayed on dirt roads. If you're looking for some sort of alibi, I stopped at a house and asked to use the phone. This old man, about as strange as I've ever encountered, charged me ten dollars to make a one-minute call. You're not going to believe it, but there was a pig flopped on the sofa, watching an Audrey Hepburn movie. As soon as my minute was up, he shoved me out the door so hard I went sprawling on the porch. After that, I came back here and tried my luck at fishing."

"What about you?" I asked Jeb. "Did you wander off to make a phone call, too?"

He spat in the fire. "Hell no. I went up on the ridge to see if I could find this purported treasure. I ate some hickory nuts and poke salat while I rested, looked around some more, and then came back here." He gestured with his thumb at Waylon. "I didn't see him."

"I went downstream to fish. You got a problem with that, Johnny Reb?"

"Showing some spunk now, aren't you?

I'm trembling in my boots."

Waylon stood up. "All you're doing in your boots is bleeding 'cause you think you've got to gross everybody out with your bullshit version of authenticity."

I intervened before this skirmish escalated. "Sit down, Waylon. Jeb, tell me who you saw while you were on Cotter's Ridge."

"A town girl by a shack. I thought for a minute she might be following me, but she didn't look as though she had the wits to follow a rock. After a time, I came across an old guy sitting on a log. He asked me if I could make sense of a map that looked as if it'd been drawn by a toddler."

"Did he have a notebook?" I asked.

Jeb rolled his eyes. "Yes, ma'am, he most certainly did. He asked me about my kinfolk who fought in the war. I tolerated his questions for a while, then decided I was wasting my time and left him scribbling in his notebook. My family's from Mississippi, and none of them was involved in engagements in Arkansas. My great-great-grandfather was killed defending Atlanta from Sherman's scum. His two brothers died of dysentery and malnourishment in a prison in Pennsylvania. Their bodies were thrown in a mass grave. No medals or citations for the three Stewart boys, or even remains sent home to their mama."

I couldn't help wincing, but it was not the time to mention the reciprocal Southern hospitality offered at such notorious prisons as Andersonville. "So after you left this man with the map, did you see anyone else?"

"I might have, but I can't swear to it. I caught a glimpse of a sickly guy in a Confederate uniform, but he was damn quick on his feet and disappeared in less than a second or two. Could have been my imagination."

"Starvation can do that," inserted Waylon. "That and diarrhea. Has anybody told you that you stink like a barnyard?"

Again, I intervened. "Waylon, it's time for you to break camp. Pack up your things and I'll tell you how to get to the low-water bridge at the other end of town. I want you to stay there tonight. The rest of the reenactors are arriving tomorrow. You can join your unit when they get here, but I don't want to see your face until then. Is that clear?" I turned to Jeb. "And I want you to stay right here. I may have some more questions later. If I come back and find you missing, I'll get some hounds from the sheriff's department and turn them loose on you. Got it?"

They both grudgingly agreed, although I

suspected Jeb was whistlin' Dixie, in a manner of speaking. I left them growling at each other and drove to Raz Buchanon's shack to have what I knew would be an unsatisfactory confrontation with the surly sumbitch. I had no doubt he'd disclaim allowing a Yankee soldier to use his phone, or even set foot on his property. He'd gone so far as to threaten me with his shotgun more than once.

Detectives on *Law and Order* do not have this problem.

To my relief, the only thing he was holding when he came out on the porch was a red-and-white-striped dishtowel. He was dressed in filthy overalls and boots that might have flattened a few rabbits come suppertime.

"Whadya want?" he hollered before I could get out of the car. "I got no time for you. Come back long about next year, or mebbe the year after that."

I went to the gate. "I need to talk to you, Raz. Don't make me haul you over to the county jail. Marjorie might pine away, and you'd come back to find nothing on your couch but a snout and a curly tail."

"You jest leave Marjorie out of this, Arly Hanks, and do your talkin' from right where you're a-standin'."

"Does this mean you're not going to invite me in for coffee? I heard a rumor that you grind your own beans. I was hoping for a steaming cup of mocha almond, with just a hint of French vanilla."

Raz ran his fingers through his beard, dislodging dried clumps of tobacco juice, crumbs, and possibly tiny tenants. "State yer business and be done with it. I ain't got time to listen to the likes of you."

I smiled brightly. "You like me? You really like me? Wow, Raz, after all the problems we've had —"

"Spit it out!" he snapped, doing some spitting of his own.

"Did you see anybody on the ridge yesterday morning?"

He considered his response. "Yeah, I reckon I might have. Bunch of damn fools, including your mama and that red-headed woman friend of hers. They's the ones ought to be at the county jail."

"Did they get too close to your still?"

"I've told you time and again I ain't got no still. If I did, they weren't nowheres near it. Otherwise, they wouldn't have never showed up in town again."

He made a move toward the door, but I held up my hand and said, "We're not finished, Raz. If this nonexistent still is elsewhere on the ridge, what were you doing?"

"Marjorie's been feelin' right queasy these last few days. She has a delicate nature, bein' pedigreed like she is, so I went to pick 'seng to make her tea. I know of some good patches."

"Were you anywhere near Hospiss's old place?"

"Mebbe."

I was actually getting more out of him than I'd expected. "Did you see anyone else?"

"I weren't lookin' for anyone else. I jest told you what I was doin'."

I thought for a moment. "Did you and Diesel have a nice visit?"

Raz squinted at me, and if he'd been holding anything more lethal than a dishtowel, I would have moved behind my car. "I disremember sayin' anything about Diesel. Why would I want to have a visit with that crazy ol' coot? I'd sooner crawl into a cave with a polecat. Why don't you take your skinny little ass up there and ask him for a cup of fancy coffee?"

"Did you come across Petrol?"

"What kind of fool question is that? He's locked up in that place by the low-water bridge, knittin' doilies or whatever it is they do." He spat in my direction. "Now git off my property afore I git riled. Iff'n I knew where this gold was, I shore as hell wouldn't tell you or anyone else. It rightly belongs to Buchanons."

I stepped back onto the road. "How do you know about that?"

"A fat ol' coon told afore I blowed his head off." He went inside, slamming the screen door behind him.

I decided it was prudent to be on my way before he had a chance to make known his intentions, and bringing me a cup of coffee and a biscotti wasn't likely to be among them. He'd acknowledged seeing people on the ridge, but getting their names or descriptions out of him would be like pulling teeth — which in his case wouldn't take long.

Gritting my teeth (all intact and clean, if not flossed), I drove to the Buchanon manor and parked. As I got out of the car, I heard voices from the backyard and headed that way. Corinne, Harriet, and Kenneth were seated at the wrought-iron table, drinking coffee. Sweetpea and Simon were at the end of the yard, standing several feet away and, from appearances, absorbed in a conversation that clearly pleased neither of them.

I sat down at the table. "I'm glad to see

you're feeling better," I said to Harriet.

"Very much so," Corinne said. "This morning when I took her up a tray with tea and toast, I couldn't help noticing how much her color has improved." She patted Harriet's hand. "That's the first thing I said to you, wasn't it? Last night I was concerned that I might have to fetch my smelling salts."

Kenneth snickered. "Smelling salts? Corinne, you're hopelessly mired in the nineteenth century. Sweetpea might get away with this girlish posturing, but in a woman of your age, it's rather pathetic."

"And you don't put on your cape and plumed hat so you can strut around like the cock of the roost? In your case, however, your admiring audience is made up of schoolchildren who're hoping you're going to stab yourself in the foot with your sword."

"Please," Harriet said, "stop this. Arly, have you found out anything more about Wendell's accident? Has his mother been informed? I was barely able to sleep last night, worrying about her."

"Mrs. Streek has been told. A friend was with her when a representative of the sheriff's department arrived at her house."

Harriet's hand shook as she put down her

coffee cup. "Wendell's fiancée?"

"I don't know," I said. "Certain things happened yesterday afternoon that have led Sheriff Dorfer to question whether or not Wendell's fall was accidental. I'm here to get statements from everyone regarding his or her movements yesterday."

"We're suspects?" Corinne said with a squeak. "Why, I hardly knew the man, and I bore him no ill will."

"Corinne's use of the word 'bore' is appropriate," inserted Kenneth, "but that's hardly a motive for murder."

Harriet looked at me. "Shall I volunteer to go first? Will the living room do, or are you going to take me to the police station to interrogate me?"

"The living room's fine," I said hastily. "I would appreciate it if the rest of you remain available for a while."

Kenneth stood up and pulled back Harriet's chair. "And I had such hopes of visiting the art museum next to the barber shop. I was told there's a very fine collection of Renoir's lesser-known preliminary sketches."

As Harriet and I went through the kitchen, Mrs. Jim Bob cut me off. "What is this I heard about Hospiss? Eula said you were at the Pot O' Gold yesterday afternoon and told her —"

"Yes, I was there," I said. "Did Eula tell you about Lottie?"

Mrs. Jim Bob's beady eyes widened as far as they could. "Why would Eula know about poor Lottie?"

I eased around her. "I suggest you call her and find out. I'm going to need to use the living room for the rest of the morning. Please let Perkin's eldest know she won't be able to vacuum and dust in there until I'm finished."

Mrs. Jim Bob was too stunned by the suggestion of Eula's complicity to do more than nod.

Harriet sat down on the sofa. "I really hadn't noticed until now that there are no draperies in this room. Is there a reason?"

"Every time Mrs. Jim Bob finds out about one of Jim Bob's . . . dalliances, she redecorates. There's probably an upholstery store in Farberville with a wing dedicated to her." I sat down across from her. "I understand you were upset with Wendell at breakfast yesterday. Something about his fiancée?"

"Well, yes," she said, sighing. "I had no intention of allowing myself to speak of such personal matters, but I simply couldn't keep it bottled up any longer. I'd counted on Wendell to advise me on every decision concerning the documentary. He and I have relied on each other for more than twenty years, and I was under the impression we had an understanding that we would be married after his mother passed away. He was adamant that the shock of even hearing of his marriage would send her into a downward spiral that could only result in her death. I resigned myself, year after year. Then, on Saturday, while we were at the Headquarters House to offer guided tours to visitors, he told me of his plans to marry Lydia Berle within a month. He was going to share this joyous news with the society at our next meeting." She discreetly blotted her nose with the back of her hand. "I'm sure a child like you can't understand the humiliation that I felt. I did not demand an explanation or attempt to plead with him, but instead left the room immediately. Lydia was sitting by the front door, collecting the entrance fees, as I went out the door."

"But he rode out here with you on Monday," I pointed out.

She looked away. "I thought we might discuss his impetuous decision, but all he did was gabble about his most recent genealogical discoveries. I don't think I said more than two words the entire trip."

"You said more than two words yesterday."

"Yes, I suppose I did," she said brokenly. "I suppose I did."

I went into the kitchen, found a box of tissues, and took it back to her. After she wiped her eyes and blew her nose several times, I said, "I won't keep you much longer. What did you do after breakfast?"

"I decided to take a walk. I went by the bridge, where I saw that two reenactors had already arrived and set up tents. I was hardly in the mood to deal with them. I chose instead to follow a primitive road of sorts up the hillside to find a secluded place to sit and examine my unseemly outburst in front of strangers."

"Did you notice an abandoned shack?"

She brightened. "I did. I studied it for quite a long time, wondering if there might be a way for the historical society to transport it to the grounds behind the Headquarters House and include it in the tour as an example of nineteenth-century living conditions in rural populations. I concluded that so much as pulling away one board would cause it to collapse into a heap of tinder. I continued on my way, and eventually found a flat rock overlooking the valley beyond the ridge. The view did much to revive my spirits and ease my pain. Eventually I returned here. Finding no one present except for the cleaning woman, I fixed myself a sandwich, fetched my reading glasses and a copy of Henry's journal, and went down by the creek. I do think Wendell was wrong when he claimed to have found a clue as to the location of the Confederate gold. I most assuredly found nothing."

"Would Wendell have written something in his notebook?" I asked.

"He wrote down everything in his notebook. If he'd carried around a thermometer, he would have kept a record of his body temperature on an hourly basis. He was the perfect treasurer for the society. Whenever the accounts were off by so much as a penny, he'd pester all of us relentlessly for receipts, invoices, ticket stubs, anything. Wendell could be" — she looked at me with a bland expression — "a real pain in the ass."

"Well, uh, thank you, Harriet," I said, flustered. "I appreciate your candor. You're welcome to go back out to the patio or upstairs to rest. If you happen to think of anything that might help us, please let me know."

After she left, I gave myself a moment, then went outside to stalk my next victim.

Corinne and Kenneth were still at the table, although their coffee cups had been replaced with glasses of orange juice. I wondered if vodka had been added.

"Ladies first," Kenneth said before I could speak. "Don't intimidate Arly, my dear. She may think you're a best-selling author with a grand mansion in Charleston, but a little Carolina wren perched on my shoulder and told me you're up to your alabaster neck in debt. Perhaps your future in-laws will let you live in the old slaves' quarters. A bit primitive, I should think, and without running water. The best you can hope for is an outhouse."

Corinne's hand tightened around her glass, but she put it down and swept into the house. She was already seated on the sofa with a tissue in her hand when I joined her.

"He is the epitome of the abhorrent, overbearing, conceited Yankee," she said, her lilting accent missing for the moment. "I'm sorry no one saw fit to shove him off a bluff yesterday. His ancestors in the army must have been among those who raped widows, burned their homes and crops, stole their heirlooms, and rode off with whatever food they'd hoarded for the winter. His revered General Wallingford Ames was a drunken pig, and so is Kenneth Grimley!"

I did not offer an argument. "I just have a few questions, Corinne. After breakfast, what did you do?"

"Simon dropped me off at the high school on his way to Springfield. I spoke to the secretary and the principal, but it seems the only person who knew anything of the schedule was not present. I was appalled that they could be so disorganized. I normally charge a substantial honorarium, although in this case I waived it."

"Why did you do that?"

"As a favor to Sweetpea. She heard about this documentary from her cousin — what was his name? Darcy? Darby? Oh, I don't know, but something like that. I'm just so angry with Kenneth that I can't think straight. I can plot a seven-hundred-page novel, but as soon as my emotions get the better of me, why, I can hardly remember my own name, much less my pseudonyms."

"The cousin's name doesn't matter. Sweetpea heard about the documentary and . . . ?"

"She thought it'd be a splendid opportunity for Simon to inveigle his way into Hollywood stardom. I did my best to point out that this little documentary was hardly an epic, but she put her foot down and insisted that I offer my services for free if Simon was given the leading role. She's a smart girl, but she can be as stubborn as any of those mules arriving tomorrow. Simon's going to have his hands full with her."

I suspected that once Simon had married the money, he'd waste no time finding a more compliant female whose dainty feet didn't reach the ground. "Maybe *The Skirmish at Cotter's Ridge* will be a big hit at the Sundance Film Festival. Where did you go after you left the high school?"

Corinne rubbed her temples. "It seems so long ago, but it was only yesterday, wasn't it? I went across the street to a funny little take-out place and purchased a soft drink, then went for a walk to admire the wildflowers. Spring is such an inspirational season. As I walked, I considered setting my next novel in this very locale. I've done more than thirty centered on the War and the Reconstruction era. Although it might not be historically accurate, it's not inconceivable that —"

"Did you see anyone in the woods?"

"A little boy heading downhill, and a bit later, a ferocious man in a Confederate uniform. He had the aura of a rapist or a serial killer. I ducked behind some rocks and waited until I could no longer hear his footsteps, then hurried on my way."

I thought for a moment about where she might have been in relation to the bluff where Wendell's body had been found. A mile, I estimated, or a shade less. "You didn't see anybody else, like Wendell, for example?"

Corinne sat back. "And tracked him down to demand he take me to the treasure? Is that what you're implying? I can't tell you about the others, but I didn't believe for a moment that he'd found a credible clue as to the location of the cave. After Simon received a copy of the journal, I read it carefully, thinking I might be able to weave an epistolary element into my next novel. Excerpts from the journal, letters, articles from newspapers, that sort of thing. And of course the novel would generate significant publicity if its author had actually found the lost gold. Ultimately, I decided not to do it, but as I said, I read the journal carefully."

"Then you didn't see anybody?"

"Repetition is a symptom of murky thought processes, Arly. So many mystery novels these days rely on the detective cornering each suspect and asking the same dreary questions over and over again. I should think a short questionnaire with boxes to mark true or false could save the reader an interminable stupor. Instead, we're subjected to an endless array of obtrusive badgering, replete with the necessity of introducing red herrings and obscure motives. I wish I could contribute, but I saw no one else. Eventually, I returned to this house, ate a few bites of potato salad and marinated green beans, and then retired to my bedroom to take another look at Henry Largesse's journal."

I had encountered a few authors during my stint in Manhattan, and without exception found them to be tedious and pretentious. I, for one, had never been afraid of Virginia Woolf. "Was anyone here when you got back?"

"The gal vacuuming the hall. She was wearing headphones and singing in an abysmally atonal voice. I'm not sure that she noticed me. I remained in my room until I heard people stirring downstairs. I freshened up, then joined everyone for wine on the patio. Mrs. Jim Bob seemed displeased, but said nothing."

"I'm not surprised," I said. "Thank you for your cooperation."

Corinne clutched my hand. "And thank you so very much for implying I'm a suspect in a case of murder. I can hardly wait to get back to Charleston and relate all this to my friends. Corinne Dawk, cold-blooded killer, stalking her victim like some latter-day Natty Bumpo in a petticoat. I only wish my theoretical victim had been someone more noteworthy, like Kenneth Grimley — and that he'd been wearing black lace panties underneath his crisp blue trousers." Before I could say much of anything (as if I knew what it would be), she said, "Oh, good, here are Simon and Sweetpea. Do give them the third degree as quickly as you can. Andrew Pulaski has invited us to lunch at a restaurant in Farberville. I simply cannot face another ham sandwich and cole slaw. I'm quite sure cole slaw was introduced by British loyalists to punish the colonists for the unpleasantness that began in 1776. I shall be waiting for you children on the patio. Do cooperate, won't you?"

Simon and Sweetpea sat down on the sofa. They were holding hands, but I felt as if it were more for my benefit than theirs. Neither exuded a desire to cooperate.

"Thank you," I began. "We'll get this over in a few minutes so you can go to lunch."

"With Andrew," Simon muttered.

Sweetpea withdrew her hand. "I already told you that we can stay here and eat leftovers, or go to that peculiar place for greasy hamburgers and even greasier fries. It doesn't matter to me one teensy bit. I just thought it might be fun. Starting tomorrow, you're going to be a lowly private in a really tacky uniform. I can hardly wait to see you sittin' astride a mule named Clementine or Gus. I brought my camera and half a dozen rolls of film."

I cleared my throat. "All I need to know is what each of you did after breakfast yesterday. Simon, I understand you went to Springfield to do the audio narration for the documentary. What time did you leave?"

"As soon as my mother hitched up her pantyhose and powdered her nose. I dropped her off at the high school and drove to Springfield, but I couldn't find the damn studio. I grabbed something to eat and got back here early in the afternoon."

"You didn't ask for directions or call the studio?" I asked.

Sweetpea giggled. "Come on, Arly, he's a *guy*. You think he's going to stop and ask for directions? If General Meade and General Lee hadn't had maps and aides to get them to Gettysburg, they'd still be leading their armies in circles and we'd be wringing our hankies and awaiting the word from the battlefield. Don't you think there's a reason why NASA includes women in the space shuttle crews?"

"I didn't have a telephone number," Simon said, unamused. "I bought a couple of bottles of booze, ate something, and came back here. No one was around, so I put some ice in a glass and took a bottle of scotch upstairs." He glowered at me, although I'd not said a word. "And, yeah, I reread that damn journal. Henry Largesse was probably a faggot. He wrote about how he and his friends would huddle together during the night, clinging to each other like leeches. Considering that none of them bothered to bathe, it must have been quite an experience."

"Poor Henry," Sweetpea murmured. "It's a shame he couldn't enjoy the amenities at your athletic club. I hear all the boys are squeaky clean."

Simon lifted his hand, then lowered it and stormed out of the room. He and Mrs. Jim Bob exchanged inaudible remarks in the kitchen. Seconds later, the back door reverberated with a resonance not unlike cannon fire.

Sweetpea shook her head. "Goodness gracious, I don't know what's gotten into him lately. He almost always minds his manners. He can be a handful, though. My mother seems to think I can make him settle down and behave, but I'm not sure. My daddy swears he's about to have a heart attack every time I mention postponing the wedding, or even calling it off. Then again, I've already ordered my wedding dress from a London designer. The flowers for my bouquet and the altar pieces are being flown in from South Africa."

"It sounds lovely," I said, refusing to allow myself to think about a certain New Jersey backyard, a bouquet of limp daisies, and barbecued ribs. "What did you do after Simon left yesterday morning?"

"I went upstairs and washed my hair, then sat on the front porch for a long while, letting my hair dry while I looked out at the stretch of road where the skirmish most likely took place. I could almost see the Yankees crouched in the pasture, fidgeting while they waited to ambush the rebels, not daring to speak or poke their heads up. They'd ridden most of the night and tethered their horses down by the creek. They wouldn't have dared make a campfire so they could have coffee. No, all they could do was wait and pray they'd survive this confrontation before they went on to the next one. And down the road were the rebels, tossing their gear into a wagon, saddling the mules, most likely ribbing each other but knowing damn well they were heading for a major battle. All of them, both sides, kept scraps of paper in their pockets so that if they were killed, their bodies might be identified and their families informed. This weekend's just a staged spectacle for the benefit of a camera and a few tourists with picnic baskets and camcorders. After all, it's only going to be fake bullets, fake blood, and fake death."

"Then why did you want Simon to participate?" I asked. "Corinne told me it was your idea to come here."

She thought for a moment. "I thought I could handle it, to come to some sort of closure. My great-great-granduncle is buried in an unmarked grave. He didn't die in a battle that merited a page, or even a paragraph, in a history book. He probably had shiny buttons and gold braid on his uniform, but that wasn't enough to stop a minié ball. If that's what it was. He could have died from any of the diseases that were responsible for the majority of the deaths during that horrible time. His parents, who'd encouraged him to enlist and sent him off with the same enthusiasm that parents in Charleston send their sons and daughters off to boarding schools, died of grief within a year after the signing of the surrender at Appomattox."

347

Her sincerity was touching, but I wasn't sure where I should be going with it. "And you thought you'd find closure at the Skirmish at Cotter's Ridge? Wouldn't a pilgrimage to a battlefield have offered a better sense of" — I opted to use her phrase despite my aversion to pop psychology — "closure?"

"Maybe so," Sweetpea said, dabbing the corners of her eye with a tissue, "but my cousin Yancy told me about this and it just about made me cry. Thousands and thousands of men and boys died in the important battles, but here just a handful died for no reason. There was nothing at stake. The Yankees didn't know about the gold, if there really was any. The Confederate boys were just following orders."

"And that's why Simon's going to put on his really tacky uniform, although in this case, on your orders? How can you think a documentary with a budget of something like five thousand dollars will launch a career in Hollywood? Do you think some hotshot producer is going to wander into the Headquarters House in Farberville, Arkansas, see this little film, and sign Simon up for a leading role in the next Civil War epic?"

"You never know."

"I guess not," I said. "After you sat on the front porch, what did you do?"

She grimaced. "Not much, since I didn't have a car. The only person in the house was a woman who made it clear that my presence was interfering with her cleaning chores. No matter where I went, she was looming with the vacuum cleaner, or a mop, or a broom, or dustrag. I finally gave up trying to escape her and walked down to the end of the road to get away from her. And, yes, I took my copy of Henry's journal with me, just to see if I could spot whatever Wendell claimed was a clue. I sat on a gravel bar by the creek for several hours before I found enough courage to come back here."

"So you were alone?"

"As God is my witness. Now, if you'll kindly excuse me, I'd like to change for lunch. And by the way, you might want to ask Kenneth about the argument he and Wendell had right after breakfast. It sounded real nasty, like when Jenna and Madison showed up at a dance at the club wearing the same dress. I swear, I thought we were going to see bloodshed in the ladies' room."

I sank back into Mrs. Jim Bob's most recent upholstery.

13

I'd talked to a lot of people, and it wasn't yet noon. Mrs. Jim Bob was not likely to offer me a sandwich and a cup of soup, but I went into the kitchen with some optimism that she wouldn't attack me with a butcher knife. She was seated at the dinette, gazing despondently at slips of paper.

"I talked to Eula," she said in a flat voice.

"Sheriff Dorfer's doing everything he can to find Lottie. If it's okay with you, I'll use your phone to call him and see if he's learned anything."

"What about Brother Verber? No one's seen him since after church on Sunday."

I almost felt sorry for her, but our shared history precluded it. "He drove away in his own car, which means he wasn't kidnapped by terrorists or beamed up by aliens. Maybe his calling sent him to Little Rock or Hot Springs to rescue wayward souls. Technically, he's not missing, so I can't ask the state police to start looking for his car."

She finally lifted her head. "And Hospiss's death has to be linked to Wendell's, doesn't it? He sat in that chair right there yesterday morning and told everybody how she claimed the Confederate lieutenant buried up on Cotter's Ridge had married her great-great-grandmother. It could have been true."

I poured myself a glass of iced tea, despite the risk of a lecture on drinking while on duty. "Would it matter all that much if it was?"

"Not to me, and not to the Stump County chapter of the DAC, from all accounts. I heard she'd been demanding membership for the last twenty years. They kept telling her that the family Bible wasn't adequate proof. I'm surprised she didn't dig up the skeleton and haul it into a meeting, the rotted remains of the uniform still clinging to the bones."

"Have you ever applied for membership?"

"The Buchanons back then didn't care one way or the other about the Civil War. I disremember hearing that even one of them enlisted. Besides, I have more important things to do than sit around and gossip about my ancestors. The Missionary Society has raised several hundred dollars over the years to bring salvation to the heathens.

The Christmas pageant at the Voice of the Almighty Lord took months of my time, what with the casting, costumes, and rehearsals every night. It was a tremendous success, except for the little angel who picked her nose the entire time. Her parents haven't dared show their faces on Sunday morning since then, thank goodness."

My mind had wandered off, but I managed a nod. "I was told you went to Farberville after breakfast. What time did you get home?"

"The middle of the afternoon, and if you're aiming to ask me about those — those people, there's nothing I can tell you. Perkin's eldest said they'd been popping in and out all day, always leaving a mess in the kitchen. She was so stirred up that I had to give her an extra five dollars. I hope she's not expecting the same when she leaves today."

"Surely not," I said. "I've spoken to everyone but Kenneth, and as soon as I'm done with him, Perkin's eldest can tackle the living room. Is he still on the patio?"

Her lips pursed. "Do you think I keep track of their comings and goings? I have plenty of more important things to do than that. I've canceled the picnic this evening, which means I'll have to find a way to feed these people yet again. If Perkin's eldest doesn't have time to iron the tablecloth and napkins, I'll have to do it myself. Not one of them has offered to set the table, much less peel a potato. And tomorrow about thirty more of these reenactors will arrive, expecting a pig roast out by the bridge." She shoved back her chair and stood up. "If you want to make a phone call, do it from your office, which the town council provides at no cost to you so you can conduct your business. I need to call Ruby Bee about her corn casserole. Lottie'd agreed to fix baked beans, but I guess that's out of the question now."

I escaped to the patio before I was coerced into making a side dish that served fifty people (unless tamales would suffice). Corinne was alone at the wrought-iron table, applying polish to her nails.

"Have you solved the mystery," she asked as I approached, "or should we all plan to gather in the parlor this evening for dramatic revelations?"

"The sherry has not yet been decanted, but you never know." I sat down across from her and let the sunshine soak into my skin. My shoulders ached, as if I'd been juggling all these statements of who was where and when and why. None of them carried much weight, however. Wendell had been on Cotter's Ridge; that much I knew. Darla Jean, Corinne, Harriet, Jeb, Kevin, Raz, Ruby Bee, Estelle, Hammet, and Andrew Pulaski had been there. It was highly probably that Petrol and Dahlia's granny were, too. Waylon might have been, and I'd yet to question Kenneth Grimley. It was amazing that they hadn't been tripping all over each other like hyperactive children at an elementary school Halloween carnival.

But only those who'd been in the kitchen the previous morning knew about Hospiss's tenuous involvement. "Did you hear about Hospiss Buchanon's death?"

"Yes, Mrs. Jim Bob mentioned it at breakfast this morning. This tiny town of yours is beginning to feel quite dangerous, Arly. Had Kenneth not offered me a morning libation, I might have locked myself in my room and called the airlines to change our reservations."

I was sorry the airlines had not canceled her flight out of Charleston two days ago. "Did Wendell say anything that implied Hospiss knew the location of the Confederate gold?"

"Not that I recall. It was really just about her ludicrous claim to be descended from an honorable officer of the CSA, who was also the scion of a wealthy family. It's possible that the uncivilized woman removed him from the road and did what she could to nurse him back to health. I can assure you that if he'd survived, he would not have spent the remainder of his years in a ramshackle hovel. That sort of thing simply wasn't done, not even a hundred and fifty years ago."

"Would it matter if she was his great-great-granddaughter? If she had proof, would she inherit the family's fortune?"

Corinne finished applying polish, replaced the cap, and looked up. "I have no idea what she might have believed, but of course she could not have made a legal claim on the estate. At the end of the War, Lieutenant Parham would have been declared missing in action, presumed dead, and the estate would have gone to the next closest relative. The laws of inheritance are quite clear."

"Even if he survived, married, and had children?" I asked. "Wendell said the lieutenant was an only child, so only his offspring would be direct descendants."

"It doesn't matter. Once he was declared dead, he was six feet under in the eyes of the court. No lawyer would bother to try to make a case. Well, no lawyer with any ethics. Several years ago a tourist from Sarasota sued me because he'd sprained his ankle while stepping off the curb in front of my house. When it was pointed out that he wasn't on my property, he claimed it was still my responsibility because he'd been backing up to take a photo of my azaleas. I will admit the azaleas were spectacular that year, but the suit was still frivolous. As an act of goodwill, I offered to pay for his visit to the emergency room, but he wanted half a million dollars. 'Fiddlesticks,' I said to my lawyer. The gentleman ended up being obliged to pay my legal fees."

I wasn't sure Hospiss had known her claim was without merit, and she certainly could have found a lawyer in Farberville who had squeaked through the ethics portion of the bar exam — if there was one. I supposed I could wait three or four years and ask Sweetpea, but it was conceivable that we wouldn't remain in touch.

"Where did Sweetpea and Simon go?" I asked, noting the yard was populated only by robins. "And Kenneth, for that matter? I need to talk to him before I go."

Corinne shrugged. "I have no idea where any of them are. I'd just as soon Kenneth stay gone until the children and I leave to go to lunch with Andrew. I don't want to feel obligated to invite him to join us, but I suppose I will. Meals have become very tense lately. I think I'll suggest to Mrs. Jim Bob that she hire additional household help."

"An excellent idea," I said. I decided Kenneth could wait until after lunch, whether he dined on crab crepes at Farberville's version of a très chic bistro, or on baloney sandwiches and the dregs of the potato salad at the dinette.

I drove back to the PD, where I found Hammet playing with my radar gun. I'd actually been given a real gun when I'd taken the job, but I kept it locked in a metal cabinet since I rarely locked the front door.

"Nailed any speeders yet?" I asked him as I made fresh coffee.

"Not yet. Do you wanna go down by the bridge and waste 'em when they come roarin' through town?"

He was looking mopey, so I gave him the chocolate bar I'd stashed away for a particularly tedious day. "Estelle and Ruby Bee didn't drag you up on the ridge today, I gather."

"Naw, they said some feller got hisself killed. They was plum crazy to think I knew where there was saddlebags of gold in some damnfool cave. I would have found 'em years ago."

"And done what?"

"I dunno, but somethin'. Her could have used 'em to buy food and shoes for us, mebbe even fancy new clothes." He gave me a guilty look. "Not that we needed shit like that. Her could always sell enough 'seng and hooch to buy cornmeal and rice, and we grew most ever'thing else. A couple of times a year we'd have fatback and black-eyed peas."

"Your foster home must seem luxurious in comparison."

Hammet grimaced. "It ain't all the time bad, but I shore miss living out here. Do you reckon you'll ever change your mind, Arly? I don't hafta stay in your apartment. I can sleep in the back room here. That way, I can make coffee for you and take care of a vegetable garden so you can have ripe tomatoes and fresh corn whenever you wants. You can have pole beans and okra and —"

"I'm not going to change my mind, Hammet," I said gently. "You'll do better in a family environment, and I can't provide it. Maybe you can stay with me for a week during your summer vacation."

"Jest a week? I got three months off."

I was searching for an argument when the phone rang. For once, I was glad to answer it.

"Chief Hanks, this is Miz Pimlico at the old folks' home. We have a situation, and I just don't know what to do. Vonetta is no help whatsoever, and the residents are becoming increasingly agitated. You'll have to come immediately."

"What's going on?"

"It's far too complicated to explain. I'll expect you in five minutes."

I put down the receiver. "It looks as though you're in charge, Hammet. Try not to shoot anyone, okay? Tourist season doesn't start until the first of June. When you get hungry, go back to Ruby Bee's and let her fix you something."

"I kin come with you in case you need backup," he said, giving me his best hangdog look.

"I'll see you later."

I drove to the old folks' home and went inside. Miz Pimlico was pacing in the front hallway, her face not technically as white as a sheet, but headed that way. "So what's going on?" I demanded, prepared to lose my temper if it had to do with stolen pudding cups or hanky-panky in the crafts room.

"This morning Mr. Whitbreedly was monitoring the pasture for signs of a Yankee invasion. He'd stand at the window all day if we didn't insist he come to the dining room for meals. Ten minutes ago, he came flapping into my office, sputtering that he'd actually seen one down by the creek. I did my best to calm him down, but he was beside himself. I finally agreed to return to his room with him so he could show me this purported Yankee. Not that I expected to see anything more than a garbage bag caught in a tree, mind you, but it seemed like the best way to snap him out of his little fantasy." She looked over her shoulder, then lowered her voice. "I was astounded to see a man in a Yankee uniform, wandering near the tree line. While Mr. Whitbreedly was busy chortling and congratulating himself, I saw a Confederate soldier approach the Yankee. They began shoving each other back and forth, and appeared to be shouting. They moved out of view — and then we heard a gunshot. This sent Mr. Whitbreedly running down the halls, screeching that we were about to be attacked. Vonetta locked herself in the pantry, and I called you."

"I have a pretty good idea who the Yankee is. One of the reenactors showed up Monday. He was camping at the other end of town, but I sent him down here. Not here, exactly. He was supposed to stay by the low-water bridge until his unit arrives tomorrow, but apparently he's not too keen on following directions."

Miz Pimlico was not charmed by my admission. "And the Confederate soldier? Did you also send him here?"

"No, I had nothing to do with that," I said hastily. "Did you hear only the one gunshot?"

"Considering the ruckus Mr. Whitbreedly instigated, I might not have heard a volley of cannon fire. What are you planning to do about this, Chief Hanks? We cannot allow anyone to fire weapons at the far side of the pasture. Bullets can travel as far as a mile, which is why we shutter some of the windows during deer season. At this moment, those gentlemen who are ambulatory are organizing a unit armed with canes and bedpans. Miz Claplander and the other women are ripping apart their nightgowns to roll bandages. Dumdiddy Buchanon got tangled up with his walker in all the excitement and sprained his ankle. This does seem to be entirely your fault, as well as your responsibility. May I assume you'll deal with it before anyone else is injured?"

"Yes, of course," I said, sighing. "Calm everyone down and assure them that I have the situation under control."

Miz Pimlico might have intended to express her doubts (which were well-founded), but an outbreak of howls sent her down a hallway. I let myself out the exit nearest the pasture and plowed through the weeds in the direction of Boone Creek. If Jeb had disobeyed my order to stay put by the bridge, he might find himself spending the weekend in the county jail. If he'd shot Waylon, he'd be spending many weekends at the state prison, along with weekdays. Or maybe Waylon had shot Jeb, or maybe they'd simultaneously shot each other. I winced as I thought about what McBeen would have to say if he was obliged to return.

When I arrived at the tree line, I found no bodies, no blood, no tent, no bedroll, no signs of a campfire. The weeds had been trampled, and there were footprints in the sparser patches. Mr. Whitbreedly's testimony might not have been convincing, but I would never dare doubt Miz Pimlico's.

I tried to figure out how best to trump up charges against the two miscreants so they'd have to spend at least one night at the jail, where they'd be served a hot meal of sorts, given the opportunity to shower, and allowed to watch TV and play cards until they were returned to cells to sleep on mattresses. Lumpy mattresses, granted, but better than thin blankets on rocky ground. Coffee and oatmeal in the morning. Complimentary copies of *USA Today* outside the cell doors, for all I knew.

Regrettably, Stump County's finances did not extend to the operation of a gulag or two. I resolved to bring it up with Harve at a later time.

Which reminded me that I hadn't called him. When I got back to the PD, I made sure Hammet wasn't crouched under a table, then sat back in my chair and prepared to badger LaBelle until I got through to Harve.

"Why, Arly," she began in a suspiciously affable voice, "how's your mama doing? I saw her and Estelle last month at Wal-Mart and we had the nicest chat. You really should settle down and give her some grandbabies."

"Is Harve there?"

"I do believe he is. I hear there's gonna be some folks making a movie out your way this weekend. Who's starring in it? Anybody I've heard of?"

"Simon Dawk. I'm sure you remember him from *The One-eyed Psycho Who Disemboweled Dispatchers*. I need to speak to Harve, LaBelle."

"I don't rightly recollect a movie with that

title. Who else was in it?"

"Andrew Pulaski, Kenneth Grimley, and a cast of dozens. Put me through to Harve, please."

LaBelle smacked her gum. "Those names just don't ring a bell. Were any of them in something else I might have seen?" When I remained silent, she added, "So how about I let you talk to Sheriff Dorfer, and then you can tell me more about these actors. Have any of them been on soaps?"

"Later," I said, then waited until Harve bestirred himself to pick up the phone. I dutifully related the gist of all the unsatisfactory interviews I'd had. "So there were more people up on Cotter's Ridge yesterday morning than there are at the Dew Drop Inn on a Saturday night. Well, there weren't any bikers or bar chicks, but I wouldn't bet the farm on it. The Cirque de Soleil could be rehearsing up there somewhere."

Harve ruminated for a moment. "And don't forget all the residents of the Pot O' Gold trailer park. It seems not more than two or three of them were home, and they were sleeping off hangovers. Hold on." He muffled the receiver with his hand and bellowed for LaBelle to fetch him coffee and a doughnut, and to tell Swilly to get off his lazy butt and go on to Bugscuffle to look into a report of stolen goats. "So where are we on this?" he went on blithely. "McBeen said that Streek died as a result of the fall and the Buchanon woman on account of her skull being smashed in. We found what looks to be the weapon in her case, by the way. There was a brass urn under the trailer, with some traces of blood. One of my boys said he'd noticed dust and ashes around the body, but couldn't see any point in vacuuming 'em up as evidence. It may turn out that one of her ancestors was responsible for her death."

"No fingerprints, I presume."

"No, and we ain't gonna order DNA tests on the cremains. Mrs. Dorfer has three urns down in the basement. She forgot to label 'em, so now she doesn't know who's who. I keep telling her to dump all three in the reservoir and let them sort it out, but she's been putting it off for years."

"I don't think the previous occupant of the urn is going to tell us anything. Have you tracked down the next of kin so arrangements can be made?"

"The deputies couldn't find any personal papers or old letters — or a family Bible — but I don't figure it's gonna be real hard to find her kinfolk. You suppose Mrs. Jim Bob would like to do the honors?"

"By all means, call her, and don't forget to mention that Hospiss most likely would have wanted to be buried in the Methodist cemetery." I stared at the water stain on the ceiling, but no inspiration was forthcoming. "We're going nowhere on this, Harve. Pretty much everybody involved was on the ridge, but there's nothing to link any one of them to the murders. I'll go find Hospiss's old place after lunch and look for an indication that Wendell was there. Unless he wrote a message in the dust, though, I don't see that it matters if he was or wasn't."

Harve wheezed, no doubt thinking about the negative publicity he'd have to deal with if the crimes remained unsolved long about election day. "The rest of the reenactors are showing up tomorrow, right?"

"And the mules, and the corn casseroles, and the folderol if the TV station in Farberville decides this will make a colorful feature to tuck between the latest arson incident and the always popular ongoing investigation of drugs in our area high schools. Updates at ten."

"I don't see what you can do except keep poking around," Harve said. "Stay in touch, you hear?"

I would have pointed out that he'd assured me that his department was going to take over the case once I'd done the preliminary work, but I would have been talking to a dial tone. I leaned back and tried to construct a mental map of the ridge, adding pinpricks for those who'd given me some idea where they were, and squiggly lines for those who'd been vague. Not necessarily intentionally vague, since there were very few distinctive landmarks. Big oaks, little oaks, scrub pines, brambles, logs, stumps, creek beds, overgrown trails. Oh, and of course squirrels, none of whom could be counted on to testify in court. If only the Confederates had brought loaves and fishes to feed the army, rather than gold to pay it, Jack and I could be spending the afternoon at Boone Creek, where I had a favorite spot for skinny-dipping. Far enough from the road so we couldn't hear any traffic, remote enough so we wouldn't be interrupted, dappled sunlight, a shady clearing . . .

The door opened. I sat upright and forced myself to remember where I was and what, in theory, I was supposed to be doing.

"Did I catch you at an inopportune moment?" asked Kenneth Grimley, who proceeded to sit down without waiting for my reply. "I'm terribly sorry I wandered off this morning, but I truly forgot you wanted to ask me questions. To save us both some time, I heard what Wendell said at breakfast and was intrigued by his less-than-subtle hint about the location of the gold. I went so far as to go to his room to try to make him understand that the gold belongs to the United States government, since it was stolen from a federal depository. Stolen, that is, in the sense this illegal coalition known as the CSA had no lawful right to act as a foreign entity. He did not grasp the fundamental truths regarding preeminent dominion based on the Articles of Confederation and the Constitution, which clearly delineates states' rights and those allotted to the federal government."

"Any chance you pushed him off the bluff and I can turn you over to the sheriff?"

"I'm afraid not. I went to my room and made sure my uniform was not in need of ironing, then went downstairs. Everyone was gone, with the exception of the cleaning woman. Although it was tempting to spend the morning on the patio, sipping Bloody Marys and reading a biography of Thomas Jefferson, I decided to go for a walk. It's an ongoing struggle to make sure General Wallingford Ames can fit into his trousers. I went to the main road and then continued up an unpaved road toward Cotter's Ridge. I roamed around for a while, careful to keep my bearings, and eventually returned to the house for a shower and a nap."

"Did you see anyone?" I asked without enthusiasm. "The Confederate ghost, for instance?"

"They all should have been put to rest on April 12, 1865, when Lee and Grant met in Wilmer McLean's farmhouse in Appomattox and the articles of surrender were agreed upon. The South shall not rise again, despite what the rednecks display on the bumpers of their pickup trucks and motorcycles. There may be pockets of delusional militants who have nurtured a hope for rebellion for more than a hundred and forty years. Don't think the FBI is unaware of them. I myself act as a covert agent, carefully recording names and license plates during the reenactments and sending in my reports. In return, the FBI avoids making direct contact with me in order to protect my status as an anonymous informant."

"Do they?" I murmured. "I've always thought they were a considerate bunch of guys. Let me repeat my question. Did you see anyone?"

"Sweetpea, but surely she's already told you she was there. She wasn't skipping along, pausing to pick wildflowers, but instead making her way quite purposefully."

"Do you think she was following Wendell?"

"I have no idea," Kenneth said, "since I didn't see him. I did wonder if . . . well, I have no business speculating. I am hardly a blue-haired Southern busybody passing judgment over a bridge table. It's just that one of Simon's remarks during breakfast caught my attention. He warned her not to consort with the enemy."

"As in a Yankee," I said. "You're a Yankee."

He smirked. "But hardly a ladies' man, as my ex-wives will cheerfully attest to. The first was a student who believed in the mystique of academia. She soon discovered the frailties that not even a Ph.D. can disguise and moved to New York to pursue a career on the stage. My second wife was merely desperate for financial security. I can't recall if we ever got around to consummating our marriage. No, Sweetpea would never lower herself to consort, as we're calling it, with someone like me."

"But someone like Andrew Pulaski?"

"I've heard rumors they found occasions for intimacy while Simon sweltered on the battlefield during the filming of the mini-series. Not that I should repeat such insubstantial stories without personal knowledge, but I wasn't there. I prefer to expend my free time educating children about the realities of war and the threat of a future insurrection. I understand that in the South, the children sing a ditty along the lines of, 'Save your Confederate money, the South shall rise again.' It's not their fault; I'm sure they've been indoctrinated since birth."

"Not all of them," I said, trying to decide if he was laughable or a little bit scary. "Thanks for coming by, Kenneth. I'm quite sure I'll see you again."

He stood up and made a swooping motion with his arm. "Not as a participant in the reenactment, but General Wallingford Ames will be there to encourage the troops to hold fast their position and take a deadly toll on the rebels."

I waited until he left before I buried my face in my hands. I was still just sitting there when Jack came into the PD.

"I saw your car out front," he said. "I was going to ask you how it was going, but I can see it's not going very well."

"When I first heard about this last Friday, I should have thrown some clothes in the backseat of my car and kept going until I ran out of gas."

"There's an upside," he said as he came around behind me and began to massage my shoulders. "Nobody's been murdered today."

"Yeah, but it's early. Kenneth was in here a few minutes ago, insinuating that Sweetpea and Andrew Pulaski were consorting yesterday morning. Did you see either of them in the motel parking lot before you left?"

"Consorting?"

"Consorting. In the same way you and I consorted after the second game of Scrabble."

"Oh, *that* kind of consorting." He sat down on a corner of the desk. "No, the only person I saw was Hammet, who was watching me from behind the corner of one of the buildings on the off chance I'd pull on a ski mask in preparation for an armed robbery at the barber shop or the supermarket. To his disgust, I had breakfast and left for Springfield without gunning down any innocent citizens. Andrew's car was parked in front of his unit, but I didn't see him. Sorry."

"And Simon never showed up at your studio. There's no way of knowing for sure that he even left town. Maybe he decided to stay and see what Sweetpea had planned for the day."

Jack pulled me to my feet. "I don't suppose you have time for tamales this afternoon?"

I wrapped my arms around him and rested my head on his chest. "I wish I did, but I need to get this cleared up before more of these aged children arrive tomorrow to indulge in their fantasies of being fierce soldiers and gallant heroes. Why couldn't the historical society have found another town? A ridge and a bridge — how hard could it be?"

"On Saturday night, we'll go into Farberville and have a nice dinner. Afterward, we can find a motel with mirrors on the ceiling and a bed that jiggles for a quarter. Maggody will simply vanish from the map."

"Maggody's never been on the map," I said, managing a smile. "Let's go have lunch at Ruby Bee's. I suppose I'll spend the rest of the day nosing around, but I should be available once all the homicidal killers have been tucked into bed. Maybe you can do a guy thing with Andrew over a couple of pitchers of beer and see if he'll let anything slip about Sweetpea."

"If you're deputizing me," he said as we went outside, "you'll have to let me wear your badge tonight."

"You're liable to hurt yourself when you try to pin it on."

"Nobody said being a war correspondent was easy."

It was very nice to laugh for a change.

Lottie had been lectured since she was in pigtails about the horrible things that befell children who snooped into others' personal possessions. Being expelled from Sunday school was the least of the punishments that would rain down with the fury of a spring thunderstorm. But she had little choice, since the Headquarters House was decidedly out of the question. She had only a hazy memory of stumbling out the back door and diving under a forsythia, where she'd lost consciousness as a result of either the nasty bump on her head or pure panic. It had been dark when she roused herself, and unpleasantly chilly. It had not occurred to her to put on a cardigan sweater before committing a felony, for surely that's what it had been.

Somehow she'd survived the night, but by the next morning she was feeling dizzy and disoriented. The yards did not look familiar, nor did the occasional cats that wandered by, pausing to eye her with typical feline aplomb before ambling on about their business. She'd sensed that it would be foolish to go inside the nearby house. For reasons she hadn't been able to define, it had seemed menacing.

Hunger and a need to deal with matters of physical comfort and hygiene had driven her into an adjoining yard, but again she'd found herself afraid to knock on the door and throw herself on the mercy of whoever appeared. She'd moved on.

When she'd found a gap in a hedge and continued into the next yard, she'd found herself confronting a very elderly woman, who'd been breaking up pieces of bread and tossing them on the patio. Perhaps the woman had seen the envious glint in Lottie's eyes as the crumbs were attacked by sparrows and finches.

Lottie was unclear what had happened after that, but she'd ended up in a lovely, soft bed in a tiny room, with a cup of tea and a warning to stay there until the woman's son had packed a bag and left on a trip. And so she had, dozing most of the day and awakening only to wonder where she was.

That evening the woman had reappeared, introduced herself as Mrs. Walter Streek, and invited Lottie downstairs for supper. They'd had soup and watched TV, neither saying much, and retired early.

By Tuesday morning, it had all come back to Lottie, but she had no idea what to do.

Was there a warrant for her arrest? Would she be apprehended if she dared set foot out of the house? She'd seen shows on TV in which the police had tapped telephones in order to overhear calls. Could Eula's and Elsie's phones been tapped in a similar fashion?

Mrs. Streek had asked no questions, despite the fact Lottie had staggered into the yard in a filthy dress, her hair in disarray and dotted with leaves, her stockings riddled with runs. And Lottie had offered no explanations, which suited them both. She'd taken over kitchen duties, fixing a nourishing breakfast and artful little sandwiches for lunch, and made sure Mrs. Streek was covered with a cozy afghan while she dozed in her favorite chair.

It had been going rather smoothly until a woman had come to the door early that evening. Lottie had hovered in the kitchen until she'd seen that the woman was not a police officer, but a somewhat frowsy creature who most likely was selling something that was overpriced and of poor quality. However, when the woman had broken the news of Mrs. Streek's son's death, Lottie had rushed in and hovered anxiously until the woman left.

Lottie realized that she had to stay until

arrangements were made for Mrs. Streek, who'd been kind and trusting to a fault. At Mrs. Streek's request, Lottie had made a long distance call to a Mondale Streek, who'd grudgingly promised to come as soon as he could get away from his office. She'd repeatedly called Harriet Hathaway, but there'd been no answer thus far.

And now, while Mrs. Streek napped in her bedroom, the blinds drawn, Lottie decided to risk eternal damnation (or at least humiliation) and snoop through Wendell's notebooks and file cabinets in search of a copy of the journal.

His office was cluttered with stacks of periodicals related to the Civil War and various genealogical organizations. Maps of battle sites were pinned on the wall, as well as newspaper clippings and black-and-white depictions of whiskered officers glowering at the camera. Four filing cabinets dominated one wall, each drawer with a neatly printed label. She found one marked "Cotter's Ridge" and removed a stack of folders to examine while she sat at the desk.

A folder with Henry Largesse's name contained several pages of notes, some handwritten and others printed from the Internet, and a copy of the journal. Lottie decided she could read it later, even while she and Mrs. Streek watched TV. It was more important to use this time efficiently. She'd always taught her students that this was the key to a household that ran smoothly and with a minimum of fuss.

Wendell had done an admirable job tracing the Largesse family in both the pre- and post-Civil War eras. He'd followed leads on Henry's sisters and their marriages and offspring, and the offspring of the off- spring. He'd determined when and where most of them were buried. It wasn't, Lottie concluded, very interesting.

She flipped through the other folders with equally detailed information about the Confederate privates who'd done their best to defend the gold that tragic morning in April. Records of births, marriages, and deaths reduced the young boys to nothing more than a compilation of factual trivia.

Only when she at last came to Lieutenant Hadley Parham's folder did she find a bit of human drama. The Parhams had presided over a vast plantation of several thousand acres, and before the war owned more than seven hundred slaves. Hadley's sister had died at the age of four, and there were no birth certificates other than Hadley's. Lottie paused to do a bit of calculation. Hadley had been barely twenty years old when he enlisted and galloped away to defend the South from Northern aggression. He'd been twenty-one when he was declared a casualty at Cotter's Ridge.

Perplexed, she stopped for a moment. A "casualty"? Acquaintances might be casual, as were impromptu gatherings in the morning for coffee or encounters in the supermarket. Picnics and potluck suppers, where most of the attendees (but not she, of course) wore shorts and sandals. But a gallant boy, hardly a man, bleeding to death on a country road? Hardly casual.

However, she realized she was not using her time wisely and continued reading. Wendell had not been content with a final notation of Hadley's death at the Skirmish at Cotter's Ridge. He'd turned his attention back to the family left to cope with the challenges of keeping the plantation productive despite the increasing rebelliousness of the slaves and the blockade that prevented the export of the cotton crop to England. The Historical Society of Crawly County, South Carolina, had provided Wendell with photocopies of the plantation's accounts, presumably in Hadley's father's own handwriting. Horace's script had been as precise as Wendell's.

More intriguing was a copy of the certificate of baptism of Felicity Louise, born of Hadley Walpool Parham and Trella, a female slave and the property of Horace Parham, Esq. An illegitimate baby, born to the master's son and a woman of color. Another document, declaring Felicity Louise to be a legal ward. The baby's skin must have been light, Lottie thought, for the family to take her into the house to be educated and brought up like a proper young lady. She'd subsequently married and procreated with success.

Lottie, who'd never bothered with frivolous fiction, found herself gazing out the window at the dogwoods and redbuds blooming in the backyards of the adjoining houses, lost in a wistful reverie of a little girl, born in tragic circumstances, her true heritage by necessity hidden, haunted by the fear of exposure, who'd gone on to make a place for herself in Charleston society.

Luckily, Wendell had left a box of tissues next to his computer.

14

Hammet was sitting on a stool at the end of the bar, as limp as a pile of sodden laundry. Waving Jack away, I sat down and said, "Bored?"

"Bored as a body can git," he said, sighing. "Last week I would've sworn that having nuthin' to do but eat ice cream and watch TV all day was all I could ever want. Even stomping all over the ridge was better'n this. You won't let me tag along, and Ruby Bee sez I can't come in the kitchen anymore after . . . well, she sez I can't."

"You didn't start a fire, did you?"

He gave me an aggrieved look. "I ain't that dumb. She said she'd give me a dollar if I cleaned the pantry. I took all the cans down and wiped the shelves, but then I decided it'd look a sight prettier if I pulled off the labels and lined up all the shiny cans. Ruby Bee dint appreciate it."

"I suppose not." I thought for a moment,

then said, "Why don't you come sit with Jack and me while we all have lunch?"

"I already et."

"Sit with us and have a piece of pie. As soon as we're done, I'm going to need your help. You know that two people were killed yesterday, don't you?"

Hammet perked up. "It must be that feller out back, the one that keeps peerin' out the window like he's waiting for the FBI to surround the motel and take him into custody. I warned you about him yesterday, Arly. He's got a real surly look to him, like a rabid polecat. His nose is all red and his eyes are real puffy."

"We'll have to wait for the FBI to show up before we tackle him. I need to find Hospiss Buchanon's old place somewhere on Cotter's Ridge. I realize you've been dragged up there for the last two days, but I promise we won't look for caves." I poked his shoulder. "I really need your help, Hammet."

I suppose I expected him to tear up with gratitude, but I was wrong. "What's in it for me?" he asked.

"I'll let you stick around until Saturday."

"My foster ma sez I ain't supposed to come back till Monday. Besides, I'm the drummer boy in this movie. I got a uniform and a drum. I ain't learned to play it yet, but

I reckon I can do jest fine when the time comes."

Ruby Bee came out of the kitchen, saw me, and disappeared as though the biscuits were smoldering and the meringue on the cream pies was turning to ash. It was just as well, since I was feeling far from friendly.

Hammet was pretending to be fascinated by the neon signs above the bar, but he was surreptitiously watching me, like a crow on a dead branch.

"Two weeks this summer," I said.

"A month."

"Two weeks here, and then a weekend of camping and fishing and that sort of primitive thing."

"Three weeks and a weekend in Branson."

I was beginning to get annoyed. "Three weeks, period."

"What about the camping shit?"

"You can pitch a tent in the pasture behind the Flamingo Motel. Deal?"

Hammet slid off the stool. "I s'pose so," he said cheerfully. "We kin talk about Branson later. Why do you want to find Hospiss's shack? There weren't much standing last I saw it. All you're gonna find is snakes, spiders, wood rats, and mebbe a nest of rabbits."

I herded him over to the booth where Jack was sitting. "Hammet has decided to become a union negotiator when he grows up," I said as I sat down. "That, or an enforcer for the mob. He made me an offer I couldn't refuse."

Ruby Bee had trailed us to take our orders. She put down menus, then glared at me. "You done anything more about finding Lottie? Joyce told me what Eula said about Lottie sneaking into the Headquarters House and getting herself arrested. But then Millicent said she'd heard that Lottie was staying at a homeless shelter on account of having amnesia and not recollecting who she was. Edwina Spitz swears Lottie's staying with the nuns that live in the old house behind the Catholic church, although I find that hard to swallow. Lottie's never been shy about talking about what she calls a papist conspiracy. You need to go into Farberville and fetch her, Arly."

"On my list," I said. I glanced at Jack, who was studying the menu, which, for the record, had not changed in the last few days or even in the last few decades. If Ruby Bee had been able to read my mind, I could expect lectures for a month on promiscuity and the necessity to keep him panting until the honeymoon. It was possible that Estelle was already looking for patterns for the bridesmaids' dresses, while Ruby Bee fretted over recipes for the cake. Raspberry or lemon filling? Pink or yellow rosebuds?

"Just a cheeseburger," said Jack, disrupting my fantasy.

I handed back the menu. "The same, and a glass of milk."

Hammet ordered an ice cream sundae with extra chocolate sauce and two cherries, but Ruby Bee merely nodded and left without asking how I'd feel about Joyce's niece as the flower girl.

In Manhattan, I could have pranced down the street in a string bikini and no one would have noticed. In Maggody, having lunch with an eligible man was tantamount to making a down payment on a cottage and subscribing to *Better Homes & Gardens*.

And making an appointment with an obstetrician.

After we'd finished, I reminded Jack to keep an eye out for Andrew, then took Hammet with me to my car. He instructed me to drive up the road in front of the Pot O' Gold, and finally turn down an overgrown trail that quickly disappeared into brush and scrub pines.

"It ain't all that far," he said as he got out of the car.

"Have you ever found it from this direction?"

Hammet shrugged as if he were a Sherpa guide who scaled Everest dozens of times and had never failed to arrive at the peak, even if it meant slinging his wealthy clients over his back for the final ascent. "It ain't all that far," he repeated. "I know ever'thing there is to know up here."

An hour later we stumbled into a clearing of sorts. Corn stalks competed with weeds and saplings, and the rotted rails of a fence lay scattered in an oddly symmetrical arrangement. What remained of the house was, as Hammet had predicted, nothing more than a heap of gray, splintery timber, tarpaper, and broken glass.

"Told ya," he said smugly.

"One more word out of you and you'll be lucky if I send you a greeting card this summer," I said. "I can feel ticks crawling all over my body, although I'm so sweaty that they may slide off. I thought you knew where this place was."

"You're looking at it, ain't you?"

I was too tired to strangle him and dispose of the body, although there was most likely a well in near proximity. "Let's find the family plot, and then get out of here."

Hammet gulped. "Where they buried folks?"

"Only the dead ones." We went around the rubble and found a patch of ground that had resisted an invasion of brush and brambles. A few daffodils competed with coarse grass and blackberry bushes. "This is it," I said. "Look for headstones."

It turned out that quite a few of Hospiss's ancestors had met their demise over the course of the last two centuries. Almost all of them had merited at least a chunk of rock, although a few had not, leaving me to wonder how dastardly their sins had been.

"Look at this one," called Hammet, scraping moss off a comparatively large marker. "It's got some letters, though I can't make 'em out."

I knelt beside him. "It could be an H and a P." I took a stick and scraped off some more moss. "And this could be 1893."

"Iff'n you say so," he said, unimpressed. "Could be a lotta things."

He was right, and I wasn't inclined to lug the rock back to the car and take it home to scrub it with a toothbrush. I stood up, then froze. "Did you hear something?"

Hammet looked at me. "You reckon this place is haunted?"

"No, it's just that . . ." My throat tightened as I saw what appeared to be a Confederate soldier watching us from behind a thicket of pines. He was as thin as a fencepost, with a pale, cadaverous face and eyes lost in the shadow cast by the brim of his slouch hat. Sunlight glinted momentarily off buttons and gold braid. Before I could find the wherewithal to so much as blink, he vanished.

Hammet tugged my sleeve. "What?"

"I don't know," I said, "but I think it's time to go back to town."

Despite his whiny protests, I dumped him off at Ruby Bee's and drove to Mrs. Jim Bob's house to have a private conversation with Sweetpea about her activities the previous morning. I didn't especially care if she and Andrew had cracked the plaster in his unit at the Flamingo Motel, but I was displeased that she'd lied to me. Then again, it was almost obligatory for potential suspects to lie over the most trivial issues. Traditional mystery fiction would never have thrived if the guilty party had raised his or her hand and admitted everything.

I was more concerned about the two bodies resting in the morgue at the Farberville hospital. Not lords in the conservatory or ladies in the parlor, but a decent if boring man and a pathetic old woman with only one small friend.

Mrs. Jim Bob was chopping onions in the kitchen. "What?" she snapped as I came in through the back door. "I would like to get this brisket in the oven, and I haven't had a chance to look through my recipe box for a vegetable casserole. Jim Bob's taken it upon himself to go into Farberville, which means I'll have to send Perkin's eldest down to the supermarket once I finish my list. One of these days, Arly Hanks, you'll find out what it's like to have to take on responsibilities. I'd gladly sit in your office all day, reading magazines and refusing to answer the telephone, but nothing would get done, would it?"

"I don't guess any murders would get solved."

She put down the knife. "So have you found out who pushed poor Wendell Streek off the bluff? He was a visitor in my home, as you well know. I feel as though I failed to provide proper hospitality. The next thing I know, you'll be telling me that more of my guests have been brutally killed."

I'd never quite seen her like this, and I was glad the knife was on the counter. I hoped Hizzoner was keeping his distance. "Although I was tempted to remain at the

PD reading magazines and not answering the phone, I've been trying my best to find out what's been going on. Are any of your guests here?"

"Most of them left to go to lunch. Did you think I buried their bodies in the garden?"

"That hadn't occurred to me. If you don't mind, I'll go upstairs and examine Wendell's files and notes."

Mrs. Jim Bob picked up the knife and slashed at an onion, sending slices all over the counter and floor. "Do whatever you want."

I eased around her and went upstairs. I could hear Perkin's eldest singing in one of the bathrooms as she scrubbed the tub. Corinne, Simon, Sweetpea, and Andrew were lunching in Farberville. I had no theories concerning the whereabouts of Harriet or Kenneth, but surely they'd both had enough sense to fix a sandwich and discreetly dispatch themselves for the afternoon. I might have considered the next county to be a prudent distance.

Simon's mess had spilled onto what had been Wendell's half of the bedroom. I tossed some clothes on the floor, then sat down on the bed and went through the files I'd found the previous day. Most of the names were of the privates who'd dutifully ridden mules from Little Rock to Maggody, barely aware of what they'd consigned themselves to when they enlisted. Custiss, Emil, LaRue, Michael, Andrew, Joseph, Zachery, Gabriel, Thomas, and Crosby — all long dead and buried, either in their family's churchyards or in unmarked graves. Boys who believed they could achieve manhood by killing their Northern counterparts. Boys who would never be men.

Henry Largesse's file was missing, as was Hadley Parham's. I was sure the files had been there when I was looking for Wendell's address book. Also missing was his copy of the journal. In that it seemed as though there were more copies of the journal in Farberville than there were copies of the King James Bible, I wasn't concerned. I certainly didn't have time to flop on my sofa and study it for whatever clue had tipped off Wendell to the location of the gold. I'd never cared for jigsaw puzzles, riddles, or games of hide and seek.

The missing files were a different matter, however. I searched under the bed and in all the drawers, but they were most definitely gone. And whoever had taken them believed there was something of significance contained within them. I was pretty sure whatever it was would have sailed right past me, but now it seemed important to give them a more than cursory look.

I was sitting on the bed, berating myself for not taking them with me the previous day, when Harriet Hathaway opened the door.

"Arly?" she said timidly. "Do you mind having a few words with me? Mrs. Jim Bob mentioned that you'd come upstairs, and I thought I might find you here. Have you made any progress?"

"In Wendell's case, no." I threw some more of Simon's clothes on the floor so that she could sit across from me. If he had half the sense of a gopher, he'd pick them up before Perkin's eldest put them in a bag and dropped it off at the Voice of the Almighty Lord Assembly Hall for the next yard sale. "It seems as though a goodly number of people were on Cotter's Ridge yesterday, including you. There were no witnesses when Wendell was pushed off the bluff. What's more, almost anyone could have gone to Hospiss's trailer and smashed her skull with a metal urn."

"Hospiss?" Harriet said blankly. "Oh, yes, the woman who claimed to be a descendant of Hadley Parham. She could have been, but it pains me to think that the young lieutenant would have chosen to desert and remain here in Maggody."

"As opposed to getting killed?"

"The sense of honor in the South, then and even now, is more than a passion. Don't you feel that way, Arly? You were born and bred here. Could you ever repudiate your ties to your heritage, to the land, to the traditions?"

"You don't want to hear about some of the traditions in Maggody," I said, sidestepping her question. "I'm here because I wanted to have a second look at Wendell's files. Someone took a couple of them, as well as his copy of the journal. Any ideas?"

Harriet looked around the room, as though I might have overlooked the files. "Why, I suppose anyone staying here could have slipped in and taken them. Could he have made some sort of note in the journal when he chanced upon what he felt was a clue?"

"I don't know, Harriet. If I had the journal in front of me, I could tell you."

"Oh, yes, I suppose you could. You'll have to forgive me. I'm still trying to deal with the shock of his death. I feel like such a fool for having criticized him for his engagement. Lydia must be as distraught as I, even though she'd known him for less than a year. It would be polite of me to call her and offer my condolences. And I really must go to Farberville in the morning to see how Mrs. Streek is doing. I suppose I'll find Lydia there."

"Or maybe not," I said slowly. "Lydia may not be the family friend taking care of Mrs. Streek. Her house is near the Headquarters House, I was told."

"Two doors down. Wendell found it convenient to unlock the house every morning and allow our volunteers to go about their duties. He had a little room behind the parlor where he kept the ledgers and . . ." She began to sniffle. "You must excuse me, Arly. Wendell and I had such happy times together. We'd sit with his mother in the living room every Saturday afternoon and listen to opera on NPR. On other occasions, we'd eat popcorn and watch documentaries of an educational and uplifting nature. I never wished that Mrs. Streek would depart this world, but her time was coming and I could imagine Wendell and me eating something as daring as a pizza and watching network TV. Now she's outlived him. She'll probably outlive me as well, since I no longer have anything to live for."

I gave her one of Wendell's handkerchiefs. "Tomorrow you're going to have to deal with three dozen reenactors, a dozen mules, a cameraman without an assistant, and Mrs. Jim Bob, who's liable to slice and dice anyone who crosses her. The pig roast is scheduled for the evening. The word's out about this, and we may be staring down pickup trucks filled with rednecks waving plastic flags, flinging beer cans, and singing 'Dixie' like a bunch of drunken coyotes. The Stump County Historical Society has given you the responsibility to come away from this with a film suitable for students. You most definitely have something to live for until Saturday afternoon. After that, you're on your own."

Harriet reacted as I'd hoped she would. "You're a cold thing, aren't you?"

"Or a pragmatist. That's part of our heritage, too. An agrarian society can't dictate the future. Floods, droughts, tornadoes, ice storms — we have to acknowledge that we can't control our collective success or failure. All we can do is keep an eye on the weather."

"I see your point," Harriet said. "Why did you imply that Lydia might not be staying with Mrs. Streek?"

"I don't know. Why don't you call her?"

"It's long distance, and I would hate to impose on our hostess. She's behaving very oddly these last two days. Then again, there is a telephone in the room she so graciously put me in. I will certainly reimburse her for any expense."

Harriet and I were giggling as we crept down the hall and went into what I presumed was Mrs. Jim Bob's vision of a ruffled rose garden in the throes of a hysterical wisteria attack. I paced while Harriet dialed a number that was well-known to her.

"Lydia?" she began. "This is Harriet." After a pause, she said, "Miss Estes? Is it possible I met you last week at the town meeting?"

I took the receiver from her and said, "Lottie, this is Arly. What's going on? Don't you realize the Missionary Society is going to hunt me down and hang me from the oak tree in front of the Assembly Hall if I don't find you?"

"That seems extreme," Lottie said tartly. "I attempted to call you earlier, but you were not at your office. I would like you to find out if the police intend to take action against me for my unauthorized entry into the Headquarters House. If so, it is my civic duty to turn myself in, although I must say I'm not looking forward to it."

"I think you're safe, but it might be best for you to stay there for the time being, if that's all right with you."

"Mrs. Streek and I are getting along very well. She certainly can't stay here by herself. Please let those who are concerned about me know that I'm fine."

"Thank you, Lottie," I said, nodding at Harriet. "As long as you're there, could you take a few minutes to look through the files in Wendell's office?"

"I did that earlier, which is why I tried to call you."

She proceeded to tell me an interesting story.

Jim Bob slapped Cherry Lucinda's fleshy white buttocks. "Go get me a beer, honey. You plum tuckered me out, just like you always do. You shore have some talents — which I hope you ain't sharing with anybody else. If I ever hear you are, I'm gonna take back those expensive diamond earrings I gave you for Christmas and find somebody else who'll appreciate 'em."

"Aw, Jim Bob, you're my man." Cherry Lucinda went into the kitchen and took a beer out of the refrigerator. Expensive diamond earrings! The jewelry store man had laughed in her face when she'd had them appraised. She'd been so humiliated she came damn near leaving them on the counter, then realized she'd have some explaining to do if Jim Bob ever asked her to wear them.

"Here's an icy beer," she chirped as she went back into the bedroom. "Whatcha reading?"

"A journal some asshole private wrote back during the Civil War. Mostly whining about how cold and hungry he was, or how he had blisters from marching. It was a war, fer chrissake, not a visit to Opryland."

Cherry Lucinda slipped into bed and tried to distract him, but he elbowed her away. "Were you ever a soldier?"

"No, but I've seen plenty of war movies. Maybe ol' Hadley should have watched some of 'em before he enlisted." Jim Bob kept skimming the pages, looking for a clue to the location of the gold. He slowed down when he came to a paragraph with a tiny checkmark in the margin. "Mind where your hand's straying and listen up on account of it may be important. 'Ma's been taking real good care of me since I got home, though I can tell from watching her that she's sick with worry. At least I made it back here. Yesterday Lester's family got word of his death down in Vicksburg. With him and his brother dead, I don't see how his pa can get in the spring crop.'"

"That's so sad," said Cherry Lucinda.

Jim Bob ignored her. "Then it goes on about this moron Lester's pa for a few more lines. Here's what may be important: 'Emil's sister came by this morning to bring some blackberry preserves and visit for a spell. Rebecca ain't but thirteen, her face all covered with spots and her knees scabby from climbing trees, but I could see she's gonna be a pretty little thing in a few years. I hope there's some young men left in the county when it comes time for her to take a beau. She begged me to tell her again about Emil's death, so I obliged her. We both got real quiet, but then she started talking about all the good times she'd had with him, fishing or just sitting on the porch. We even got to laughing about the time Emil tangled with a copperhead and came darn close to losing his foot from the blood poison. His ma's poultices saw him through it, but he was always scared to go in the woods again, even to hunt. I guess he reckoned the war was gonna be fought in town squares and churchyards. Custiss used to sneak up behind him and hiss, and Emil'd darn near jump out of his skin, then take to cussing something awful while the rest of us laughed so hard our bellies ached. I never could figure out how he'd be much using farming when we got home. I sure ain't these days.

It's all I can to do use my crutch to hobble out to the porch and sit in the sun for a spell. I don't reckon I'll be a burden much longer.' "

Cherry Lucinda used a corner of the sheet to blot her cheeks. "That is just too sad. Think of that little girl with her dreams of getting married and having babies, but all the boys were soldiers who'd marched off to war."

"So maybe she had to settle on some old coot. It don't matter, since she's been dead a hundred years." Jim Bob finished the beer and squeezed the can. "What's interesting," he said as he lobbed it in the direction of the trash basket, "is that this Emil was scared of snakes."

"I'm scared of snakes," Cherry Lucinda said. "I thought I'd die when Indiana Jones fell in that pit and —"

"Fetch me another beer. I got to think."

Sweetpea came into the PD, winced at the decor (yellow and white gingham curtains, bluish-gray mold, and cobwebs dripping with dust), and sat down across from me. "I suppose we'd better talk. When we got back from lunch, that weasel Kenneth pulled me aside and admitted he'd been talking out of school. God only knows what he'll say to

400

Simon. The only way I could see to shut him up was by using his saber to cut his throat, but I was afraid you'd be even more annoyed with me."

"Not necessarily," I said. "So exactly what did you do yesterday morning after breakfast?"

"I sat on the front porch and let the sun dry my hair, waiting until I thought everyone was gone. I called Andrew and ascertained that he was . . . in the mood for company. I didn't want to walk down the main road and risk being seen, so I found a trail of sorts along the bottom of the ridge and came across the pasture to the Flamingo Motel. If I'd had any idea Kenneth was following me, I would have hidden behind a tree and bashed him with a rock. Some of my best friends are Yankees, but he's just arrogant and hateful. I pity the students in his classes. He must drone on interminably, lulling himself into a stupor by the sound of his own voice. He should keep an alarm clock on the podium so the students wake up in time for their next class."

"What time did you get to the motel?"

She fluttered her fingers. "I don't know, since wearing a watch would interfere with my tan. I have to wear the ring Simon gave me" — she extended her hand so I could admire it — "but I don't wear any other jewelry in the spring and summer. I don't want people whispering that I have some sort of degenerative skin disease."

"Are those amethysts?" I asked.

"Yes. The diamond's not quite what I'd hoped for, but the ring belonged to Simon's great-grandmother and has sentimental value, or so he says. And it pleases Corinne, who's just such a dynamic person. My mother's never earned a penny in her life. After her husband abandoned her, Corinne had to struggle to provide for herself and Simon. She took menial jobs and wrote every night until she sold her first book. After that, she was the talk of Charleston society, especially after she bought her house and spent a fortune on remodeling. Of course she'll never quite fit in, since her family was in trade, but she's been on talk shows and knows celebrities. I thought my mother would have a hissy fit when she found out that Corinne had gone out to lunch in New York with Katie Couric."

"Big time," I murmured. "So you went to Andrew's motel room and stayed there until . . . ?"

"Early in the afternoon. I took the same circuitous route back to the house, fixed myself something to eat, and went down to the creek to study Henry's journal. Once I'd given up finding anything of note, I did a few watercolors of wildflowers, read for a while, and arrived back just as Kenneth was pouring wine." Her girlish dimples faded and her eyes narrowed. "I came in and told you this of my own free will. I don't see why Simon needs to hear about it. Andrew and I have an understanding that our relationship will never go beyond the rare opportunities that may arise at these reenactments. He knows that if he so much as attempts to make contact with me while I'm in Charleston, his wife will receive a thick packet of proof of his infidelities over the years. Her family owns the car dealership. I have no idea what she does in her spare time, but I suspect she could replace Andrew for a model with lower mileage without bothering to cancel a session with her personal trainer."

"I've heard that Simon was suspicious, perhaps so much so that he didn't go to Springfield to make the audio tape."

"And stayed in town?" Sweetpea said in a thin voice.

"I won't know until I've checked the mileage on the odometer of the rental car and compared it to the number on the paperwork in the glove compartment, if that's where Corinne put it. Farberville is twenty miles away; Springfield's roughly a hundred. It doesn't require advanced algebra to do the calculation."

Sweetpea sat back and did some calculating of her own. "He said he couldn't find the place and eventually gave up. That's his approach to life, you know. When the going gets rough, Simon goes to the club for a drink. In this case, I hope to hell he didn't go to that bar down the road and sit by a window where he had a view of the motel. It'll be one big ol' bother if he did. He'll feel obligated to stomp around and mutter about defending his honor. I'll cry, of course, and swear I must have lost my mind. Simon will forgive me, Corinne will pretend she wasn't listening outside the door, and we'll all go back to the issue of the flowers at the reception."

"Simon wouldn't threaten to call off the wedding?"

"Oh, please," Sweetpea said as she stood up. "He wouldn't call off the wedding if I told him I had every imaginable sexually transmitted disease and have been giving the pool boy blow jobs since I was sixteen."

"Have you?"

"That's hardly your concern, is it? Now you know where I was yesterday morning, and with prodding, Andrew will tell you the same. May I rely on your discretion?"

I gave her a cool look. "Yes, you may rely on my discretion. Every family needs its secrets, right? No matter how fine the pedigree, there's always a mongrel in the mix. Ruby Bee swears that my great-grandmother on my father's side of the family was a full-blooded Cherokee."

"Then I'm sure you must appreciate your heritage all the more, knowing you have some tiny indigenous claim to the mountains and the prairies, as well as the casinos with tax-exempt status. Are we finished?"

"I believe we are." I went over to the door and opened it for her. "I won't bother any of you tonight. Please let Simon know that we'll be having a rehearsal of sorts tomorrow after the rest of the reenactors arrive. I'd like to make sure everyone understands what to do when we start the actual filming on Friday and Saturday."

"I'll tell him," she said, hesitating in the doorway. "You're going to talk to Andrew, aren't you? He may squirm around a bit, but keep after him and he'll tell you the truth. He's very nervous about the possibility of Simon punching him in the nose or some such display of machismo. Don't worry about a duel at dawn in the motel parking lot, though. Neither of them has the balls, musket or otherwise, to put himself in danger. Blustery little boys, both of them."

I couldn't imagine Simon scheduling anything before the middle of the morning. I waited until she'd walked out of sight, then went down the road to see if Jack might be in the mood for a swim.

And other things.

Hammet was sitting on the gravel in the parking lot, lobbing bits at the bugs scuffling through the patches of weeds. "You'd have thought," he said as I approached, "that they'd at least give me my drum. I ain't gonna learn to play it by whacking a pillow with a couple of pencils, which is what Estelle keeps saying I'm s'posed to do. She sez when the time comes, it'll all come together. I shore as hell ain't gonna come marching down the road with no pillow strapped to my belly."

I sat down next to him. "You keeping an eye on the felon?"

Hammet nodded. "He keeps peeking out the window. It's likely he's aiming to make his break afore too long. He ain't got a car, so I reckon I can follow him till he holes up, then come fetch you to shoot him."

"I'll try to stay available. What else is

going on in this hotbed of crime and intrigue?"

"Jack's in there with him now. I shore hope they ain't partners. You'd be more tore up than an armadillo what got caught under a combine. I saw one last year when our class went on a field trip to some stupid farm where we was supposed to get all excited about petting lambs and goggling at chickens. I offered to show ever'body how to wring a chicken's neck, but my teacher hung on to me after that so I dint get a chance. She wouldn't even let me collect the armadillo and bring it back to school."

"I'm sure your classmates were all disappointed, but you can always hope you'll go on another field trip next year. So Jack's in Terry's room? What about the other guy, the one with silver hair?"

I fully expected my runty detective to demand payment before he passed along his vital information, but he merely shrugged. "He had breakfast at Ruby Bee's, then drove off for most of the morning. He came back, changed into a fancy jacket, and then left again. He's back now. If you look at his window, you can see the flickers on the wall from the TV. I thought he might be a master criminal, but he said he was a car dealer and gave me a dollar for fetching him a limeade from the Dairee Dee-Lishus. He called it a mixer, which dint make a whole helluva lot of sense. If you ask me, anyway. Nobody ever does, not even you."

"But here I am, permanently dimpling my butt by sitting next to you. I'll bet you a dollar you've already forgotten what all happened here yesterday morning."

"I already got a dollar."

I tried to stop myself, but my mouth just wouldn't listen to my brain. "You want to go swimming this afternoon? The water'll be cold, but the sun's shining."

"Jest you and me?"

"I was thinking I might invite Jack. We'll talk him into buying some sodas and cookies. Is that okay with you?"

"Yeah," he said without enthusiasm. "Anyways, yesterday morning I was waiting for Estelle to show up and take me on what she called a picnic, but she was later than she'd said she'd be. When she finally got here, she had dirt and grease all over her hands from changing a flat tire, and was near to blubbering like a baby on account of breaking a fingernail. Her always said the only thing fingernails was good for was chewing on."

"So you had to wait most of the morning for her," I said. "Must have been boring."

"Yeah, I was gonna just watch TV, but Ruby Bee came bustling in to vacuum and leave some clean towels. She was all fidgety 'cause she had to do the other rooms afore she could start fixin' lunch. I offered to help her, but she said the best thing I could was to stay out of her hair. I went down to the end of the building and sat in the dirt, watchin' grasshoppers and waitin'."

"You didn't see anyone coming up from the woods?"

He shook his head. "I dint see nobody. I did later, though, after I got tired of traipsing around the ridge, with Estelle breathing down my neck and poking me in the back. A lady with dirty yellow hair was cutting through the pasture. She went into one of the motel's rooms afore I could catch up with her. I reckoned she was part of the gang. All of the killers in the movies have girlfriends, 'cept most of 'em get shot before the end."

"They do, indeed. How long was this before you found me?"

"Not long. I was watching when you went into that feller's room, and as soon as you came out, I figgered I'd better warn you."

"You got a pair of shorts to swim in?" I asked. "Go grab them and a towel, then we'll collect Jack and take the rest of the day off."

"He's gotta come, too?"

"We can't play gin rummy without three people."

Although it only takes two to tango.

15

Maggody was abruptly yanked out of its rustic stupor early Thursday afternoon. Horse trailers were being parked in Earl Buchanon's pasture, some with horses and others with loud, disgruntled mules. A cannon lashed down on a flatbed truck rumbled by the PD and continued toward the bridge. The reenactors began arriving in pickups with dogs hanging out the window, their tongues flapping, and in station wagons jammed with children, their tongues flapping, too. A convertible packed with half-naked fraternity boys with rebel flags painted on their chests rolled by, entertaining spectators with a raucous rendition of "Dixie."

Harriet Hathaway had taken her post on the edge of the road in front of Ruby Bee's Bar & Grill. She waved each vehicle to a halt, ascertained the identity of the pertinent player, and then directed each either in the direction of the bridge or the hillside below Mrs. Jim Bob's house, depending on political affiliation. Camp followers and tourists were advised they'd be pitching their tents and setting up their grills on the lawn surrounding the Assembly Hall. Jim Bob had assigned Kevin and Idalupino to a long table in front of the SuperSaver, with an array of bottled water and sodas, sandwiches wrapped in plastic, candy bars, cookies, and fresh fruit. And a gizmo to take credit cards, just in case any of the reenactors or their families assumed the Chamber of Commerce was welcoming them with complimentary goodies. Cheerleaders pranced around in front of the table, shaking blue and gray pom-poms. I had little doubt that most of them had stitched rebel flags on their underpants for more festive cartwheels.

Hammet, Jack, and I watched from the PD parking lot. We were, I think, all feeling better after playing hooky the previous afternoon. Jack and I'd played other games after returning Hammet to Ruby Bee's grudging custody. She'd held her tongue, a first for her, but as Jack and I left, I could hear her meddling mind whirring away.

As well it should have.

"Look at that dude!" Hammet said, hopping from foot to foot as an enormous Harley-Davidson purred past us. "I reckon he can kill all the Yankees, big hairy guy like him."

"Nobody's going to get killed," I said. "This is a reenactment. They all know the rules, and one of them is that ammunition is forbidden. They can't even use paper wadding in their muskets because of the risk of fire. Smoke and mirrors, Hammet. That's all it's going to be."

"He could too kill 'em," my bloodthirsty protégé muttered as he took off down the road to catch up with the motorcyclist and try to wheedle a ride in the sidecar.

A pickup truck laden with a crate stopped in front of us. Its toothless, greasy driver leaned over and unrolled the window. "Got the pig," he said. "Who's paying fer it? Iff'n you want me to butcher Beauregard, it's gonna be an extra hunnert dollars."

I couldn't quite find a response. Jack came to my rescue and directed the man to Harriet, who was undoubtedly prepared to dispense funds, if not the tools necessary to facilitate the transformation of placid porcine to barbecued ribs.

An RV somewhat larger than a tract house pulled up. The passenger, a woman with sequin-adorned sunglasses and a crude Confederate flag painted on her cheek, leaned out the window and shouted, "Hallelujah, sister! The South shall rise again! Until then, where do we park so we can get a hookup?"

I sent her back toward the Assembly Hall. I wasn't sure with what she intended to hook up, but I hoped it wasn't Mrs. Jim Bob or Brother Verber after they'd assessed the damage to the lawn. Some questions didn't warrant further investigation.

LaBelle and three of her women friends, all hefty and crammed in the subcompact, pulled over. "This is so exciting, Arly," she gurgled. "We just came today to see the movie stars. I still haven't figured out who this fellow named Simon Dawk is, but I just know we'll recognize him when we see him. How should we go about finding him? I promised my niece I'd ask for his autograph."

"Down by the bridge at the other end of town," I said, although I doubted Simon would poke his head out of Mrs. Jim Bob's house anytime soon. Then again, Kenneth Grimley and Corinne Dawk had spent the morning at the schools, alarming the children with their parallel tales of death and destruction, and might deign to sign autographs, one with blue ink, the other gray.

The strains of "Dixie" competed with "The Battle Hymn of the Republic" as cars continued to inch past us. I was about to suggest to Jack that we retire to the bar for pie and coffee when Andrew Pulaski joined us.

"I thought you might come knocking on my door yesterday," he said to me. "I was prepared to offer you a martini while I made my confession."

"Sweetpea called you, then."

"The poor girl is distraught. She's young and liberated, but she can't put aside her previous persona as a debutante in a white gown, clinging to her daddy's arm as she's introduced into society. However, she did come to my motel room Tuesday morning so we could discuss the economic penalties imposed during Reconstruction on families such as hers that had managed to hang on to their plantations. It was very enlightening to hear her perspective. We also, um, experimented with other perspectives. She arrived shortly after I'd finished breakfast and stayed several hours."

"So she was there from around nine until one or so?"

"Close enough. I wasn't wearing a watch."

"I'll tell her you did a fine job sticking to the script," I said coolly.

Andrew frowned. "We're supposed to

stick to the script, aren't we? A reenactment's not the place for ad libs and pratfalls. My lines are rather repetitive, and I have no doubt most of them will be muffled by musket fire. I saw no mention that the cannon will be utilized."

"No," Jack said, "they couldn't use the cannon because none of them had been trained. From what I gathered in the script, about all you do is ride back and forth behind your troops, shouting at them to steady their aim and that sort of thing. Eventually you send them running up to the road, but only after the Confederates have fled on the mules. I believe your only line of significance is, 'Let the bastards keep their damn cannon. General Alessio is waiting for us to get back before he moves on Farberville. Head out, men.' "

"And a fine line it is," Andrew said, glancing uneasily at me. "I guess I'll see you tomorrow at the pig roast."

"Before then," I said. "Once we start the actual filming tomorrow, it's going to disrupt traffic. I realize this isn't an interstate, but a lot of tourists come through here headed for Branson, and farmers in the area use the road to get to Farberville to shop with wild abandon at the co-op and Wal-Mart. Today at four o'clock everyone is going to assemble in the SuperSaver parking lot, and then block out the movements. Costumes are not required."

"I have a uniform, not a costume," Andrew said haughtily. "I am not an actor."

"Oh, I think you are," I said.

He turned around and left. Jack was agreeable to pie, and I was fairly sure I'd set everything into motion, with some flexibility in case of unanticipated reactions. Now all that remained was to wait until four o'clock.

Jim Bob was more than startled when he came around to the patio and saw his wife sitting alone at the wrought-iron table, her skirt hitched above her knees and her feet spread so far apart he couldn't help but get a glimpse of her thighs. To add to his bewilderment, there was a half-empty wine bottle on the table and a glass set in front of her.

"You okay?" he said.

She refilled the glass. "Why shouldn't I be?"

"It's just that, well, it's just that . . ." he said helplessly.

"You think you're the only one in this marriage allowed to indulge in sin? Is that what you're trying to spit out, Jim Bob? Oh, excuse me. I meant to say Mr. Mayor. You run all over the county like a tomcat in heat, sniffing up every female. You'll be glad to know that I don't do *that*, Mr. Mayor. I stay right here so I can iron your shirts and make your dinner and bury your whiskey bottles in the trash."

"Because it's what you agreed to do when we took our vows. I'm the one what provides, and you're the one what honors and obeys. That's what Brother Verber said, anyway. Shouldn't you be thinking about dinner tonight, or getting ready for the pig roast tomorrow?"

"I should be, but I'm not. Have you seen what's happening on the main road? I might as well have told Earl to plow up his pasture so they can put up circus tents and parade the elephants through town. This was supposed to be a dignified affair, a tribute to Maggody's contribution to the annals of history. But, no, we've got people being killed, truckloads of hooligans braying louder than the mules, half a dozen wine bottles in the garage, and unmarried people fornicating in one of my tastefully decorated guest rooms."

Jim Bob glanced at the windows on the second floor. "Fornicating? You mean that young couple?"

"As if I couldn't hear them through the door, plain as day. There was no question about what they were doing." She gulped down the wine and refilled her glass. "I ordered new draperies for the living room. You have a problem with that?"

"No," he said, "I'm sure they'll be right nice. Are you planning to sit here and drink the rest of that bottle?"

"I might, and there's another one in the refrigerator. They keep showing up like mold on bread, or maggots on spoiled meat. Maggoty Maggody, such a quaint little place to live and die. I'm not real sure which I've been doing all these years. Maybe dying's a gradual process and I just never noticed till now."

Jim Bob was so lost as to how to respond that all he could do was awkwardly thump her shoulder. "I don't think you're dying as of yet, Barbara Ann."

"You haven't called me that in ten years."

Jim Bob was going to refute that, but he couldn't for the life of him remember when he'd last addressed her by her given name. Mostly, he didn't call her anything, but if she was the only one in the room, she shouldn't have had any problem following him.

"You heard that Arly wants to have a rehearsal for this reenactment later today?" he said.

"That's nice."

"Maybe you should go watch."

"Maybe you should take that rake over there by the garage and shove it up your ass."

On that note, Jim Bob exited.

Millicent licked her lips as she tried to think how to respond to what Darla Jean had just told her. Spiriting Petrol out of the old folks' home, losing track of him, and then sneaking out of her bedroom to look for him. Millicent could imagine what her sister would say about how this was bound to happen, what with Darla Jean being spoiled since the day she was born and allowed to have a phone in her bedroom since middle school. Millicent's sister hadn't allowed her own daughters to talk on the phone till they were eighteen. Now one of them was a lap dancer in Las Vegas and the other had joined a cult, shaved her head, and supported herself by panhandling in airports. Neither of them called home except at Christmas.

"You aren't gonna tell Pa, are you?" Darla Jean said, sniveling.

"I don't know, but I suppose I should.

What you did was wicked and deceitful, Darla Jean. You put me in the uncomfortable position of having to tell the secretary at school on Tuesday that you'd gone tearing off to your grandma's nursing home because they thought she was dying of pneumonia. I hope you've prayed for forgiveness."

"That's about all I've been doing since Saturday, except for going all over Cotter's Ridge shouting Petrol's name."

"What did Arly say when you confessed to her?"

Darla Jean wiped her nose. "She didn't say much, but I think she's more worried about that fellow that got killed, along with Hospiss out at the trailer park. She acted like she thought Petrol could take care of himself."

Millicent sat back and thought for a long while. "He might have gone back to his house. When's the last time you went there?"

"Monday. If you recall, you grounded me when I got home Tuesday, and the only place I've been allowed to go since then is school. Are you gonna let me go watch when they make this documentary on Saturday?"

"Your pa and I will discuss it this evening.

I'm inclined to be in favor of it, since it's educational. Is everybody at school all excited?"

"Sort of," said Darla Jean, not sounding all that excited herself. "We had an assembly today, where this man and woman dressed in costumes pretended they'd been alive back then. There was so much whoopin' and booin' when the Yankee strutted in that the vice principal had to start threatening to pass out detention slips."

Millicent clucked, then said, "All right, Darla Jean. I'm going to let you take the car and go over to Petrol's house to see if he's there. If you even drive by the Dairee Dee-Lishus, you're gonna find yourself grounded till you turn twenty-one — and this time your pa'll nail your bedroom window shut. You'd better come straight back here, you understand? I don't want to smell cherry limeade on your breath, either."

"Yes, Ma." Darla Jean took the keys and went out to the car. She didn't have much faith that she'd find Petrol sitting on his porch or hunkered in a back room, but it couldn't hurt to have a look. And go straight home and offer to fix supper, and feed the damn dogs without being asked, and maybe even sit in the living room afterward and pretend to listen to her parents jabbering at her.

Petrol's house was out past the Pot O' Gold, set way back from the road and almost invisible behind the bristly weeds and brush that'd taken over the yard and rutted driveway. She parked as close as she could and walked the rest of the way. The house was in better shape than Robin's shack, but not by much. She'd decided earlier that the porch wasn't safe, so she went around to the back and opened the door, intending to call out Petrol's name a couple of times and then leave.

As she stepped into what had been a kitchen, she heard a shriek from another room. It was followed by a progression of moans and groans, each getting louder. A woman's voice, scratchy and shrill, hollered, "Lordy, lordy, lordy! Don't stop now, you old goat! Hallelujah, Jesus! I'm a-comin' through those Pearly Gates!"

Darla Jean felt her face turning hotter than the steering wheel when the car had been sitting in the sun on a blistering August day. She stumbled back, nearly falling over her own feet, and somehow made it down the drive. She figured she'd found Petrol, and Dahlia's granny, too, but she sure hadn't been about to go one inch farther into the house to make sure. Not when they were doing what they were doing — and at their age. It was nauseating, a whole lot worse than when she'd walked into her folks' bedroom and saw them doing it.

After sitting in the car and thinking, she decided all she could do was go home and tell her ma that Petrol hadn't been there, then find a minute to sneak upstairs and call Arly. With luck, she'd get the machine and be able to leave a real short message, 'cause she sure as hell wasn't about to go into detail about all that disgusting moaning and groaning and shrieking. All that had been missing was squeaky bedsprings.

No way, not ever, not even to Heather.

At four o'clock, the Confederates began to show up in the parking lot in front of the SuperSaver. Some of them wore tattered uniforms and had unkempt greasy hair, as obsessed with their need for authenticity as Jeb Stewart, who was chawin' on tobacco and watching me through hooded eyes. Others were plumper and pinker, or in the case of the biker, close to popping the buttons off his coat. A quick count determined that only Private Henry Largesse (aka Simon) was absent.

Jack took over and described the scene he wanted to shoot early in the morning when there might be lingering fog in the valley. "Have your mules saddled by six, please. Since you'll be arriving, you'll need to wear your backpacks and —"

"Haversacks." Jeb spat on the asphalt for emphasis.

"Ah yes, haversacks. Have your bedrolls, canteens, and whatever other gear you brought. We'll go down to the far edge of the pasture on the other side of the creek, and then I'll film you riding toward me, with the mountains as the backdrop. With some careful camera angles, I can keep the road out of it, since the dirt won't be put down until Saturday morning."

"Ain't all of us gonna ride," said a squatty man with a high, shiny forehead and side-burns so bushy they nearly concealed the lower half of his face. I presumed he had not chosen his countenance as an homage to Ambrose Burnside, who'd been a pesky Yankee general. "Fred and me went down to have a look at the mules earlier. Ain't but eleven."

"That's ridiculous," said Miss Hathaway as she stepped forward with a clipboard. "I made it very clear that we

425

were paying for twelve mules."

"Whatever you say, but there ain't but eleven."

She turned to me. "Oh, dear, this is terrible. Shall I call the man and demand that he produce another mule before six o'clock tomorrow morning? What if he refuses?"

"Can't we just sort of jam them together and hope nobody counts?"

She gave me a level look. "That wouldn't reflect what was in Henry's journal, would it? Ten of the men were riding, while two of them walked alongside the mules pulling the caisson. I daresay most of the students who'll watch the documentary are capable of counting to twelve."

"I'll find another mule, okay?" I looked over her shoulder. "Oh, good, here come Simon, Sweetpea, and Corinne. I wonder what's happened to the cavalry?"

"The Yankees are saddling up their horses," volunteered Dahlia, who was maneuvering the double stroller through the tourists with the practiced ease of a NASCAR driver. "I just came from there. The one with the most stripes on his coat said they'd be along shortly."

Jeb crossed his arms. "Can we get on with this? It ain't right for us to be standing here surrounded by cars and telephone poles and women with babies. In fact, if that lady" — he gestured at LaBelle — "doesn't stop taking pictures of me, I'm going to rip the camera out of her hands and stuff it in her big fat mouth."

"Well, excuse me," said LaBelle. "I just assumed anybody what goes to all that effort to make hisself ugly as a catfish is doing it so folks will take his picture."

"Please," I said loudly as the crowd of nearly fifty people began edging forward, "I need you to back up and give us some room. We're about to have two dozen soldiers on horses, and I don't want anyone to get hurt."

"Yankees," mumbled a fraternity boy sitting on the asphalt, his back propped against a truck and a beer in each hand. "Goddamn Yankees right here in Stump County! We ran 'em off before, and I say we ought to do it again."

"You are poorly schooled in Arkansas history, young man," Harriet said sharply. "I trust that some morning when you're not debilitated by a hangover, you'll take time to visit the Headquarters House and learn about the Battle of Farberville."

Jack went back to describing the scenes he'd be filming, from the arrival to the establishment of the camp beside Boone

427

Creek. "We should be done in a couple of hours. After that, I expect you'll have visitors with lots of questions for you."

"Always do," said the big, hairy dude, as Hammet had dubbed him. He leered at LaBelle. "You come around tomorrow, little lady, and you can take all the pictures you want of me."

Simon joined his compatriots. "I don't see the point of this," he said. "Surely even these cretins can follow instructions, as long as they're given in words of one syllable."

"How about 'shut the fuck up, jerk'?" Jeb said.

The cavalry trotted up in the nick of time, with Andrew Pulaski in the lead. Neither he nor Sweetpea acknowledged each other with so much as a glance. The men all dismounted, some of them calling greetings to their soon to be mortal enemies, if only for one small skirmish. The horses were jittery, as was I.

I stepped forward. "Now that we're all here, Miss Hathaway has an announcement about a change in the script. We've added a scene that will affect only those rebels who were killed during the exchange of musket fire and left behind."

"Just a few of you," Harriet said apologetically, as if she felt it was unfair that only half of the Confederates had been shot like fish in a barrel. "As the script now stands, after the surviving rebels ride away, the Union soldiers come up to the road to collect the mules left behind and then determine that the caisson is damaged. Colonel Ricketts" — she nodded at Andrew — "orders his men to mount their horses and prepare to ride back to join their army. They depart, at which time the camera will linger on the bodies of the dead. After a poignant moment, perhaps with a fife playing softly, a mountain woman in a thin cotton dress and bare feet comes walking down the road. She kneels beside each body, searching the pockets for coins or trinkets. She removes a pair of boots from one body, a cap from another, a belt from yet another. When she nears the crumpled body of Hadley Parham, she freezes as she hears a groan. Is he still be alive?"

An expectant hush had fallen over the parking lot. All eyes, except for those of Waylon Pepperstone (and mine, obviously), were fixed on Harriet. He looked oddly agitated, as if he had a sudden need to relieve himself. If he'd been adhering to Jeb Stewart's diet, he probably did.

"Is he?" Dahlia whispered.

Harriet nodded, to everyone's relief. "She

uses the hem of her dress to wipe the blood from his face, then helps him stagger to his feet. She drapes his arm across her thin shoulders, and they move slowly down the road."

"Who is she?" said Kevin from behind the refreshment stand.

"She is, or to be accurate, was, the great-great-grandmother of a woman named Hospiss Buchanon, who was living right here in Maggody until a recent and most unfortunate incident took place. As of yet, we do not know this mountain woman's name or have much information about her descendants, but a record was kept in the family Bible. What's more, Hospiss included valuable information in the letters of application she submitted to the DAC. She even attempted to make contact with her cousins who live today in South Carolina. Wouldn't it have been heartwarming if she could have met her cousins one hundred and forty years later to share family stories?"

"I'm sure Oprah would have invited them on her show," said LaBelle.

"Yes, indeed," I said, taking over from Harriet before she began to fumble her lines. "Two cousins embracing on the porch of the mansion, or glaring at each other across the courthouse steps. Certainly a worthy human interest feature for the media in either case. We don't have all the information yet. Wendell Streek, who was the genealogist for the historical society before his tragic accident, had compiled much of it in detail. The only copies of his files remain at his mother's home. Miss Hathaway has found another member of the society who is willing to sort through everything and put it in publishable shape as a memorial to Wendell. I'm planning to drive into Farberville this evening and take the files to this accommodating volunteer."

"That just twangs my heartstrings," said Dahlia. "Mebbe someday I'll write up my granny's memoirs, assuming I can ever find her."

"I told you I'd find her, Dahlia," Kevin bleated from behind the table. "Soon as I'm off work, I'll jest go right back up on the ridge and stay there as long as it takes."

"Dahlia," someone murmured.

Jack took over from me. "Okay, everybody, let's block out the skirmish so we can do it most efficiently on Saturday morning. Colonel Ricketts, I want to shoot some footage of you and your unit arriving slightly before dawn on Saturday morning, when we have just enough light. Have you determined where you'll tether your horses?"

"Trees at the back edge of the pasture," said Andrew. "We'll ride across the creek and —"

"Dahlia!"

I stared at Waylon Pepperstone, who was moving slowly but purposefully toward Dahlia. His eyes were wide and very bright, his mouth gaping, his arms extended to grasp her voluptuous assets.

"What in tarnation is wrong with you?" she said. "You just stop right there, mister. Don't you come any closer to me!"

"Dahlia, you know I love you," he said in a plaintive voice. "I came all this way to tell you."

Jeb snorted. "Some damn fool must have given that boy whiskey."

Waylon kept closing in on her. She shoved the stroller at a woman standing nearby, then began to back away. "I'm warning you," she said. "Don't make me slap you silly. Kevvie, do something!"

Waylon lunged at her. She reeled around and took off running toward the side of the SuperSaver, moving with amazing alacrity for someone of her size.

"Kevvie!" she howled as she disappeared around the corner.

"Dahlia!" Waylon howled, but with different intent. He, too, disappeared.

Kevin finally came to what limited senses he possessed and took off after them. "I'm coming, my goddess!"

"Why, that Yankee aims to rape one of our women!" yelled Jeb. "Come on, men, we'll catch the dirty bastard and string him up."

The Confederates, with the exception of Simon, ran after Jeb, jostling each other, tripping over the spectators, and shouting threats that sounded more unpleasant than a straightforward lynch party.

"What are we gonna do, Colonel?" said one of the Yankees. "We can't let those rebs beat up on one of our own!"

"No, we can't!" Andrew barked. "Mount your horses, men, and prepare to charge!"

Charging across a grassy expanse must have worked somewhat better than it did in a crowded parking lot. Several of the women began to shriek as the horses pranced and shied, their hooves clattering on the asphalt. Most of the men were yelling obscenities as they tried to get out of the way. The fraternity boys scrambled onto the hood of their car and began to sing "Dixie." LaBelle screamed as a horse bore down on her. Children crawled under cars and trucks, or stood bawling like calves. Idalupino jumped up on the table, which promptly fell over, sending bottles, cans, apples, bananas, and oranges bouncing and rolling all over the parking lot.

"If you pick it up, you gotta pay for it!" shouted Jim Bob from the doorway of the store. "I'm watching every one of you!"

Although this particular battlefield lacked resounding cannon fire and smoke, bodies were falling every which way as people skidded on Jim Bob's finest produce and bottles of designer water. The drunken fraternity boy bellowed as a hoof came down on his knee.

Jack drew Harriet and me away from the escalating chaos. "What was that kid's problem?" he asked.

I shrugged. "Whatever it was, it just got a whole lot worse. The Confederates are hot on his heels, and the cavalry is charging. Dahlia's the only one I'm not worried about. The Buchanon blood, you know." I looked at Harriet. "Which one of them slipped away?"

"Sweetpea, I'm sorry to say. She's had time to go back to Jim Bob's house and collect the rental car. I didn't see her drive by, but I might have missed General McClellan and all seventeen thousand of his troops marching down the road. I don't believe I've ever seen anything quite like this. Is this what you expected?"

"Welcome to Maggody," I said with a faint smile.

I told Harriet I'd keep her informed, then Jack and I walked down the road to Ruby Bee's. She and Estelle were standing in the parking lot.

"What in blazes is going on?" she demanded. "It sounds like one of those riots you see on the news."

Estelle raised her artfully drawn eyebrows. "Shouldn't you be doing something?"

"I was thinking Jack and I should order a pitcher of beer," I said, "but we can always go over to my apartment if you two prefer to stay out here and rubberneck."

Ruby Bee shot me a look that hinted of blistering lectures in the future. "No, I reckon I can fix you up with beer and pretzels, or maybe even some popcorn. It ain't any of my business, but it seems to me you and this fellow here have been spending more than enough time in your apartment lately. Folks are beginning to talk."

"Beginning?" I echoed.

"Well," she said, squirming, "some of them have been wondering just what his intentions are, him being from out of town and all."

"A fascinating question." I looked at Jack. "Do you have any intentions, honorable or otherwise? Be specific, please, so that Ruby Bee can put all those inquiring minds to rest."

He grinned. "My apologies, but I'm fresh out of intentions at this time. I may have some back at my office in one of my desk drawers. If I find any, you'll be the first to know."

Ruby Bee was harrumphing as she stalked into the bar.

"You aimin' to tell us anytime soon what happened down at the SuperSaver?" asked Estelle as we followed suit. "I ain't heard such a ruckus since the Lambertino boy set off a box of Roman candles at the Fourth of July picnic last year and Elsie McMay's straw hat caught on fire."

"When I get it sorted out," I promised. I told Jack to make the big decision between pretzels and popcorn, then went over to the pay phone and called Harve. The dispatcher substituting for LaBelle put me through without a fuss. I wished the substitution would be permanent, but Harve could never fire LaBelle without incurring the wrath of Mrs. Dorfer, who was some sort of cousin.

"Sweetpea," I told him. "You have

someone there waiting for her?"

"I saw to the details, myself. The companion agreed to invite whoever showed up to go right upstairs to Wendell's office. Mrs. Streek doesn't have what I'd call a real firm grip on things. She'll most likely offer her guest tea and cookies." He paused to light a cigar. "Guess you made the wrong call on this one, Arly."

"At least I made a call, while you sat around assuring me you'd take over the case as soon as I did the dirty work. I want four deputies on Saturday morning, Harve, starting at five-thirty. There's going to be some real bad blood between the two sides, some of it possibly being shed right now. Call me back once Sweetpea's in custody."

I joined Jack at a booth, where we had both popcorn and pretzels. "How'd you pull that off?" I asked him.

"I told her she looks more like your sister than your mother."

"She does not," I protested, but very quietly. Said topic of discussion was watching us from behind the bar, and Estelle from her usual roost.

"I was hungry."

"You may have to fill up on carbs. I've got so many loose ends to tie up before I call it quits that I may be indulging in macramé until midnight." I took a swallow of beer. "Sheriff Dorfer accused me of making the wrong call, but both options were possible. Sweetpea had her family name and family fortune to defend. On the other hand, Corinne might have recognized Hadley Parham's name when Wendell first mentioned it, but Wendell stated unequivocally that Hadley was an only child — and therefore not anybody's great-great-granduncle. Corinne did know that Sweetpea's insistence on coming here was questionable. A low-budget documentary isn't likely to lead to a Hollywood blockbuster — no matter how talented the cameraman is."

"So Sweetpea already knew about the connection?"

"I'm sure her family talked about it after the children were sent to bed. Hospiss wouldn't have recognized the Yarborough name, but she certainly knew the Parham name from the entry in the family Bible. She might have known the name of the plantation if it had been passed along in the family lore, and sent her letters there. I'm sure her claim of consanguinity caused quite a ruckus, as Estelle would say."

Jack waited silently, allowing me to keep sorting through what I knew and what I'd theorized.

"Corinne wasn't worried about the Yarborough fortune," I added. "She knew that the passing of the estate to Felicity Louise was irrevocable. She must have done research about that sort of thing for some of her novels. She probably didn't know the child was illegitimate, with a mother who was a slave. Sweetpea did, though, and she knew it would cause no end of crude jokes at the country club. The Yarborough family would never have engaged the services of a genealogist to produce a flowery family tree."

"But along came Wendell," Jack murmured.

"Wendell, with plenty of free time to search out every tedious detail about every last Confederate soldier at Cotter's Ridge. He'd already tracked down the certificate of baptism. He knew it would make more than a dry little footnote. And with the journal to be made widely available in the next few weeks, he might have nurtured hope that his literary effort might attract some attention. A reporter drawn to the romance of buried treasure might have come across the family link between the genteel Yarboroughs of Charleston and the mutant Buchanons of Maggody. We still may see Sweetpea's photo next to Hospiss's on the cover of a tabloid."

"But did you make the wrong call?"

"No," I said, nibbling on a pretzel. "I just let Harve think I did so he'd feel magnanimous when I demanded two more deputies on Saturday. I knew for sure when Sweetpea came up with her second round of defense, the tryst with Andrew. Hammet didn't see her until late in the morning, and frankly, they would have been hard-pressed to keep Ruby Bee from vacuuming the room. Sweetpea was scrabbling for an alibi; innocent people don't bother." I looked back at Ruby Bee. "Where's Hammet? I thought he'd come marching down the road this afternoon, banging his little heart out."

"I told him the truth," Estelle said, "which was there wasn't any drummer boy in the script. He was pretty sore."

"I liked to wash his mouth out with soap," added Ruby Bee. "You never heard anything like the vocabulary he has."

Estelle rolled her eyes. "But then he calmed down, and the last we saw of him was when he came to get some cheeseburgers 'cause he was playing checkers with that sickly boy out back."

Jack squeezed my hand. "You sure you'll be tied up tonight? Beginning tomorrow, I'm going to be working almost as hard as you. After I get the footage in the morning,

I'll drive back to Springfield and take a look at it in case I need more. Then I'll drive back here and steel myself to get up at five on Saturday morning."

"I wish I could," I said, "but I need to tell Corinne and Simon where Sweetpea will be residing until her rich daddy gets her out on bail. I've got to go to both camps and make sure we won't have any midnight raids. Oh, and I've got to see a man about a mule."

16

"I just have no idea what to do," Corinne said to Simon as they came in the back door. "Should I call Sweetpea's parents, or let her do it? I did not accompany her as a chaperon, so I don't feel responsible. Perhaps you should be the one to call them, Simon."

"Let's ask Mrs. Jim Bob to do it, since she's a distant cousin. Why, the whole clan could come to South Carolina for a family reunion. We can have pork rinds and chitlins."

Corinne swatted at him. "You're absolutely hopeless."

"But the perfect product of my upbringing, *ma petite mère*. Shall we have wine on the patio — or would you prefer a jar of moonshine?"

"Wine, I think. I wonder where everyone is. Kenneth mentioned he might take a nap. It's too bad he missed the spectacle in front of the supermarket. If it hadn't been so ludicrous, I could have used it in a novel. But, alas, it was stranger than fiction." She went to the doorway into the hall. "You open the wine and take it and some glasses out to the table. I'll see if Mrs. Jim Bob might want to join us and hear what happened. She must know some of those involved."

Simon smirked. "But you're not going to rouse Kenneth. Oh, wait, you did that earlier this afternoon, didn't you? Aroused him, to be more precise. Don't you think you should show some decorum at your age? I could hear the two of you from my bedroom."

"Don't be impertinent," Corinne said. She went into the living room and stopped. "Simon! Come here!"

When he came into the room, they both stared at Mrs. Jim Bob, who was sprawled on the sofa and snoring boisterously. An empty wine bottle lay on the floor.

"She's snockered," Simon said, awed.

Corinne crept closer. "And wearing a most peculiar dress, as if she'd planned to go to a fancy ball this evening. The material is some sort of heavy brocade. Really most attractive, although likely to be oppressive in this weather. When she has recovered, I believe I'll suggest she use something similar for drapes in this room. The effect would be quite lovely."

Harriet was in the bedroom, debating whether she could swallow enough of her pride and make the phone call. At last she picked up the receiver, glanced at the number she'd carefully recorded, and dialed it.

"Lydia," she began, "I just wanted to tell you how sorry I am about Wendell. I know you and he were looking toward some very happy times together. He seemed so enthusiastic and self-confident his last few days." She listened for a moment. "That's very kind of you, Lydia. Wendell and I were dear friends for quite some years. I do think the society should have some kind of memorial service at the Headquarters House in the next few weeks. Wendell would have liked that, don't you think? How is Mrs. Streek holding up? Has the shock been hard on the dear old thing?" She once again listened, this time with a faintly impatient expression. "We've all been busy, Lydia. Please let her know that I'll come by Saturday afternoon, and stay with her until her son arrives to see to her future care. I may offer to stay with her indefinitely — unless, of course, Lydia, you're planning to do that. After all, she might have been your mother-in-law."

★ ★ ★

I called Harve from the PD. "Everything go smoothly?"

"Like an oil slick. She knocked on the door, introduced herself, and offered some glib reason why she needed to fetch a few documents from Wendell's office. Once she'd loaded a stack of them in her arms, Les and Swilly stopped her in the hall and transported her here. She's down the hall, denying everything. I ain't sure how she's going to explain away the notebook, files, and family Bible in the trunk of the rental car. Guess she was planning to toss 'em all in a Dumpster on her way back to Maggody. I just don't understand how a pretty little thing like her could be so cold-blooded as to murder two people, both of them harmless senior citizens."

"Even cold blood's thicker than water, Harve. I'll come in to your office tomorrow and help you write up the reports, this having been your case all along."

He wheezed for a moment. "I reckon we can stick your name in somewheres."

"Thanks," I said, then hung up and drove out past the bridge to the Confederate campsite. None of the soldiers sitting around sipping whiskey seemed unduly bruised or battered.

"We shore got started off with a bang, didn't we?" the biker-in-another-life cackled as I walked past him. "Ol' Snaggle here got so excited he damn near had a stroke, and that Yankee peed his pants when I took a rope and tossed it over a branch. 'Course we weren't really gonna hurt him, not with all the tourists watching. Besides, that woman he was chasing laid into him and liked to break his nose before we could haul her off of him. God, I love these weekends."

I found Jeb sitting a goodly distance away from them, no doubt fearful of farb contamination. "We aren't going to have any more trouble today, are we?"

"Nah, they're all too fat and drunk to bother. One of 'em brought chips and dip."

I sat down next to him. "Were you and Waylon down past the low-water bridge yesterday afternoon?"

He turned as pink as his pallor would permit. "Yeah, the dumb fuck left his canteen, so I took it to him. We got to talking, and he said he'd seen some of my fine bloating at Chattanooga a couple of years back. He wanted me to teach him how to do it, as if I hadn't spent years perfecting it. I told him to shoot me, so he did and I took the fall, gulped in as much air as I could, and then focused on forcing my abdomen to expand. He tried, but it was a pitiful thing to watch."

"You given up on finding the gold?"

Jeb looked at me from under his bushy eyebrows. "Until it's found, you can count on seeing me every now and then. Or maybe not, unless you look real quickly."

"Oh," I said, then went back to my car and went to see a man about a mule.

The man, and that was a polite designation, was Raz Buchanon. I knocked on his door and waited, but he did not appear. His truck was parked at the edge of the road, indicating he wasn't up on the ridge supplementing his income by preparing to sell 'shine to the reenactors. Even Jeb might buy some, since it was, after all, authentic.

I walked down to the barn. The door was partially open, and I could hear Raz grousing and cussing. He came to the doorway and blocked me.

"Whatta ye want?" he demanded, puffing up like a bullfrog.

"We need another mule for the reenactment tomorrow morning."

"I ain't got a mule, and iff'n I did, it wouldn't be in the barn."

"Raz," I said with a pained sigh, "you and I know that you stole Perkin's mule a while back. I don't see it in your field."

"It ain't in the barn. Now git off of my property afore I fetch my gun, Arly Hanks. It's time somebody taught you some manners."

I pushed past him and went into the barn. "Where's the damn mule, Raz? You can have it back Saturday . . ." I slammed to a halt. "What have you done, you sumbitch? You get your sorry ass in here and untie Brother Verber before I — I take Marjorie down to the rebels for their pig roast! Do you hear me?"

"I ain't gonna let him loose till he eats ever' mouthful of that ham he brought right to my front door. Marjorie was so tored up that she came close to cryin'. How'd you feel if I chopped up Ruby Bee and brought you her hind leg as a present?"

Brother Verber looked up at me with piteous eyes. His face was smeared with grease and flecks of white fat. "Help me, for God's sake."

"Raz!" I said. "You are in bad trouble. I don't know what the charges will be, but I'll think of something. Start hacking at those ropes if you want to live long enough to go to court!"

On Saturday afternoon, Jack and I at last

found time to escape to my private sanctuary on Boone Creek, far away from where the Confederates were packing up their gear and congratulating themselves despite their loss. I presumed the Yankees were equally cheerful, if not more so. In this case, there were no spoils to go to the victors, but they'd had a fine time popping up and down in the pasture to take shots at their enemy.

"Tired?" said Jack.

"More than that," I admitted, resting my head on his chest. "Do you think the documentary will come out well?"

"It's hard to say, but with Terry's and Hammet's help, we got as much footage as possible. I have a feeling Simon won't show up in Springfield to do the auditory, but Frank can do it as soon as he can walk again. That was one helluva nasty bite that horse took out of his . . . buttocks."

I took a tamale out of the sack and offered it to him. "Enough about this madness, okay? I just want to lie here for a week and listen to the water ripple by. Maybe I should have gotten more tamales and beer."

"Tell you what," he said, sounding as lazy as I, "let's stay here until it starts getting chilly, then go back, get cleaned up, and have a nice dinner in Farberville. Tomorrow I need to get back and prepare for the more mundane work that pays the bills."

"Planning to come back here?"

"I'll think about it."

"Good idea. Are you going to bring any intentions with you?"

He held the tamale so that orange splotches dripped on my belly. "Do you want me to?"

I thought about it for a moment. "No, not yet. We're both locked into our present situations for the time being. You can't uproot your kids, and I'm not ready to abandon Maggody just yet. Then again, you're self-employed and I might as well be, considering how much I'm paid. Surely we can arrange some vacation time."

"In Branson?" Jack asked as he began to lick up the mess he'd made.

I tried not to giggle, but it was impossible to keep my composure. "Okay, but let's not tell Hammet."

Jim Bob's throat was tight with anxiety as he crept toward the cannon. All the damnfool reenactors and their families and the houseguests had left town, and if any of 'em had stayed around, they wouldn't be wandering around at midnight. Mrs. Jim Bob had locked herself in her bedroom long about the middle of the afternoon, and he doubted he'd see her for another day or two. He was the only one next to the bridge, and he was relying on moonlight instead of a flashlight that might attract attention.

He knew where the gold was, or he was damn close to sure he did, anyway. The private, Emily or whatever his name, had been so scared of snakes that he wouldn't have gone very far up on Cotter's Ridge, looking for a cave. There was as many copperheads and rattlers up there as there was acorns, along with harmless blacksnakes and even little grass snakes. No, the boy'd skedaddled back down and stuffed the gold in the cannon for safekeeping. He probably figured they'd turn everything around and whomp the damn Yankees, and be able continue on their way to Farberville, pulling the cannon with them.

Jim Bob swallowed, then started to stick his arm in the cannon, aware that he was likely to have to dig past spiderwebs and maybe critters that had gotten trapped and died. But it was gonna be worth it.

"Don't bother," said a voice from the shadows. "It ain't there. Well, it ain't there anymores."

"Raz?" croaked Jim Bob. "What the hell are you doing here, and where do you get off sneaking up on me like that?"

"I jest came to see if any of you slick ol' boys might come lookin' for the gold."

"You said it ain't there anymores," he managed to say in a more neighborly voice. "Where is it?"

"I collected it 'long about Thursday night. There weren't all that much, but I reckon it belongs to me all the same. I took it to a coin dealer in Farberville, and the feller liked to split his britches. It weren't millions, if that's what you're thinkin'. Then again, it weren't peanuts, neither. Mebbe I'll buy a fancy new truck or two, and one of those satellite dishes so Marjorie and me can watch movies all night. If I weren't so fond of makin' 'shine like my great-grandpappy, I could retire. Mebbe I'll look into condos on a beach somewheres so Marjorie can wallow in the sand. She's pedigreed, ye know, and has a delicate nature."

Jim Bob tried to make him out in the shadows under the tree. "Why are you sayin' the gold belongs to you, you old coot?"

"On account of how all those long years ago when the rebels showed up, they stole a pig from my great-great-grandpappy. I've been hearing the story of how he watched the soldier boy put the gold in the cannon since I was knee-high to a polecat, but nobody knew where the cannon was till now. Now they's paying for the pig. You got a problem with that?"

Jim Bob heard the sound of a shotgun being cocked. "No, Raz, I reckon I don't."

About the Author

Joan Hess is the author of twenty-eight mysteries, including fourteen in the Maggody series. A former president of the American Crime Writers League and current president of the Arkansas Mystery Writers Alliance, she lives in Fayetteville, Arkansas. Visit the author at http://www.maggody.com

The employees of Thorndike Press hope you have enjoyed this Large Print book. All our Thorndike and Wheeler Large Print titles are designed for easy reading, and all our books are made to last. Other Thorndike Press Large Print books are available at your library, through selected bookstores, or directly from us.

For information about titles, please call:

(800) 223-1244

or visit our Web site at:

www.gale.com/thorndike
www.gale.com/wheeler

To share your comments, please write:

Publisher
Thorndike Press
295 Kennedy Memorial Drive
Waterville, ME 04901